MW00577743

Cashdown's Folly

Cashdown's Folly

Stephen Preston Banks

FIVE STAR
A part of Gale, a Cengage Company

Five Star Publishing, a part of Gale, a Cengage Company
All scripture quotations, unless otherwise noted, are taken from the King James Bible.

This novel is a work of fiction. Names, characters, places, and incidents are either the product of the author's imagination, or, if real, used fictitiously.

LIBRARY OF CONGRESS CATALOGING-IN-PUBLICATION DATA

Names: Banks, Stephen P., author.
Title: Cashdown's folly / Stephen Preston Banks.
Description: First edition. | [Waterville, ME] : Five Star, 2022. | Identifiers: LCCN 2022013035 | ISBN 9781432895129 (hardcover)
Subjects: BISAC: FICTION / Action & Adventure | FICTION / Westerns | LCGFT: Western fiction. | Novels.
Classification: LCC PS3602.A6623 C37 2022 | DDC 813/.6—dc23/eng/20220328
LC record available at https://lccn.loc.gov/2022013035

First Edition. First Printing: December 2022
Find us on Facebook—https://www.facebook.com/FiveStarCengage
Visit our website—http://www.gale.cengage.com/fivestar
Contact Five Star Publishing at FiveStar@cengage.com

Printed in Mexico
Print Number: 1 Print Year: 2023

Cashdown's Folly

CANADA
Spokane Falls
Cheney
Latah
Rosalia
ROAD
Oakesdale
Farmington
ERRITORIAL
WASHINGTON
Thornton
IDA

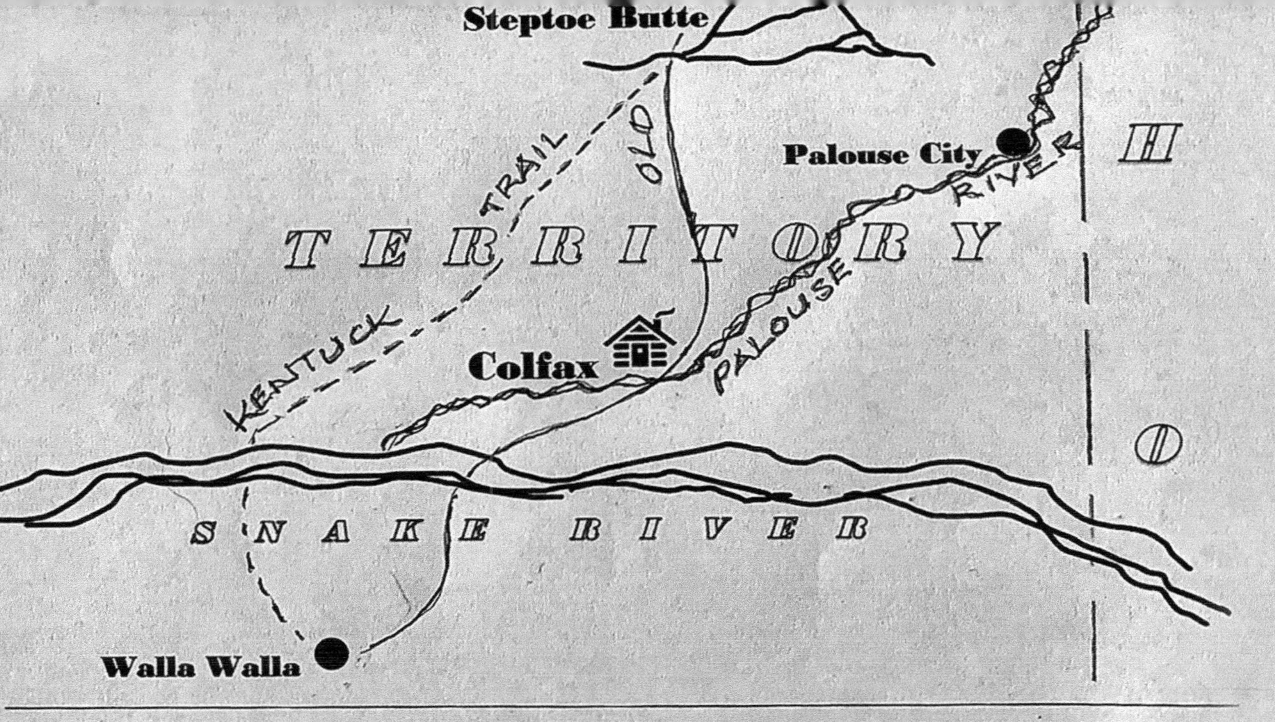

Palouse Region Ca. 1880

ACKNOWLEDGMENTS

My appreciation goes first to Tiffany Schofield, Diana Piron-Gelman, and the staff at Five Star Publishers/Cengage for their careful guidance and production of this book. I am indebted also to the research librarians who helped me with sources at Washington State University and the University of Idaho's Special Collections. Special thanks to Dr. Edwin P. Garretson and his colleagues at the Whitman County Historical Society, for guiding me through their archives of pioneer records, personal papers, maps, and research files; to Dr. Jeff Kline, for information on frontier medical practices; and to Prof. Rodney Frey, for his critical reading of sections about the Paluse People and neighboring tribes. Any errors and misrepresentations of tribal history are mine alone. Thanks also to Robert Baron, Meggan Baumgartner, Nick Gier, Peter Haggart, Kevin Riddle, Elizabeth Sloan, Bert Thomas, Penny Trudeau, Ann Warrington, and many others, for encouraging discussions about the project as it took shape. I am grateful to Mars F. Davis for information about the family history of James S ("Cashup") Davis, whose life story piqued my curiosity at the beginning and inspired my imagination throughout the writing. This novel is based in part on Cashup Davis's adventures as a migrant from Hastings, England, to the Northwest frontier.

Last, but also always first, my everlasting gratitude goes to my family for their patience and encouragement: Russell, Chase,

Kathy, and especially to my wife, Anna, for her continuing belief in my work and her decades-long tolerance of my follies.

★ ★ ★ ★ ★

Part One

★ ★ ★ ★ ★

The amity that wisdom knits not, folly may easily untie.

—William Shakespeare, *Troilus and Cressida,* act 2, scene 3

Chapter 1

"Do you have a stake, Mr. Musgrave?" James Perkins and Hamish Musgrave sat knee to knee before the fire, sipping from tins of Arbuckle's ariosa.

"Aiming to make one, sir. That's me purpose."

"Any idea where you'd find your site?" Perkins was a long-limbed man, middle-aged like Hamish, but, unlike him, smooth shaven and dark haired, a bachelor. He already had a reputation down in Walla Walla for being a wellspring of information about the region and an avid promoter of its possibilities. People found him solicitous and generous.

"We could use a recommendation, Mr. Perkins. Never been in the Palouse country before, though I carry a good map." Hamish patted his breast pocket, replying as amiably as his headache allowed. His rusty hair was flecked with grey and sprung wildly around his head. His beard flew out dense and coppery.

He had come up from Walla Walla, riding and walking from the grey light of predawn until long after darkness fell, for it was late in the year, and snowstorms would soon blow in from the southeast. Five days on the rough track to Belleville, he had forded the Touchet, Toukanon, and Pataha, summited Alpowa, and crossed the Snake shallows at Almota behind the Nez Perce guides who helped swim his mules across.

At Belleville he would rest some hours before continuing northward. James Perkins, who was building a sawmill at the

Palouse River confluence, offered the hospitality of his board-floor shanty and a hot meal served up by his houseman. Hamish had left Elizabeth and the children at camp outside Walla Walla to follow later under the care of Callum. They were seeking a homestead in the bunchgrass of the Palouse country, he told Perkins, a new place to improve their herds. They hoped it would be a gain over the Willamette, where the seasons were mild and gardens came in well enough, but forage for the livestock was modest at best and the floods unpredictable. Now, he was warming from a bone-deep chill. But the pain pressing against his skull was quickening, and he felt surges of nausea.

"A person might consider the drainage above Pyramid Peak. Cross the river here. It'll be slack enough this time of year where the track goes in by the mill. Head due north on the Fairfield Indian Trail and stay on it till the peak aligns just northeast of two streams that join below a rock bluff. Hard to miss. Some fifteen or so miles northwest of that spot you'll see a north-flowing drainage. Area's called Thornton. There's cottonwood and poplars in the bottoms. Above, the woods give up to broad stretches of bunchgrass."

Hamish laid out his map and asked Perkins to indicate the area. Tapping a spot north of Elk Creek along an unnamed watercourse, Perkins said, "Around here it's mostly unclaimed and generally safe. If you pass this way on your return, the mill superintendent serves as our land agent. That'd be Osgood. The survey's been done, and you'd be best off registering here. Osgood will take the papers to Walla Walla for you."

Hamish winced as he scrutinized the map. Perkins asked, "Are you well, Mr. Musgrave?"

"Tolerably so, thank you."

"I see you're undressed. Do you carry anything with your gear?"

"I've a Colt Army on the ride and a Spencer repeater on the

follow mule above me spokes. You see hostiles hereabouts?"

"Sometimes the Snake Paluses will run settlers out, but lately all's been quiet. Beware a band of horse thieves, though, half a dozen greybacks who take inventory along the Columbia and trade up near Fort Benton, so I've heard. We've become aware of claim jumpers, too. I'd keep your Spencer closer by."

It was just after dawn when Hamish departed Belleville. The settlement then was James Perkins's lumber mill—two unfinished structures of rough-sawn timbers and boards—and a scattering of dirt-floor tents and green-log shacks linked by muddy cart tracks. Perkins had named the mill site Belleville to honor Belle Bond, his girlfriend back in Dayton. A few years on, after receiving a "Dear James" letter from Miss Bond, he would decide the growing village at the Palouse confluence should be renamed Colfax, after President Grant's running mate. Perkins would eventually convince the territorial legislature to legalize the name and designate Colfax as the county seat. It would continue to expand and prosper. Its wide main street with raised sidewalks of milled planks would be graced by tall storefronts and hotels of brick hauled in from the kilns at Palouse City and Idaho's Paradise Valley, which in time would be called Moscow.

Hamish scanned the scenery as he traveled north, trusting his mules to keep their footing and stay in line. Occasionally he dismounted and walked ahead of them for a mile or so. He was a compact man, trim and muscular. Despite his modest stature and his mules' great size and power, he would unburden them from time to time of any portion of their load, as a kindness and a salve to his fatigue. Besides, he wished to put his feet on the turf of the enchanting territory he had entered. Dun hills rose and fell like gentle sea swells to the limit of his vision in all directions, and at the far edges rose dark crenellated ridges, some already snowcapped. Tall clumps of June grass and fescue and wild wheatgrass bent in the wind like spume. Here and there in the distance sudden buttes disrupted the horizon like sailing ships.

He passed several small creek beds along the way, in this season dry gullies edged by leafless osier and hackberry, and at sundown he arrived at the point where the two year-round streams joined. To the northeast, just as Perkins had said, loomed a steep-sided mountain shaped like a tall, extinct volcano. The late sun burnished its stony cap to gold, and Hamish stood transfixed as he watched the shadow line slowly climb the treeless flanks toward the summit.

"Pyramid Peak," he pronounced aloud.

He camped there for the night. At daybreak he headed west along a descending draw until he came across a winding creek. Instead of turning north in the direction of Thornton, he chose to follow the draw toward the southwest, yielding to the charm of the shallow valley, with its stream glistening like quicksilver in the autumn sunlight amid stretches of water birch and aspens and willows. He also was yielding to the pain enwrapping his scalp. He needed to find his destination quickly and identify any promising spot to set his stakes, a place from where he might quickly depart in search of relief from his intensifying torment.

At noon he consulted his map, calculated his location, and decided he was nearly at the corner of contiguous quarter sections. The terrain looked promising—a broad valley defined by rounded loess slopes on the north and south sides, the meandering stream, abundant bunchgrass, and, still standing sentinel over his shoulder, the bare top third of Pyramid Peak. He removed two stakes from the pack mule: wagon wheel spokes, metal tipped and hewn from locust heartwood. After scouting around for basalt boulders of convenient size, he knocked one end of each spoke flat enough to penetrate the soil. He located good spots on rises within the two quarter sections and drove in his stakes. On each stake he had carved his name and regimental unit: WISC 3rd VOL CAV REG.

It was warm enough by midafternoon for Hamish to bathe in the stream. He made camp streamside among a stand of willows and golden currants. While the mules grazed, he lay in a makeshift lean-to and chewed willow twigs for the pain and after a while felt relief enough to make a meal. As he gazed at the mules he sensed movement on the north rim of the valley. Five riders briefly appeared, seemed to look in his direction, and then vanished. He went to the pack gear and pulled out his Spencer repeater. The riders—he couldn't tell if they were Paluses or white men—had been nearly a thousand yards away, just beyond the range of the .56-caliber rifle, but the span of the valley assured him ample forewarning if any threat approached.

He kept watch until dark, through his meal of brined beef and coffee and stream-soaked bread, and even afterward he remained vigilant for several hours before sleeping. He kept his saddle gun and the rifle beside his bedroll.

The morning dawned overcast, and pellets of snow came in with a cold rain. He packed up and bushwhacked on a diagonal back to the Palouse River crossing. He wanted to save time returning to Belleville, where he would register his stake and seek treatment for his headache. It was now a pulsing torture engine, a deep, throbbing pain behind his eyes that blurred his vision. From time to time it would rise to agonies of such wrenching intensity that he was brought near to vomiting. It had come on two days earlier as he was crossing the Snake River, and he remembered worrying then for Libbie and the children and wondering if Callum had arrived on time to bring them north. His brother was rarely undependable, but he might be waylaid, and lately he had become moodier and distracted.

Hamish Musgrave was not easily given to worry. He had been celebrated back in Oregon and, before that, in Wisconsin as a gay-spirited man. He loved music and dancing, and he was tenderly indulgent with children and all animals, wild and domesticated. People found his devotion to Elizabeth admirable—Libbie, his forbearing and resilient wife, who would have been all alone in the world but for her sister Adelia and their chance meeting with the Musgrave clan in Wisconsin. Hamish was ardent in all his relations with the world, most devotedly with Libbie. But now his high spirit was assaulted by the pain.

He intersected the Palouse River east of where he had intended and made his way along the riverbank through snaking valleys thick with stands of huge ponderosa pines and cedars and past high cliffs of granite and basalt rimrocks. The spitting snow and rain continued all afternoon. He pulled his collar up and his storm hat down to his ears. At dusk he crossed the southerly branch of the river above Belleville. Wood smoke from the shacks drifted in thin ribbons across the damp valley as lamps and fires were lit inside. He unpacked his mules at the same pen as before. James Perkins welcomed him into his shanty and sat with him by the fire.

"You look somewhat travel worn, Mr. Musgrave. I can make a willow tea, if it would please you. Goes well with a sip of whiskey."

"I am grateful for your kindness, Mr. Perkins. And, yes, such a tea should help restore the heart," Hamish said.

The fortified tea brought only brief relief, and soon he began to feel the nausea and a more dizzying compression around his skull. As they talked on about the location of Hamish's stakes, the nauseous pain became nearly unbearable. Perkins eyed Hamish's face with care. Abruptly he said, "You seem to be in a great discomfort. Are you ill?"

Hamish looked up with a weak smile. "Was wondering if there's a doctor."

"No, not hereabouts. None closer than Dayton." He thought for a few seconds. "My man's friend is a wrangler, Chinee.

Knows their medicine. This wrangler—name's Pinky—this wrangler recently came up here and looks after the stock for the mill men. Sometimes helps with potions and such when someone's ailing, too. Pinky's always willing when I ask."

Perkins, his Chinese houseman, Wang-an, and Hamish trudged through the sleet down the rutted, half-frozen road to a shack near the river. It was dimly lit inside by a kerosene lamp and a fire on the hearth. A woman in a coarse ankle-length robe opened the door. Her wide, ruddy face glowed darkly, and her teeth glistened like a string of copper pearls. Perkins asked his man to introduce Hamish and explain that he was in pain and needed relief. Wang-an and the woman had a brief exchange in Cantonese.

She bowed slightly—an exaggerated nod—eyed Hamish up and down, muttered something, and gestured for him to follow her. She led him behind a heavy sheeting partition to a plank bed beside a low chest of drawers. The woman sat on the bed and bade Hamish sit beside her. She spoke in a quick, hushed voice. "I am Ji Ping-tien. Pinky. Where is your pain? Say how long." Hamish told her about his suffering. When he finished, she said, "I can fix you up okay."

Hamish studied her a moment. He saw an impassive face, confident and canny, he judged. Her hands were muscular and, like her face, weathered to amber; the nails were chipped and burnished. She had wide shoulders and a thick body conveying strength beyond mere toughness. It was impossible to estimate her age. The bulge under her robe suggested that she wore a revolver. "Okay."

Pinky told him to take off all his clothes and lie on the bed. She busied herself with a large leather wallet and some philter vials. She swabbed wire needles with something resinous smelling and lined them up on a towel. She flicked her fingers on his skin, and immediately he felt a tingle. For half an hour she stuck the wires into dozens of spots on Hamish's scalp, face, torso, and extremities. Needles went into his wrists and between his thumbs and forefingers, in his earlobes, and between his toes. Pinky passed a candle flame next to each needle for a few seconds and moved on to the next. After a while she removed them and told him to turn over.

He had been depleted by his pain and travel, and he began to feel very tired. He drifted into sleep. A while later he became aware, as if through a veil of mist, of Pinky removing the needles and rubbing the spots with ether. She mixed liquids from the vials, put a drop in his beard, and rubbed some on his chest.

"Put on clothes now." She watched him dress and was smiling when he turned around to thank her. He smiled as well, for he already felt renewed and nearly without pain.

"You like cheese much?" She spoke softly, in a rapid-fire whisper.

"Aye. A hard, strong cheese packs well."

"No more. Cheese good for everybody, not for you. What is your name? Sorry, I forget."

"Ah. Hamish," he said. "Hamish Musgrave."

"Where you come from?"

"Down Oregon way. Before that from Iowa. Before that Wisconsin, Ohio, England. Family came down to Hastings from Edinburgh near fifty years ago."

Pinky's eyebrows raised questioningly. Lamplight sparkled in her jet-crescent eyes.

"Always looking for opportunities," he explained.

"Hmm. Hard to be happy," she said. The pearly smile returned. "You got wifes? Kids?"

"Aye. One wife, named Elizabeth, Libbie. Twelve kiddies, two still down in the Willamette, ten coming up from Walla Walla."

"Ah, okay, good," she said brightly. "Come by and by I go visit you and lucky wife. You get pain again, come see me. I fix you up good."

"How much do I pay you?"

"Later. Maybe sometime trade."

"I always pay me debts in cash, laid down now. When I buy something it's cash down on the counter. And when I sell something I expect cash down. That way there's no mistakes, and you know how much the deal is for."

"Oh, very strange. You got cash. Okay, good. Twenty-five cents please."

Hamish paid her and thanked her for the treatment. She said, "Please say nothing to James, okay? I am just some China face, goddamn know-nothing, just wrangler with some secret medicine. Better like that."

"I understand," Hamish said. He put on his boots and walked into the front room to join Perkins and Wang-an, who had been catnapping.

It was after midnight when a clamor outside James Perkins's shanty roused Hamish from a deep sleep. He had been dreaming he was watching dawn's light edge down Pyramid Peak. He heard dogs barking, then several people talking, followed by horses and wagons being moved off to the pens and sheds. He had almost returned to his dream when Perkins pulled the drape aside and told him his family had arrived.

Chapter 2

Hamish dressed quickly and, still pulling on his shirt, came out to greet Libbie. He hugged her off her feet and nuzzled her neck. He kissed her lips and her eyelids, her nose and chin, her mouth again. He squeezed each of his children and kissed them on the forehead. Standing behind them was Callum, gangly, somewhat taller than Hamish but stooped, still clutching his wet hat. Hamish clapped him on the back and said, "How are you, Cal? You must have driven all night?"

"Seemed necessary, Hamish," said Callum. He wore a worried expression, but Hamish was unalarmed. Callum always worried. He worried that something wrong might have been his fault and so was apologetic. He often spoke with cautions about the future and regrets about the past. Hamish knew his brother did not lack courage and resourcefulness. Cal had proven his bravery during the war and shown his toughness throughout the many long travels he and Hamish had undertaken—from Hastings when they were young adventurers crossing the ocean to New York and Ohio and much later, after the war, on the harsh migration from Wisconsin to Iowa, then to Oregon, and now into the Washington Territory.

But Hamish also knew the family's late-night arrival signaled a disruption of their plan. He wished to comfort Callum and Libbie and, as usual, to make all as hopeful and high spirited as he felt, as if he could will them to a happy optimism merely by the strength of his love for them.

"Surely it must have been," he said. "I'm only glad all of you are safely here. What happened?"

"A band of mounted warriors stopped us. I counted thirty, all brandishing arms," Callum said. "They wanted their livestock back and accused whites of rustling from their lands to the east. Might've been Shoshoni Sheepeaters. We told them we brought our herds up from the Willamette, but they circled 'round us for two days. The second night I dispatched Tray and Elbourne to the fort, and the next day the boys came back with a rifle company who ran the Indians off. The lieutenant took our stock and the big wagons back to Walla Walla for safekeeping—I have the papers—and he told us to move north smartly, as there's been increased threats from the Cayuses and Shoshonis. We brought the charabanc and the surrey and four of the good pulling teams."

"Well done, Cal. Must not've been easy." Hamish turned to Libbie. "And you, dear heart, you survived the ordeal well?"

"It's done, Hamish, and we're here." She was an ample woman, shorter than her husband, sturdy and round shouldered, as if heavy labors were her lot, including ranch work and the births of her many children. Her hair was a dense mass of black and silver curls, and her eyes were jasper brown and inquisitively alert. Hamish always elicited a wail of objection when he would announce she had the appealing look of a Cumbrian ewe.

Hamish well knew from Libbie's stories how terrifying any encounter with Indians would be for her. She told each new child about the attack. He had heard it a dozen times, about when Libbie's mother was a girl of seven and living at a marshy place called the Big Bottom on Ohio's Muskingum River. The child had heard the adults talk about how trustworthy the natives were around the inchoate settlement. But the Lenape and Wyandots harbored covert plans to push the white invaders out of tribal lands. The Ohio Company would offer no security for those pioneers who had bought into its Big Bottom land scheme, leaving Libbie's ancestors on their own for safety. There had been too little money and too little time to build a blockhouse or stockade, and no sentry had been posted, so the adventurers—intruders, to the Indians—were taken completely by surprise. At dawn of a clear, cold January day, two dozen warriors entered the village from the east bank of the river. Before the settlers could grab the few flintlocks they owned, the adults were struck down by hand axes and jawbone clubs. Most died from the first blows, and some of those were immediately beheaded or scalped and dismembered. The few who did not die were carried away, to become slaves or hostages. Within minutes mutilated bodies lay strewn throughout the settlement, all the livestock were slain or run off, and children were run down and clubbed to death. The village was put to flames.

The company of soldiers from Marietta who arrived the next day surveyed the butchery. Nothing was left alive that they could see, not even the vegetation, and the smoking ruins were acrid and silent. After a while, however, they heard a child crying. As they approached the sound, a bloodied little girl crawled out from within the charred carcass of a flayed cow. The child was gravely wounded, her glistening skull cracked open, a leg dragging behind like a string toy. She was returned to Marietta, where over many months she was nursed back to health and eventually adopted by an immigrant German family on their way to Wisconsin.

That child was Libbie's mother, and for the rest of her life she retold her story to her children, always warning them about the dangers of meeting with Indians in the wilderness. Libbie continued her mother's practice, recounting the tale to each new Musgrave child. She would distrust the natives wherever she wandered.

Perkins turned over his cabin and Wang-an to the Musgraves

and passed the rest of the night at his sawmill. Hamish tried to pay for the hospitality, but Perkins refused his cash offer. Instead, he provisioned the party for their short journey to Hamish's stakes and their three hundred and twenty acres. Osgood the land agent was away at Walla Walla for a few days, but Hamish cheerfully said he would return to register his claim within a week. He was feeling buoyant again.

It was a grey, frosty Saturday when the two wagons splashed across the Palouse River above the new mill. Callum drove the charabanc, with six young ones on the benches and the spare teams tethered behind. Liam, the oldest boy, drove Libbie and the rest of the children in the surrey, while Hamish rode his big saddle mule, Peppermint, and ponied the pack mule. When they arrived at the convergence of the two year-round streams, Hamish told the family he would someday own the cone-shaped mountain rising to the northeast.

"Fasten your eyes on the work just ahead, if you will, Hamish," Libbie replied with a cautioning smile that showed her small, even teeth. "We have a farm to build first."

Hamish's imagination, she'd repeatedly observed, was always over the horizon, and she knew he would never lack for dreams of new adventures. There were times when she preferred Callum's tame appetites, so different from his older brother's great ambitions and dissatisfactions, but, in the end, all those years and children ago when they'd met in Wisconsin, that difference was a main reason she chose Hamish over Callum. She never regretted her choice, despite the continual necessity for restraining her husband's enthusiasms. But she had feared boredom more than exhaustion and preferred surprise to predictability. As it happened, Callum so lacked in forwardness that she often wondered if he fully accepted her decision or if he'd even meant what she understood to be his early, tentative interest in her.

After camping at the confluence overnight, the party continued toward their new homesite. Hamish intended to set up a tent camp while they constructed rough sod houses and sheds for the winter. They would build a real house and proper outbuildings the following summer. First they would need to survey the acreage to identify springs and favorable locations for the soddies. As they moved down the swale toward the site, Hamish spun out plans for winter corrals, a trash dump, and an outhouse with a deep cesspit. They would have to harvest and protect a supply of firewood and make a good cold hole for storage. With such plentiful wild game on the prairie, the hunting would be easy.

Near noon they approached a gentle rise half a mile from the stakes. Hamish, riding in the lead, saw smoke ahead. He pulled up and signaled for the wagons to halt. He dismounted and walked to the crest of the hillock and studied the scene. Two men were cutting turf and clearing a dugout foundation at his first stake. Three men holding rifles and wearing sidearms stood around a campfire nearby.

Returning to his family, he said, "Company at our site. Looks like claim jumpers, and they're well armed. Possibly the riders I spotted three days ago. Cal, maybe you can stay with the others and wagons, and if there's trouble, all head back to Belleville with wings on. I'll go have a word, sort it out."

"Hamish, I don't think it . . ." Callum stammered, but Hamish had already turned and mounted Peppermint. He rode at a trot directly to the five men and stopped a few feet from the digging. The guards leveled their rifles at him. He ignored them, dismounted, and ground tied the mule.

A tall man in the dugout hole leaned on his shovel, tipped his hat back, and squinted aside at Hamish. "Where you headed, nester?" he said. His off-eye wandered.

"Right here," Hamish said. "This is me claim. I believe you've made a mistake. And anyway, I would not dig a house quite on this spot." He smiled at the man with the shovel.

"Maybe you forgot where you planted yours. We know what we're doing." He went back to digging.

"Don't suppose I could have me stakes back, do you? Sentimental attachment." Hamish scanned the ground and spotted bits of flattened metal in the smoking ashes of the cook fire.

The guards moved a few steps toward the conversation, but the tall man with the lazy eye motioned them off and pulled his hat down to his eyebrows. "You got papers?"

"Mr. Osgood is away just now."

The man huffed a dismissive laugh. "Look. We don't welcome no jumpers here. You don't want trouble, stranger, so you'd be wise to ride off as far away from here as that beast will take you and consider yourself lucky. We have this section all staked and patented, and we'll damned well cut the balls off anyone who tries to snatch a blade of grass or cup of water on any part of it."

"Just so I remember to steer clear," Hamish said, smiling again, "what's your name, sir?"

"Bragg. *B-R-A-G-G*, Odis Bragg. Best you remember it. If you'd've checked this section at the land office before coming out here trying to steal my claim, you'd've already known."

"Where will I find me stakes?"

"Don't know what you're talking about. Now I'm tired of conversing, and my friends are getting impatient."

Hamish slowly mounted Peppermint and returned at a dignified walk back to his waiting family. "Claim jumpers all right. Leader named Odis Bragg. Prickly chap. No need to get into a shangles when there's so much fine territory hereabouts. I saw another good valley just a few miles south of here."

When they arrived at the new location, Callum and Libbie

agreed that it was as promising as the claims taken by Odis Bragg and his men. There was a generous stream meandering through a broad plain. It was sheltered on both sides by basalt rimrocks etching the hilltops as far as they could see to the southwest. The land offered the same rich bunchgrass and deep loess soil they had seen across the lower Palouse, and along the stream banks grew many varieties of trees and shrubs. There would be abundant land for planting and grazing and a good supply of timber in the deep draws for firewood and building materials. They spotted numerous wet patches indicating springs near the surface. Looking up the valley they could see the top of Pyramid Peak, and Hamish was comforted.

Using a wire saw, they made claim stakes from the bench rails of the charabanc and planted them in two adjoining quarter sections bisected by the stream. Hamish asked Callum to remain with the stakes and care for the children and horses while he and Libbie returned to Belleville to register the claims. The jumpers would not bother them, he said, because they were busy gloating over their theft of the first claim.

When Hamish and Libbie returned two days later they carried with them a receipt for provisional title to their land and the tools to begin work on the dugout lodges for the coming winter. "This Bragg," Hamish told Callum, "had no claim, sure enough. He's known for removing other settlers' stakes when they're away and jumping the claim. Depends on people just moving on, then registers it as his later. Sells it afterward as a farm, probably. Or maybe they're accumulating acreage. Before long, if something isn't done, all the good land will go the way of our first claim. Somebody better form a club."

Chapter 3

The six founding members gathered around James Perkins's desk and negotiated each clause of the charter before Hamish put the words to paper. Hamish's handwriting, he had told them, was exceptional. He said when he was still a child his writing was judged so elegant and precise that he was hired at sixteen as penmanship and literature teacher back in Hastings. Besides, forming the claims club was his idea, and he had vigorously lobbied for it in town and gained support at remote ranches around the lower Washington Territory.

Perkins agreed immediately to the club idea. He already had seen too many settlers come to the land office to find their claims already offered for sale by jumpers. Also among the founders was Taylor Osgood, the local land agent. Lycurgus Ames, a recently arrived journalist from Minnesota, eagerly joined the others. Ames would establish a Radical Republican newspaper, starting with a hand-printed weekly he named *The Guardian.* Ivar Nyberg, another founder, had wandered westward from the Swedish whiskey-maker settlement near Paradise Valley, aiming to farm grains on the Palouse Prairie. He had just completed his sod house but twice earlier had lost his stakes along Union Flat Creek before successfully registering a claim.

The last to join was the most recent migrant to the region. Two weeks earlier, Cushing McBride had staked his claim on a half section south of Colfax at the shore of the Snake River. The

Nez Perce ceded the spot to him in exchange for a sack of apple seeds and a promise of future trade. He hoped to resume the orchardist's life he'd left behind in the Georgia uplands before the Klan began torching farms of unionists and white Republicans. Odis Bragg and his men had run McBride and his family off his claim before he had a chance to register it, and when he traipsed to Walla Walla to submit his paperwork, he learned it was already claimed and sold.

Hamish attended to the club members' discussion and carefully wrote:

> The mission of The Palouse Country Claims Association is to assure the true and lawful apportionment of land ownership in this Territory and to protect all persons who do or may hold claims, against the interference of any person who shall attempt to deprive such claim holders of their claims and improvements, by preemption or otherwise.
>
> Any member who initiates a request for action by the Association shall do so only with the strictest proof of prior right and honest intent in making his claim.

Ivar Nyberg wanted to include a plan of dispositions. "It would be only right to lay out in a public paper how our mission would be achieved." Future club members would need guidance, he explained, and the founders knew how things got out of hand back in the Dakota Territories, how vigilante hangings and tar-and-feather parties could easily become a habit. Such actions always led to the forced disbandment of claims clubs, sometimes by the army, sometimes by circuit lawmen.

The PCCA founders decided that a civilian posse would be maintained for enforcement, and the punishment for claim jumpers would be forfeiture of property and a fine payable to the grievant as determined by the district court. Imprisonment would follow if a judge found it fitting. There was in fact no such court and no judge, but James Perkins was unfazed.

"I am confident that within the next year our territorial governor will approve a judge for the Whitman County district. And I'm at work on my lobby to recruit a county sheriff."

Hamish rode his saddle horse Cricket throughout the region to distribute copies of the club's document and enlist volunteers for a posse. At each stop he regaled the settlers like a preacher, telling stories of claims thefts and arguing for a posse. Whitman County as yet had no law officer; the nearest to a government official was Taylor Osgood. But Osgood, who also was the mill foreman, had authority only to receive claim registrations and fees and transfer them to the land office in Walla Walla. It would be six more years before Colfax had a land registry of its own. Hamish nonetheless persuaded Osgood to join in any posse the club ordered out, to help with legitimacy, he said.

For the week Hamish and Cricket were traveling, Libbie and the children worked under Callum's supervision on the sod houses and livestock shelters. All had to be made ready for winter, and much remained to be completed. Pens and run-in sheds for the horses and mules were up, and a loafing station for the cattle now had a stick roof and fencing enough to impound the entire herd. The family no longer lived out of the wagons and tents. But the big soddy needed floor pallets and caulk. It was damp underfoot and soon would turn muddy, and the front wall still would not hold together. Palouse topsoil was unlike the densely matted prairie sod of Iowa and Kansas. Here, it was a silkier loam of sparser bunchgrass roots interlaced with rhizomes of native wildflowers and shrubs. Here, settlers had to cut and build with smaller bricks of sod and often had to find underlying clay deposits to use as mortar. Here, soddies required more roof and wall support, and the new settlers had to learn by errors. But the soil was incomparably rich, the scant clay turned hard as concrete, and, unlike the treeless Midwestern prairies, plentiful wood was at hand in the Palouse ravines and creek bottoms.

When Hamish returned home, Callum was dismantling the roof on his soddy. It sagged and had to be redesigned. Together they fashioned a web of sticks and bark that would support the patties, set upside down to minimize cascades of dirt inside, and covered it all with cedar branches. They split cedar for his window and door frames and topped up the walls by cutting more sod with the grasshopper plow and immediately laying it on, again upside down so the roots would attach to the next layer above. Then came the caulking. It was hard labor, and the brothers stopped only for supper and toilet breaks. They talked as they worked.

"Doesn't look like you could well sleep here while I was away." Cashdown eyed his brother obliquely.

"Libbie lay with the girls. I was with the boys," Cal muttered, without looking up.

"Are you still agreeable to fetching the babies?"

"If you can spare me the weeks it'll take. Don't want any absence to be a burthen."

"Adelia wrote, y'know. Said they're all fine now."

"If I left soon, we might be back before the weather turns too bad."

By midnight the small soddy was habitable but for the cook-stove, which still hadn't arrived at Colfax. Until it came, Cal would eat with the family, but now he could sleep in his own shelter.

With the help of Liam and the twins, it took the brothers two days to rive enough timber to make floor pallets for the ten-by-twenty-foot main house. Hamish had bought glass panes at the new Colfax mercantile for the windows, two for the face of the main soddy and one for Cal's. Liam, the oldest child at seventeen, was given the honor of glazing the window in Uncle Callum's house, carefully laying pitch all around and snugging the panes into the frame.

When the soddies were enclosed and Callum's stove was installed, the family gathered before the main house under galvanized skies. A cold wind had picked up, and approaching snow squalls were visible on the southern horizon.

Hamish made a speech as if launching a ship. "We have traveled a long way to come to this place at this moment. We have weathered a winter and the blistering summer on the trail to Oregon. On the way we escaped devastation by storm and predation by hostile natives and wild beasts. We have survived many illnesses and injuries. We suffered a flood by the Willamette and prevailed by grace, with bodies, property, and livestock intact. We have been blessed to find this Eden of such great promise." He gestured grandly with outstretched arms, a corked whiskey bottle in his right hand. "And now we embark on a new life in these humble abodes. May they see us and our beasts safely through the coming hard season, and may we have strength and wisdom to create here a grand new house and fruitful farm that all others across this territory will proclaim as a model of prosperous and joyful living. And may Henry and Mindy, our babies, come home to us healthy and safe."

He pulled the cork from the bottle, and each of the three adults took a ceremonial swig. The children cheered and clapped. That night the family gathered around the cookstove while the first snowstorm of November howled outside. They ate a meal of rabbit stew and root vegetables. Hamish had brought in the cider barrel to keep it from freezing, and his face, flushed with excitement and a big meal and several cups of cider, glowed in the light of candle lamps and the fireplace. He pulled out his hornpipe and tossed a concertina to Callum, and they began to play a round of reels. For an hour the children sang and slapped their thighs to the old tunes, and the celebration went on until Libbie stood and announced that it was time for the young ones to go to bed.

"There are chores in the pens yet to be done. I will pick up here."

The men put away the pipe and concertina. Hamish stretched and said, "Aye. We'll have much work to do tomorrow, so we'd better get to it." The three oldest boys—Liam and the twins, Elbourne and Trayton—rose and put on storm coats. Libbie shooed the rest—Holly, Laura, Ferdy, Willie, Jack, Charlie, and Frances—off behind the curtain of sheets, girls to one corner and boys to the other.

An hour later the men came in from tending to the stock. They shook off snow just inside the door and placed their coats and boots around the stove. The boys went to bed, and Hamish and Callum sat on low stools near the fireplace, poured out whiskies, and relit their cigars. There were some moments of silence before Libbie could be heard rustling behind the curtain. The glow of her candle lamp moved back and forth as she prepared for sleep.

"It's luck we covered the wood pile," Callum said.

"Aye, 'tis," Hamish sighed. "We should keep the open fire going through the night. Is yours set?"

"I've makings inside."

Hamish studied his brother's somber face. "Good." He paused. Then: "I wonder how you feel now about fetching our Mindy and Henry."

"I could go in a few days, after we finish the well. It'll be freezing up soon, and we should get the rock in, so we don't have to work in mud or, God forbid, a collapse come spring. But I should go shortly."

Both had been well builders and dry-stone masons back in

Hastings, apprenticed to their father. They also had worked side by side through their teens in his lumber mill. Lachlan Musgrave had milled timbers for the Hastings shipbuilders during the Napoleonic campaigns and prospered greatly. The clan built the new town of St. Leonard's-on-Sea, laid all the foundations and all the dry-stone walls, dug scores of wells, and milled poles for the hop fields and turnpike gates. Those had been profitable businesses, but Lachlan died in his prime, when a well he was restoring collapsed on him. His sons thereafter took special precautions in wells. With help from Sussex uncles and aunts, the family stayed together until they decided to emigrate to America, the two eldest first.

"Aye, it'll be a long journey in foul weather."

Hamish wished to be sure Callum still accepted the plan they had made in Oregon. When the babies were well enough to travel, Cal would go to the Willamette and bring them back to join the family, while Hamish and Libbie and the other children would get the new farm started in the Palouse country. In her letter Aunt Addie, who was caring for Miranda and Henry, remarked on their restored health and confided their eagerness to rejoin their family and her reluctance to let them go. The alternative to Callum would be for Liam to make the trip, but they agreed it might be too risky for a seventeen-year-old to travel that distance alone in late autumn and then back with two toddlers. No other options were discussed.

Three days later the wells were rocked up and filling with clear groundwater. Callum had been unusually reticent recently, pensive and brooding as if he were working out a difficult problem. Whenever his brother asked what troubled him, Cal would mutter, "Oh, naught but aches and pains, just nothing proper."

When the time came, Callum climbed aboard the wagon in a gathering sleet storm and clucked for the team to move off for

Oregon's Willamette valley. Hamish shouted, "Godspeed, Cal, and may all three return safe and happy." Callum hunched over the reins and waved without looking back.

It would be over four months before Hamish and Libbie were to greet their two youngest children. The winter snows would block the northeasterly routes over the Cascades, and the Modoc War, having spilled over the territory west and north of the Klamath country, would menace them until the peace commission talks resumed. When little Miranda and Henry finally arrived late in March, the main obstacles on the route were axle-deep mud and creek washouts.

The wagon and trailing herd of horses and mules slogged down the track to the Musgrave homestead in a fading twilight. Over the sounds of the team's and herd's snorting and tack leather creaking and wheels groaning, an adult's hail of arrival and youngsters' squeals of joy reached Hamish and the older boys where they were working on the new house. They ran up to greet the weary travelers. It was not Callum, however, who clambered down from the driver's seat and lifted each child from the back.

CHAPTER 4

Still clutching Mindy, Uncle William scanned the property and beamed. "We've had a fine time of it! Henry helped me out of many a mud hole, and sweet Mindy sang and kept watch every day until she'd fall asleep atop the dogs. A jolly company all the way."

"William, how grand to see ya, and how can we ever repay your kindness?" Hamish's eyes brimmed with tears as he covered the kids' faces with kisses. "But what became of Callum? Unwell, is he?"

"Nah, he's fine last I saw. Don't know where he is, though. Went off somewhere south over a month ago, best I could tell. Said he'd return, but we haven't seen hide nor hair of him since."

Libbie ran out and scooped up the two children, kissed her brother-in-law on the cheek, and told the twins to see to the horses, mules, and wagon. "Come inside by the fire. We'll get the stove going and have a good supper," she said. "Come, come, bring those cases and bags in."

They talked into the night over brined salmon and potatoes and the last of the winter squashes. They drank ale and sang ditties, exchanged news, and told old family stories. Hamish would have danced, but the soddy was too low and crowded. The children listened carefully to the anecdotes, as if collecting gemstones from the creek bed.

After Libbie settled the young ones for sleep, Hamish asked

William what his plans were for his return to Oregon City. "If you could stay on here for a while, 'twould be a great help to the boys and me. The foundation's in, and we've set the sills and first posts. And Cal's sod house is vacant for you."

William stroked his beard and grinned. "Made fast time coming up. My plowing's already done—appears it happens sooner down there. Adelia and our boys can see to the first planting. It would suit me well to stay on for a few weeks so I can see more of the Palouse. It is an inviting country around here. And I'd be made glad to help with the new house. I'll write and let her know."

Hamish clapped him on the shoulder. "We'll be even more beholden to you and Addie. You must consider moving up here once the territory is more laid out and your herd is built. The cousins could be together. Maybe by then Cal will be back." He paused in thought. "Probably out right now scouting for a mate, someone to help him settle once he returns."

For the next two months work went on through all hours of daylight to raise a two-story farmhouse drawn from Hamish's memory of construction at St. Leonard's. It was three thousand square feet of post and beam framing with a central staircase and a shed mudroom out back. There was a stone foundation—rare in northwestern settlements of the early 1870s—and stove flues for each room. Liam kept a little sawmill operating at the new millrace on the creek to produce the necessary lumber. Hamish, Uncle William, Elbourne, and Trayton did the carpentry. They welcomed the help of nearby settlers and new friends from Colfax. For three or four days at a time, Taylor Osgood would close his office, ride out early, and camp overnight at the building site; Ivar Nyberg would come out with his boys, three gangly teenagers already skilled as woodworkers; and sometimes James Perkins and Cushing McBride would ride up for a day's volunteer labor. Libbie and the older girls prepared meals for everybody, and the little children helped by carrying materials and tools, doing barn chores, and cleaning up. The livestock now could be pastured, so work on the house went on mostly uninterrupted, dawn to dark, day after lengthening day.

Sometimes the men would pause while pegging a rafter or raising a framed wall and attend to the song of a meadowlark. The cascading melody would ring in the light breezes, the dry air would smell of pine resin and syringa blossoms, and the ocean of new bunchgrass would ripple like chartreuse swells.

One bright morning Libbie set out on foot in search of the new season's wild onions and ramps. The five youngest children, carrying baskets and cloth bags, trailed behind her. She also wanted to see where she might harvest camas roots and wild carrots later in the year. The troupe hiked down the valley and scrambled up over the north rimrock, chittering like house wrens as they went. They descended again to a wide marshy meadow with a sky-blue haze blanketing its far side. Libbie led the children to the blue flowers, and all squatted down to examine the dense camas lilies. She pointed out the delicate starbursts of indigo petals cradling blooms like tiny blue pine-cones.

"When summer's over," she said, "we'll come back and dig up the roots. They taste like sweet potatoes when we roast them. And we can make flour with them, too." Henry and Mindy picked a couple of the flowers and put them in a basket. Frances, Holly, and Laura said to save the flowers for later, so they'd have plenty of roots to dig up.

A horse snorted, and Libbie and the girls looked up, startled to see half a dozen stone-faced warriors peering down at them from tall grey mounts. How they managed to approach without making a sound was a mystery. But the girls and Libbie were so enraptured by the camas flowers they hadn't been paying attention.

The riders were Paluses, mostly young men, half naked in the spring sunshine and themselves out scouting flowers to predict the coming harvests.

"I am Tomeo, son of Kamiakin," announced the Indian on the nearest horse. "Why do you take my *quamash*?"

The girls gathered around Libbie's skirt. She straightened and looked up, shielding her eyes from the morning sun. Her heart pounded, but she tried not to show the riders or her children how stabbed by fear she was.

"Chief Tomeo," she said, "we are not taking your flowers. The children are being children. They . . . they just made a mistake."

He gazed down at her, then at the horizon. "I am not a chief. We know you are from the new farm. We have seen your fences. More whites are coming. You are changing the land, bringing the railroad." A long pause. "Do you want the railroad?"

Libbie delayed before replying. "We did not come to plant grains. We raise horses and cattle. And plant fruits. That's all. No wheat. We have no need for the railroad."

"But will they build it?"

"I . . . I don't know. Probably. Not for many years, I think."

"Tell your men to come visit us. We can talk." The six horsemen turned and moved off northward at a slow walk.

Libbie fanned her breast, smiled weakly at the girls, and said, "Maybe they have little children where they live, too. Now let's go find some onions."

When Libbie told Hamish about the encounter with the Paluses, he asked for details of everything she could recall. "So, the chief's son, a strapping young man. But no guns?"

"None that I saw. Knives . . . they had knives. Oh, I think one rifle on a sling. Or maybe I just thought I saw one."

"Paint?"

"None I could see."

"Did you feel threatened, Lib?"

"Scared to death. But once we spoke I felt better—the way he looked at me, as if we understood each other. He was most interested about the railroads. I was thinking then he'd maybe heard about Mr. Davenport coming this way."

"It'd make sense they'd be worried. The rail line would cut through their land like a broadsword. They'd lose fifty thousand hectares or more right off."

"He's been paying farmers to come out to the territory, you know," Libbie said. "It told in *The Union* that we've doubled our numbers just since Christmas."

"Aye, that's the threat to us all, not just the natives. Turning good grazing land over to grains, and their wheat and barley and such needs shipping out. It all but guarantees the rails will come one day. It's a wonder the Paluses aren't on the warpath over that."

Libbie would feel very differently about the local Indians five years later, and it would be nearly a decade before Davenport's railroad reached the Palouse country. By then it would pose a different sort of problem for Hamish and his family.

That night when putting the children to bed, Libbie noticed that Mindy felt feverish. Mindy complained that she was "feeling choky." Libbie moved her mat to a place next to where she and Hamish slept, to keep the little girl as far away as possible from the others.

By morning Mindy was gasping for breath and scorched with fever. Henry began to show the same symptoms. The adults talked over the possibilities. Maybe the two had not completely recovered from the mountain fever they had suffered going into Oregon. Yet, had they not been well for the long trip up to the Palouse Prairie and robust for the past many weeks? It must be something contracted from visitors, or maybe from the Indians they encountered yesterday.

Hamish rode Cricket at a gallop to the nearest settlement, the sprawling Ewing place well east of Pyramid Peak. The Ewings had lived in the area for eight years, since before the Coeur d'Alene gold rush, and they knew everyone from Colfax to Spokane Falls. They might know of a doctor.

"Could be the strangler," Orrin Ewing said. "You'll want to get Doc Kenoyer, from up Farmington way. Training was more Biblical than medical, but he apprenticed a physician in Philadelphia 'fore the war. So he says, and it's true he's helped many a settler."

Hamish thanked Mr. Ewing and immediately headed north to fetch Dr. Jeremiah Kenoyer. Doc Kenoyer was a soulful servant of the ill and injured, and a charismatic preacher of the United Brethren Church. He immediately packed up his bag, kissed Mrs. Kenoyer and his children goodbye, donned his buffalo coat, and mounted his mare to ride back with Hamish.

They arrived at nightfall. By then both Miranda and Henry were gagging and wheezing, and their fevers continued to rise. Libbie had separated them from the rest of the household by a curtain of sheets, but it was dark and close in that corner, and the rest of the soddy was getting crowded. Doc Kenoyer examined the sick children and said, "Yes, it's surely the strangling angel. They'll need quiet, complete quarantine. What about that other little house? Can they go there?" He looked worried and tired, an antiquated frontiersman in his beaver Cossack hat and fur coat with long fringes that swayed like willow branches.

Libbie asked Uncle William to take a front corner of the big soddy; Callum's could become a hospital ward. Doc Kenoyer asked Liam and the twins to find some snails and earthworms, so he might make a mash for medicine and poultice. He compounded them with some herbs and wild mustard seed into a paste, instructed Libbie how to dose the patients, and said he would pray for them on his return journey.

The next morning, after Doc Kenoyer left, the adults set up a vigil. They took turns sitting by the sickbeds in the little soddy, applied moist cloths to the toddlers' foreheads, and turned them to help clear their throats. By dawn's light the following day they could see that Henry was much worse, near suffocation, and Mindy was delirious with fever.

Hamish declared, "Prayer's not going to help our babies. They need air and nourishment, or the bloody disease'll take them. I'm going to go see those Paluses, find out what they've had. Maybe it'll help us. If there's no satisfaction, I'll try Pinky. Let me have some trading supplies—some of that sugar and those beans. I'll take a cider jug, too."

He packed the bags and rode off on Peppermint to the Palus encampment near Thornton. The lodgings were arrayed in a semicircle of half a dozen clusters of four or five tepees. He stopped in the center and dismounted, but nobody appeared to be around. He removed the saddlebags and dropped them and stood quietly. Some of the tepees were made of tule mats, others of hides; all looked tattered and stained. A pack of dogs came and barked at him. Shortly he was approached by eight men carrying old rifles and sidearms.

Tomeo stepped forward, scrutinized Hamish up and down, and held out his hand. Hamish shook hands with him and said, "I'm Hamish Musgrave. Some of your people met me wife and some of our kiddies awhile back. We wish to thank you for your hospitality of allowing us onto your land." He gestured to the saddlebags. "Brought a few gifts." He pulled out the sacks of sugar and beans and two jugs of cider.

The Indians nodded appreciation and murmured among themselves. Tomeo thanked Hamish for his generosity and invited him to talk and smoke with them. "You are the cash down man. I hear that you breed good horses and mules. They say you train and treat them with respect. That is good."

"How do you know about cash down?"

"Pinky."

"Ah, f'sure, Pinky."

They sat in a circle under an enormous black cottonwood. The seed cotton drifted down softly like tiny feathers. Tomeo wanted to talk about the railroad coming, and Hamish knew it would be useless to hurry things if he wanted any hope of help here. He confided that he thought there indeed would be rails on the Palouse territory someday but not for many years to come.

Tomeo studied the westward horizon and asked, "What do you think we should do?"

"The Palus people? Or all of us?"

Tomeo stared steadily at him without answering.

"I canna say what you should do. But it gains none of us a thing to look back and wish for the old times," Hamish said. "We only have today and tomorrow and whatever follows after that. We can try to help the tomorrows to come as friends, and we can learn from remembering, but we will not overcome every force in the future. Some forces will be good for us, like the water and sunshine for this great tree. Some will change us forever in ways we cannot know, like windstorms and drought. This tree is mighty. But it will not last. It can resist fire, but it cannot resist time or disease or hard luck. It will become something else one day—a lodge or a fence, a bridge for crossing a creek. But it will not be the same."

Tomeo stayed silent for a while. He gazed up at the giant cottonwood. A pipe went around the circle. "We have always been keepers of the old times. We do not resist the storms and the dry seasons. But we have had disease and too much bad luck," he said. "If the railroad comes, we will see what can be made of it for us. And for you, Mr. Cashdown."

"Nae, I'll have no need for the railroad. But maybe it will bring us good luck anyway. I too have much bad luck now. I have sick children." He paused, looked beseechingly at Tomeo, and continued. "Has there been a sickness here, Chief Tomeo?"

"I am not a chief. No sickness here in some months. But many of my brothers and children are buried in the ground near the Yakama because of sickness brought by the white soldiers and miners. We are less than half of what we were when I was a child. What is wrong with your children?"

"Strangler's disease, I think," Hamish said, looking like a man who confronts a force he cannot overcome or even fathom.

"They are choking and hot?"

"Aye, almost to the death."

He stared at Hamish as if deep in deliberation. "Mostooshish, our wisest medicine man, has seen many people with the strangling disease. He can help."

He gestured to a withered elder sitting quietly across the circle. The ancient man was wearing a soiled Laredo hat and tattered shirt, vest, and breeches. Mostooshish nodded and talked quietly with Tomeo in the Palus Shahaptin dialect. "He says we should go now," Tomeo announced.

Hamish left the camp with Tomeo, Mostooshish, and six braves, and they rode at a gallop to the Musgrave settlement. When they stormed into the front yard and dismounted, Trayton and Elbourne came out to collect Peppermint and the Indians' horses. The twins had to break the grim news to their father.

"Mother is inside Uncle Cal's house with Mindy. Henry . . . he didn't make it. Mindy's worse," Elbourne blurted.

"Uncle W-willie is w-w-with him," Trayton added. He gestured toward the big soddy.

Tomeo told his men to stay outside. He and Mostooshish followed Hamish inside the big soddy. Henry's corpse was wrapped in a blanket and laid by the back wall. William had been sitting vigil. In the little soddy, Mindy lay in a front corner, gasping and writhing as Libbie tried to soothe her with compresses.

Hamish told her the Paluses were going to help Mindy. He introduced Mostooshish, but Libbie looked away to hide her tears and exhaustion. "What good can they do, Hamish?" she whispered. "We've just lost our Henry. Dear Mindy is not long behind him." She began to sob.

Hamish put an arm around her, helped her stand, and guided her outside. They sat on the threshold, while Mostooshish attended to Mindy. Tomeo came out and asked if one of the boys could help. Liam immediately volunteered, and Tomeo told him to fetch a hard stick of dry grass bur and some soft tallow and bring them to Mostooshish. He told Trayton to find a hollow reed, at least a foot long.

The old man breathed into Mindy's mouth until Liam brought the stick and tallow. Mostooshish wrapped a glob of tallow on the burr, pulled her jaw open, and immediately plunged the burr down her throat. Liam recoiled in alarm, but Tomeo placed a hand on his shoulder and told him to just watch. When the medicine man twisted the stick and withdrew it, Liam saw a dripping membrane like a sow's placenta clinging to the burr. The sac glistened with pus and mucus. Tomeo told Liam to put on gloves and take the thing far away and bury it deep. Miranda was crying loudly, but her breathing was strong and clear now.

The Indians somberly mounted their horses and gathered to leave. Hamish and Libbie went out to thank them. Tomeo told Libbie, "If the child cannot breathe again, put the reed down her throat. She will live."

Hamish gave his hand to Tomeo and said, "Will you come for the burial?"

"That is for your family. We will not join you."

"Then I hope someday I will be able to repay you for this kindness."

Tomeo shook his hand and said, "Maybe you will speak the truth. That is enough." The Paluses walked their horses slowly out the gate and up the trail to where it cut through the rim-rock and disappeared in the grass-covered hills.

Chapter 5

They laid Henry's body in a flat-sawn cedar box. Casket would be too elegant a name to call it, for Hamish had to build it quickly, as the disease had to be confined. Libbie stayed back at Cal's soddy with the convalescing Miranda while the rest of the family, including Uncle William, silently filed out and stood in a semicircle around the hole Liam and the twins had dug on the south slope of the valley. They kept a few yards distant, for safety and to be respectful. It was a shimmering green morning in early June.

Hamish carried the box, wrapped in a coarse shroud, the quarter mile from the house to the grave site. He strode ahead, never lifting his eyes above the ground before him. He knelt and placed the box in the hole and gazed down at it, as if he were remembering every detail about his son's four years of life.

He stood and turned to face the gathered family. "Our hearts are filled with anguish," he eulogized, "because with the passing of our little Henry we will have fewer moments of inspiration, and we will know only uncertain love in the future. We will no longer hear the special song of his laughter, no longer witness his happy curiosity and the wonder on his sweet face, no longer feel his loving arms around our necks at bedtime. Yet here we remain." He paused, took a few deep breaths, and continued. "And we can do naught but mourn and then try to learn from this devastation. We can let him teach us to be better persons, more cheerful and loving persons, truer in our actions and stronger in our ambitions. And we must be thankful that our Mindy has escaped the same fate and is now on the mend. For each of you, my beloved family, I say goodbye to our dear son, nephew, and brother."

Hamish stripped off his gloves and tossed them into the grave. He picked up a shovel and started filling in the hole, his eyes glistening with tears. It took half an hour, and the rest of the family waited quietly while he worked. At last he smoothed off the rounded crest of soil and replaced and tamped down the sod. Later, Hamish and the older boys would build a grave marker of ponderosa heartwood and inscribe it with Henry's dates and the words *Fortuna Caeca Est.*

Miranda would never completely recover from the illness, though her spirits and mind would quickly rebound. As she aged, she would lack physical stamina, suffering shortness of breath and heart pain, and she would sometimes have difficulty with her balance and hearing. There would be a painful surgery and no children. But for the rest of her life she would speak from time to time of her wondrous journey from Oregon to the Palouse country with her older brother Henry and kindly Uncle Willie.

For many weeks Hamish said nothing about Henry's passing, except to comfort Libbie whenever grief seemed to overwhelm her. As summer came on, he began to divide his time between grimly finishing the new house and tending to his animals and orchard and gardens. When the house began to reveal its final form his mood brightened, and he could be heard once more singing or cheerfully telling stories to the children who happened to be working alongside him. William returned to Oregon, promising to send any news he heard about Callum. Friends came by to give their condolences and often stayed on for a day or two to help with the house and barn construction. Ivar Nyberg stayed away this time: he told people in town the Musgraves were getting too friendly with the savages.

Hamish began going to Colfax each week—for supplies, he said, or for a mug of ale with James Perkins and Lycurgus Ames, or sometimes for Pinky's acupuncture treatments. She had become his physician and a boost to his good civic reputation. The Territorial and Kentuck Roads were improved that year, which made the travel back and forth faster and smoother.

"Pinky. Are you here?" Hamish called from the front door of her newly expanded shack.

"Hello, cash-down man. You need me to fix you up?" Pinky was still in her wrangler clothes and had just come in the back way to the laundry from the mill paddocks. She beat dust off her pants and pulled off her gloves as she spoke. She had started a laundry near the mill, the first north of Walla Walla.

"Bloody headaches again, Pinky."

She came up to him and peered intently into his eyes, examined his tongue, turned him around and felt his neck, took his pulse, and examined his hands. "You eat cheese again?"

"Aye, sometimes. But not like before."

"You got troubles, Cashdown? I know your boy died from sickness. Too goddamned bad. So sorry." She was facing him again, and her eyes looked up searchingly, registering deep sadness.

" 'Twas a hard loss, he was so young. Now I just want to get on with me work."

"Okay. You wait. I can fix you up good." She went behind the curtain to clean up, then called him to the back area for his treatment. When she finished and was ready to see him off, she said, "Stage line starting soon to Spokane—Walla Walla to here, and here to north, each section fifteen miles on Territorial and Kentuck. Going nearby to your farm. They say more new people, more driver jobs."

"Good. The coach will be civilizing for the Palouse country. Come out to see us on it—we'll have a big party. Now, let me pay you."

"Okay, Cashdown." Pinky grinned and accepted the coins.

Strolling along the wooden sidewalk on the main street of Colfax, Hamish was bumped by a fashionable woman exiting the mercantile, a wrapped parcel in her arms.

"I beg your pardon," she said in a tone suggesting that she expected him to ask her permission to pass. She looked him up and down, and her offended expression changed to one of approving interest.

Hamish tipped his hat, smiled, and said, "Sorry." He stepped to move around her just as she moved in the same direction. He immediately moved in the other direction, and she did, too. They laughed at the awkwardness. The woman was handsome and stylishly decked out, in a high-necked morning dress in shades of slate and charcoal and a straw sun hat tied under her chin by a rose ribbon. She was middle-aged, full-figured but shapely, pale under her hat brim. Hamish detected a seductive cast to her face.

"I wonder if you might help me with this burden, sir? I need to take it across the traffic to Riverside." She thrust her package toward Hamish.

He reflexively grabbed the parcel and followed her to the other side of the street, dodging wagons, riders, and mounds of horse shit, and on into the Riverside Boarding House & Hotel. Over her shoulder she told him it was just upstairs. He followed her bustle up the polished staircase to a room where she had taken, she said, "temporary residence" until she could find a permanent place to settle. She said her name was Mrs. Lettice Wheeler and explained that she had recently arrived, a bereft widow looking for a place to establish a new life. Her brother down in Dayton recommended the promising town of Colfax.

She told Hamish to put the parcel on the bed, thanked him, and asked him if he would like to share a lemon ice with her.

" 'Twould be swell, Mrs. Wheeler. But I have many errands to run before I return to me farm and family. I'm Hamish Musgrave, from up Cottonwood Creek way. Livestock and apples." He looked around the room and saw a child asleep in a cradle beside the dresser.

"My niece," she said. "My brother could not care for her just now, so I am helping out."

"Ah, I see."

"Well then, Mr. Musgrave. Perhaps I shall meet you again one day in town, and we can have tea or something together." She gave him a sidelong glance and a demure smile.

Before he left Colfax that day, he was hailed by Lycurgus Ames. "Cashdown, come in. I have a matter for the club."

There had been another incident of claim jumping, and the victim said Odis Bragg and his men did it. The newcomer, Payton Williams, had come up from Utah with his family intending to farm wheat. They had established a stake on the eastern edge of the recently chartered Whitman County. Bragg had forced the family away at gunpoint, raced to the federal land registry in Walla Walla, and filed the papers, saying he had bought it. The theft was a great loss to Payton Williams, especially because the new territorial agriculture station was soon to be built near his claim site.

"Looks like it's time to bring our posse together," Hamish said. "I'll come back in two days so the club can vote to go ahead. When will that new justice be here?"

Lycurgus Ames—his tiny wire-frame glasses riding under bushy eyebrows, unruly dark curls falling over his wide shoulders—said he wasn't sure, but the Whitman County commissioners had promised the appointment of a circuit judge before the end of summer. "I'll verify with Mr. Williams that he's willing to testify," he said.

Arriving home, Hamish told Libbie he might soon need to ride the circuit to gather a posse. "If we don't put a stop to Bragg, he'll become the biggest landowner in the whole of Washington Territory."

"Just be careful, Hamish. And how do you feel now?"

"All's well. Pinky sorted it. She said there's to be a stage line through here on the way to Spokane Falls. I reckon they'll be needing a depot for rest and supplies right about here. There's a new widow in town, a Mrs. Wheeler, real smart dresser."

"Where'd she come from?"

"Dayton. Don't know before that. She's looking for more permanent lodgings. Has a niece with her, just a wee one, not much bigger than Mindy."

"I'm not taking in any boarders. And clear the idea of a coach inn from your mind. We're farming, remember?"

Hamish grinned but said nothing further. He was whistling as he went out to finish nailing up the last of the eaves' trim.

The club voted to raise the posse and bring Odis Bragg and his bunch to justice. Hamish rode to all the county settlements, enlisting volunteers. Within three days a dozen settlers had joined the Claims Club founders in Colfax, all well-armed farmers and tradesmen, all determined to bring safety and order to the region. Payton Williams rode in from his new homestead on the Idaho borderland to join up.

They gathered under a grove of tall ponderosas next to James Perkins's cabin. Hamish asked the posse how many had been in military service. Nine of the twelve had seen battlefield action during the war and now carried their military-issue rifles. The other three gave accounts of their expert marksmanship and displayed their armaments. Lycurgus Ames said he didn't know a muzzle from a buttstock, but maybe he could carry supplies.

Ivar Nyberg muttered, "Don't have no supplies." The rest silently toed dirt around until James finally said they would need a reporter to record what happened, and it was agreed to include Lycurgus.

It was widely believed that the Odis Bragg gang had a cluster of cabins in one of the ravines between the Palouse highlands and the Snake River. The canyons were steep clefts that dropped over fifteen hundred feet to the powerful river in less than two miles. Clogged with dense, thorny brush and rocky debris, and almost vertical at the sides, they were ideal hideouts for rattlesnakes and bandits. James Perkins and Lycurgus Ames believed there might be at least six in the gang, possibly some women and children, too.

Hamish began briefing the posse on procedures for a quick and safe capture—there needed to be one speaker at the encounter, one leader only, he said.

James interjected, "That should be Cashdown Musgrave. I nominate him."

"Second," someone shouted.

"Cashdown, Cashdown," the posse responded. The acclamation was unanimous.

Hamish grinned broadly when they called him by this nickname. His virtue was branded on it, and it suggested a distinctive identity among his new friends. He replied that he would be honored to take command, and he resumed his briefing. Everyone, he said, should watch his hands—he demonstrated some signs he would use if necessary—and unquestioningly follow his orders, spoken or otherwise. There was to be no violence except as a last resort. When they located Bragg and his men, they would break into two groups, six or seven staying behind in case the capture didn't go smoothly. He asked Payton Williams to lead the backup riders. "It'll prove better if Bragg doesn't get a look at you right away, as you're the recentest to receive his shenanigans. We want to avoid a fuss if we can."

They set out to the southeast early the next morning, a clear, hot Friday in mid-July. The posse rode along the ridgeline above a series of ragged gorges descending sharply to the Snake. On the far southern horizon loomed the snowy peaks of the Seven Devils. They searched through thickets of cow parsnips as tall as a man's head and spikes of mullein and bear grass and clusters of pink-topped thistle. These could signal the roughed ground of old trails heading into a ravine. The riders occasionally stopped to listen for the sounds of horses or humans.

At the top of one draw a shallow spring made a little pool, and they stopped to water the horses. One posse-man said he could see a wisp of smoke rising from down the grade. Soon they all saw it and agreed it couldn't be fog or mist or dust. Cashdown told him to walk down with caution and find the source of the smoke.

Half an hour later the scout returned. "They're there. Looks like only three, Bragg and two others. They're clearing more land 'round the cabins—four rickety shacks. Burning brush in little piles so's not to make much smoke."

"See any firearms?" Cashdown asked.

"Stacked long guns by the near shack. Bragg for sure has a revolver, border style. The others, maybe. But I didn't make it out clear."

"Horses?"

"Didn't see no horses. No mules or wagons, neither. No women or kids."

Cashdown separated the posse into the two groups. They rode down the canyon, slowly negotiating narrow spots where huge boulders had fallen into the gulch, limiting passage to one or two riders at a time. They split up a quarter mile above the cabins. Cashdown and eight posse-men raced into the encampment at a gallop and halted, facing Bragg and his men. Bragg reached for his sidearm but froze when he saw the riders already had their rifles trained on him and his men.

"Kindly unbuckle that rig and toss it well behind you," Cashdown said.

Bragg did as he was told. "What do you want?" he growled.

"First I want to know where your horses are."

"Pastured down the draw."

"Bloody shame. You'll have a long walk back to Colfax. And the rest of the company?" Cashdown suspected there were others near the camp, given the size of the corral and the four shacks.

"Just us three," Bragg said. "Ain't nobody else around here. My friends are off to Montana, 'round Fort Benton."

Bragg's men were eying their rifles stacked against the nearest cabin wall. "Lycurgus, would you fetch those weapons over there?" Cashdown said.

Lycurgus dismounted, gathered up the rifles, and handed them to other riders. As he was moving toward his horse, he passed one of Bragg's gang, a tall, skinny boy with a downy chin and shifty eyes. The boy lowered one hand, drew a derringer from under his shirt, and trained it on Lycurgus. "Drop all those guns or this man loses his head!" he screamed, trembling and wild eyed with excitement.

Everyone stayed still for a few moments. The posse-men looked toward Cashdown's hands for a signal. He held out his left hand, palm down, and his men slid their rifles into their scabbards. "Everybody off. Off!" the boy yelled, and the posse dismounted.

The boy turned toward Bragg and started to ask him what he wanted to do next, but Payton Williams and the remaining posse-men jumped out from behind one of the shacks. Williams put the barrel of his revolver to the boy's neck. "Give me that, butt-end first," he said evenly. Now it was evident the boy was shaking from fear, and they watched as he wet himself.

The posse secured the claim jumpers by tying their wrists behind them and looping the cord around each man's neck. They yoked the three together by their necklaces and marched them in a line up the ravine. About halfway to the ridge, the trail entered a defile among boulders and brush. At the upper end of the narrow gap the trail opened onto a small clearing. Across the trail above the clearing lay a tree trunk that wasn't there when they descended earlier.

James Perkins dismounted and inspected the downed tree. He saw it had been dragged into position. Before he could say anything, six riders with revolvers leveled at the posse sprung from the brush around the clearing.

One of the gunmen shouted for the posse to dismount and stand together. He got off his horse and removed Bragg's neck cord and rope shackle.

Sneering at Cashdown, Bragg said, "Thank you, Leo. These farmers think they're lawmen, but here they've gone and broke the law themselves, dragged innocent, hardworking settlers off their own property, stole their firearms, run off their stock—I think they deserve justice for such lawlessness. What d'you think, Frank?"

A squat, slovenly man leered and said, "Looks like maybe they should take a swim."

The gang laughed as they freed the other two and tied up each man in the posse with his own belt. But first Bragg ordered the captives to take off their clothes, boots and all. Looking at the boy, he said, "See if you can find some pants that'll fit you." The rest of the gang jeered, and the boy turned away.

They gathered the clothes and guns and tossed them aside. The posse-men were forced to walk in their stockings back to the claim jumpers' shacks and corral all their horses. Cashdown's feet were bloodied by the rocks and briars on the trail. From there they were driven like sheep slowly down the gorge toward the Snake River.

Although it was July, the river was running full and fast. The Snake, treacherous even in the driest months, drained much of Idaho's southern plain and the high mountain ranges bordering Oregon and Washington Territory. Where the bound men were taken, it was a powerful torrent more than a hundred yards across. Ancient boulders deep in its bed created moguls dozens of feet high, followed by sluices and sinks surging with countless tons of roiling water. Gigantic tree trunks and root stumps could come swirling down as lethal debris in any season.

The posse-men stood at the roaring riverbank, the gang behind them. Bragg told two of his men to bundle the posse into a circle by cinching the neck rope. He saw Cashdown working his hands free of his belt and said, "Hit that farmer with a stick. And re-fix his belt." The two men swatted Cashdown across the shoulders with tree branches and tightened his belt and neck rope.

"Matter of fact," Bragg said, "give 'em all a lick." The two men were joined by other gang members, who picked up driftwood by the riverbank and began striking the cluster of naked men. Bragg bounced excitedly on his horse and egged them on: "Hit 'em! They were going to kill us. Hit 'em again!" His off-eye wandered wildly.

It became a frenzy of beating, the gang members laughing and whacking the captives on the arms and chest and legs, the posse-men cursing and dancing in a jumbled, stumbling circle.

Chapter 6

Blood flew and spattered the cringing posse-men, and dark bruises rose in fat welts across their exposed bodies. As the mad beating went on, they were driven in a scrummage toward the river's edge.

Just as the desperate captives were about to be forced into the Snake, the ground heaved open with a thunderous roar a dozen yards away. Erupting like a volcano, rocks, shrubs, and tons of gravel and dirt shot violently into the air, branches flew off nearby trees, a boiling cloud of dark smoke and fire filled the vale, and burning debris came down in crackling and sizzling showers around a huge crater. The crazed beatings instantly halted, and the gang members and posse-men stood frozen as statues.

They faced a massive figure striding toward them through the drifting debris and smoke. The gigantic man moved unevenly, one leg straight as a post. He was carrying a large-bore coach gun in one hand and two sticks of blasting powder in the other. He strode straight to Odis Bragg and with a rattlesnake strike of his coach gun knocked him clear off his horse. Placing his straight leg's boot on Bragg's back and the gun's muzzle against his head, he scanned the gang and drawled in a deep voice, "Dismount. Throw your rigs to that hole and lie facedown, hands behind your heads."

In short order the possemen were free to secure the gang members' guns. Horses were rounded up, proper wristbands were tied, and the prisoners were roped together by the neck.

The rescuer grinned and, nodding toward the river, said to the posse-men, "Go take a swim if you want." Nobody moved. "Let's walk them back to your gear." His voice was calm, orotund.

On the way up the ravine they collected the posse's horses and clothing. The skinny lad had to put on his wet dungarees.

Heading for Colfax, Cashdown rode next to their rescuer. "Hamish Musgrave, farmer and breeder. We raise horses, mules, and apples. Your name, sir?"

"Orestes Alton Banks, legal nomad, ex-politician, buffalo hunter, sometime cowboy."

"Well, Mr. Banks, we owe you much, and I'll start with me own thanks for your rescue."

"Any man that's been treated unkindly has choices, Mr. Musgrave—to retreat from all others, to be himself unkind, or to redress unkindliness. I prefer the last of these."

Cashdown appraised the man's tack and weapons. The rescuer wore a brace of Dragoons under his black duster. "You're a veteran?"

"Cavalry, Fifth—Hopkinsville to second Saltville, then the Tenth. I was admitted into the Tenth because I could read. Had a Spencer, too, when most everybody in all the regiments still carried muzzle-loaders."

"I was cavalry, too," Cashdown said, "Wisconsin Third under Colonel Barstow, and then after late '62 down to Kansas and Arkansas. Mustered out at Leavenworth."

As they rode along—Orestes Alton Banks on his dun warhorse and the diminutive-looking Cashdown on Cricket—they talked about the war and the recent history of the Bragg gang and the new settlements around the Palouse country. They also kept a watchful eye on the tethered men trudging ahead of them.

"What brought you here, Mr. Musgrave?"

"Came up from the Willamette with the wife and eleven kids—ah, there were twelve, but we recently lost a boy. And me brother. Came for better grazing land. Wife says I also have a bit of the wanderlust. And people hereabout call me Cashdown now. On account of a habit of laying cash down to pay."

"Sad to hear about your loss. But lucky you to have cash. I well know the pull to wander, Cashdown. Been doing it since I left the Tenth, though I hadn't intended to." Orestes Alton Banks spoke slowly and pensively. "Believed I was going to be a practicing lawyer for the duration."

"Lawyer?"

"Had a practice once in upland Georgia, but I got ambitious and managed to get elected to the legislature." He laughed at the miscalculation. "By then the Black Codes were in, and then the Klan chased most of us off, all the ambitious Negroes and progressive Whites. Lost my family there, so I headed west. Did some cowboying, little of this, little of that."

"Terrible about your family. We're hearing the backlash was a cruel thing."

"Well, the Freedom Amendments don't mean much now in Dixie. Maybe not anywhere."

"Aye, we fear it's spreading. Grant's been too politic. And what's your attraction to these parts, Orestes? You can see there's no lack of small-minded people here, too."

"Why would anyone come this way? Freedom to restart a life. It seems a place to get away from the war, putting together a long distance and a good stretch of time. I heard about the gold strikes up in Idaho country, soured on hunting buffalo, didn't want to kill Indians, and so I cowboyed in this direction. It's too late for the gold, but you never know where you'll find something better. I need to settle sometime soon, though. Fought and rode too long and can't move as well as I used to."

Cashdown was stunned to think that this ferocious man, easily over six and a half feet tall and quick as a cougar, could move any better than he did just now at the landing. He mused that Orestes must be at least in his forties, maybe older, but there were few grey hairs on his head and none in his woolly beard, and his mocha complexion was smooth as a saddle seat. "Injured in the war, were you?"

"Just the leg. They took it off at the knee. Damned good surgeon, but it took three years to get my wood limb. Finally made it myself. How about you?"

"Nae," Cashdown replied. "Had me hair parted a few times, holes in the kepi. Got nipped in the ass one time at Prairie Grove, but I was horseback again in two days. Cut me saddle tree in two, but I obtained a better replacement." They chuckled like conspirators.

The Colfax light fades in July around ten o'clock. When the posse-men and their captives arrived, it was full dark. The Claims Club founders had designated the basement of the new mercantile as their jail. They secured Bragg and his gang there with Taylor Osgood, who pretended to deputize two mill workers to keep watch until the gang would be arraigned.

"Where could a person like me find a lodging?" Orestes asked.

"I have a friend who can help," Cashdown said.

Pinky said he could stay at her wash house. "I have back room for drivers, but nobody staying now. Still just Colfax business." She had been taking in laundry for townspeople but hoped to soon serve the new stage line transients. The wash house was now making more money than her wrangling for the mill men, and she would need to hire help.

She looked up at Orestes. "You have job, big man?"

"Right now, Miss, I have nothing but what I carry on my horse."

"You want work, I have work. By Jesus Christ, maybe you do

my horse job, so I can do laundry."

"We'll have to talk it over. Right now I'm in need of sustenance in the form of food and a good beverage."

The three went out to the Riverside Hotel for a midnight supper. Over trout fillets and wild rice, Pinky pressed Orestes to take on her wrangling work. They cut a deal. He shook his head and grinned. "Back to cowboying I guess."

Before he left for home the next morning, Cashdown went with James and Lycurgus to see the new circuit magistrate about the Odis Bragg arraignment. On the way he spotted Lettice Wheeler strolling up the sidewalk toward them. He ducked into a doorway until she passed, then quickly caught up with his friends. James told him Mrs. Wheeler had been inquiring around town about his reputation and background. "Seems she's taken an interest in you, Cashdown."

"She is a looker, ain't she?"

They checked on the magistrate's calendar: there would be a hearing in a week.

When Cashdown arrived home, Libbie was sorting berries in the afternoon sun on the side porch of the new house. She rose from her work and greeted him with a smile. He lifted her off her feet and twirled her round and round. He nuzzled his beard into her neck. She called him a redheaded monkey and laughed so loudly some of the children came running up from the garden—Jack, Charlotte, Frances, and Mindy. He greeted each one with kisses and said how much he'd missed them.

Libbie asked about the capture, and Cashdown said they had been outfoxed by Bragg and then rescued by a gigantic gunfighter toting explosives. "So much for the amateur posse. We almost took a swim in the Snake," he said.

"You're not much of a swimmer, Hamish. We just give thanks to God you got home in one piece."

"Aye, and there's work to be done here. Where are the boys?

We need to finish before the party." The house christening event was set to happen in four weeks.

CHAPTER 7

They invited neighboring homesteaders, including Cushing McBride and Payton Williams and their families, as well as new friends from Colfax: James Perkins and his girlfriend, young Jenny Ewart; Lycurgus Ames and his new bride, Genevieve; and Pinky, who in turn invited Orestes Alton Banks. The Ewings and a few other farm families in the vicinity came, too. The guests arrived by buggy and horseback, the larger families by buckboard carriage and charabanc. They brought baked casseroles and breads and cakes, fresh fruits and all the vegetables of the season. Elbourne and Trayton as usual saw to the horses' livery.

Liam was unavailable. He had accepted work as assistant at Overman Powell's new Colfax bank. OP, as Powell was called, established the bank as a branch of the one he'd opened in Walla Walla a few years earlier. Now he was teaching Liam how to keep accounts. OP came up to Colfax in search of new opportunities, he said, and to get some distance on the memories of his late wife, deceased from smallpox after she refused to be vaccinated. Though there were no variola pesthouses in Walla Walla and Mrs. Powell declined at home, OP was not infected, perhaps because he was not so religiously persuaded and had gotten his scratch. But his wife had suffered amid fervent prayers through fevers and blisters, and then vomiting and bleeding pustules, and finally a painful, choking death. OP declared that her pious devotion wasn't a very effective curative and thereafter proclaimed himself a healthy atheist widower.

OP arrived at the Musgrave celebration in the company of Mrs. Lettice Wheeler, leaving Liam to mind the bank. Mrs. Wheeler had heard in town about the plans and exclaimed to OP what a grand opportunity it would be for a lonely widow to meet some of the better people in the surrounding area. She had clutched his arm with both hands as she made her gentle plea. His instinct was to help her adjust to her new life condition; after all, he was in a similar situation and well knew how isolating widowhood must be. Though he equivocated, at the last moment he told her he would be pleased to have her accompany him.

When OP and Lettice Wheeler arrived, the visitors were gathering in the backyard between the new house and the vegetable garden. Pyramid Peak rose protectively over the northeast horizon, the early afternoon sun turning its western flank golden and making it look like a colossal haystack. People remarked about how comforting it must be to live in close view of such an inspiring mountain, so like a sentinel guarding against danger and a beacon showing the way home.

" 'Tis indeed a constant inspiration," Cashdown said. "Always in mind, and sometimes I go up to the top before dawn to be first in the territory to see the sun rise. One day I will be gathering fruits over there."

Libbie emerged with the girls after preparing the meal. She instructed all the youngsters to lay the enormous banquet table—a twenty-foot slab cut from an ancient ponderosa pine and set on sawhorses in the yard—and joined Cashdown by the garden. OP approached and introduced Mrs. Wheeler.

"I have met Mr. Musgrave, on more than one occasion," Lettice Wheeler said, smiling demurely and offering her gloved hand to him.

Cashdown gave her hand a quick pump and said, "My darling wife and mother of our industrious brood, Elizabeth Musgrave." He pulled Libbie to his side and grinned. The two women inspected each other up and down.

"Welcome, Mrs. Wheeler. Hamish has told me you're thinking of settling at Colfax. It's a coming place. You'll surely find a proper situation and a good church there, if you choose to stay on."

Lettice pursed her lips into a weak smile, and Libbie cocked her head and turned to Cashdown. "I'll just check on the children," she said. "We're almost ready to eat."

Seated at the long table, the family and guests passed around platters of roasted venison and salmon, fresh vegetables, tureens of game-bird stew, and casseroles of chicken and rabbit. They poured pitchers of cider and ginger beer. Soon the valley was filled with their raucous gossip and laughter. They told stories of Indian encounters and swapped lore about farming methods and ways to handle the challenges of raw nature.

At the table's far end Cashdown talked with OP, Lycurgus, James, and Orestes about the magistrate's decision. "They made a restitution, all right, gave over the stolen lands and paid the fines. But a year's prison time seems a tot light to me," he said.

James said he was hoping Bragg and his entourage would be banished from the county. "Or we might be chasing them again next year. They deserve worse, and our town deserves better."

"The purpose of punishment, gentlemen, is to correct and educate, not to gain revenge. The problem for the law is to find a proper measure of the one and to avoid an inclination toward the other," Orestes interjected in his deep baritone. "We call them judges because they must exercise judgment, not just on guilt or innocence but also on fitting the penalty to both the crime and the defendant. Too much penalty and some criminals will seek their own revenge. Same crime with too little penalty and there's insufficient learning. In both cases there will be no correction. Since there was no jury to be taught the case and the principles of jurisprudence, the task for our magistrate was to properly fit the penalty to the guilty party, and that means he had to properly read Bragg's character and temperament. Only time will tell how well he did his reading." He smiled and scanned his companions, as if he'd given a successful defense of the magistrate.

The others looked at one another, perhaps thinking the same inspired thought. James was first to speak out. "Orestes, do you plan to wrangle horses and clean stalls the rest of your life? Or might you put some of that training in the law to better purpose?"

Orestes smiled and said, "Cleaning stalls does no harm to my dignity, and I enjoy working with the horses. Maybe you have something else in mind, James?"

"Whitman County's growing, Colfax is prospering—the future looks bright. People here have already taken to you, Orestes. They accept you and like you, and I'm confident they'd vote for you for a town or county office. You should settle here for good."

Orestes began to shake his head *no.*

Cashdown said, "Now that Mr. Nosler is leaving the territory, we'll be needing a new sheriff. Seems a natural choice, Orestes. Come November there will be an election, and we could form a committee. I'd say it's not too soon to start preparing your acceptance speech."

Shortly thereafter, Cashdown clinked his knife on a pitcher. He stood and announced to the celebrating visitors, "Mr. Orestes Alton Banks, Esquire, our esteemed rescuer and recently arrived townsman, has just declared his willingness to be drafted for the soon-to-be vacant position of Whitman County sheriff. We congratulate him and join together in our vigorous support of his campaign to win that office. He will make a grand law officer!"

He raised his glass in a toast. People cheered and clapped and toasted to Orestes and his forthcoming campaign.

After the tours of the big house and barn were over, after the vast table was cleared and dishes were washed and restored to their rightful owners, after the sun dropped below the rolling hills to the west and left the valleys in cooling semidarkness, and after the last visitors disappeared down the Territorial Road and all the night chores were finished and the children were asleep in their new bedrooms, Cashdown and Libbie carried a lamp to their room and sat on the edge of the bed. Libbie withdrew a letter from her skirt pocket and handed it to Cashdown. "It's addressed to you." she said.

"What's this?"

"From Callum."

Cashdown carefully opened the envelope and held the letter toward the lamp. He read it, then slowly read it a second time. He sat for a long while with the letter in his lap, staring at it and saying nothing.

"Bad news?"

"Hard to say. I'll read it to you."

> My Dear Brother, I am ashamed that I did not return to the Palouse with Henry and Mindy, and I can only beg for your Understanding and Forgiveness. I was drawn away by Something I could not resist. I was visited by a Temptation and ran off in a swoon. When I awoke from my stupor I found myself in Utah in company of several Gentlemen who encouraged me to establish myself independently and in harmony with my True Spirit. It might occur to you that I have fled because of an affection I cannot express even within our Family. You might think it regards only, or in

the main, your faithful Wife, my Sister-in-law, but that would be mistaken. I hope someday to make this clearer for both of us.

I am now residing in Colorado, and I do not know when I will return to the Washington Territory. Until I do, my blessed Hamish, I will think of you and all the Family with Love.

Your Faithful and Admiring Brother,
Callum

CHAPTER 8

"He was always a bit off, don't you know. Not that he wasn't clever and given to many talents. Oh, he was a binnacle, I swear, with a magnetic compass grown into his head, never in his life got lost, but maybe that was because he took such care and was so watchful. And in school he was an apt pupil and loved mathematics and history. It's just that he had little joy, and strangers made him uneasy, always did. I remember before we left Hastings for Southampton and the ship, and he said he'd changed his mind and didn't want to go to America after all. So I say, 'What now, Cal? I can't manage all this cargo alone, the team and trap and our trunks and the crates for Uncle Granville. I'll have to see them all the way to Ohio m'self.' And he looks at me like I'm speaking Swahili. Just looked so sad and balled up inside, like he often did. Well, you've seen him like that, Lib. Eventually he replied, kind of sheepish like, to say he was afraid to be confined with all those people—forty days on a ship crowded with strangers, everyone pushing to hear each other's stories? It wasn't the stink below or the rotten food or the pinched quarters he feared. No, it was those people. He was never happy outside the family and took little joy inside."

Libbie was trying to stay awake while Cashdown reasoned his way through the oblique statements and lacunae in Callum's letter. It was long past the time everyone else was asleep, and the two were in bed in the new house. But he needed to talk. He had a puzzle, and his usual way to reach understanding of problems and puzzles was to talk until something suggested itself as a way into the true heart of the mystery. He would encircle the unknown with a seine of language, trawl through any relevant memories and anecdotes and stories, and pull out any quirk or deviation as a clue.

"Then why would he go off to Colorado like that, away from all he has of family out here?" she said.

"There's the rub. All his life he's had only a few close friends. I've been the closest, if I do say, and I miss him so greatly now you'd think he'd miss us. Surely you know he never wed, but he was once engaged to be married. In Ohio it was, the first girl he'd gotten to know, little thing only fifteen but already in the puddin' club and the father desperate to get her sorted. They lived on the next settlement to Uncle Granville's, flock of Norwegians, and when we arrived with our fine carriage and team and educated speech and spare coins, they must've thought they'd found a plum match. I was having none of it, but Cal took the girl as a victim that needed a rescue, like a puppy that's been whipped. They ran off somewhere, but something about it didn't appeal to Cal, because within a week the girl—Astrid something, if I recall right—came back in tears, and her clan went off chasing someone else.

"I asked her what happened with Cal, and she said he never took advantage of her, though I suppose they'd had relations, but he'd protected her until they met up with a bunch of Lutherans, and he left her in their care, and they sent her home. I think she married one of the Lutherans. When he came back Cal told me he had reconsidered and decided he was too young for fatherhood. I think he was embarrassed to say what he thought about the girl. But that was the last time he ever showed any interest until you arrived. So, to answer your question, m'love, I'm still stumped."

"Cal is now fifty-two, isn't he."

"Aye, two years junior to me."

"Might he be troubled by some spiritual matter? His letter says he got a revelation and was finding his true spirit. I've often spied him gazing skyward with that lost look on his face, and whenever you two finished the day and sat before the stove you'd be talking away and Cal would be downcast as if he was in prayer."

"Ah, prayer. We weren't a churchy family back in Hastings. I've told you that before, Lib. And he never mentioned wanting to attend services, though he did like to sing hymns, and we both could quote from the King James. He especially liked the verses about order and cleanliness and often repeated his favorites. 'Let us cleanse ourselves from all filthiness of the flesh and spirit,' he'd say. And—and, 'Wash you, make you clean, put away the evil of your doings.' That one he'd say like he was singing a song when we'd got muddy and would be washing up for supper. I thought he was just being clever, but now I wonder. I wonder if he senses some guilt about something, and that's the spiritual trouble he can't wash off, what's chased him away."

"Hamish," Libbie murmured sleepily, "in time the truth will be revealed. Be patient and go to bed."

"Aye, right, of course. Still, I think I'll write back to him one day soon and try to comfort him."

But as so often in the past, he quickly forgot about his urgency to write to his brother. Harvest season was fast approaching, and preparations for the Palouse winter were soon to start, so letter writing and gadding about in Colfax would wait. Besides, he had a political campaign to run.

The sun was now rising later each morning and farther to the south of Pyramid Peak, and Earth's shadow chased the cone of brassy light up the Peak's western flank earlier each evening. The wheat fields had turned to blond seas with golden waves rolling in the dry winds. Geese in their thousands barked high in the twilit skies, and choruses of waxwings and grosbeaks and mated kinglets adorned the black hawthorns and bitter cherries. The world smelled of baked earth and ripe grains and pine resin. Creeks were low, and the wells were down, but there was enough water yet for the livestock, and travel was eased by the long dry season.

For a while Cashdown and the boys—now not only Elbourne and Trayton, but also the younger Ferdy, Willie, and Jack—joined the three neighboring families to move equipment from farm to farm for the harvest: the shared reaper and threshing machine and dozens of pulling mules and horses, the supply wagons for grain sacks and straw, and the cook wagon and foodstuffs. As it had to be finished before the fall rains came, there was a continuous press of dangerous work. Someone, often one of the younger boys, would get sliced on the leg by the thresher belt, a wagon would run off downhill and spill over, a crouching fawn would be shredded in the reaper, and everyone would be scorched by the relentless sun. But after three weeks of dawn-to-dark labor, all four farms had sacks of wheat stacked to the rafters and bays full of chopped straw in the barns. Sales and trade would follow, some at the new mills in Dayton and Waitsburg, and, for flour ground from the grains, at docks far to the west in Portland and Astoria. Cashdown didn't grow it but took payment for his harvest work in grains and straw. It was as good as cash, he instructed the boys.

During the harvest, whenever enough energy remained in their tired bodies late at night, Cashdown and the family worked an hour or two copying handbills and posters for Orestes's sheriff campaign. While they worked, Cashdown entertained the children by singing frontier songs of work, love, and war—"Pop Comes the Rhino," "The Fisherman's Bride," "Dancing Cowhand," and "When This Cruel War is Over":

Dearest Love, do you remember, when we last
did meet,
How you told me that you loved me, kneeling at
my feet?

Oh! How proud you stood before me, in your
suit of blue,
When you vowed to me and country, ever to be
true.

Weeping, sad and lonely, hopes and fears how
vain!
When this cruel war is over, praying that we meet
again.

He would sing in falsetto and pretend to weep at the end, and the young ones would cackle with delight.

Cashdown had a talent for songs, happily playing his pipe or fiddle at every opportunity and recalling lyrics to hundreds of standards of the day. At celebrations he would dance endlessly—the reels and jigs and hornpipe steps, the polkas and waltzes and quadrilles. In addition to his reputation for being an astute and honest merchant-farmer who always paid cash and expected cash in payment, he was gaining renown as a man of high spirits and gay temperament. On many Saturday nights he welcomed dozens of settlers and Colfax friends for an evening of revelry, converting the entire downstairs to a dining room and bar. After dinner they would move the festivities to the rough floorboards of the barn, where there was band music and singing and dancing, often going on till daylight. This was when he began to put up oysters in quantity for treating his guests. At first, he would buy them from traveling coastal Indians; later, tinned or iced oysters were shipped up the Columbia, and he would buy them from roving Nez Perce brokers from Almota.

Cashdown and Libbie were invited to all the dances and parties and holiday events in Colfax and elsewhere around the Palouse. If he heard a musician he particularly admired, Cashdown would enlist him in the Wheatland Whirlwinds Frontier Band, a group of entertainers he assembled and managed. There were fiddlers, pipers and horn players, percussionists and a guitarist, and an accordionist who would take to a piano or concertina if one was available. With musical roots in the Midwest and Appalachia reaching back to ancestors across Europe and Africa, the players were Colfax shopkeepers and millworkers, and farmers from around the Palouse country. They played for pleasure and donations and enjoyed widespread acclaim, and they learned from one another so that in time they came to justify their fame.

They played for Libbie's grand suffrage party one evening in September, after the big traveling event in Colfax. On a second circuit of the West, following a tour two years earlier that stopped only in Walla Walla, Abigail Scott Duniway brought Susan B. Anthony to the Palouse for lectures, rallies, and pamphleteering. Colfax was their second stop, and they attracted a crowd of three hundred women and their male supporters, all dressed in Sunday finery. A noisy fringe of anti-suffrage marchers—mostly men but also some women wearing headscarves and homespun aprons—circled the gathering and tried to disrupt the rally speeches. But they were booed and shouted down until they skulked away.

Libbie stood so close to the speakers she could see the sparkles in their eyes and hear the rustling of their crisp dresses when they gestured. Cashdown stood at her side. She knew what to expect because Miss Anthony's speeches had been quoted in Wyoming and Utah newspapers and reproduced in all the regional editions. But to hear the appeals in person and this close, to witness demands for equality of the sexes and races delivered with such passion and conviction, was electrifying to Libbie and the local women. She knew then that the women's vote was more than just a fanciful hope.

She exclaimed, "I want to help gather the women here for the vote, Hamish. I must do something."

He flashed his broad grin. "Grand. Of course I'm with ye, and all the women hereabouts. And across the nation, too. Shall we invite these to dinner? Mrs. Duniway's husband, too?"

She turned a stunned look to him. "Oh, Hamish. No, we're not important enough. Besides, they're off right away to Spokane and Olympia. But we could hold a gathering at home to form an association. We'd set a feast, and your band could play, and we'll have a fit celebration to start things off."

While Mrs. Duniway was handing out copies of the *New Northwest* and Miss Anthony was instructing her entourage on arrangements for the rest of the tour, the crowd milled about and socialized. Local plans were laid for adding temperance and wage equality to the Northwest suffrage movement. Networks were formed of farm wives and employed spinsters. There was talk of joining in a march planned for Walla Walla.

A hand touched Cashdown's arm, and from behind a woman's voice cooed, "I'm sure we ladies can count on your support, can't we, Mr. Musgrave." He turned to face Lettice Wheeler. With a nod and smile to Libbie, she had eased herself between them.

"Ah, Mrs. Wheeler. You have me right," he said, launching a pre-emptive verbal barrage. "In fact, Libbie and I were just now discussing our plan for a grand gathering at our abode to sort out the issues and make a committee and find our way toward establishing the women's vote, and, oh, we'll have a festive meal and fitting music at our little place—songs of liberty, songs of women's suffrage, songs of honor and duty. I've got the band already, and they're ready to play, might even deign to play a tune or two m'self, and there will be dancing, oh aye, there must be dancing, and we'll dance till the cows come home, won't we, Lib!"

With that he spun around, reached behind Lettice Wheeler and grabbed Libbie by the wrist. He reeled her into his arms and began to dance a jig on the jammed main street of Colfax, singing and whooping and laughing. Soon another couple stepped out to dance, and in a few moments most of the assembled crowd were embracing and singing and dancing. Lettice stood in befuddlement and watched until she had to get out of the way of the surging, wheeling dancers. She retreated into the Riverside Hotel & Boarding House before Cashdown and Libbie headed off to their gig and team.

Chapter 9

The big table was set up outdoors near the garden. By dusk it was covered with heaping platters of meat—fresh roasts of pork and venison, wild pheasant and quail, slabs of salmon—and bowls of summer squashes and carrots and wild roots, and plates of greens and nuts and cheeses. Casks of cider and ale were set on cribs near the table, and people lined up to draw pints into their mugs. Cashdown came from the house bearing a wide tray of oysters, both spiced patties and fried. He pinged a glass with his knife and called for attention. Thirty people gathered and sat down around the table as Cashdown delivered an opening speech.

"How happy this occasion is, bringing together you good people, new friends and neighbors, fellow settlers all, fighting for passage of the universal franchise. Welcome to our home, and thank you for coming here and giving joy to this old heart. Indeed it is not our place to lead the fight, we men. That is yours, you women and the other disfranchised of the land. I therefore am going to clam up and give the floor to anyone who wants to take the lead and show the way. Meanwhile we'll enjoy the vittles and the rest, and later we can dance till the sun rises on a new day." He passed around the oyster salvers amid chatter of who should speak first about suffrage.

A voice rose above the din. "Let Elizabeth speak. She knows what we want!" Shouts of agreement and applause encouraged Libbie to stand and say something.

"I don't know where to start, except, of course, like Hamish, to thank you for being here. I know only that hearing Miss Anthony speak so well about the need to recognize women as people and citizens was, well, just one of the profoundest things I've ever heard. I was moved to tears when I realized the power in her vision. Imagine women being able to vote, being eligible to take office, at last being free to petition on our own." She paused and looked around searchingly. "I say the time has come for us, if only we declare it so. We must form an association here on the Palouse Prairie, like they've done in Walla Walla, and speak up for our part of humanity. Who has an idea about how we should start? Will someone make note of our ideas? Thank you, Mrs. Parker. I'm hungry, so just speak up, anyone." She sat down, but in a short while she was asked to stand again to accept the nomination for president of the Palouse Women's Suffrage Association.

The feast and discussion lasted for two hours. The band arrived and set up on the barn threshing floor. The animals were tended, cleanup was finished, and fresh casks of ale and cider were moved inside the barn. Music and dancing and laughter started up, and the sounds flowed out the wide doors and spread like a spicy fragrance across the valley. The twins had prepared a bonfire in the east yard and lit it at midnight; its ashes were still flickering in the early glow of dawn when the last buggy left the place and disappeared down the Lapwai Trail.

Libbie turned in, but Cashdown stayed out and watched the bonfire fade to a few curls of white smoke. In the grey morning twilight he looked to the northeast and watched the dawn's aura brighten around the top of Pyramid Peak. He shifted his gaze toward the northwestern horizon and saw there the silhouette of a dozen horses, the riders standing and squatting alongside, as if they had been watching from the bluff for a long time. The riders swung up on their bareback mounts and vanished.

He went in and sat by the kitchen stove. He lit a pipe and sat watching the dawn rise and pondered his ambitions and all the changes he'd seen. After a while, he took up pen, ink, and paper and very slowly began composing a reply to Callum.

My Dearest Brother Cal,

It cheered this heart to receive yours of the 18th last. I am well pleased that you have found a place in Colorado, though I confess we all wish you were here with us now. You have no cause for shame nor reason for seeking forgiveness. If anything, it is I who should be asking for your forgiveness, as I was not attentive to your sufferings. It matters not what the reasons are for your changed sentiments, we all harbour secrets in our hearts, and we all struggle in the eyes of Providence. What's right for us is only to continue loving one another as heartful as we can. You remember Father saying that love is not a something, and I always took him to mean that love is some actions we can learn to do with growing effect and satisfaction over time. So, we're just on a ride, dear Brother, traveling on a trail toward a destination we will never reach. The traveling is all that can matter, and you are smack in the heart of it.

Things here are much different than when you left. The stage line is soon to come up the Territorial Road and the Kentuck to Spokane Falls, possibly within the year, although the railroads still talk of extending lines into the Palouse Country. Pinky says she will buy a Concord and promises she will stop here when her coach comes up. Our friend Orestes Banks will be soon installed as Colfax and Palouse sheriff. He is a first-class man and will bring order and dignity to the country. James Perkins now is running things in Colfax, and Liam and Elbourne both are working at Overman Powell's bank. Tray is farming, and Ferdy and Willie are not far from it. Young Jack is learning the printer's trade. The Paluses have been kind and peaceful, but there are rumours of Nez Perces coming on the warpath, and they say the Paluses and Cayuses might join them. Libbie is frantic, and I'm trying to assure her that we are safe and the bands nearby us are our friends.

We all send our most affectionate good wishes for your safety and vigourous health. I hope it will not be very long before we see your face once again. You know you always will be welcome here and remain secure in my heart.

Your Loving Brother,
Hamish

Cashdown would receive no reply from Callum that year, nor for some years after. The time would pass quickly, though, for the Musgrave household was a hive of continuous labor and entertainment. Cashdown would expand his herds and hay fields, begin construction on a new barn, and design a small general store in anticipation of future stagecoaches; he would play in the Wheatland Whirlwinds Frontier Band at events around the region and go to Colfax weekly for what he called "the public service"—politicking and socializing with his friends. When Orestes brought Lucinda Callison to a Baptist congregation supper at the Colfax Academy, it was Cashdown who welcomed the couple into the social circles of the city and outlying farms. Orestes told him in confidence about Lucinda's Indian heritage, and Cashdown responded, "We're all some sort of mongrel, ain't we?"

The office of sheriff had gone by a landslide to Orestes, who would earn a reputation as a sober, wise, and fearsome lawman who brought order along with justice to the Palouse country. During his years as Whitman County sheriff, he would bring civility and peace to Colfax; a district court would be established there, and local constabularies would be started in many towns. He tamed the fractious prostitution trade, which was consolidated into an orderly house run by a madam known as Big Kay. By his second year in office, the hand-written weekly *Colfax Guardian* had evolved into the machine-printed daily *Palouse Gazette,* and a recurring column of news about the sheriff's law enforcement actions was added. Orestes quickly became known and respected by settlers throughout eastern Washington.

Before his term expired, Orestes was drafted for another public office. He was elected by a large margin as the first Black representative sent from eastern Washington to the territorial legislature and would long be remembered as a tireless advocate of women's voting rights and defender of Constitutional rights for Indian tribes in his region. Cashdown managed his campaign.

On the eve of Orestes's departure for his first legislative session in Olympia, he asked Cashdown and a few other close supporters to join him as his guests for drinks. They were seated around a rear table near the Rumford stove at the Frontier Hotel and Public House, Colfax's first brick structure. Orestes wore a black pinstripe suit with a grey waistcoat and a watch fob. His boiled white shirt was set off by a floral tie and matching pocket square. Cashdown arrived outfitted as a gentleman farmer: high-collar shirt under a wool sweater and tweed hacking jacket, all in shades of brown and tan, and twill pants that covered most of his tooled riding boots. He wore his silk stovepipe hat. OP, James, Lycurgus, and local teacher Sam McCroskey joined them.

"You, my friends, have been my staunchest supporters, both during my brief years as sheriff and in my campaigns. This gathering is a way for me to express my gratitude for your diligence and goodwill." Orestes raised his whiskey glass. "Thank you, one and all, for your faith in me and for welcoming me and my new bride into your lives. We will be maintaining a home here in the Palouse country, even as we travel often to Olympia."

They toasted their congratulations and wishes of good luck, each in turn, and by the time the first course was brought to the table the conversation was a lively chatter of stories about crimes solved and attempted jailbreaks averted, campaign mistakes and triumphs, crop harvests and population growth, flood control, and Indian encounters.

OP said the election was proof that Orestes had been a fine lawman. "But you never once executed a capital felon, in spite of the magistrate's order. I've wondered how you dared that."

"If you mean why I dared disobey the bench, Overman, it was a philosophical quarrel. I cannot carry out such a form of punishment. I will not kill another person, man or woman, except in direct defense of my life or under threat of imminent death of an innocent. My position is that I'm dedicated to restitution plus recompense, correction, and restoration. Justice reaches out to both the victims of crimes and the perpetrators. My position, my friends, has reflected the full meaning of justice."

"But how do you repay for a life already taken from the innocent?" OP demanded. "The death sentence is handed down to only the most incorrigible criminals, and it's the broadest and fairest kind of recompense, a life for a life taken or a herd stolen, and the strongest kind of correction, because it warns onlookers of the consequences of such a crime. Execution only happens to persons who are incapable of correction and restoration. And if it's the law of the land, across the entire republic . . ."

Orestes held up his hand. "Any person incapable of correction is a mental defective and should be in a madhouse, not dead. Otherwise, there are always contributing circumstances, and of course it's possible to get the wrong miscreant. Law of the land? Consider that it's still the law of the land that women can't elect me. If Mrs. Elizabeth Musgrave tries to vote, am I to drag her away or arrest her? My cousin in Georgia still cannot sell the fruits of his farm at night—that's the law of the land in Georgia, and the United States government will do nothing to overturn it." His voice slowed and grew more solemn as he talked. "The law still says our red friends must stay on patches of land we've generously given back to them after stealing and diminishing it. What happens if I'm told I must capture a Coeur d'Alene or Cayuse brave because he's wandered off his reservation? Am I to say, 'You don't belong here in freedom, you must return to your confinement?' "

Cashdown nodded in conciliation. "Aye. Our circuit judges surely did back away from insisting on such punishments, and Orestes was right for us. And now he takes his lofty ideas to Olympia, where he can help shape the laws."

OP shook his head. "Those ideas will indeed be tested in Olympia."

When dinner was over and the cigars had been smoked down to stubs and the others had departed for home, Orestes and Cashdown remained to say their goodbyes.

"This was a spare country when I came up a mere half dozen years ago," Cashdown mused. "Almost empty. Hardly another person for ten miles in any direction then, even counting the Paluses. And now we've new villages and towns, sprung up like spring mushrooms, brickworks and mills and bridges and roads, aye, and people, enough people to warrant our own representative, and by God we've got the best one of any."

"You've a flair for flattery, *amigo.* But I surely wouldn't be heading west without your wisdom and hard work, and I hope I can justify what you and all the folks here in my adopted homeland have done for me and the faith you've placed in me. I'll do my damnedest to bring us statehood and establish some control over the railroads and get the currency straightened out."

"It's you who've done the hard work. Pity the poor places where there's lawlessness and brutality—you've protected us from that, and your policing and good example have given me and settlers like me the freedom to start our businesses, work up our herds, and set our crops. And the heart to dare something new. Ah, I don't know what I'll do for company with you off to the coast."

"There's plenty to occupy you, I'm sure—your cows and mules and horses, your orchards. And most of your kids still need education. That can't be left solely to Sam McCroskey. I worry more about you getting into mischief over Lettice Wheeler in my absence."

"No telling who she'll muckle onto. But truly I'm afraid I'll be lonely, not seeing you riding in at our place all the time on your rounds. OP's accounts are growing so fast he hardly has time for a friendly beer on an afternoon, and, besides, he's soon to marry Florence Higginbotham. Lycurgus is all tied up with his new presses and trying to keep aboard a good reporter or two. James is running the city now, so he has no time for me, and Pinky's away most of the time on that Concord coach she bought. And Libbie, Libbie's away half the time, too, teaching and preaching on the Suffrage Association. My Liam is in town all week at the bank, and the twins are now thinking of claiming a place of their own. Good Jesus, no, I expect it'll be lonelier around here without your constant presence."

It was a long ride home on the Territorial Road under the cool October moon. Cricket, eighteen this year, was slow and distracted—six hours of saddle riding in one day was a lot for her. As they neared the farm Cashdown looked back at the moonlit spire of Pyramid Peak, hovering like a ghostly cone on the northeast horizon. It seemed the only permanent feature of the country, the only comfort in his times of loneliness and a lodestar of self-location.

After breakfast and his early chores the next morning, he came in for some coffee. Libbie was busy in the kitchen with the girls. "I've been thinking," he mused, "about why I feel more lonesome now. Orestes says I have plenty to distract me, folks to keep me company. But I still feel isolated. I believe I miss my people, the Scottish way of life, my heritage, don't you know? I've been thinking, we should leave here and move up to British Columbia. We ought to do it before the young ones go much further in school. I can have things all settled up by the end of the month."

★ ★ ★ ★ ★

Part Two

★ ★ ★ ★ ★

Every man is said to have his *peculiar ambition.*

—Abraham Lincoln

CHAPTER 10

She debated him through the winter and on into spring. What about her suffrage campaign? How could they leave Liam and the twins here on their own? What about *their* family? The schools in Canada's territories might be poor. His responses were always the same: life is a series of adventures, and if we stop chasing the adventures we die of boredom. The real roots of England and Scotland are transplanted in the north, he'd argue. She persisted in the face of his intransigence, but in the midst of April's rains and deepening mud Cashdown announced that he was leaving for British Columbia come May, no matter her objections. He would go with or without her, he said, but he was going, and he would take the children and the livestock with him. Libbie recognized his desperation; still, she struggled to reason with him, and a standoff ensued. He had laid down his final card and so made his preparations.

The shrill courting of redwing blackbirds and warning honks of nesting Canada geese twirled up from the swollen stream on the morning she relented. For the first time, Libbie acknowledged how weary she was made by the struggle. He had worn her down, she said, and she recognized this was not the time or issue when her principles and desires could turn him toward renouncing his restless imagination. She paused, stared at him solemnly, and said simply, "Your romantic heart is a danger to your good intentions, Hamish. So, we'll go."

Within days he had a buyer for the farm, and two weeks later he had completed plans for packing the wagons and moving the stock northward. OP wired Cashdown's considerable assets to a bank in New Westminster. The older boys would be staying on in Colfax, taking over James's original cabin and corrals for Liam and all working at the bank. Tray now also had a farm, and Elbourne would soon join him on an adjacent section. But the other children were coming to an age when they could help with home and farm chores and the demands of such a move as Cashdown envisioned. They began to realize they would not be planting this spring and so there would be no fall harvest, they would not be starting at Sam McCroskey's academy, and the spirited all-night revelries at home would stop. Cashdown tried each evening to convince them that the excitement of the adventure and the family's improved future circumstances would happily justify their new labor and sacrifices. Nobody shared his enthusiasm. Ferdy and Jack said they would not go, insisting they could stay on with their older brothers. But their father forcefully overruled them. Late at night the children grimly rehearsed their farewells to friends, to their daily routines, to their life at the big house.

The final evening at the homestead they camped in the yard, the house and sheds having been emptied and the line of wagons loaded chock-full with furniture, tools, clothing, food supplies, and all the goods that make civilized, if not gracious, frontier home life possible. Cashdown was up before dawn the next day and roused everyone from their bedrolls. He made coffee and inspected the herds and pull-horses and mules and the idling wagon train. He would travel on his big riding mule, Peppermint, and keep the herds in order. Libbie would take the lead wagon. The children worked in pairs, each pair driving a freighter: Holly with Frances, Laura with Jack, Ferdy and Little Mindy, and Willie with Charlotte. The first three wagons drew supply trailers, the last two ponied the charabanc and surrey in tandem. After breakfast was finished, all were ready to start out as the rising sun lit the top of Pyramid Peak.

The entourage eased onto the trail amid the clicks and whistles of drivers, creaks of axles and harnesses, grunts and farts of horses, and the heavy rumble of following livestock herds. Cowbirds flew up and quail skittered ahead of them, the morning breeze ruffled manes and tails, and the early sun mocked nine stolid faces. Only Cashdown seemed happy to be moving. He whistled a tune as he encircled the herds and rode up and down the slowly moving train, never looking back at the homestead receding below the grade behind them. Within an hour the train had settled into an orderly pace and spacing, and by noon they had arrived without incident at the Kentuck. Less than a mile beyond Pyramid Peak, they turned north and a short while later stopped for lunch.

After seeing to the animals and setting out lunch for the children, Cashdown and Libbie sat by a water-birch grove near a swollen stream and ate.

"What's this stream called?" Libbie asked.

"Cottonwood Creek, same's what runs just north of our place, only here it's called Clear Creek."

"Pretty place, this."

"Aye, 'tis. And now the peak is right near, just a bit more southerly."

They sat quietly and ate their cheese and pickle sandwiches. After some minutes Libbie said, "Hamish, what are you going to do with nobody to call you Cashdown?"

He stopped chewing and stared straight ahead. After a long pause he replied, "Never thought much about it. A blessing, I'd say, to have a reputation and a name to go with it. I believe I shall miss that indeed."

"You will miss our friends and neighbors, Hamish. You have missed them much lately, I know, and you have been emptied by their absence from you. And now here you are trying to fill up your emptiness by heading off in the opposite direction of where you need to go."

"What're you saying? We're heading north to join my people."

"I just realized why you're so fixed on doing this. Your people? You know no one in the North. Your people, Hamish, are right here with you. That's not it."

"Ah, not this again. It's plain to see, Libbie, nobody needs me here. They'll get along famously without me. I'm taking my people with me, then."

"Your boys need you. Even though they're grown up men now, they still need your counsel. Your strength and love. But it's not that you don't see they need you."

"Aw, they know I love them, and we'll be only a letter and a week distant from them."

She thought for a moment. "Cal is only a letter and a week distant, too, but I'll bet you prefer that he was here at your side, so you can lend him your strength and reassure him of your love. I think it's that you miss Callum, and you fear he's not coming back, and you resent it. That's why you want to leave."

Cashdown went silent and stared at the blue mountain ridges to the east. He turned and gazed back on Pyramid Peak, stood, and continued gazing at it for a long time.

Finally, perhaps emboldened by her insights, Libbie said, "Hamish, I've changed my mind. I'm not going. I have my friends and my work on the vote to do here, I want the young ones to go to Sam McCroskey's academy, and I want you to be at my side when we win the battle for suffrage."

"Oh, I will. But you don't have to be here. Besides, we didn't start here, did we."

"I love this place, and we've adopted each other. You forget, it's *my* home country, and it's here I want to die, not in some foreign land." It was her turn to throw down the last card.

"You're not going, then?" He stared at her in disbelief, like a parent suddenly realizing his child had become an adult.

"No. I'm not going one foot further. I know why you're running away. But you'll be just as lonely above the border. Lonelier."

He paused again, looked around as if evaluating the terrain, and turned his pain-filled face to her.

"Are you having one of your headaches, Hamish? How would you go on without Pinky's treatments?"

"Ah, Libbie. What can we do now but go? We've sold the place, lock, stock, and barrel."

"We won't go backward." She scanned the area. She had been picking at her lunch and brushing crumbs off her lap. But now her arms were folded defiantly across her breasts. "What's wrong with this spot? There's the creek, there's your mountain just over your shoulder. We have the herds and enough in the wagons to begin anew right here."

Cashdown again gazed around and remained silent for several minutes. Then, as if emerging out of a dark cave into the noonday sunlight, he squinted and grinned, smacked his thigh, and shouted, "By good God, the stage line will soon be coming this way. Pinky said so, right past where we now stand! And they'll need a stop. This is the perfect spot for a new inn. You're a wonder, Lib. We could build the finest roadhouse between Walla Walla and Spokane Falls and have it up by summer's end."

They gathered the children and explained that a new plan was being laid. They would camp here at Cottonwood Creek while Pa would go to Colfax to see about the land and have his money returned from New Westminster. They would be attending Mr. McCroskey's school the following autumn after all.

In Colfax Cashdown learned that the Cottonwood Creek land was available from the railroad, and he immediately bought four square miles for six thousand dollars. Before the first stagecoach made its way up the Kentuck and the Territorial Roads, Cashdown had the framing for his new inn and store erected upon a stone foundation. He diverted some of the water from the creek to a twenty-foot-long trough so that several teams simultaneously could be refreshed with flowing water. When the main structure was finished there were five visitor suites, a four-hundred-square-foot dance floor, a tiny general store, and a large private wing for the Musgrave family's home. Neighbors and townspeople were so eager to help with the construction that the barns, pens, and storage sheds were finished by early July. The place was to be the biggest and finest roadhouse on the Palouse. Cashdown and Libbie no longer were just farmers and ranchers; they also would be innkeepers, merchandisers, and entertainers. Cashdown said they soon would be commercial orchardists again as well. Nobody thereafter mentioned the aborted emigration.

But there were dire distractions to their work that summer. Travelers to Colfax from the south told about Indian massacres of settlers and military encampments—non-treaty Nez Perces led by Chief Joseph and some Paluses under Red Echo, they said, had murdered men, women, and children at two sites in revenge for past humiliations. Others who came to Cashdown's Pyramid Inn roadhouse spoke about gatherings of warriors across the prairie and warned of an impending large-scale war. Mindful of Libbie's anxiety about natives, Cashdown headed to Colfax, saying he had to "suss the truth behind the rumors."

He found Lycurgus bent over his big Boston press in the newspaper office, muttering to himself. "Goddamned devil goes dry right in the middle of . . ."

"Ah, me blasphemous editor, what're we up to now?" Cashdown slammed the door when he entered, and Lycurgus glanced up.

"Damned bucket of gears and bolts keeps losing oil, always in the midst of a run. Thank you for interrupting my interruption. And to what do I owe . . . ?"

"What do you hear about braves on the warpath? Libbie's fit to collapse over the rumors."

"Oh, well she might, but it's uncertain," Lycurgus said, wiping oil from his hands. "There's been a major battle down near White Bird Camp. Two companies of the First Regiment went down there—armed cavalry about a hundred strong—and they had a dozen civvie volunteers and another dozen or so Nez Perce scouts with them. A couple of days of hard travel to get there, and they were tired out by the time they came across some seventy non-treaty braves under Chief Joseph and his brother."

Cashdown frowned. "The troops run 'em off?"

"Reports I received say it was a rout, but not the way you'd think. The troops had to retreat all the way to Mount Idaho. Thirty-four soldiers killed and four injured but rescued; far as I've heard, no Nez Perce casualties. Reporting said the used-up army horses bucked and bolted, so the troops couldn't shoot off them. But the Indian mounts were rested and strong, and, besides, the warriors usually get off and shoot from the ground, plus they know that country like their own beds. They had inferior guns; some even used bows and arrows. But they ruled the battle. Now, they say, they're on the run, God knows where."

"So, there's something to it after all."

"I heard most of the non-treaty bands are headed for Montana, but all the Paluses have turned back to go home. Libbie should rest easier, Cashdown. This might not become a general war."

"I'm obliged, my friend, but 'might not' won't be assurance

enough for her."

Cashdown gave encouraging news to Libbie when he returned to Pyramid Inn. But the rumors continued, and her panic grew. She soon determined to join fleeing neighbors, who formed a train to seek shelter at Fort Walla Walla. A platoon of cavalry soldiers came up to escort the settlers. Cashdown and the older children would stay, but Charlotte, Frances, and Mindy were to go south with their mother.

Chapter 11

A few weeks after Libbie and the girls departed for Fort Walla Walla, Cashdown heard rumors that the railroad was willing to sell off some land around Pyramid Peak. The newspapers and territorial maps were now calling the mountain Steptoe Butte. The new name honored a military battle near Rosalia twenty years earlier, when Colonel Edward J. Steptoe and his troops suffered an unseemly defeat by a force of Coeur d'Alene, Palus, and Spokane Indians. Despite Colonel Steptoe's humiliating retreat from the Pine Creek battle, stories spread of his battlefield courage and skill in earlier and subsequent engagements, and sympathy for him grew. The retreat gradually was transformed by patriotic memory from ignominy to wisdom. Some mistook the peak for the site of the battle and retreat, and so it began to be called Steptoe's Peak, over time evolving to Steptoe Butte. Later a new town would be named after Colonel Steptoe, and the actual site of the defeat would be rehabilitated to the Steptoe Battlefield State Park. Eventually, geologists around the world would label bedrock pinnacles exposed by erosion of lava deposits as "steptoes."

The coach inn duties and farm work were becoming routine business, so Cashdown was left with excess energy and time. Following his natural impulse, he began looking for new opportunities. He searched out the Northern Pacific Land Division agent—the spherical, flamboyantly dressed Cliven Cleary—and intercepted him on his circuit ride through Colfax. They met one early autumn noon at the Riverside Hotel, and Cash-down bargained a purchase of eight hundred acres that included most of Steptoe Butte's eastern and southern skirts. Upon his return home, Cashdown unhooked the sign that said *Pyramid Inn* and replaced it with one that said *Steptoe Station.* He engraved the letters in a plank two feet high by eight feet long and suspended it from the entrance gate's top bar.

Some days later, while working on a new extension for the horse barn, Cashdown spotted a spiral of dust above the ridge opposite. A fast-riding group of twenty or more Palus braves descended into the yard of Steptoe Station. Tomeo dismounted and walked over to face him.

"Your wife and children have left with soldiers and the other women. Why did they go?"

Cashdown looked at the implacable faces of the mounted Paluses. He studied Tomeo's expression and saw only serene self-possession. "They are afraid there will be a war," he said.

"No war here. We have other business."

"What is that, Tomeo?"

"Eeyomoshtosh, what you call Pyramid Peak. Now you call him Steptoe Butte. I see your sign."

Cashdown had dreaded this confrontation. The mountain was a sacred place for the Palus people, certainly for centuries, possibly for millennia, as a site for youths to go alone on spirit quests. A power spirit resides there, they said. Cashdown had seen the blackened campfire spots and animal bones left by boys during their conversion to adult braves. From their quests within the wildness of the peak—the dangers they faced from beasts and storms and the visions they saw in trance—they would find their manhood and their name. And now he owned much of it.

"What is your wish about Eeyomoshtosh?" he asked.

"The railroad man Cleary took your cash for the papers. You

made a treaty with him about it, and now you want to do something with Eeyomoshtosh. We do not honor treaties anymore. They tell us nothing. Mr. Cashdown, we want to know, what will you do now?"

"Ah, I see, yes. My wish is only to plant trees, Tomeo, sweet, blessed apple trees, around the feet of Eeyomoshtosh. It's to help our great Mother Nature honor him in the gift of her bounty, and to share the wonder of her fruit with every human in this region. I have no wish to interfere with your doings there, and I will be pleased to share my apples with the Palus people."

Tomeo and the braves looked askance. They had often heard confiscation and paternalism twinned in the settlers' talk. Even in this peaceful man, who had been kind to them and had become almost their friend, they were hearing it. They looked away, as if embarrassed by his presumptions. But Tomeo remained placidly focused.

"No fences?"

"No fences."

"No animals?"

"Aye, no livestock. No cattle, no horses."

"Sheep?"

"No sheep."

"We will still go to the mountain."

"Yes, of course."

"You will bring us apples?"

"I will bring all the apples you want."

"When?"

"Three, maybe four years. It takes time to grow the trees, get them producing."

A flicker of satisfaction crossed Tomeo's face. He returned to his horse, mounted up, and led his braves slowly away.

Cashdown immediately began plotting his orchard on the

east flank of Steptoe Butte. Cushing McBride heard about Cashdown's purchase and made a similar deal with Cliven Cleary for a smaller, adjacent section. The two friends met in Colfax and talked about joining forces as orchardists. They would pool their purchases of seeds, grafting supplies, and seedlings to gain buying leverage, they would share what each might learn about varieties of apples and husbandry, and they would share tools and the labors of planting and harvesting. Eventually their acreages would be joined, and their families would be joined by marriage.

Cashdown was excited by all the new activities at Steptoe Station and the butte. All that was missing, apart from Libbie and the young ones, was Callum. If he were to return, it would be a perfect time indeed. But there was no sign of him, and no letters from him came in on the stagecoaches. Cashdown decided to continue to write to his brother; maybe that way Cal could share in some of the improvements and excitement and would be more likely to consider renewing contact with the family.

My dearest Brother Callum,

We think of you every day with fondness and high hopes for your good health and prosperity. We are making good headway with our Coach Inn, which we are now calling Steptoe Station. It is named after the mountain you recall as Pyramid Peak, which is now known by most hereabouts as Steptoe Butte, and which I have recently purchased with intentions of creating orchards for the production of cider and eating and pie apples. We have a small crowd of travelers and drivers arrive twice each week and, on special occasions, more often. Pinky now owns the laundry and runs her two Concords. She was first to drive a coach here, and she foiled a highway robbery by Bragg and his gang on the Kentuck. When they arrive we put passengers up in the five guest rooms and feed them grand meals and entertain well into the night. We really do need your squeezebox and zither, though, for the dancing. The oysters have been fat, and last year's cider was especially fine.

Libbie and the three babies have gone down to Fort Walla Walla for a time, because of a Natives uprising. She feared there would be a wider range war, as did many in the Territory. She sends sorrowful letters home—she so misses the Palouse Country—but also is so fearful of the warriors and worried for the family's safety. All has been calm nearby here, though, and I hear the Nez Perces have been chased to the Canadian borderland in the Montana Territory. I'm sure she sends her highest regards and her wishes to see you again. Please give consideration to coming back to us. It's a splendid country and fertile, and full of game and fish, and populated by upright and vigorous settlers. All here miss you. I await your next letter with faithful anticipation.

Your abiding brother,
Hamish

Libbie and the girls stayed in Walla Walla until just before the autumn rains. Following the widespread panic from early reports of Indian attacks, an atmosphere of calm had returned to Whitman County. The papers in Spokane and Lewiston were reporting on the army's pursuit of Chief Joseph into Montana's northern wilderness, and the tribes in Washington Territory had resumed peaceful ways. The Indian bureau and the army encouraged settlers who sought shelter to return to their homesteads. Libbie returned in company of a dozen other mothers and their children, all escorted north by another cavalry unit from the fort.

Libbie told her husband she still was paralyzed by fear of an Indian attack. "You were right after all, Hamish. We should not have turned back from our plan to go north. I think we should give British Columbia another thought."

Cashdown gazed at her with a mask of adoring sorrow. "I understand, Libbie love, how alarming it must have been to hear all those stories. I'm sorry it pains you so and gives you such worry for the family's safety. But they have war parties up there, too. And Tomeo tells me the Paluses don't want war, and he is going to make it possible for me and Cushing to grow our apples without being troubled. We have dedicated ourselves anew to this place, Lib, and it's our duty to make good of it. Besides, you have much work to do right here for the vote. And the stage line depends on us now."

In time Libbie gained confidence that the family was in no imminent danger of attack, and she returned to the demands of her farm chores and duties as mistress of the inn. She also returned to her women's group and the campaign for suffrage.

Orestes and Lucinda returned to Colfax during the fall recess of the territorial legislature. Cashdown and Libbie were invited to dinner at the Banks home, along with several other leading citizens of Whitman County. Over glasses of young wine brought up from Lewiston, Orestes regaled the guests with stories of wild schemes to pass or defeat proposed bills, of backbiting and skirmishing among lawmakers, of bribes by conniving lobbyists, and of lessons learned from deal-making public servants, who had introduced him to the ways of the new legislature. While the problems were different, Orestes said, the process was much the same as he once saw in Georgia. He told them soon there would be a convention in Walla Walla to draft a state constitution, and he had created two petitions related to it that he would present to the legislature. One petition would allow women as delegates to the Walla Walla convention, and the other would add a clause in the forthcoming state constitution calling for universal suffrage. Even if there were enough signatures, however, the petitions still would have to be read out in committees before full hearings.

"So, what are our chances of gaining statehood?" Lycurgus asked.

"Less than even right now. But if we can fund a delegation to go to the national Congress, we might be able to press our case. Obadiah McFadden, our delegate-at-large, was an advocate, but he died last June and hasn't yet been replaced."

When the vote was taken in Olympia the following month, the petition for women to be delegates to the convention died in committee. The suffrage petition was moved forward and placed on the calendar for later floor debate in the legislative session. Most of the legislators were distracted by scandals in the East, and gossip flowed around the chambers and through the halls of Olympia. Little territorial work would be finished while the consequences of the snarled election were still unknown.

With the eventual compromise election of Rutherford B. Hayes, federal control over policies in Reconstruction states quickly shrank to nothing. All protections for freedmen and citizens of the territories were handed over to states and local governments, and it seemed to most citizens that the railroads and bankers were controlling the economy. A nationwide strike had been called by rail employees and another by miners. Federal troops were called out to battle the strikers, the same troops who no longer would be called out to protect Blacks in the South.

By the opening of Olympia's fall legislative session the rail strike had been broken, but the miners held on. Settlers farming in the territories and their legislators were unsure how much and what kind of support they might expect from the national government. It was clear, however, there would be a shift of control and funding toward local sources. Washington needed a replacement for the territory's nonvoting delegate-at-large, the legislator who would represent Washington in the national Congress. Olympia Republicans turned to their rising star to replace the late Obadiah McFadden.

A note arrived from Orestes saying he needed Cashdown's help with his campaign. Elbourne and Trayton would take leave from the Colfax bank and their farms on Tuesdays and Thursdays to manage Steptoe Station, while their father was away with Orestes and their mother was traveling the circuit to promote universal suffrage. Cashdown would hire farm labor for the twins. OP would be away with Orestes's campaign, too, which left Liam in charge of the bank on those days.

The autumn rains began as the campaign got underway. Cashdown had first to meet with the advocates from Whitman and adjoining counties to create strategies to influence legislators who might turn public opinion toward Orestes. The inaugural strategy meeting was held in Walla Walla, and Cashdown went on Peppermint as he expected muddy roads, and his mule would be dependably strong and surefooted. His expectation was warranted by the downpour that lasted all that day and into the following night. He was twice delayed when he stopped to help wayfarers in buggies stuck on Alpowa Grade and at the stream crossing in Waitsburg. The traveling doctor he rescued on Alpowa found half his wagon stuck in the ditch, and his exhausted filly was unable to pull any more. Cashdown eased the little horse out of the traces, replaced her with Peppermint, and hauled the buggy back onto the center of the road, itself a linear bog that snaked up the steep pass. At the Waitsburg crossing the bridge was down and a team balked. He rode across the swollen stream with the headstall of the team's off-mare in his hand, leading the way to safety. Tired but jubilant, he arrived at Walla Walla sixty hours after leaving home.

On the same Tuesday Libbie set out in the opposite direction, answering a plea from women of the Rosalia Church to help them create a suffrage group. She packed spare clothing against the weather and carried gifts of food and her flyers in a map case. She hitched their trusted mare, Cricket, to the little surrey and headed out in a steady, cold rain. Late in the afternoon, as the rain increased to a major storm, she came to the bridge across Rock Creek. The creek, now a roiling river, was above flood stage and surging under the bridge with mere inches to spare. Libbie urged Cricket ahead, and she dutifully crossed the unsteady bridge, carefully placing each hoof to avoid slipping. Once across, Libbie looked back and commented aloud, "If one old log came racing down . . ." and shook her head ruefully.

She lodged at Pastor and Mrs. Grandlund's farm and remained until Friday, and still the rains came. Half a dozen women from Rosalia and Oakesdale arrived to see her off. They thanked her and wished her a safe journey home. In the best of weather it was a five-hour ride, but with the storm and an elderly horse on muddy roads it would take twice as long.

An hour after leaving, she approached the Rock Creek bridge. She could see it was now underwater, a fast-moving current flowing over its riprap bed and side logs. She pulled Cricket up and looked through the sheeting rain for debris upstream. It was common for travelers in high-water times to ford streams on flooded bridges, so Libbie was undaunted. She was eager to get home and relieve the children, worried that Cashdown would have trouble returning from Walla Walla, and reluctant to turn back and impose again on the Grandlunds. She estimated the depth of water, guessed it was shallower than her surrey sole, and decided to go ahead.

She clucked and flicked the reins, and Cricket pulled forward onto the bridge. They were almost halfway across when a surge of water and a submerged tree hit them broadside, knocking out the bridge, overturning the surrey, and pulling the horse off her feet. The front axle, wheels, and spring shafts, made to separate in a crash, broke free of the surrey box and rear wheels, leaving Libbie to spin in the floating box until it capsized downstream and she was thrown into the current. Cricket flailed ahead of her, both screaming in the roaring stream, and the remains of the wagon and bridge threatened to chase them down from behind. Libbie yelled and gasped, but her voice was lost in the torrent and the blast of the storm. She flailed in her heavy clothing, took in water as she began to sink, and struggled until she lost consciousness and flowed as one with the swirling debris.

CHAPTER 12

It was a poor time to hold the council, as the weather was bad and promised to grow worse. The pit houses had yet to be restored and cleaned, and the tepees would be taken down and replaced with dugout huts. The deer and elk hunting had just begun. Soon the meat and fish would have to be smoked and put in. But Tomeo, his brothers, and the elders were obligated to go, leaving the others to continue with the work at home.

All day they rode northward in the cold rain to Colville. There they sat with leaders of the Spokane and Schitsu'umsh tribes, with the Okanagan and Wenatchi and their kin of the Yakama. The Paluses wore their best furs and exchanged gifts of drums, beaded bags, guns, and belts. For two days the leaders talked of reservation alignments and the railroad rumors and new mining claims, of the hunt and outbreaks of illnesses, and of battles to the south and east. At the end they planned the annual Jump Dance festival. There was a banquet, and on the third morning the Paluses donned their fur cloaks and returned home in the same steady, cold rain.

They skirted Rosalia to the east at Hangman Creek and headed toward Rock Creek. As they descended the grade to the crossing they could see that the bridge had been washed away in a fury of floodwater and storm flotsam. A small wagon body was rocking on its side in an eddy by the bank a short way downstream, and they rode at a gallop to see if anybody was near it. The torrent rumbled, and rain fell in undulating curtains as the Indians dismounted and pulled a woman's body from the water. She had been pinned between the wagon and an outcrop of dead willows. She was unconscious and grey as the rain. They laid her facedown on the mud bank and pounded her back. Water and vomit of thick phlegm pulsed from her mouth, but she remained limp. Tomeo lifted her and held her upside down for a moment before grasping her under the arms. He violently shook her up and down. The woman choked, gagged, and spit up more water and phlegm. She gasped and cried and clutched his neck.

Tomeo draped her over his horse and remounted behind her. As they turned to head for Rosalia, he saw three legs of a horse rising clear of the water further downstream. The rest of the horse lay beneath a logjam in the swirling current.

Cashdown came up later that day on Peppermint. He knew there must have been trouble, and he was desperate to find her. By tracking her probable route in reverse, he eventually found her recovering in a quiet bedroom at Parson Grandlund's home where Mrs. Grandlund had been attending to her needs, following advice from Doc Kenoyer. Cashdown tearfully embraced Libbie, touching her face and hair all over like a child with an injured pet.

"When you can travel, dear heart, we'll get you back home. The children and our friends are worried sick for you and will be greatly relieved to learn you're going to be all fine."

Libbie smiled weakly and whispered, "We are blessed, Hamish" and returned to sleep.

On his way back to Steptoe Station, Cashdown found the remains of his surrey. He lashed the toe rail to his saddle horn and pulled it out of the muddy and littered creek bed. Downstream he discovered the remains of Cricket. He calmed Peppermint, who was made balky by what had happened, and together they hauled the corpse up the slope to a grassy area, where Cashdown knew in a few days nothing but a bare skeleton would remain. "From nothing to nothing again," he said aloud and turned away downcast.

Using the spring-shafts for rails, he made a travois and lashed on as much of the surrey as he could recover—box and wheels and axles, some of the tack. It was a slow, cold ride home, and he was grateful for Peppermint's strength and steadiness. Upon arriving at Steptoe Station he gathered the children and told them of the calamity. "She'll be right in time. Her spirits are good, and her constitution is firm. She will be right soon enough. We should mourn for old Cricket, poor lass, but now she will feed a family of coyotes or bears for a season. Ours is to go on and make good of our work."

In time Libbie came home, and the autumn chores gave way to winter routines at the inn. The working horses and mules were brought in each night, the others set to pasture with the cattle. Tools and tack were repaired and oiled, and the gardens were top-dressed with rotted manure. The coaches came less frequently, but few that stopped each week went on without spending at least one night at Steptoe Station. When the coaches stayed, Cashdown and Libbie worked tirelessly to feed, lodge, and entertain each group of six or eight travelers, despite frequent snow and temperatures that often dropped below zero. Day and night, ice dams in the horses' water trough had to be broken up; feeding, grooming, mucking, and farrier work had to be done for each relay team; and cooking, serving, cleaning up, and laundry had to be done for the visitors. Merriment had to be on offer, too, which was joyfully supplied by Cashdown. If they were able to get through from Colfax, his Wheatland Whirlwinds Frontier Band joined in the revelry. There would be dancing and kegs of cider, and at midnight a round of oysters would be set out.

By February family wagons from Colfax and Palouse City and Oakesdale began showing up for the nighttime gatherings. Word had spread, even beyond Whitman County, that Steptoe Station was the jolliest and cleanest stage stop in the entire region. Libbie bemoaned the added work, as there sometimes would be a dozen extra revelers for dinner and dancing. One evening in late March, as the weather improved enough for the smell of spring to begin rising from the valleys, three charabancs from Colfax arrived bearing twelve couples, all eager for a night's entertainment. Libbie looked out to the yard and covered her mouth in shock.

"Good Heavens. Hamish! What have you done? Did you invite these people here?"

"I merely said all were welcome. There's no harm, dear Libbie. We have plenty of provender."

"But who's going to cook and serve it all, and who's going to clean up after this crowd?"

"Aye. Maybe we'll have to hire someone," he said, and he went out to greet, whistling.

The business of Steptoe Station was expanded to include a restaurant and dancehall. Cashdown found migrants looking for work and a place to settle. If they were healthy and impressed him as trustworthy, he hired them. He trained his new employees in hospitality skills and sanitation and helped them find homesites in the nearby Palouse country. Some were lodged temporarily in the barns and helped with farm work.

With improving weather and his employees assigned to the inn's chores, Cashdown devoted renewed effort to work with Cushing McBride at their orchards around Steptoe Butte. He often told Libbie he cherished the ride out. It followed a trail branching east of the Territorial Road just above the inn and winding along drainages scarcely over two thousand feet high. The slopes on both sides offered him a seasonal palette—flecks of wildflower yellows, pinks, whites, and blues winking within quilts of new grasses marbled in chartreuse and bright green. He was charmed by songs of western bluebirds and meadowlarks and warblers heard over the rush of the wind, and he was comforted by the familiar smell and creak of his saddle leather and the easy rhythm of Peppermint's stride. Along the trail the peak of Steptoe Butte loomed like a sentinel, as if the landscape he traveled through was an enfolding diorama. He told her the mountain was like a gigantic friend looking over him all the time, and it put him in mind of Orestes.

Much labor was needed at the flanks of Steptoe. Weedy brush had to be removed. Young trees had to be pruned, and more acreage was marked to be cleared. They had stock to plant or graft for new apple varieties and additional fruits—plums, cherries, and pears. They built double fences, one a shoulder's width inside the other, to keep deer and elk out of the orchards. Cashdown said he would explain the need to Tomeo one day soon. Cushing brought up wagon loads of poles and posts from his woodlots, and Cashdown built gabions and filled them with stones for post anchors on rocky patches. The young trees from last year were flourishing; within a few years there would be abundant apples and perhaps in time pears and cherries or plums. The two friends talked quietly as they worked on the new fences.

"You think the railroad will be coming up to Colfax one day soon?" Cashdown pulled on the end of a braided wire.

Cushing drove in the staples and headed to the next post. "They've been running that little line with the hearse car down at Whitman Mission for some time now. But nothing's come of it," he said over his shoulder.

Cashdown spooled out the low lines as he followed. "Aye. They put up all that money for the Seattle and Colfax line, but nothing's happened there, either. I heard the Northern Pacific got more land out here, and there's some plan to run a line down from Spokane. Don't know when that'll happen."

"Maybe they could use some of that Seattle and Colfax money to bring it out this way."

"Someone said the Whitman line's up for sale. But wouldn't it be a boon to have a spur out here, so our produce and meats could be shipped? I'm thinking we ought to get on the list while they're still planning." More pulling and wrapping and stapling.

"Maybe," Cushing suggested, "we could ask Orestes to put in a good word."

"Aye, perhaps I'll do that. The towns and cities will grow, and life for everyone'll be more civilized, I warrant."

Cushing stopped his work and frowned. "Railroads bring riffraff, y'know. Chinks and gypsies. More thievery and prostitution."

"Now, Cush. We both know Pinky's done everything to better our Palouse country. Her kind work harder'n the rest of us. She'll own half of Colfax one of these days. Sure as God's in Heaven we've no lack of prostitutes hereabouts, but since Orestes was sheriff and Big Kate took over, why they've been no more harm than gnats to a few over-refined ladies. And a good time for lonesome miners and cowboys."

"Well what about your station? A rail line out here'd mean the end of the stages."

"Maybe I'll turn it into a hotel," he said with a grin.

It was at the August congressional recess when Orestes and Lucinda next returned to Colfax. People clamored to talk with the legislator—Mayor Perkins and his civic leaders needed a consultation about funding a library building; the new sheriff, Arvind Carscallen, wanted some advice on policing; Lycurgus asked him for an interview for the newspaper. But Orestes needed time away from the pressures of official business, so he was gratified when Cashdown asked him and Lucinda to join friends for an afternoon and evening at Steptoe Station.

"I'm cheered to see you so lively, Elizabeth, after your accident," Orestes said upon their arrival.

"Why thank you, Orestes. I'm now recovered, but I will be staying closer to home in the next storm."

"Your inn has gained business since we left for the East. And a high reputation that now spreads across the territory and into Oregon."

"We owe much to Pinky," Cashdown replied. "As her business grows, so our patronage grows alongside."

"Everybody ask me to stop all night at Cashdown Station," Pinky said.

"So," Orestes asked, "you have more passengers than before?"

"More trips, now each week four times. And now I haul sometimes from Walla Walla to Cheney."

OP said, "Prepare for more traffic in the future, Pinky. There's talk of a rail line down to Cheney once the northern route's completed. People will want to go north on your stage so they can go west on trains."

The party went in and sat around the big dining table. Holly served ale and appetizers.

Cashdown said, "Orestes, what about the Palouse country? Any news about rail plans for us?"

"Some. The Tenino route from Olympia was opened last month, so now there's service from Seattle to Tacoma and Olympia down to Tenino. That's good progress. I heard a rumor in the district that the Northern Pacific line through Spokane will restart construction from the west end. The route and money are set, but even if they start work this month it'll be three, four years before the last spike goes down at Spokane. Then there's still the link east to Montana. Could be most of five years before the entire northern route's done."

"I hoped we'd sooner have a fast way to get me fruits and grains out to market."

"You're growing wheat now?"

"No, no. I just help the neighbors and trade for clean wheat. All sacked and ready to sell. I still put up hay for my herds . . . might rent out some acreage one day."

"Well," Orestes said, "it's more likely that a line will come up from Walla Walla first, and the Palouse goods will move down the Columbia, instead of north to Spokane. Maybe someday we'll get both, and you'll have a choice."

Pinky was listening with a keen and skeptical interest. "It will happen, won't it?"

"I'm trying to influence anyone who can help it to happen, Pinky. But I have no vote."

"I mean, someday railroad comes and bang—no more stagecoach. Mail going on trains. Freight going on trains. People going on trains. So goodbye old ways."

"I see. I guess I've become an agent for change and the uncertain future after all. I think it's inevitable. We have to stay one step ahead of it, Pinky. Do you have a plan?"

"Maybe just settle down, sell coaches, find good sugar daddy. Maybe I'm too old."

"If I may ask, Pinky, how old *are* you?" Orestes smiled and gazed down on her like a kindly teacher.

"Don't know. Maybe forty, maybe fifty. Too old for, you know, make face." She looked around to check for offense, but she saw only grins. "Came here as baby and my parents die . . . died, in mining dynamite mistake. I never know how old I am."

"Suppose you don't find your sugar daddy," Orestes went on. "What *will* you do when the railroads come?"

"Okay. Soon I will buy Riverside Hotel, after I sell my Concords to Mr. Hailey and sell my laundry to Wang-an. I think . . . thought, *hmm,* railroads coming. So I will make a big restaurant, make Riverside into top class hotel." She eyed Lycurgus. "Still is my secret, so not for your newspaper yet, please? We are not all done talking about money deals."

"Well done. Good plans, Pinky," cheered Cashdown. "You'll run a fine hotel and restaurant. And the trains will bring crowds of people who will come just to eat your food and enjoy your grand lodging. Just what we need. And you can tell them of your high adventures."

"You'll be needing a lawyer, too," Orestes said. "We're finally becoming governed by laws, and you'll want to make sure you have control, and nobody tries to take the properties away from you."

"Okay. So you are too busy, I guess. Where can I find other good lawyers?"

"I know someone in Walla Walla who can help. I'll write to him."

"By Jesus, you are a goddamned big friend, 'Restes!"

As preparations went on in the kitchen, Cashdown brought out bottles of Lewiston wine, explaining that he'd traded a foal for three cases of last year's best French varietals. The friends toasted to Orestes for completing his first session in the United States Congress. They toasted to Libbie for surviving the accident at Rock Creek. They toasted to OP for opening a new branch of his bank in Dayton. Orestes made a toast to all the women present for their efforts to get legislation on universal suffrage started in Olympia.

Chapter 13

"Much work is yet to be done," Orestes said, staring into his wine glass. "The '75 bill died quietly in the House. Even if I'd been in office then, it still would've failed, fourteen to twelve. When it comes up again—and I know it is destined to come up—I will be there to vote and horse-trade everything I have, even put my reputation at stake."

"Your fine reputation," Cashdown objected, "in the end is all you have, aside from your talents and training, and none of those can be traded. A man who trades on his reputation would be made a charlatan, and in jig time he would be trading on a false reputation. It's self-defeating. I say trade on others' foolishness. Grant favors and curry gratitude, then put those gains on the auction block, if needed."

"I suppose, but I will fight to the end for it."

Libbie said, "Your influence will be a blessing. But by now we've learned that petitions don't help much. We need to get to the right House members. And do our own horse trading, too. We women need to figure out what we can hold back as something to trade on, just like we've always done."

Genevieve Ames said, "But we also need to rouse prominent people outside government who favor universal suffrage, in Olympia and in Seattle and Walla, all around the territory. We need to make a committee of the association just for influencing bigwigs." Libbie concurred, and they agreed it would be done at the next meeting.

Genevieve was well qualified to assemble a political committee. The daughter of a prominent attorney and legislator in Wisconsin, she grew up in a household where politics was a favored subject for discussion at the dinner table. Legislators and judges and professors from the new college orated and debated in the family parlor, the same parlor where Lycurgus had courted her. She was a graduate of Mount Holyoke Female Seminary in Massachusetts and had returned home to Wisconsin to teach civics in a boarding school at Madison. Lycurgus had proposed marriage in a letter and traveled back from Colfax when she said yes. The Ameses were ideal allies for Libbie and the suffrage association.

The women met the following week in Colfax. The first task for Genevieve and Libbie was to neutralize tensions created by factions within their own organization. Genevieve said those factions could be brought together amicably in time. "Temperance can help us in many ways, but we must avoid talk of prohibition," she hinted.

"Yes," Libbie said, "like Mrs. Duniway's notion of temperance the way President Lincoln wanted it. Drink in moderation, without drunkenness."

Genevieve cautioned about another, more serious distraction. "Mrs. Wheeler is a member of the association now, but something odd has been happening. She has stood against every proposal that's come to a vote. And she encourages the discord around temperance. She refuses to say temperance, always insists on prohibition."

"You have to wonder why she joined us."

"And ever since she began attending meetings, she's been accompanied by that dirty man, Mr. Tuttle. He's her helper, and he's deaf, so she says, but I see them whispering, and he makes notes in his tiny handwriting while it looks like he's pretending to read the programs. I've asked her what he's doing, and she says he's a self-taught poet and is writing down ideas for his poems. He surely doesn't look like a poet."

"Lettice has been seen with him at breakfast," Jenny Perkins mused. It was hard to imagine Mr. Tuttle as a secret lover, especially in view of Lettice Wheeler's refinement. His suit stretched almost to splitting over his bloated torso, and his soiled shirttails flagged at the belly. Stains marked the front of his waistcoat and pants, and the cuffs were frayed. His porcine face was blotchy and patchily shaved. Lank hair hung here and there from under his greasy derby, which he never removed.

They agreed the key was to find out more about Mr. Tuttle. "I wonder if Pinky knows anything about him," Libbie said.

On her scheduled stop at Steptoe Station two weeks later, Pinky reported what she had learned from the Chinese territorial underground. "Not Mr. Tuttle. His name is Frank Souwer." Pinky had difficulty pronouncing it, so she spelled it. She added, "He is some kind of agent man for people who sell liquor. He comes up from Nevada, but people see him all over, in Colfax and Walla Walla many times. He knows bad people, they said."

Cashdown slapped his palm on the table. "Crickey. I smell a rat, a dirty, fat rat." He said if Libbie and Genevieve wanted it, he and Lycurgus and Orestes would investigate Mr. Souwer and find out who was behind him and what their game was. Libbie thought it might be better if the sheriff looked into it, but when the association brought their suspicions to Arvind Carscallen, he said there was no clear basis for a complaint because so far there was no injured party and nothing more than an unease about this Mr. Tuttle or Frank Souwer. Cashdown and Lycurgus wrote to Orestes, who agreed to make inquiries about the illicit liquor distribution matter.

Lycurgus contacted his newspaper friends in Walla Walla and Cheney and across the border into Idaho Territory. From Lewiston he learned that, a year ago, Frank Souwer had been run out of Pierce for trying to influence Nez Perce men to become distributors of alcohol. Souwer had told the Shoshone County sheriff he worked for a businessman named Bragg, but he didn't know how to locate his employer. Lycurgus also learned from his journalist contacts that temperance rallies in Walla Walla had been disrupted by protesters advised by Frank Souwer.

Cashdown sent a letter to Orestes to warn him of Odis Bragg's possible involvement. Orestes wrote back that the territorial marshal, Orange Fairbairn, was investigating a wildcat whiskey and beer ring that had been growing throughout eastern Washington Territory. He suggested that Tuttle might lead them to Bragg, if indeed Bragg was boss of the illegal liquor trade. "If I were there now I'd happily go after them, but you can work with Marshal Fairbairn," he concluded.

Orange Fairbairn had a long reputation as a diligent and dauntless lawman. His appointment as territorial marshal was meant to be a sinecure in his old age, but he was finding more business than expected. It also was more fascinating than he had expected: the crimes turned over to the marshal's services were the bafflers, the schemes and cover-ups that eluded other lawmen or were too complex and widespread for local sheriffs and constables to handle. Nobody in the West wanted to hire the Pinkertons anymore. It was feared they couldn't be trusted to protect working people. Marshal Fairbairn had never been a Pinkerton, though from time to time in his career he had hired out to stop unstoppable gunmen, and there was no lack of shootists on the frontier. He had even taken leave of his command during the war to bring in gunslingers, so much in demand were his skills.

At Arvind Carscallen's suggestion, Marshal Fairbairn stopped at Steptoe Station on his circuit through the Palouse country. Cashdown and Lycurgus greeted him as he dismounted at the gate and escorted him inside for lunch. Cashdown made introductions. "My wife, Elizabeth."

"Pleasure." Fairbairn eyed the table. "You make an attractive dinner, Mrs. Musgrave." He spoke in a soft, melodious voice.

"How d'you do, Marshal."

As soon as they sat for the meal, Marshal Fairbairn turned to business. "Your Sheriff Carscallen tells me you have some interest in the liquor trade hereabouts. How so?"

Cashdown explained. "A man noteworthy because he doesn't fit expectations has been coming to me wife Libbie's suffrage group meetings. He's been in the company of a local woman—well, she's recently arrived, like all of us, but is known in Colfax and generally respected—and this man isn't who he claims to be. His name is Frank Souwer, and some of Lycurgus here's newspaper friends have linked him to alcohol distribution in the region. Trying to sell to our Indian neighbors. Now we think he might be working for a longtime thief and highwayman named Odis Bragg."

While Cashdown was talking, Fairbairn watched his face with intense focus. For a few moments afterwards he wiped his thick, drooping mustache and turned silently to his beef stew, as if his mind was fixed only on eating. Without looking up he said, "Who is this Colfax woman, if I may ask?"

"Mrs. Lettice Wheeler, a widow most recently from down Dayton way," Libbie said.

"Sure of that?"

"That's what she's told us. Since five years ago," Lycurgus said. "And she introduced Souwer as Mr. Tuttle, a deaf man and self-styled poet who just helps her out with chores and such."

"When's the last time you saw Tuttle?"

The other three looked to one another. Libbie said, "About three weeks ago, at our last meeting."

"I heard he was seen more recently breakfasting with Mrs. Wheeler in Colfax at the hotel," Cashdown added.

Marshal Fairbairn attended to mopping up his stew with bread.

"More?" Libbie asked.

"That would be nice, Mrs. Musgrave," he said, a grateful smile deeply lining his face. He wiped his mustache again. "You know where this Bragg holes up?"

"We're not sure," Cashdown said, "but he's been known to favor the breaks south of Colfax down to the Snake. He and his gang once had a holding in Wawawai Canyon. That was back when we got them for claim jumping. Orestes Banks actually nabbed 'em when they were about to drive the posse into the river."

The marshal took a long draught of his ale, pushed back from the table, and folded his arms in apparent satisfaction. He nodded his thanks to Libbie, looked slowly around the room, and said to the vacant space above their heads, "Good man, that Orestes. I'd heard something about that at the time. Now, Mr. John Stahl and his wife, Catherine, have a licensed brewery, fine ale-making place, in Walla Walla. Nice people. Took over the old Meyer firm years ago. They're good business for Walla Walla, and they sell all over. John tells me there's a sinister competition, and he thinks it's coming from a renegade brewer, and it's somewhere north of there. Taken a toll from his business, he says. I hear the same story from other licensed brewers along the mid-Columbia all the way into Cheney. At each town with a licensed distributor or producer I hear about a strange little fat man, a newcomer who tries to interest people in starting bawdy houses or tries to get hotels and inns to change their distributor of ales and liquor. Sometimes he appears to be working to choke off temperance groups. Did that in Walla Walla, much as you've described. There he called himself Frank Estes, and he befriended a woman who had a scarlet past but had come to Jesus and joined the Christian temperance group."

"Sounds like our Tuttle," Cashdown said.

"Could be. The woman complained that Estes was trying to bribe her to sabotage the temperance group, and he was run out of town by some of John Stahl's friends. But damage had been done, and many places receive their deliveries of liquor and beer in plain bottles after dark. As to your Mr. Bragg, I know of him. I'm after him, and eventually I'll smoke him out."

Lycurgus said, "How can we help?"

"We might start with your Mrs. Wheeler. Maybe she can be convinced to come clean about Mr. Tuttle. We box him in, we'll find out if he's Mr. Bragg's man."

They agreed to meet in Colfax upon Marshal Fairbairn's return from Cheney. Libbie was to draw Lettice Wheeler to a tea at the right time, and within a week all was arranged.

Chapter 14

"How thoughtful of you, Elizabeth." Lettice pursed her lips in a little smirk as they brushed cheeks. They sat at a small, round table by the front windows of the Riverside Hotel lobby. Tea and sweet cakes were brought by an elderly Chinese man. The women chatted pleasantly about the new Methodist church and its reception by St. Patrick's parishioners and the Baptists, until Lettice abruptly changed the subject.

"You didn't invite me to tea to discuss Methodists, did you. Just why are we here today, Elizabeth?" The smirk turned reptilian.

"Well, I've been surprised somewhat, Lettice, by your opposition to the temperance women who want to join us for the vote." Libbie tapped her fingers softly on the lace tablecloth.

"It's a mistake to include anything about alcohol. Not that I approve of drunkenness, of course, but men will forget all about women voting if they must give up whiskey to allow it. I believe alcohol should be kept out of the home, and I speak from experience. The home is a moral sanctuary and our proper sphere. I, too, want the vote. But at what cost?"

"Temperance after all doesn't mean prohibition," Libbie replied, "and accepting those women into our association gives us a chance to talk about different ways to get what's right and moral and to convince them to temper their ardor. Women will solve problems with liquor in their homes in their own ways. If we keep the temperance group out, they'll draw attention away from our campaign anyway. It doubly weakens ours."

Lettice was about to respond when Cashdown entered the lobby. He was followed by Orange Fairbairn. "Oh," Lettice exclaimed, brightening, "here's your charming husband."

The men approached and said hello. "This is Territorial Marshal Fairbairn," Cashdown said. "Marshal, Mrs. Lettice Wheeler."

Lettice's expression went blank, and her eyes searched from face to face.

Libbie said, "Please join us for tea, won't you?"

Orange Fairbairn nodded his greeting and turned to face Lettice. "Mrs. Wheeler? I believe I have something of importance to discuss with you, and perhaps it would be better if we took tea at the back of the room."

She looked confused but rose when Libbie got up, and they followed the men to a table at the far corner of the lounge. The marshal started speaking as if pondering a vague memory. "Now, I understand you came up from Dayton some years back. Would my understanding be right?"

"Yes, I did. I was recently widowed and seeking to establish a new life on my own." She smiled, a bit saucy.

"And before Dayton, now let me see, where would you have resided?"

"Near Denver."

"Near Denver." He lowered his head and stared at her over his generous mustache. "If I recollect rightly, and please correct me if I'm wrong, you in fact lived near the Market Street teens. Is my recollection accurate, Mrs. Wheeler?"

Lettice looked away and said nothing.

"And at Dayton you lodged with?"

Lettice frowned and shrugged.

"Hear tell a while back you and the child you call your niece stayed for some months at a place called The Goddess. Is that so?"

A long pause. "I knew my lodging as The Garden."

"Then you would be acquainted with a woman called Hattie Soames?" He studied Lettice's eyes.

"That name doesn't ring a bell just now." She looked away again, as if combing her memory.

Marshal Fairbairn pulled a document from his waistcoat pocket. "Now, this docket summary says you and Miss Harriet Soames appeared together on July the twenty-seventh of 1870 at the Columbia County Court of Assizes." He hesitated a few seconds. "Shall I go on?"

Lettice turned ashen and looked searchingly around her. "No. Please. As I just said, I am trying to establish a new life here on my own. It's all changed now."

"Why don't you tell us about your Mr. Tuttle."

"Oh, that. Well, I'm sure he has nothing to do with this Hattie Soames. He's just a poor wanderer who offered to do chores for me for a fee. A poet. He's deaf, you know, and so I try to be of help to him, too."

"And how did you meet the so-called Mr. Tuttle?"

"Well, I can't really remember. Probably on Main Street or West. I remember him helping me cross the street."

"Can you recall anything else about that first encounter? Time of day, maybe?"

"I'm sure it was at noon. The bell on Saint Patrick's rang the noon hour just as I was crossing."

Marshal Fairbairn continued to study her face. "And why would you need help crossing the street in full daylight, let alone from a deaf man? You appear to be an able-bodied woman."

"I can't recall. Probably my niece."

"Ever talk to you about Miss Soames, this Tuttle?"

"No. Never."

The marshal examined the document for a few seconds. "Do you have any idea why, all during the five months you and the child lived at Miss Soames's house and your Mr. Tuttle worked as her handyman—must've been on the property about every day—you never came across him? Why would you never come across him?"

"No idea at all."

"Well, Mrs. Wheeler, Miss Soames tells us you had a considerable acquaintance with Mr. Tuttle, only then he was known as Frank Souwer, and he was said to be the child's uncle. And not deaf, either. Should we talk about him?"

Lettice covered her face with a napkin and sobbed. "I . . . we're going to be sacrificed either way," she cried.

"Would you like to talk with me in a more private location?"

"Yes. Please." She continued sobbing.

Marshal Fairbairn escorted Lettice quickly out of the hotel and across the street to the sheriff's office.

"What was that Denver business about?" Libbie asked Cashdown.

He shrugged. "Not sure, but I've heard a part of Market Street's a gathering place for all the camp followers."

"Why would Lettice be following the army around?"

"Ah. It's a place for ladies of joy. Pleasure girls, that sort of thing."

"Lettice?"

"Well, I know The Goddess down in Dayton is said to be a bordello."

"But, Lettice?"

"There's all kinds, my dear. Poor Chinese, Negroes, Mexicans, even Indians. Smart, most of 'em, but adrift, and refined white women, too."

"Shameful filthy business! It's against the law. Those people should be jailed. But it couldn't be Lettice."

"If our Lettice once was such, maybe we should have mercy. Think of it this way. Many, many women don't have the tranquil life you've had. They come West, often with a brood of kids, and their men get killed or they run off, the wives're alone and unable to find respectable work to support themselves, they're tired and broke and in the wilderness, and there's a ready market for the only valuable trade they have to offer. They're sullied by it, sure, but if there were no customers there'd be no business. And there will always be customers, so making it safe is the right aim. The ones who should be jailed are the politicos and the generals and the lawmen who allow the trade to keep going but pretend they aren't any part of it, pass laws against it for political reasons, savage the girls and let the uncles go, and they don't do anything to make it safe. I warrant there's more to Lettice Wheeler's background we don't know about, something maybe sad and desperate."

"My life, tranquil? Hah! But think of that child, Hamish."

"Aye, think about the child."

Marshal Fairbairn learned the information he needed. Tuttle indeed was Frank Souwer, Fairbairn said, and he had frequented The Goddess when Lettice was staying there with a child she now confessed was her daughter. She had come from Denver, where for the previous three years she had run a prudent and opulent brothel, only to be fleeced of her mortgage and most of her savings by a banker who had been her best client and main source of income. The banker had arranged for her to be run out of town. Harriet Soames had once been one of her top girls. It was to Harriet that Lettice fled with her infant daughter, Angela, seeking solace and a hideaway. She worked at The Goddess for a time and managed to steal sizeable sums from drunken clients. In consideration of her child and when her savings seemed adequate, she decided to quit the trade and try elsewhere for a legitimate marriage and respectability.

Sometime after she settled in Colfax, Frank Souwer found her. He offered to pay her in exchange for cooperation in his efforts to derail the women's suffrage movement in Whitman County. At first she refused, but he threatened to expose her past and ruin her chance at returning to social acceptance. For the last year she had been suffering alone under Souwer's bribe and threat: she feared being shunned by her new friends and agonized that exposure would humiliate her daughter. Moreover, she had become dependent on the money Souwer was paying her.

"We've made a deal where we'll be sure to collar Frank Souwer," Orange Fairbairn told Cashdown. They were sitting on the broad south porch facing Steptoe Station's barns, their booted feet on the rail, and drinking coffee in the autumn sun. The marshal had come out to tell Cashdown and Libbie the news and to enlist their help in luring Souwer into his trap.

"Sure and I'm happy for that, and I'm glad to help, but I feel sorry for Mrs. Wheeler," Cashdown said.

"I regret that I had to put the tongs to her, but in the long run she will feel liberated. She's been imprisoned by her past long enough."

" 'Tis so. I feel sorry for the pain that woman must've felt through all her years in the trade. Heaven knows it's hard enough to keep 'em out of the Station here. They come out from town and say they're looking for dance partners, all just fun. Those pitiable girls are so run-down, beaten down, you can spot 'em right away, looking around for a hurdy-gurdy. And then they get disappointed whenever I grab me pipe or fiddle. I have to point to the sign that tells 'em no single women after eleven o'clock. So far, they've departed all orderly by then. But they keep coming back because they must, they have such a short time to make their income, nobody wants an old whore, and there's no rest home for them. So, I try not to be a fussbudget with them."

"They steal from their johns, you know. Carry the venereal and Chink black pills. They're dirty, they vex legitimate businesses, and they don't pay taxes, so they're kept on the run."

Cashdown shook his head. "They're the victims. And, ah, but isn't it rare that one of those unfortunates can make a breakout for an honorable life? Few women have the moxie of our Lettice Wheeler to secure the wherewithal and the skill to play the fashionable widow. Takes nerve. I'd always thought she was a tad too proud and superior, but now I'm thinking whenever it looks like she's being uppity, she's probably just overplaying her role because she doesn't quite know what it needs. Frankly, Marshal, I admire her nerve. What's her real name, anyway?"

"Let's just go on calling her Mrs. Lettice Wheeler. Courage she has, and I admire her quick thinking. She caught the end of this game right off, knew what her hand was, and found a way to fold with a good chance of coming out winning the pot."

"So, what's the plan for bringing Souwer in and putting your tongs to him?"

"If we go after him with the right bait, we won't have to squeeze him at all. We'll get him to lead us straight to his employer."

"Aye, the right bait. And what would it be?"

"Mrs. Wheeler will have to tell one more convincing lie. And we'll have to enlist Mr. Powell and Congressman Banks to make it work. I wonder, would you take care of that part, Cashdown?"

He agreed eagerly, for he had a passionate desire to be present when Odis Bragg was captured. Orestes was to compose a letter to Lettice responding equivocally to her inquiry about a rumor that Washington Territory would soon outlaw all alcohol consumption. OP was to float the rumor in Colfax. Souwer would know the implications, and Lettice was to embellish the story. It would be risky for her: although Souwer was not known to have killed anybody, he was a suspect in several earlier murders. Orange Fairbairn couldn't predict how Souwer would respond upon seeing his and Bragg's business under threat. But he was certain that Bragg would want to see the letter before changing directions.

Within a week the rumor of prohibition was circulating. Lycurgus printed an anonymous letter about it in the *Gazette*. A vigorous exchange in letters to the editor among local liquor sellers followed. Orestes wrote under his at-large congressman letterhead:

Dear Mrs. Wheeler,

Thank you for your enquiry dated 14th October 1879, regarding certain rumors that the Washington Territorial Legislature is presently considering a Bill to prohibit the sale and consumption of alcoholic beverages throughout the Territory. While I am not privy to any such deliberations in their particulars, and in my present Position will not be accorded a vote on the matter, I am aware of certain sentiments among Legislators in favor of total Prohibition. I moreover cannot assure you with certainty that any such Legislative effort will successfully be blocked in Olympia. In the case of passage of the Prohibition Law, it is clear that immediate and swift implementation and enforcement of the Law will be necessary so that inventories can be recorded to prevent stockpiling and the closing down of establishments can be done in a timely manner.

Would that I were able to be more specific in answering your letter, but I trust this will convey my interest in the matter and the limitations of my freedom to speak on it.

Very Truly Yr Hmbl Svt & Representative,

Orestes J. A. Banks, Esq.

Lettice had a messenger take a note to Mr. Tuttle inviting him to join her for breakfast. She had urgent news for him, it said. Frank Souwer promptly appeared as Mr. Tuttle and pulled a chair close to her.

"What?" His grunt emitted a sour smell.

"The Palouse Women's Suffrage Association met and voted to end any connection with the prohibition women," Lettice said. "I wasn't invited this time. They're moving ahead as a separate campaign."

"That it?" he wheezed and stared at her. He looked and smelled foul, like a neglected boar. Despite the chilly fall morning, he was bleary-eyed and sweaty, and he had fresh tobacco stains on his waistcoat.

"You've heard the rumors about the new prohibition law, haven't you?"

"*Pah.* Rumors. People always make rumors 'round their worst fears."

"Some important people think there's much to them. Mr. Powell at the bank has announced that he will buy out any liquor merchant who wants to sell. And their inventories. The letters in the newspaper said the same. He boasted that he can sell the inventories in Idaho and Oregon Territories at a profit and that the buildings will expand his real estate holdings. He sounded serious."

Tuttle pondered silently awhile, picked up his knife and fork, and stared at them. "He's kinda sweet on you, ain't he."

Lettice smiled at the opening. "In fact, I think Mr. Powell is about to propose marriage to me. And when he does I will no longer need your payments or this arrangement."

He scanned the dining room and refastened his glare on Lettice. "Dare not forget the rest of our deal. Wouldn't want your banker and that little girl to hear your dirty secrets. You belong to us, and you just keep to your part," he growled through clenched teeth.

The elderly Chinese waiter came over and asked Tuttle what he wanted. He ordered without looking up: biscuits and gravy, eggs, bacon, beans, coffee.

"He wouldn't believe you," Lettice continued. "Our arrangement might be over anyway, Mr. Tuttle. I'm convinced it's going to happen, the prohibition law. Representative Banks seems to be saying it's under active consideration, and he seems to be warning us to get ready for some change." She pulled the letter from her purse and handed it to him.

Tuttle skimmed the letter, then re-read it slowly, moving his finger from word to word. He stared at it and grunted. His breakfast arrived, and he folded the letter, stuffed it in his coat pocket, and began to eat. Lettice watched him, smoothed her skirts, tidied her hair, and waited.

After some minutes of watching Tuttle slurp and smack his way through the food, she said, "I would like my letter back, Mr. Tuttle."

He wiped his mouth on the back of his hand. "No. I need it." He ran a finger around the insides of his cheeks. "You know all them temperance girls, don't you?"

"Not all."

"You know where they meet up."

"I'm not sure."

"Find out. And find out if they're hitched up with the other ones around the territory. We gotta get 'em to pull out, pronto."

He scraped his chair back and barged out the Riverside Hotel front door. He headed directly to the town stables and quickly saddled and mounted his horse. Marshal Fairbairn and Cashdown were waiting behind the sheriff's office and followed him out of Colfax at a distance. He turned north along the Kentuck for several hours and veered east near Hangman Creek. They saw him enter the cedars and willows along the creek bottom and ride toward the settlement of Latah. They followed atop a ridge half a mile to the south. When he moved out of the ravine and up the hillside where the town was spread out, Marshal Fairbairn and Cashdown rode to the creek and waited to see what direction he would take from the center crossroads. He moved higher into a stand of ponderosas and disappeared into the forest. Cashdown and Fairbairn rode up to the edge of the woods, dismounted, and walked toward their last sighting of Frank Souwer.

When they next saw him, he was about to get off his horse at the hitching rail in front of a large cabin a quarter of a mile into the trees. A curl of smoke rose from the stone chimney. Behind the cabin was a barnlike structure with a tall metal stack rising from its roof. Some horses were standing in a nearby pen. Marshal Fairbairn motioned for Cashdown to lie flat behind a small rise fronted by a boulder between them and the cabin. They were close enough to hear Souwer's wheezing as he dismounted. A man came out of the cabin and said, "What are you doing here?"

"Tell Odis I have something for him."

"Hey, Odis!" the man yelled over his shoulder.

Bragg came out, and Souwer handed him Orestes's letter. "Better read this," he said.

Bragg looked quickly at it, glanced around, and gestured that they should follow him inside.

"Eight horses, far as I can see," the marshal said. He pointed to the barn. "That looks like their still and brewery."

"Shall we take 'em in?"

"Let's wait a while to see if they make a move. If not, I'll come back with a small posse. Now we know where they're holed up."

They kept silent and watched for several hours, until it was growing dark. The only movement had been some men going back and forth to the liquor barn and feeding the horses.

"Looks like they don't plan on riding tonight," Cashdown said. The marshal agreed, and they returned to their rides and headed south under a brilliant harvest moon.

Chapter 15

Orange Fairbairn received a warrant from the federal circuit judge to arrest Bragg and Souwer. Orestes had returned from Olympia, where he had attended the legislative sessions while the national Congress was in recess. When Marshal Fairbairn asked him if he would consent to being deputized for the pursuit of Odis Bragg, he said it would make him happy. The following day, November first, the marshal and a posse—comprised of Orestes, two railroad detectives, Sheriff Carscallen, and Carscallen's deputy, who had been a Nez Perce scout for the army—set out for Latah.

Libbie tried to persuade Cashdown to stay home and work at his fields and orchards, but he said he knew Orestes would be going, and he wouldn't miss it for the world. He saddled Peppermint and rode early to Thornton. He was waiting when the posse approached on the Kentuck, and the marshal welcomed him to ride with them and deputized him.

They reined in at the edge of the woods above Latah and sent the deputy to reconnoiter the cabin and still. He returned and reported that it was a hive of activity, a train of freight wagons being loaded with cases of liquor and beer, men moving back and forth between the cabin and still, and two men were busily tending to the seven horses in the pen. "I counted seven men," he said, "but no sign of Bragg. Looks like they will make deliveries tonight or tomorrow night."

Marshal Fairbairn said, "Go down to Latah and see if you

can requisition a large freighter or farm wagon and a good team."

The posse approached the cabin site and moved into position near the horse pen. When the wranglers finished their chores and returned to the liquor barn, Fairbairn asked Cashdown to point out the lead horse in the herd.

He studied the horses moving around and said, "That little dun mare's the honcho."

At the marshal's signal Cashdown slipped into the corral with the two detectives, put a halter and lead rope on the dun mare, and slowly walked her out of the pen and into the woods. The other horses quietly followed in an orderly line. As soon as the gang's rides were tied out of sight, the posse mounted up and went directly to the still, four at the front and two at the only other exit, on the north side. Orestes rode to the cabin, dismounted, and strode to the door. Outside the front of the still, the marshal fired a blast from his shotgun at the pipe chimney, knocking it clear of the barn roof in a clattering crash. At the same time, with one kick Orestes burst the cabin door off its hinges.

Five men came running out of the barn like frantic ants, searching wildly for the source of the blast. They were confronted by Orange Fairbairn, the deputy sheriff, and two railroad detectives on horseback with revolvers drawn. A few seconds later two more men ran out of the side door, only to face Sheriff Carscallen and Cashdown, shotguns already trained on them. Orestes paused, listening, and then entered the cabin. The fire was low, but in the dim light Bragg's absence was palpable. He searched all the rooms, pulled back drapes, turned over beds, and saw that nothing belonging to Bragg remained.

Cashdown gestured toward the three loaded wagons. "This probably would be their last shipment," he told Marshal Fairbairn. They tied and gagged the gang members and loaded them into a farm wagon and moved off for Latah, followed by the contraband liquor and beer wagons driven by three of the posse-men. At Latah, Marshal Fairbairn and Orestes selected the member of the gang they thought would be the most viable source of information. They knew it should be the youngest, the one with the most to lose and least to gain, and the least experience in such situations.

The marshal pointed to one of the men who earlier had been in the corral and told him to stand. The young man, by appearance barely in his teens, didn't move. Orestes strode to the side of the wagon next to him. Marshal Fairbairn told him they weren't going to kill him, they just wanted to talk with him. He still sat frozen. Orestes reached over the rail, grabbed him by the belt, and lifted him backward out of the wagon. He carried the youth overhead out of sight to a shack behind the town livery.

They removed the gag, sat him on a bench, and stood over him. The youth stared at the marshal and then at Orestes and looked around the shack in confusion. Marshal Fairbairn began to talk to him in a soft, slow voice. "We need to know where Mr. Bragg is and what your plan was. You know that information, and you're going to tell us."

The young man stared at him without a twitch. The marshal went on, in the same even tone. "If you don't tell us what we need to know, I'll see to it that you go to jail for a very long time. It will not be fun. They will beat you. You'll cry for your mother. You'll wish you had a girl. You'll wish you had a private place to shit. You could end up passing the next fifteen, twenty years in a cell with some smelly, boy-raping sonofabitch who would have you for lunch every day. You could get sick and die from the venereal. We see it all the time. You could end up breaking rocks for the rest of your godforsaken life in that hellhole in southern Arizona. They feed you so bad there'd be nothing left of you at the end but dried bones." He paused to let it sink in. "So what'll it be? I'll give you half a minute to think it over."

The prisoner continued to stare stonily and said nothing. His chin began to quiver. Orestes whispered to the marshal, "Suppose we let Cashdown fill him in on the rest."

They left the young man sitting in the semidarkness of the shack and told Cashdown the boy was unresponsive so far. Cashdown said, "What'd you tell him?"

"Threatened him with a bad future," Orestes said. "We're ready for the next step. Maybe you could give him some proper encouragement."

Cashdown entered the shack and squatted down in front of the young man. He cradled his coach gun across his lap, turned a solemn and sympathetic face to the boy, and placed a hand on the bench next to his knee.

"You're a young chap with possibly many good years ahead of you," he began. "But you've gotten yourself into a tad bit of trouble here, and it could go very poorly for you. Marshal probably told you so. But we don't want to see that, and I'd lay odds you don't want that, either. Now, you look like a smart young lad, and I'd wager that with the right breaks you could turn things around and make good, get anything you wanted the respectable way. Sure and every last one of us has made mistakes along the way. Every one of us has had to turn things around to stop being someone else's errand boy. And when it happens, somebody's given us a break, and we've been better men for it. If you help us, we can help you get the right breaks."

Tears began to crest over the youth's eyelids. "He'll find me and kill me," he whispered. "I'm only fifteen, and already I'm a dead man."

"Guarantee it won't happen. That giant that carried you in here? He once personally captured Odis Bragg. Walked right up and slapped Bragg off his horse. One blow, *poof.* Put him and his whole gang behind bars. He'll see to it you're kept safe."

The young man stopped blubbering. He looked into Cashdown's smiling face. "I didn't mean for it to go this far. They offered me a job, said the pay was enough to clear all our debts. I don't know what to do. I . . . I just want to go home."

Cashdown nodded and stood his coach gun on its butt end. "I'll sort that. You tell us where to find Bragg, and we'll take care of the rest."

The boy looked at the ten-gauge, studied the detailed etching on the receiver and the precise checkering and engraving on the stock. He seemed to gain confidence just looking at the fine machine in Cashdown's gnarled hand. "I don't know I can trust you."

"My word as a cavalry officer."

The young man thought it over, then nodded. "We're supposed to meet him with the freight tonight at Wilder Gulch outside Cheney."

"Any particular time?"

"As close to dark as we can."

"Who else'd be with him?"

"Just Souwer, far as I know."

"Then what?"

"He was gonna tell us where the deliveries was supposed to go. Two to a wagon, driver and brakeman. We're using horses 'cause we couldn't find no mules to take."

"After that?"

"I'm not sure. He was going to quit the operation in Latah, wait to see if the rumors was true. Guess he was going to pay us off, and we'd break up till there was more work."

"What's your name, son?"

"Northrup, sir. Silas Northrup."

Cashdown patted Silas Northrup on the knee and said he

was going to replace the gag for now and would look out for the boy's future. He left, taking his shotgun, and told the others what he'd heard.

There was no jail in Latah, so Marshal Fairbairn instructed Sheriff Carscallen and his deputy to take the prisoners to Rosalia, where they could be held until the posse returned from arresting Bragg and Souwer. The marshal asked the sheriff to be sure to tell the jailer in Rosalia to safeguard the boy, and then he and his deputies were to rendezvous with the rest near Wilder Gulch. The contraband was stored at the Latah livery in the charge of the local land agent.

A cold front was approaching from the southwest, and as darkness came on the wind picked up, and the trees closed in like shrouds. Marshal Fairbairn and the posse rode at a slow walk along a path in Wilder Gulch. Nobody spoke, and the only noises were the wind in the black trees, the tack creaking, and an occasional snap of a twig under a horse's hoof. A pin of lamplight could be seen ahead, and the posse came to a halt a few hundred yards from it. Orange Fairbairn motioned for everyone to dismount and quiet his ride. He whispered cautions to keep arms ready but not to fire unless receiving fire. "Let's just take them in," he said.

The two detectives circled around to the right of the lamp, and Sheriff Carscallen and his deputy went to the left. The rest walked down the trail toward the glowing light. When they approached close enough to see, it was clear there was one man holding a kerosene lantern outside a rough shack, as if waiting for somebody.

The man saw the posse approaching and yelled something. He dropped the lamp and ran off into the night. Immediately another person came out of the shack, working the lever on a Winchester carbine. With lightning speed Orestes moved in and snatched the rifle from his hands. It was Odis Bragg, and he looked up at Orestes in astonishment. He backed away a couple of steps and put his hands behind his head. "Enough. Don't kill me."

Cashdown and Sheriff Carscallen quickly returned to their rides and headed off in search of Frank Souwer. A full moon had risen behind the clouds, turning the sky to swirling mercury. Above the wind and the horses' hooves, they followed Souwer's snarls and panting grunts as he crashed through brush in the ghostly light. They were almost on top of him when he turned around and fired three times. Peppermint hopped a step and then stood still. The muzzle flashes marked Souwer's position, and the sheriff fired his shotgun. They heard Souwer moan and cry out for help.

Carscallen said, "He might be faking."

"I'll sort him out," Cashdown said. He dismounted and walked toward Souwer's voice. After a few minutes he called back, "You got him. Dislodged a sack of fat, but he'll live."

Souwer had been hit around the lower back and thighs, the buckshot tearing into his buttocks and some shot smashing his left hip. When Cashdown dragged Souwer back to the sheriff, he could make out a glistening on Peppermint's front legs. "Oh, my Peppy, I think you've been hit."

They loaded Souwer onto the sheriff's horse and walked back to the posse, who by now had relit the lamp and carried torches. Marshal Fairbairn had examined the shack, removed everything of possible use, and packed the trussed Odis Bragg and sacks of evidence onto Bragg's horse.

"Bring that lamp over here so I can get a look at me mule," Cashdown told the deputy. He saw that a slug had gone through Peppermint's left shoulder. A hand-sized flap of flesh was hanging at the exit hole, and she was bleeding from both areas, but it was a clean flesh wound.

The deputy said he could help. He walked down into the

draw and found a cedar. There he collected a patch of resin in his water cup. As he applied the resin to Peppermint's shoulder, Cashdown talked calmly to her, assuring her he would take care of her and telling her how nice and easy it will be when they arrive back at Steptoe Station. She nickered and stood unflinching.

Man and mule arrived home two days later, Cashdown having walked Peppermint the forty-two miles, shouldering his saddle and gear. He led her to a run-in shed, doctored her properly, and fed her generously. He greeted Libbie with a hug and twirled her off the floor. After kissing each of the young ones, all in their beds, he ate heartily. He rubbed ointment on his feet, went to bed, and slept for ten hours.

When he arose, it was nearly noon Sunday, and the older children who had been at the academy in Colfax were back for the holiday. Come fall term, a new schoolmistress, Ursula Hartjes, would take over from Sam McCroskey. Knowing his Colfax students would be well served by Miss Hartjes, Sam had accepted an offer to build a school in Farmington. Next year, if the family could afford it, Frances would join her siblings at the academy, leaving only Mindy to be schooled at home. Holly was back, too, as she now was one of Cashdown and Libbie's employees at the inn. Laura planned to do the same after her graduation.

"How is Peppermint?" Libbie asked over dessert coffees in the kitchen.

"She's strong, and I don't see any pussing. It'll take some time, but I think she's going to be all fine."

"You took a dire chance, going after that Souwer alone. I'm happy you weren't hurt."

"Had to be such. Arvind would've finished him off. And so it's done. They're in jail now, and the rest is all up to Orange and a judge. I hope they hang 'em all."

"Hamish! Your temper's talking."

"All except for the boy. But I had to use great restraint to keep from killing Souwer m'self the other night."

"You suffer to kill a chicken. And remember Orestes saying that everybody's a victim? And justice must be done for everybody? Don't you think those two, Bragg and Souwer, could learn to behave right and one day be good citizens?"

"Nae. The youth could, but so far in seven years Bragg hasn't shown me any encouragement. Justice, the kindly rehabilitation of the sort Orestes believes in, that needs trust. The good citizens and the wise judges have to trust that these rotten apples can be restored to civility and, more, that they'll want to be restored, presuming they have some passing acquaintance with civility. I might guess those two unfortunate devils were born into incivility, into a cruel and criminal world of their making. It's all they know."

"Well, maybe so, but how would you know, if the courts don't take a chance on them?"

Cashdown let that be the final argument on fates he preferred not to interfere with. But he had another fate on his mind that constantly gave him much worry.

"No word from Cal?"

"Nothing came while you were gone. I thought he might send a birthday wish for Mindy. But nothing."

Cashdown sipped his coffee in thought, then suddenly banged his cup down on the table. "Good Jesus and God in Heaven! What's the matter with that defective brother of mine!"

"Hamish, calm yourself. You'd have an apoplexy. He's just troubled, and he's troubled because he loves you and admires you so."

"Ah, Libbie, I just wish I'd hear from him, learn what's vexing him so to cause him to be absent and silent. I'm all tongue tied over it."

"Why don't you try writing to him again? It would be good for both of you."

"Maybe it would be better if I go to see him. I'll bend him to come back with me."

Chapter 16

Libbie glanced up from her work on the kitchen table. She was composing a resolution for the Palouse Women's Suffrage Association. Cashdown was seated opposite, delaying his last trip to the paddocks and stalls for the nighttime check of the herds. Winter was at the door, and he would have to put on his greatcoat and hat, the stiff gloves and liners, and his heavy felted barn boots. He would have to carry the lamp and trudge through the new snow to each gate and inspect each stock pen, each gather of horses and mules. It would take nearly an hour. He ordinarily enjoyed the late rounds, but tonight it was cold outside, too raw for this early in the season, while in the big kitchen it was pleasantly warm. Besides, his time was passing quickly, and he was distracted, pondering how best to find Callum.

"You wouldn't know where to look," she said.

"I'd know where to start. Just ask around for the best wellman. Can't be that many well builders in Colorado."

Libbie rested her pen and gazed at him. "Now, you don't know that. Even if he is building wells, and even if there was only four or five, they might be scattered all over God's creation—it's a big territory, you know. Or it could be everybody down there finds their own water, like we do here."

"Then I'd just have to go ask, town to town. He did say he was near to Golden, didn't he?"

"You wouldn't traipse all the way down there this time of year."

"I've still a few weeks afore winter really sets in, and I only need to get to Walla Walla. There must be a rail train south from there."

"You'd be derelict not to inquire first. I don't think it's wise."

"I'll get started in the morning." Cashdown was gaining confidence and enthusiasm and was hardly listening.

But Libbie had other objections. "You're not going to leave me here to run this Barnum show by myself, Hamish. It's unfair and a fool notion for you to go running off like that."

"Aw, Libbie, 'tis selfish of me, I know. Maybe we can hire on a few more wanderers to help with the work."

"And just who will train them and keep watch on them? No, Hamish, you're more needed here than down in Colorado looking for your runaway brother!"

Cashdown hung his head in thought before speaking. After a while he looked up brightly. " 'Tis a big Barnum funhouse, ain't it, Libbie, a circus every other day and night? And we truly are tied to the circus by more than just the hullaballoo at our station. My great-great Uncle Ricketts brought the circus to America, you recall. Became quite the sensation."

Libbie had heard the stories of Uncle Ricketts before. She smiled: he had turned agreeable again.

Cashdown stood, donned his greatcoat and boots, grabbed his gloves and hat and the lamp, and went out.

The next morning before anyone else was up, he was at the kitchen table, drinking tea and composing a letter to Callum.

My dear Brother Cal,

I only hope this letter finds you well, in good humour, and ready to come back to the Palouse Country. Another season is behind us, and we had a fine harvest and stock sale, though I would have treasured your company and help. It was a gentle autumn this year, dryer than last, thank Heavens, and the smoke was cleared by Michaelmas, and we've clear skies since. You would have enjoyed the pretty evenings on the porch.

James Perkins sold his mill interest, then Mr. Hollingsworth sold the entire mill two years and more ago. It was fortuitous for James, however, because the Colfax floods last spring took out the better half of the structures, killed poor Willard Jones, whom you never met, trapped him in fallen joists and pinned him under the floodwaters. The mill is all rebuilt now, also grinds grains. It is going great guns. I am doing all my milling there before shipping the flour off to Portland. We are making good profits here, Cal, and you could, too.

There is a revised school in Colfax, run by a furious woman from back East called Ursula Hartjes. She is a mound of energy—near 15 stone—and an exacting teacher; and even at ten dollars per term, her school is already full up with every kid in the Palouse Country, including all ours but Mindy and the older boys. Liam now is second at the bank to OP. Tray and Elbourne are talking of leaving the bank, to start a new farm of their own. Tray already has a full section he has been working, all paid up, over near Endicott.

We as yet have no railroad service, tho' trains now come all the way through to Walla Walla from the West and South. Orestes Banks tells us it will not be long before we see the iron lines coming to Colfax, and I aim to get a spur built out to Steptoe. When that happens, Cushing and I will expand our orchards and ship all our produce directly from Steptoe Station and the butte. I have good acreage there in reserve for you, if you wish to raise fruits—apples do especially fine here, and we've all the materials.

Two weeks ago, I put Odis Bragg and his gang in the hoosegow for the final time. We were a posse made by Territorial Marshal Orange Fairbairn, augmented by our new Sheriff and his Deputy, and by Orestes Banks, who was home from the Congress and Legislature. It is a fair exciting tale that I would cherish telling you upon your return home. I do so look forward to the times when we can swap stories and hatch plans again by the fire.

Please write back right away, we worry so about your well-fare and miss you greatly. I hope this reaches you, as it is going out to the only address I've known there.

Your Loving Brother,
Hamish

Too eager to wait for the late stage arriving from Cheney, Cashdown shortly headed for Colfax to post the letter. He thought he might also try to contact the Northern Pacific agent, Cliven Cleary, about his idea for a branch line to Steptoe Butte. Cleary, however, was rarely in Colfax, so Cashdown would have to reach him by telegraph to arrange a meeting. A decommissioned army line to Fort Walla Walla had been taken over by the town, and the terminal was now installed in the *Gazette* offices.

"The editor is in," called Lycurgus. "Take a seat over here, Cashdown. I'm working on the Bragg arrest." He had been writing at his spacious desk and welcomed the interruption.

"Eyewitness I am, and not at all averse to spill the beans," Cashdown joked.

"Devoting all your time to spreading heroic tales about yourself and the bandits now?"

"Nae, I'm after that agent, Cleary. Want to talk with him about getting a line built to me butte."

"You don't want to talk with Cleary. He just disposes of land now. The line planning honcho is a man called Anders, Willard

C. Anders. He's working at the NP office in Walla Walla. We can reach them by wire. You want the operator?"

"Might's well."

"He's at the compositor. I'll get him. Then we can have a lunch." Lycurgus fetched a pimply, lanky youth who came in wiping his hands with a rag.

"You got a message to send?" He gawked at Cashdown, who examined him without confidence.

"Where'd you learn to tap on this thing?"

"Army. It's all I did for two years. Actually I'd prefer to set type, sir."

"Well, if you'd set down my message just this once," Cashdown said with a smile and handed him a hastily scribbled note.

The youth sat at the terminal and started wiggling the toggle key. Shortly he turned to Cashdown and said, "It's gone. Want me to wait for an answer?"

Cashdown looked to Lycurgus, who nodded. "Please. We'll return in a short while."

At the hotel, Lycurgus and Cashdown were joined by Pinky. "Mr. Gus, you can make articles now about my hotel," she announced with a grin.

"Your hotel. Well that's wonderful news."

"Congratulations, Pinky, well done," Cashdown added.

"What shall I print?" Lycurgus went on. "Let's see. When did you complete the purchase, and what are your plans for the future of your business?"

"Deal finished Thursday. I still got some money for changes. No more rooming house for me. Now it is all hotel, and I will move hotel up higher, so floods just go past."

"You mean you're going to raise the building where it stands?"

"Yeah, raise it. Make a new bottom, on rocks, bricks. Too many floods over and over, so I lift it up this high," she gestured shoulder height, "and we don't get so wet. So, everybody inside can be happy and safe and just thinks about how smart Pinky is."

"And who will do that work?"

"Mill guys I know. They got some big screw jacks. We close maybe only three weeks, maybe in April, or maybe May. Maybe only small floods before that, so I still have my hotel to lift up, hah!"

"So what about your laundry, Pinky?" Cashdown asked.

"Oh, Wang-an leasing from me now, maybe buying it later. Good business for both, I think. More hotels coming in, so I must get better, make my hotel more special. New name, I think. You gentlemen have ideas? Riverside not such good luck, maybe, so I am thinking change to Belleville Hotel, pretty name. I hear people . . . heard people talk about Belleville."

"That might not sit well," Lycurgus said. "James is the true pioneer hereabouts and much loved, and he would be dead against Belleville."

"Okay. Maybe Perkins Hotel?"

"You might ask him, but you might also consider something pretty about the Palouse countryside. How about the Camas Hotel or Arrowroot Hotel?"

James Perkins came in just then and, spying his three friends at lunch, asked if he could join them. Cashdown explained their discussion with Pinky. "She was thinking The Perkins Hotel sounded right fine. What say you?"

"I'm flattered, Pinky. Thank you for honoring me. But there might be confusion, 'cause my home is lately being called the Perkins House, and I wouldn't want to have to answer the door at all hours of the night to send your travelers away."

"Okay. You got other ideas?"

"We were just talking about the natural scenery as an inspiration for a name," Lycurgus said.

James thought a few seconds. "How about the ponderosa? Our main-most tree is the big bull pine, and to us it means not just beauty but strength and progress. After all, we build the biggest buildings from it, your hotel for example, and all kinds of critters take refuge in bull pines, just like travelers in a hotel. And it's true, the bull pine is a thing of great beauty."

Pinky frowned, as if she didn't like what she heard. Then she brightened. "Oh, okay. So maybe not Bull Pine Hotel but call it Ponderosa Hotel. Right?"

"Right," James said. "The Ponderosa Hotel, finest lodging in the Inland Northwest."

When Cashdown and Lycurgus returned to the newspaper offices, Aaron the telegraph operator told them he had received a reply from Walla Walla. He handed his transcript to Cashdown.

"Ah, this Willard Anders will be coming up day after tomorrow. I'm to meet him at the Riverside, ha, soon to be the Ponderosa. Here we go, my friend." Cashdown clapped Lycurgus on the shoulder. He paid Aaron for his services, collected Peppermint, and headed home.

Two days later, he was greeted by Anders at the hotel front door. "How'd you do, Mr. Musgrave?" Anders offered his gloved hand. He was a spare, angular man, sallow and humorless looking in his brushed grey suit and clean boots. His eyes shifted about, and his eyelids fluttered as he spoke. His Adam's apple was prominent and bobbed up and down. Cashdown gave his hand a vigorous shake and, grabbing him by the elbow, steered him into the lobby dining area.

"You said you wished to discuss a profit-making proposal, Mr. Musgrave. For whom would that proposal be of benefit, sir?"

"Undoubtedly, Mr. Anders, 'twould profit both the Northern

Pacific and our Palouse agriculturalists. And benefit the whole of Washington Territory. I and me colleagues and neighbors propose that the Northern Pacific plan a line into the farming area at the Steptoe Butte. Once built, from there we could ship carloads of fruits and every sort of grain, hay, and straw, plus our livestock and fresh meat harvests. Freight rates would be competitive with our current methods by less than half, and the time savings to markets would vastly improve our efficiency and aid in the settling and development of the entire Northwest."

Anders looked left and right and replied with a flutter and a little sneer. "The products of your fields and orchards, Mr. Musgrave, are seasonal only. What do you propose as uses of such a line for the remaining ten months of each year?"

"Oh, there will be much more commercial development at the new town of Steptoe, where my inn and store are now located. We envision both mercantile traffic and passenger needs for a rail line that could connect settlements in the area to Colfax and Cheney and stops beyond. Right on today's stage route, don't you know. Surely it would carry sufficient business aside from the agricultural freighting."

Again Anders frowned and looked aside. "Such a plan, Mr. Musgrave, would prove awfully costly to the company. How would you conceive to mitigate the construction expense?"

Cashdown sipped his tea as he invented and calculated. "We were thinking we would mill the lumber for the roadbed. That's a lion's portion of the expense, and we presently have the highest quality wood and the mill nearby."

Anders told Cashdown the railroad already had plans to be in the Palouse country within three years. The new lines would link the transcontinental route across the northern sector with communities southward to Walla Walla and Wallula. "You must understand, Mr. Musgrave, we are no longer interested in laying track and operating trains. We are in the business of land trading, railroad leasing, and business acquisitions."

"But you chaps determine who gets the rail lines and where, don't you?"

Following a long pause, Anders said, "Your proposal is interesting, and your enthusiasm appears genuine, Mr. Musgrave." His eyelids fluttered like a hovering kestrel. "For your proposal to become reality, you and your friends must be committed to seeing it through and be totally dedicated to Northern Pacific's profitability."

"So, you're interested in the idea?"

"We will see what we can do. It has possibilities."

After their meeting, Cashdown rushed over to the *Gazette* to tell Lycurgus about the discussion. But Lycurgus was out of his office, Aaron didn't know where. On his way to the town livery, Cashdown met Lettice Wheeler on the plank sidewalk. He tipped his stovepipe hat, and they exchanged greetings.

"Mrs. Wheeler, you did a brave thing last month," Cashdown said. "You served the territory well. I wish to thank you for your courage."

"You flatter me, Cashdown. Few choices were mine. But I'm happy I got free of my burden, and I feel like I truly do have a new life now. I owe my future to the marshal, and to you and the good people of Colfax."

"You're going to go on with the women's suffrage work?"

"Please tell Elizabeth I'm with her entirely. It's past time for women to have a voice in the laws and rules that control us. And assure her I have not really favored prohibition. She was right—it's every person's own responsibility to decide what to do about strong drink."

"Aye, right I will. And your, um, niece? She's now in school?"

"My daughter. Angela has been accepted into Miss Hartjes's academy. I'm soon to be employed by Miss Ji at the hotel, so I can afford to send my child to the school." Lettice smiled, without a trace of aloofness. "I will be keeping the books."

A gust of cold wind blew down the street. They said goodbye and went their respective ways, holding onto their hats and pulling their collars tighter. Cashdown visited his three oldest boys at the bank, left word for James and Lycurgus that he'd started things rolling toward a rail line to Steptoe Butte, and returned to the livery. Halfway home, wisps of snow began to fall.

After dinner that evening, after cleaning up for the night's festivities, after the cider and ale barrels had been brought out and the first round of dances had been concluded, Cashdown stood on a chair and clinked his blade on a bottle for attention. The stagecoach guests applauded and eagerly turned to hear what he would say.

"My new friends, old friends, and dear family, I have an announcement to make of potential historical import. Before revealing my news, I wish once again to welcome you to our humble but warm establishment." He gestured with the bottle toward the humming wood stoves. "No matter if you've stopped here just overnight on your way to Cheney or Walla Walla, or if you reside hard by and visit often, you are always welcome to come and enjoy what we have on offer in food, libations, and uplifting music.

"Now, with apologies to my friend, your stage driver and protector Lucius Pringle, we must agree it has proven tiresome and time-wasting, the way we travel over this bountiful territory—afoot, on horseback, in carts, traps, wagons, and stagecoaches. Why, in the best of circumstances it takes near three seat-sore days to get from Colfax to Cheney. The inefficiency of our modes of transport has proven a hindrance to the proper development and prosperity of our towns and region. Ah, but such is no longer so out on the coast, where the towns between Seattle and Tenino have grown and flourished, and that region of the territory has become a lodestone for developers. The difference"—he slowed and lowered his voice theatrically—"is the railroads."

He paused to let his point take root, then continued. "I recently learned that the rail line from Seattle to Olympia and beyond, now opened more than a year, has influenced unprecedented prosperity in all the stops along the route. The industrious people of Puget Sound made it themselves, by raising the monies and doing the hard labor. And look at what they've got—a ticket to the future, a future of wealth and happiness unheard of before the railroad. And so, thinking that we might accomplish something similar here, I put the question to a high official of the Northern Pacific, who as much as guaranteed me they would sanction and design and lay out a line into this very spot where we celebrate tonight. To make the deal, I offered him our facilities and labor, mainly in the manufacture of wooden crossties and bridge braces. He agreed it was a fine idea, and we shall be hearing further from the Northern Pacific soon as he confers with his officers."

A buzz ran though the group of enthralled guests. It was widely believed that the east-west route would be completed within a few years, and most people knew the history of how the railroads caused towns to flourish and how bypassed communities stagnated or disappeared altogether. The guests cheered and applauded. Cashdown raised his hands and shouted over the noise, "Now back to our entertainments, and later there will be a special treat!"

Oyster stew was served at midnight. In the meantime, Cashdown made his rounds of the livestock and saw that the storm was intensifying, with snow now half a foot deep. He cautioned the revelers that an early start in the morning might be necessary, and the giddy party dispersed to their rooms long before the usual hour.

Chapter 17

At first light Cashdown was up with Lucius Pringle, readying the coach and team. "Best to get out now, Lucius," he said. "This might become a serious blow, and you've near twenty miles to cover 'fore the next stop." Lucius nodded and went inside to round up his reluctant passengers.

The snow continued to fall, sometimes in light showers and at other times driving almost horizontally on the wind in dense white assaults. It drifted around the buildings and the lee sides of fences and scalloped behind ridges. Cashdown passed most of the day getting restocked for the next stage arrival. "We must be prepared," he told Libbie and the staff, "for the time when some storm will keep our guests here for a longer stay, maybe up to a week. Could be more. We don't want to lose anybody, including ourselves, for lack of provisions or heat."

He split five more ricks of firewood and added them to the supply stacked under the back shed-roof. The children moved stores of meat from the ice house to the cold hole beneath the porch. The snow scraper was pulled forward in the barn and winter harnesses brought out. By dusk Cashdown was tired enough to sit by the fire with a glass of ale for half an hour before going back out to check the water for ice.

"You know what day this is, Hamish?" Libbie kissed him on the forehead.

He turned a puzzled look to her. "Wednesday . . . I think it's Wednesday, right?"

"It's your birthday, dear. You're sixty-five today, and you don't act a minute over sixty-four."

"Ah, should've thought of that! Right now I'm feeling me age."

"Well, it happens that you're the same age as Mrs. Stanton."

"She must be older than me. And clearly more important, too."

"Don't be sour about it, Hamish. We need to celebrate your birthday."

He brightened immediately, and after dinner there was a fruit pie with a candle, and cheeses and a round of whiskey; later there were more whiskeys and songs and storytelling until it was time for the children to go to bed.

The wind and snow let up during the night, and the dawn's iron sky turned ragged, with black shreds and curlicues scudding overhead in a turbulent mottle of greys. The temperature had sunk to near zero, and the stock water needed to be cleared of ice again. The return stagecoach from Cheney arrived on schedule just as a new front moved in from the southeast. Cashdown knew it would be a major storm whenever it came from that direction, and he told Lucius to prepare his passengers for the possibility of an extended stay at Steptoe Station.

The dinner and revelry that evening were as usual, but no friends from Colfax or Palouse City braved the worsening weather to join the stagecoach people for dancing and midnight oysters. Before turning in, Cashdown confided to Libbie a concern about the storm. "I worry about the range stock. They'll have to find shelter in the draws. I suppose the forest will give them some relief. If the creeks don't freeze down to the stones, the horses and mules should be able to get water, but I'm not as sure about the cattle. They don't graze well in deep snow. Maybe I should haul out some feed."

"Not tonight, Hamish. It's three o'clock, and we can see

what's what in the morning's light." Libbie was struggling to keep her eyelids from dropping, and she knew he would be up in a few hours.

At dawn Cashdown, already dressed in woolens, tiptoed out of the bedroom carrying his Templar cap. At the back mudroom he donned his oiled coat and knee boots, tied his checked deerstalker over the cap, and put on rabbit-skin gloves before pushing the door open. He stepped into a foot of rippled snow and saw through the swirling blizzard that shoulder-high drifts had formed between the barn and access road. He pulled up his collar and headed to the stables to saddle Peppermint.

He knew the terrain intimately and could tell where to expect impassible drifts. In several places he urged Peppermint to go around a berm covering the trail; her instinct was to keep to the known route, but Cashdown knew the snow in those spots would be more than belly deep, and even his tall mule would struggle to get through. He found a herd of his cattle gathered in a long ravine within a copse of firs and cedars. They had waited until the horses had broken the creek ice, and now all were drinking. His horses were scattered across the snow-covered pastures bordering the ravine, and all had found browse and were busy grazing. He counted the cattle and horses and moved on. A few mules were gathered on a nearby hillside beneath a rock overhang.

Whenever he put his livestock on range, he would keep them within his own eight hundred acres, much of which he and his boys had fenced. He rode Peppermint in a circular route past the unfenced areas to see if there were any signs of his animals wandering off the property. Satisfied that all one hundred cows and forty horses and mules were collected in naturally sheltered areas of his ranch, Cashdown patted Peppermint on the neck and said, "Let's head home, girl."

At Steptoe Station he checked on the stabled animals, mostly the babies and the ailing and oldest cattle, the riding mules and horses, and the pulling teams. The children would see to the chickens and rabbits and pigs later. When he returned to the house the guests were just stirring, and Libbie and the older girls were preparing breakfast.

"Coffee and cakes, that's a grand way to welcome a man in from a storm," he declared. The kitchen smells and buzz of activity cheered him as he beat snow from his coat and hat. He entered the kitchen in his stocking feet and embraced Libbie and twirled her around. He nuzzled his frozen beard into her neck.

"You're raving mad!" she shouted.

"Better stay away from me," Mindy chirped. She was mixing batter for griddle cakes and shook her spoon threateningly toward her father. He leapt at her with a pucker, and she flung a clot of batter in his direction. In seconds he was chasing Mindy around the table and stove as she continued to fling batter at him, both giggling and panting, yellow coins of batter in their hair and on their clothes. He caught her in his arms and danced her back to the huge bowl she had been stirring. As he let go and turned away, he spun around and stuck his wet beard in her neck. Mindy screamed, and amid an uproar of laughter the staff rushed in to see what was going on.

"Just Papa being Papa," Libbie said and brushed them back to their chores.

The wind rose to a rumbling din and occasionally accelerated to blasts that caused the Steptoe Station sign to bang against the head-gate arch. Cashdown had hung storm windows all around the inn, a caution deemed a luxury on the Palouse prairie. But he had calculated that it would save him time, effort, and money in firewood and maintenance, and at moments like these their muffling of the wind gave some comfort to the people indoors. The snow, blowing across the Palouse like a white hurricane, continued to pile up and drift.

Just as darkness came on, a stagecoach and six from Cheney plowed its way into the yard, and passengers achingly clambered down. Cashdown rushed out to greet them and direct the stabling of the team. Without a messenger, Felix Warren was a lone, snow-caked driver.

"Good thing you had your big team, Felix. They must've pulled fair well in this snow," Cashdown said.

"It was touch and go in places, Cashdown, 'specially this side of California Creek on Mulouine Hill. Can we take cover here till it blows over?"

"Come join the party. Lucius and his travelers are here. With yours we'll be twenty-three in all, but we have ample victuals and ale."

There were the usual feast and songs that night, and the next, but by the third morning of the storm, snow was over the porch rails and reaching to the windows like a rising tide. Cashdown and the younger men worked outdoors in relays for short periods to open access to the barns and stables. They strung storm lines between the house and outbuildings to guide their way; they shoveled paths and stacked more firewood; they fed and watered livestock and tended to the sick or very old animals. There was cheer among the hardy ones who helped outdoors. They joked about the follies of wintertime travel and the perils of following guide lines to the frozen gates of hell, and they sang happy songs about sledding in the snow and sad ones about loves lost in bad weather. But there was quiet fear among the travelers who remained indoors, many of whom had never experienced a Palouse winter storm. They sat by the stove and attended watchfully to the blizzard and relentless wind.

Among the Felix Warren passengers was Ursula Hartjes, at whose Colfax Academy the younger Musgrave children were now enrolled. She was a massive woman about thirty years old, half a foot taller than Cashdown, firm in her opinions, and ready to level a withering glare on those who disagreed with her. She joined the men in their outdoor chores, carrying a large share of firewood and feed; she was among the first to go out in the morning to re-clear the paths to the barn and sheds; and she stayed up late at night with Cashdown, arguing and debating, drinking and laughing.

After two more days and nights with no letup in the storm, Ursula declared that she should be back at her academy in case any children might make it in. "Damn this snow! I'm needed at my school, and there's no way to get there," she groused.

"One thing this land teaches us, Miss Hartjes, is patience," Cashdown replied. He drew on his churchwarden. Ursula and half a dozen other guests were seated with Cashdown around the big stove in the main hall. It was long after midnight, and they nursed glasses of warm port.

"Patience? Well, Cashdown, if I may, my patience with our legislators and common schooling officials is fragile as a cobweb. Coming on a decade we've had the territorial superintendent of schools and the fund, yet neither has ever made an appearance here. Are we or are we not in Whitman County and part of Washington Territory? If our academy is to remain standing and our children are to be taught responsible citizenship, the principles of truth and proper social behavior, and the basics of literacy, well, it's left to me to do it alone. And I thus feel an urgency to be at my school."

"Ah, Ursula, I shouldn't disagree with ya. But you are not alone responsible for the schoolhouse and its contents, nor for the complete education of our kiddies. We pay our tuitions, and as landholders of Colfax and the county we've taxed ourselves to help support the academy, just as we did with Sam McCroskey's makeshift school. Our legislators in the capitol worry only that Olympia should remain the center of the universe, which means only for their own improvement." He winked slyly and went on. "This is not to offer excuses for them, no. The virtues they say must be taught are only for orderliness and continuity of public affairs, to make life easier for them and the rulers. That's what legislating really is, don't you know—harvesting money and distributing it, with the main aim of making life easier for the legislators and administrators. And that includes keeping their sinecures in Olympia and helping their well-set friends." He sipped his port, sucked his pipe, and grinned.

"You're denouncing categorically, Cashdown. Surely there are good men in Olympia." Her tone changed to something more measured and reasoned. "Perhaps it's just that they don't appoint good men to run the common schooling enterprise."

Lucius Pringle said, "What about our own Orestes Banks, Cashdown? You think he's just in it for himself?"

"Nae. Orestes is the one exception in a million politicians. Alas, he won't stay. Last time we talked about his positions in Olympia and the national capitol, he said he was uninterested in making it his life's work. He has the finest principles and grand new ideas, and he has the dedication of a plow ox—and the strength, don't you know. But he said the political life is poisonous and too much exposure will rot a man's soul. Or a woman's, though women needn't worry much on that score, 'cause the rotten-souled men have always kept them from the field."

"That will change one day," Ursula said, punctuating her declaration with a wagging finger. "In some future day women will not only have the vote, but women will be voting as legislators and will govern cities and could even become elected heads of nations."

Some of the men scoffed, but she quickly silenced them with a stony glare. She would have known Cashdown agreed with her, for hadn't he been at Libbie's side in all the suffragist events? And hadn't he just last night spoken passionately about the need to modify the Fifteenth Amendment to include all persons, men and women of all skin colors?

Cashdown chunked more wood into the stove and sat again in his oversized chair. The chair was one of many pieces he had ordered from Europe—France, Germany, and England—bought through an agent in London and shipped across the Atlantic, then by freight wagon over southern Mexico, up the coast and the Columbia by sail and barge, and by rail and freighters along the trails to Steptoe Station. There were sideboards, tables, bed frames, and settees made of the finest oak, chestnut, and walnut carved and fitted by the best craftsmen. Among them was his favorite polished chair, with the carved lion heads atop the chairback and great paws at the feet and armrests. Seated next to the fat, nickel-trimmed stove, he looked incongruously like a diminutive potentate on a medieval throne.

"Aye, it will change, but only in consequence of right, secular education. We all need to be citizens who can read and acquire a love for it. Our country, my adopted land, depends wholly on that. All people must learn about the truth, the facts of history, and the highest of previous thinking before they can vote in the best interests of every man, woman, and child. And of the nation. Nowadays, though, we let any fool white man vote and don't bother to ask what he understands about the moral ground for human decency or about the proper balancing of safety and liberty, or the costs of war. Some God-fearing voters think men have natural dominion over women and Whites have dominion over all the other colors, and they know so little about economic facts as to think newcomers like our own Pinky are ruining their markets and taking their jobs. What nonsense! We're all newcomers, just arrived at different times, driven or drawn to where we are by different forces."

As he talked he was staring under bushy, silver eyebrows at

the nickel woodstove. "But nobody's above anybody else by nature, and we must ask permission and make compromise before taking someone else's land or labor or privileges. That's why we depend so dearly on our teachers and schools and why we should be thanking and honoring educators like Ursula Hartjes and Sam McCroskey and demanding that our legislators do their jobs and move the funds out to the backcountry, as they promised to do."

Felix Warren was skeptical. "And just who owns truth, Cashdown? How can even a teacher tell the real facts from some other person's ideas about history or our natures or, or whatever?" He folded his arms and smiled, as if he'd landed a fatal blow.

Ursula pounced on him. "Books! The labors of scholars, centuries of learning, for heaven's sake!" she spluttered.

"Seems they're always changing what they think they know. Every new book takes over some earlier one, excepting for the Bible," he answered.

"Here's my reply to you, Felix," Cashdown interjected. "My old country gave America at least two blessedly unbiblical tools. From England the migrants carried the idea of civil deliberation. That means reasoned and orderly debate. It's the tool the congresses are supposed to use for deciding how the power and money get distributed and who pays. The basics of reasoned and orderly debate—the rules to go by and measurements for judging who wins a point—come from a century earlier, don't you know, and those came from even earlier ideas going all the way back to the Romans and to the Greeks before that. Rationality will rule the day, different kinds of logic and rigors laid over a common and practical learning. The law is based on that. And the second tool was the unholy idea of compromise. When all the debate is said and done and there's still some disagreement on practical matters, we follow the rule of splitting differences and trading off one point for another. It's not perfect, but it's a way of doing business that allows for facts to change based on what's possible to learn from observations and careful thinking. And then just and civil discussion. We could have no trade if it weren't for these."

Felix shook his head in disagreement, unconvinced. "So why isn't it working now?" he said.

Cashdown nodded toward Ursula, who gestured dismissively toward Felix. She rose from her chair, and the others stirred and all drifted off to their rooms. Cashdown cleaned up the wine cups, stoked the fires, tapped the ash plugs from his pipes, and went to bed, humming contentedly.

The next morning's sky was brighter, with slivers of blue visible above the southwestern horizon and a warming wind gusting from that direction. By midday the temperature was above freezing, and before nightfall the huge snowdrifts had sagged by a third. On the sixth day the roads became passable, and the two stagecoaches with their passengers departed amid cheerful goodbyes and thank-yous and promises to spread the word about the splendid hospitality at Steptoe Station. Cashdown went out to survey the storm damage and check on the range livestock. Three cows had died in the snow, but the rest of his herds were safe. Some fences would need repairs, and soon the creeks would be flooded, but all else appeared unharmed.

Two days later the stage arrived from Colfax bearing eight passengers and a week's mail. Libbie sat at the kitchen table sorting through envelopes and packages. When Cashdown came in from restocking firewood, she handed him a large envelope. "From the railroad," she said.

He quickly read the letter. "Hah. Says they like my idea. 'We find your proposal of interest and will include it in the company plans for future expansion,' they say. Signed by some vice president. We might be in business."

Then he asked, "Anything from Callum?"

She gave him another envelope. "It got returned. Never opened. It says 'Addressee Not Known: Return to Sender.' "

Chapter 18

Snowfall resumed after Thanksgiving and continued without letup for more than two months. The region was snowed in for the holidays, no movement between settlements, no stagecoach deliveries or resupply trips to town, and scarcely a soul stirring in Colfax unless it was a dire emergency. At Steptoe Station the storm lines to the barn, granary, and sheds hung slack and frozen in head-high trenches. Drifts rose over the barn, leaving caps behind the roof peak like cresting waves. Every day Cashdown and the older children shoveled enough space open by the barn to pull the plow out with mules and clear the way to the main gate and access road. But there was nowhere to go and nobody coming in: by New Year's the snow had drifted to five and six feet deep in places, and the mules couldn't move through it. A train had been snowbound for days on the tracks below Cheney. Cashdown knew he would lose more range cattle, even if they had followed the horses into forested draws.

Some mornings when the snowfall abated for a while, Cashdown would stand atop a drift over the main gate fence and gaze around the hushed countryside. Glistening and muted shades of white on white like linen flowing into rice paper wrapped around moonstone mountains that etched the horizon at the edges of the implacable zinc sky. He always looked eastward, so his eyes and mind could linger on the porcelain cone of Steptoe Butte jutting defiantly upward, as if resisting a smothering god. Sometimes he would go in the house and tell

Libbie how beautiful the scene was. "The view from up there must be damnably grand today!"

"Looks to me like the most forbidding place in the world," she would reply.

They were well prepared for their long isolation and withstood it stoically, and by mid-February a warm front from the southwest pushed the storm systems into Idaho and Montana, leaving behind shrinking snowbanks and rising streams and rivers. Cashdown went out to investigate the winterkill among his herds. He discovered some of his cattle by their legs pointing skyward from swollen streambeds, others by ragged hides on humps left by receding snowdrifts. But more than half had survived and stood with the horses and mules yarded up in ponderosa stands, all gaunt and bony and wild to get at the sleigh of hay he'd hauled to them.

The Palouse River rose and surged at the Colfax confluence. Townspeople stood on higher ground north and east of downtown and watched the river rising a foot an hour along Main Street. It overflowed its banks and within a day had covered the streets in the center of town. The next morning, with the warming temperature, it continued to rise and soon soaked the boardwalks and lapped at the doors of shops and offices. Lycurgus had stuffed oily rags in the front and back entries to the *Gazette* offices and stacked sandbags three feet high across both sides of the building. He went in and out by ladder to the second story.

The swirling waters reached under buildings and steadily inched up to joists and floorboards, lifting and twisting and seeping into interiors. Lycurgus could see shops and stables being prised off their foundations, whole buildings beginning to rise and slowly rotate and move downstream like gigantic rafts adrift. The mercantile came floating down Main Street, tearing off porch roofs and smashing into other buildings and dislodging them. It became a monstrous wrecking ball as it careened downstream. He heard groans and squeaks from the bowels of the *Gazette* building, but the massive printing presses and heavy files and supply barrels and trunks helped the structure remain anchored to its pilings.

Pinky had sandbagged her hotel on all sides, and its brick foundation was sounder than the wood posts most buildings sat upon. Still, she watched anxiously as the floodwaters rose over the porch and crept up the sandbagged walls. She had nearly two dozen lodgers, many previously confined there for weeks by the storm, and she had to decide when it would be necessary to evacuate them. Yet her plan for evacuation was drowning with the roiling debris swirling down Main Street. She had no good alternative to the academy and Methodist church to relocate her lodgers, and the way to those shelters now looked forbidding. She asked herself why the town fathers had decided to move the main commercial center of Colfax from the hillsides to the river bottom. Maybe because James Perkins had built his cabin—the first seed of the settlement—next to the river? When all the flooding was over, she would have to ask him.

In time the floodwaters receded, leaving a battlefield of debris in the center of Colfax. Entire buildings were crushed or otherwise deposited intact like rubbish into the riverbed; piles of downed trees and torn out sidewalks and porches, clusters of overturned and smashed wagons, and the furnishings of countless stores and homes that had been gutted by the torrent were strewn everywhere. Gradually people emerged from safety and began clearing up the wreckage. When the roads became passable once more, Pinky's guests resumed their travels, and she turned her energies to cleaning up around the hotel. James Perkins told her, when she asked him, that Main Street had been relocated because newcomers found it inconvenient to haul carts uphill.

Flooding had plagued the territory's coastal cities as well, and travel was long delayed. As soon as it was possible to reach the Columbia River, Orestes and Lucinda Banks made their way home to Colfax. Orestes surveyed the damage in the town and called for a citizens' meeting to discuss funding recovery work. Two hundred and twenty people packed the sanctuary of the Baptist church on North Mill Street. Orestes received testimonials about losses to homeowners and farms and promised he would press his fellow legislators in Olympia for relief money. He helped organize cleanup teams.

"I also wish to report to you," he announced in his deep, mellow voice, "that the Northern Pacific is coming close to completing the transcontinental line to Spokane. It won't be long before Whitman County will be connected by rail to the wider world, both to the south and to the north. We should be prepared to meet this change," he warned. "I'm pleased in addition to announce that a renewed effort to gain statehood for Washington has started up in Walla Walla, possibly to include a constitutional provision for universal suffrage. I aim to take the lead in Olympia for legislation to carry to the national Congress." The last announcement drew cheers and applause, and dozens of people clamored to shake hands with their representative as the meeting broke up.

An hour later at the hotel bar, Orestes was seated for drinks with half a dozen gathered friends. "It's a great pleasure to see each of you again," he toasted them. "I have been away from Whitman County far too long this time, and my heart has pulled me for months in two directions—to work afar for our people and to come home to our peaceful Palouse country and be among real folks."

"Ah, we surely have missed the comfort of your presence, Orestes," Cashdown said. "We appear to've made it through a savage winter in your absence, my friend, but there isn't a one of us who'd not want you and Lucinda constantly here among us, where you've become a cornerstone."

The others around the table—James Perkins, now County Executive, Pinky Ji Ping-tien, Lycurgus Ames, Overman Powell, and Sheriff Arvind Carscallen—nodded and voiced their salutations.

James said, "It must've been savage for you, Orestes, holding the line against the Democrats all around us. Would suffrage strengthen the petition for statehood?"

"It was unpopular in '78, less so in '76," OP said. "I think the depression influenced the vote, and the Walla Walla Democrats trying for secession to Oregon scared a lot of voters. But much has changed since then, both in politics and in finance."

Orestes slowly sipped his whiskey. "I agree entirely," he said. "Add Colorado's statehood, so their fear of throwing future elections to the Republicans also interfered. Now, all of that looks to be settled—some people even think Mr. Garfield was fairly elected—and the main opposition worry is loss of subsidies. With the coming of the railroad, that shouldn't be a problem for our petition. The approval of women's suffrage is overdue, and now it's properly severed from prohibition. If we can't get it into the constitution, we'll do it by separate referendum. James, I won't comment on the savagery of our political culture, except to tell you I've met a lot of fools and otherwise flawed men, but I've also met a few honorable, learned, and honest men. I've strived to work as one of the latter group, but Lord knows we pay our dues—we're always tarred as rebels and dissidents."

"Well might you be, and that's grand," said Cashdown. "We're the bastard children of the territory, we here on this Palouse prairie, and we depend, Orestes, on your strong dissenting voice in Olympia and the nation's capital for our welfare and advancement. We'd prefer you and Lucinda here, but you do well by us there. Through all those quiet days of imprisonment by the weather, I got a rare opportunity to have a good think about our future, and I've been wondering of late how you plan your campaign for next year. What can we do to promote your re-election?"

Orestes eyed Lycurgus. "This must be off the record."

Lycurgus nodded. The rest also signaled agreement.

"I have a lot on my agenda for my coming years. But not included is my re-election. We've decided to return home to Whitman County and truly settle down. Repeated migration across the territory and across the continent is proving too demanding, especially on Lucinda. And we don't want to bring up little ones in such a life. When the time is right, soon, I will announce my resignation from the legislature. My only regret will be not representing the Palouse people in Olympia and the District of Columbia."

For a few seconds a stunned silence fell on the group of friends. Pinky was the first to speak. "You going to have babies?"

Orestes laughed. "Lucinda seems to think that's possible."

"Ah, wonderful!" Cashdown exclaimed. "May you double the population of Colfax with your progeny. You belong here as much as any of us. We're all migrants, Orestes, and our lives have been, for many of us, just a selfish wandering." He turned serious. "But others, like you and Pinky, you were driven out of your homelands and arrived here by luck and main strength, and you well deserve a place to alight permanently. Others of us, we've always been hungering for the gold mine at the end of the trail. And then the next trail, and the next. There's always something to lure us over the horizon, and we'll surely push anyone out of our way, take what's not ours, brutalize the land and animals, even put our families in danger, just to satisfy that hunger."

"Yours appears to be always over the next horizon, Cashdown, though it's not likely you'd put your family in danger now," quipped Lycurgus. "Mine? It's always my next editorial to put my family in danger. You'll have to speak for yourself on the wanderlust."

Cashdown chuckled. "Well, migrants like me, because of it we're destined in the long run to be satisfied with less than the best, or else continue to itch. The clever mercenaries stayed put back in New York or Boston and profited greatly from our foolishness, the wandering and suffering and hard work of us pioneers. You know what a pioneer is? He's a greedy, adventurous fool whose folly is his belief there's a gold mine awaiting just for him, if only he goes far enough into the wilderness, if only he grabs enough of what others don't dare to, if only he takes the next step over the far horizon. There's smarter swine lazing at home in Philadelphia and getting rich off our hunger for railroads and market loans and timber. We cut the trees and lay the tracks; they make the profits. We dig out the silver and gold; they keep the minerals and pay a pitiable wage. You and Orestes and Pinky, you just had the misfortune to end up here, with a community of romantic fools."

"Your brush is too full of tar, Cashdown," OP said. "We're as different from each other as bats are from doves. We've arrived here for many different reasons and from many origins. Why, just at this table we have Lycurgus, who searched for and found a place in need of an honest newspaper. And we have Arvind, who arrived to continue the policing work he loves. Both these friends and good citizens are helping our town prosper in a safe and well-informed way. I could say the same about many of our citizens, including Miss Hartjes and, particularly, James here." He gestured toward Perkins. "You came here as a pioneer to start a mill with your partner, creating something out of nothing, and you've devoted your life and work to building the city of Colfax and the county of Whitman. And my intuition is none of us, including myself, longs to leave this community of fools."

"I can't leave, because I'm about to build a house too fancy and dear to abandon," James replied.

"I possibly would leave for the chance to run a bigger paper in a big city somewhere else in Washington or Oregon," Lycurgus said. "Genevieve would approve. She says I have the journalist's itch, but she enjoys cities, too."

Arvind Carscallen cleared his throat. "I admit, I know I'd leave Whitman County if I could double my pay, but only if I could cut my work demands in half."

Pinky looked around thoughtfully. "You men worry so much about whys and maybes, why this, maybe that, all the time. I think I just worry about solving this problem right here"—she pointed in front of herself—"and then solve next problem and go ahead to next bigger job, just happy to eat good, breathe nice air, sleep safe."

"I admire your practicality, Pinky," Orestes said. "And that is part of the spirit of people who arrived on the frontier from the beginning. But, with gratitude, Cashdown, I think you are partly right. Some of us were put on the track to the frontier by circumstances we had little choice about, and some came because, for one reason or another, they were wanderers with high spirits and a romantic nature. And do not overlook the government's inducements. But there are many ways to wander and many reasons to settle. All the good people I've met and had the privilege to serve here in the eastern territory are honest, industrious, compassionate, and, maybe above all else, brave souls. I do not know many fools among them, and the greedy or condemned ones are noteworthy for their small numbers. We know them all by name. We know the most dependably generous ones, too, and among the most generous are you and your Libbie."

Cashdown pouted while rotating his whiskey glass on the tablecloth. "Might be just talking about m'self," he said. "I am always a skeptic and the most restless wanderer you've ever known, and there've been times when I've aimed to leave and start over. And I've come to think I've intruded into someone else's home, taken what is not mine to take, as if there was nothing important here before I came. I am both ashamed and grateful. But I also am a resentful soul. It might be that I wander because I am in a constant anger at the gouging we take from manufactory moguls and the big Eastern bankers and all the abuses we suffer from the politicians, present company excluded. OP, you've been a godsend, and without your bank many of our neighbors couldn't've gotten started. And then I look at all the mayhem and ravaging we've heaped on our Indian brothers and the way all the Reconstruction benefits have been sullied, and, well, I am in danger of becoming nothing but a raving cynic. If it weren't for each of you and all the grand times we are having, I would fall into despair."

"Despair, according to Cervantes, is the greatest folly," Orestes said. "Cheer up, *amigo,* soon enough you will be hosting your parties at Steptoe again, the crops will be coming up, and the blossoms will blanket your apple trees. You will always find new windmills to subdue."

"And," Lycurgus said, "we have the good news that Orestes and Lucinda will be back with us again."

Just as Orestes predicted, with the return of the stagecoach runs the revelry did resume at Steptoe Station, and Cashdown's mood did brighten. His inn became a favored venue for observing weddings and wakes and anniversaries, and the Wheatland Whirlwinds Frontier Band often was on hand. Cashdown would join the music with his hornpipe and fiddle. After young Silas Northrup demonstrated his mastery of the banjo, the band would expand by one. In time, Pinky would hire Silas to clean hotel rooms and entertain guests after dinners.

It wasn't all merriment that year for Cashdown. He fretted about Callum and often said to Libbie, "Maybe I should try writing again to Cal." She heard it so many times, she began to just shrug her shoulders in reply. By midsummer, however. she had grown weary of his self-doubt and responded, "Yes, Hamish, I think you ought to write to him. And then you can feel doubly bad when it gets returned again."

He persisted but equivocated until, on a trip to Moscow, Idaho, Cashdown put the question to the new postmaster. Sam Neff told him a letter would not be returned to him if he sent it in care of general delivery to his brother's last known city and asked that it be forwarded. He returned home full of optimism, ready to try again. It was necessary to update the news from his previous letter.

Dear Callum,

I have tried on numerous past occasions to get a letter to you, but you seem to have relocated. I include herewith my last to you, which was returned, and so I try again. We here all miss you and send our hopes that you are well and prospering. My wish is that you will one day return to the Palouse Country and live and work alongside us.

Our winter lasted well into April, and so we were late into the fields and orchards. There was some die-off from the deep snows, but the herds are coming back, as we had a goodly number of foals and calves this spring. From all signs, we can look forward to a grand harvest come autumn. I am now making flour at the grist mill in Colfax and shipping mostly to Tacoma, estimated at 83 cents per fifty. We might get 20 bu. per acre for wheat this year, and the price has held steady at 55 cents. When the railroad comes to Steptoe Station, our shipping cost will go down by half, and our bulk wheat and milled flour will be at market in half the time. I expect the first train in less than three years.

Some of the neighbors gave up and sold out, the Rheinhardts and Trappens. Two families from the Paluses bought those holdings from OP at the bank and now are working up the acreages as good cropland. The rest of the Tribe are in danger of being sent up to Colville's Reservation or out to Yakima. The new Indian Agent, a man named Milroy, believes all the farmland was made for White settlers, and he wants the Indian Homestead Act voided. Orestes Banks is going to see if he can move Olympia to oppose the Bureau and Milroy, but his time in the Legislature is short, as he and his wife are returning to make their future at their home in Colfax. He is a splendid man, and he will continue to give his generosity to the people of the Palouse Country.

We are all well. Mindy asks after you often, and the twins are still holding onto a quarter section for you, should you choose to come back and make a farm. I would surely love to see you again, no matter what changes have drawn you to where you now are. Please let us know right away that you are well; we worry after you so often.

Your loving Brother,
Hamish

He sealed both letters in an envelope addressed to General Delivery, Colorado Springs, and sent it in the mail pouch on the next stage. It would be another six months before he learned if it reached Callum.

Chapter 19

When the harvest was done and the grains and flour and sold livestock were shipped, and after the year's accounting and preparations for the coming winter were completed, Cashdown could again devote time to his orchards. He and Cushing McBride wrapped young tree trunks with burlap, replaced damaged fences and stakes, harvested late fall apples, and worked on trellises and spreaders. But he sometimes went off alone or with Peppermint and coiled up the butte to the summit, where he would sit for hours gazing to the distant horizons in all directions. On morning climbs his eyes would trace the snowcapped crests of the Cascade peaks to the west. Evenings, he watched dusk edge up the sunlit flanks of Idaho's Bitterroot Mountains to the east. In all directions he traced the sensuous curves and lines of yellowed hills and dark river valleys.

One evening after retreating from the peak he said to Cushing, "Someday I'm going to put something up on the top, something so I can share me love for this place with everyone."

Cushing regarded him with skepticism. "Pretty hard to get up there, Cashdown. You'd be sharing the great effort it takes to gain the top, too."

"I'll sort it out," he replied with a grin.

"You'd better do it soon. You're no spring chicken anymore."

Cashdown had noticed on his hikes that there were no new fire rings or animal bones on the peak, nor was there any other evidence of Palus Indian activity. He hadn't seen any Paluses near Steptoe Butte for at least a year, and he told Libbie he thought they might have abandoned the ritual site. "Maybe they think we've profaned it. Don't know where they'd go otherwise, though. Those Indian boys won't become men just will-ye nil-ye."

"Maybe they've gone up to Colville. Or they decided to farm."

"I think I'll have a look."

"Why would you want to spend your time stirring them up? Don't we have better things to do, Hamish?"

"Just curious. I'll take Ferdy with me."

Cashdown and his middle son rode out to the last Palus encampment they knew of, but they found the site cleared of tepees and stock pens. Only some rotting debris from the trash pit remained scattered around.

"What happened to them, Papa?"

"Hard to say. Looks like they left all orderly. Dogs have been here, though. Let's go ask somebody."

They rode east to a tidy farm on the route to Rosalia and talked with the settler, Kellen Dybdahl. He greeted Cashdown and Ferdy as if they were old friends.

"They've all but disappeared, Cashdown. Once they got wind of the government plan to pay to get 'em on reservations, they just vanished. A couple families are farming down near Endicott, but I have not seen a shadow of Tomeo and his band. Can't imagine them on a reservation. Nontreaty to the bone."

"Aye, that's true. I wonder if they might've joined up with some of the Spokanes or Coeur d'Alenes?"

"A man could probably find out. I know there's a band of Spokanes just north of Rockford, and I've had good talks with them. Ka'ashish-tu is their leader, but he's not a chief. They're kind of independent. Nice people . . . helped us with our crops early on."

"Thank you, Kellen. We might just do that."

On their way back to Steptoe Station, Ferdy asked his father, "How do you know Mr. Dybdahl, Pa?"

"We stayed there when Peppy was shot the night we caught Odis Bragg and his men. He was very kind, but I paid him well for the fare."

When they arrived home, Cashdown made plans to visit the Spokanes. Libbie asked him again why he thought it was necessary. He replied that he didn't know, but it was nagging at him badly, and he wanted to learn if they still had use for the peak and still held it sacred.

It was late autumn once more, and the golden hills were turning dusky. The limbs of poplars and bitter cherry were bare, and the ocher needles of tamaracks drifted down to mat the valley floors. Rushing waters of creeks and rivers harmonized with the melody of fresh winds, and more frequent rains became mixed with sleet and fleeting snowfalls. Cashdown packed up Peppermint with gifts and overnight supplies, put on his oiled greatcoat and winter hat, and headed north to Rock Lake. He was greeted at the Spokanes' settlement by a dozen men and boys. They led him to Ka'ashish-tu, who was resting before a fire in his bark-shingled house.

Cashdown and Ka'ashish-tu exchanged gifts and talked about the government's plans for relocating nontreaty tribes who still had land on the Palouse prairie. The old leader looked unmoved—neither pleased nor skeptical—when Cashdown told him many Whites did not agree with the new government policy. He showed more interest when they talked of the railroads.

"When railroads come, we must make a hard choice. The old ways will be gone forever. We must choose to honor our ways or give them up and be like Whites. We must choose to live or die as a people. Some say to live is only possible on the reservations. Others say we die no matter. What do you think, Mr. Cashdown?"

"It will be hard, for certain. Our great father, our president, is not a wise man, and he is not a good man. This one is different from your Chief Big Thunder. But he will not be our president for a lifetime—our Constitution says it will be only a short time before we will have another president, and maybe his spirit will be stronger, and his heart more generous, and his mind wiser. We have had wise and kind leaders before, so maybe in time your choice won't be so hard. You will be able to raise your families and have your farms, and you can have your dances and religion and keep your language—our Constitution guarantees that as true."

"I think we will die, no matter what your Constitution says."

Tomeo and his band were lodging with other Spokanes, Ka'ashish-tu said, just west of Rock Lake—Cashdown had bypassed them on his ride up. The Rock Lake band were relatives of Ka'ashih-tu's wife, and they had been farming there for a decade.

Cashdown went to talk with Tomeo. They met in a hide-covered shelter.

"What brings you, Mr. Cashdown?" Tomeo's black, braided hair now showed streaks of grey, and there were long creases across his broad forehead and down his face.

"I hope you and your family are well, Tomeo. I have seen that your people no longer go to Eeyomoshtosh. My wish is that you did not leave the peak because of my orchards. Last year and again this year I could not find you to bring fruits for your people. I have some small bags with me, but there's more for you, if you want them. I have new plums coming on, too."

"We do not ask for your gifts. We want only to be left alone on our land. You may leave those bags, but we do not need such help."

"Right. But I think of me sacks of fruit not as help for people in need but as an act of sharing. I wish to share, just as you have shared your mountain and your medicine know-how with me."

"You have a strong spirit, Mr. Cashdown. But we face troubles your spirit cannot help. The land we always traveled and hunted on and lived on is being eaten, more and more, faster and faster." He spoke rhythmically, slowly, low. "Whites are building fences around our camas fields and game. Without the land, to live as Palus we must go hungry or go through the fences. We cannot travel to see our friends and relatives beyond the Snake. The Whites complain about our horses and dogs; they think we steal from them, so they chase us to reservations. We have talked among ourselves. Many say we can have our Washani spirits if we go to the reservations. But we will have to give up our lands and freedom. Some say we must bury Washani under the grasses and trees, so we can live on our lands and stay free. But if we stay free, we will not be free for long, because the Whites will continue to come, they will come like a big storm, and they will change the land and build fences, and they will call in the soldiers to keep us from hunting and traveling. Some say our Washani already is lost. You cannot help, Mr. Cashdown. The storm will grow worse until all is destroyed and we are gone."

"I know too well the choice you have to make. I am indeed sorry. But maybe I can find something useful for you. What if we could make a little treaty, just you and me."

"I have no faith in treaties. But we can talk."

Tomeo and Cashdown parleyed for an hour more. Cashdown left the sacks of fruit and rode back to Steptoe Station in the enclosing darkness. As he approached the inn he saw the amber light of lamps and woodstove fires glowing from windows all around the main floor, and he smiled while he dismounted and led Peppermint past the house, behind the massive barns, and into the paddocks and sheds. As he passed, he heard the after-dinner songs and shouts and laughter of his family and guests indoors. He groomed and fed the mule in the dark, whispered his thanks for her two days of work and companionship, and went to the house.

"Ah, here he is!" Libbie declared. "Hamish, are you satisfied with your trip?"

"I am, m'love. They're in such a sorry state, but we now have an understanding that might improve things somewhat. For them and for us. And what remains of supper?"

He ate like Tomeo's storm, consuming everything left on the table. He drank two pints of ale, packed and lit his pipe, and joined the gathered guests, staff, and family in the great hall. They sang and danced until midnight, when Holly and the night maid served trays of fried oysters and jugs of Lewiston wine.

Three times during that winter and the following spring Cashdown went to the land office in Colfax. Each time he would purchase a master list of all available public land parcels between the Snake River and Cheney and between the Columbia and the border of Idaho. Each time he would then ride to Tomeo's winter encampment, hand over the plat roster, and read the words on the maps to him. Tomeo would ask questions about who had adjacent parcels here and there, what the claimed lands had been used for, and how much had changed since Cashdown's previous visit. At the end of each visit Cashdown would thank Tomeo and Chief Big Thunder for peace and return home to his usual business.

Business was better than usual that summer. As sallow-brown hills turned into the brilliant greens of new wheat, and as pastures became lakes of blue camas and yellow balsamroot, a new generation of healthy foals and calves was born. The orchards came thickly into blossom, the finest bloom yet; Cashdown told the family the clouds of colors and fragrances were dizzying. Through the summer there was just the right amount of rain, and just the right temperatures held for the crops. By harvest time the wheat was abundant and fat and the hay tall and dense. Cashdown milled the largest shipment of flour in the county. No word from Callum arrived, but Cashdown took it as a good sign that his last letter might have been received.

At the end of the 1882 legislative sessions, Orestes said his farewells in Olympia and Washington, D.C., received accolades and testimonials from his colleagues, and packed up his temporary household for the return to Colfax. Lucinda had gone ahead to reopen and re-stock their cottage on Hillside Avenue. Orestes had a small pension and some savings, but he would need additional income. He told his colleagues he was restless to discover a new calling and was eager to get to work at it. In the meantime, he was looking for a space to open a law office. First, Cashdown had something for him to do.

"The militiamen from down around Union Flat are behind that Indian agent, John Monteith. They're still pushing the Paluses onto reservations so they'll have all the land to themselves. And they're afraid of the Ghost Dances and fighting again over the camas patches. So, there's more watchfulness and possibly some real mischief ahead."

Over lunch with Lycurgus at the Ponderosa Hotel, Cashdown was bringing Orestes up to date on the Whitman County Indians' situation. Outside, the last of the oak and poplar leaves were drifting down and skittering in dry little eddies along the board sidewalks. Now that the harvest was in and the fall sales of weanlings and milled flour were behind him, Cashdown could afford more time in Colfax with his friends. Lycurgus had hired the youngest Musgrave boy, Jack, as his apprentice. Jack was proving so able that Lycurgus, too, could enjoy more leisure time away from his work.

Lycurgus said, "They're behind the Yakima agent, Robert Milroy, too. And he's said to be equally determined to keep the nontreaty Paluses from homesteading. They're all against the act."

"Do the tribes have any advocates?" Orestes asked.

"None. And they can't represent themselves," Cashdown said. "Most of them can't read English, so they don't know what the act really says, don't even know what they're entitled to. Entirely dependent. I told them I'll help sort it out. I've fetched them the maps and plats for available land and read them for Tomeo, but so far they haven't done anything about it."

"Who besides us and some of our neighbors supports their homesteading?"

Lycurgus said, "General Howard for years has been outspoken about their right to settle on public land under the act. If only we could find him and possibly join up with him."

"I had little admiration for him in battle, but since the war he's been a paragon for Blacks," Orestes said. "I would not have been educated if it weren't for General Howard. And say what you might about his campaigns against the Nez Perces, lately he's been plenty vocal to Congress about his support for native homesteading."

Cashdown said, "I recollect he helped some lower Paluses claim a big chunk of shore land down near the Snake. I heard he's no longer assigned to Vancouver, though. Back in Nebraska or Dakota country somewhere."

"Probably Fort Omaha," Orestes said.

"Could you talk to him?"

"Pits the army against Interior and the Indian bureau, but it's worth a try."

Oliver O. Howard was not difficult to find. Lycurgus wrote to the editor of the *Omaha Daily Republican,* who helped Orestes contact the general. Following an exchange of letters, General Howard, who thought he was meeting a retired army captain, agreed to come to Colfax on his next swing through the Department of the Columbia. He arrived during the winter thaw in late February 1883. The general and Orestes met in a private dining salon at Pinky's hotel.

When Howard and his aide entered the room, Orestes stood, saluted, and extended his left hand to the general. Howard ignored the hand but gazed up with penetrating blue eyes at Orestes and brusquely demanded, "How did you lose your leg?"

"Sir, I was hit at the second assault on Saltville, December twentieth, 1864."

"You appear well and able bodied. You have been blessed, Banks."

"It was a fine surgeon, sir, and I returned to duty and joined the Tenth Cavalry afterwards."

"Commendable, commendable," the general muttered, while looking around for a chair. He sat, and Orestes and the aide, a first lieutenant, followed suit. General Howard looked older than his forty-three years. His heavy torso, clearly once the body of a powerful man, now slumped at the shoulders, and he moved as if in deep pain. His right sleeve was neatly folded above the elbow and fastened with an engraved brass clasp. He wore a thick, full beard and wide moustaches that flowed into his chops like the wings of a scouting harrier. He was going silver-grey all over his broad head. "Now, refresh my mind on this militia business, Banks."

Orestes told him the history of dwindling numbers of peaceful, nontreaty Paluses and the threats over hunting and root lands by ethnic Germans, who had recently come in from the Midwest. Newly arrived Russian settlers had been doing the same in the north. He described the militias, who were pressing for abolition of the Indian Homestead Act and enforcing White settlers' demands, agitating to remove all Paluses to Colville and Yakima. When he began to relate the history of settlement on the Palouse prairie, General Howard interrupted him.

"I served as Columbia Division commander, and I am well aware of Whitman County's history. I am not interested in the quality of social life of the tribes and bands here. That would not be my assignment anyway, had I remained at Vancouver. I am interested only in keeping peace and enforcing existing laws. The law says native peoples have the right to claim vacant public lands, and, until the law is changed, I shall assure that happens."

Orestes stared steadily at the general. "Sir, if I judge by your humane administration of the Freedmen's Bureau, I find it difficult to understand your lack of care for the well-being of the Indians."

Beneath wiry eyebrows, Howard's watery glare fastened on Orestes. "We are a Christian nation, Banks, and you and your people are among the most devoted of Christians. The natives, in contrast, believe in a dangerous magic. They shun the holy order of God's supremacy in the universe, and they are against progress and the natural order of human supremacy on earth. I could not countenance abetting their savage way of life."

"Sir," Orestes answered, "I can see that the least and the most we can agree on is the necessity for laws and the orderly enforcement of existing laws. Regardless of the question about whether or not ours is a Christian nation, it is written into our founding documents that ours is a nation created first and foremost on the law. The first three grievances specified in our Declaration of Independence all name the rule of law as the genesis of a just society and the abjuring of laws as justified reason for revolution. We both know that, General. My plea is that you use the powers of your office, your long association with both military and civilian leaders, and your great respect for the law to influence all parties to cease the deportation of the Paluses from their ancestral lands."

"You address me as a lawyer would, Banks." General Howard puffed his chest and scowled with contempt.

"Perhaps that is because I am a lawyer and learned my lessons too earnestly when at Howard University."

"You attended my institute?"

"Inaugural class of the law school."

"Hmm. Do you have a legal practice?"

"I have served in law enforcement and politics, the Georgia state legislature, and most recently as Washington Territory's at-large representative to the United States Congress."

General Howard blanched. "Well then, sir, I have misjudged you. I shall do my utmost to sway our Congress toward upholding the act." He turned to the lieutenant to make sure he was taking notes. "And to earn your confidence. I also shall direct my subordinates to maintain surveillance on conditions among the natives here in Whitman County."

"Thank you, General. May I call on you if I pass through Omaha?"

"I would be pleased, sir. However, I expect to reassume command at Fort Vancouver shortly, and perhaps you would join me for dinner there, when I arrive."

"I will look forward to that time."

"Thank you, sir," the general said. He gestured for Orestes to precede him into the lobby and extended his left hand to shake in farewell.

As Orestes was watching General Howard and his lieutenant leave the Ponderosa Hotel, Cashdown was sitting down a block north on Main Street in the Northern Pacific office of Cliven Cleary. Willard Anders was up from Walla Walla and had joined

Cleary to receive Cashdown's latest inquiry.

"Well, well, Mr. Musgrave, how can we help you today?" Cleary's fat cheeks shone like buffed apples. He rose from his desk and rushed to shake Cashdown's hand. He wore a pinstriped suit with a crimson silk puff tie and matching pocket handkerchief. Anders remained seated next to Cleary's desk. His suit and full waistcoat of somber grey matched his complexion and hair. The two sat side by side, a peony nodding next to a granite post.

Cashdown removed his greatcoat and stovepipe hat. "Morning, Mr. Cleary. I'm pleased to catch you here, Mr. Anders. I wished to find out the latest news of the railroad coming out Steptoe way. There must be significant progress, eh?"

"Indeed, indeed," said Anders. His eyelids began fluttering. "We expect to bring the first train into Colfax this year, Mr. Musgrave. We're very optimistic that passenger service to Hooper and Wallula will be established before autumn. Plans are finished for the new bridge across the Snake, and it'll be built this summer. It won't be long, Mr. Musgrave, not long at all."

"Ah, that's grand. But what about our line out to Steptoe Station?"

Cliven Cleary and Willard Anders exchanged glances. Cleary said, "It's in the mill, the planning mill, Mr. Musgrave. We certainly want to be able to serve large shippers like yourself, and if development continues as we predict, there'll be a passenger market in the mid-prairie as well."

"So, may I assume that it is still on?"

"Still on indeed, Mr. Musgrave. No worries on that."

Anders concurred: "Yes, still on. Rest assured, Mr. Musgrave, we'll be giving full consideration to your needs and ideas." He rose and made a sweeping gesture toward the door.

Cashdown got into his greatcoat, tapped on his stovepipe hat, and turned to the railroad agents. "Thank you, gentlemen. I will be expecting to hear more good news near the end of the year."

He went out whistling a little jig tune and hummed and sang all the way back to Steptoe Station. When he came in the door, the lamps were already lit, stagecoach guests were milling around, and dinner was warming in the ovens. Libbie was supervising the kitchen staff, and he grabbed her from behind and spun her around.

"Hamish, Hamish, let me go!" She turned around to greet him. "What did they say, the railroad men?"

"Seems all fine. They make no promises, but it's almost as good. We should be under construction by next year."

"And Orestes?"

"The general did come to town, and they met. That's all I know for now."

"Oh, the mail came on this afternoon's stage. There's a letter for you from Colorado. Looks like Callum's hand."

CHAPTER 20

Cashdown slammed the letter down on the kitchen table. "What *is* this?" he blurted. "What in bloody hell on earth is Callum trying to say?" He scraped a chair out and sat. The face he turned up to Libbie was rouged by befuddlement and rage in equal measure.

"What does it say, Hamish?"

"Says he's been sorting out his feelings. Says he's doing just fine. Wants to take care of our kiddies. He's gotten bloody rich, but he's poor in spirit. Says he can't abide m' presence. Me very *presence*, for God's sake!"

"Why don't you calm yourself and read it to me."

"Well, salutation, et cetera. Then he says,

> You deserved a response from me long before now, but in truth I continue to try to understand why I have travelled away and remain at such a distance from my family, and how my spirits are troubled. I miss all of you, but I must seek my own way, to save my soul and honour. It would be unfair of me to mislead you, Hamish, and when I am sure I understand, I will tell you. Of one thing I am certain, and it is that I have stood in your shadow always, for too long, and have never learned to be my own person. Until I am confident of my independence, I am compelled to remain at a distance, and I ask only that you not travel

here to see me just yet, for I cannot stand in your presence.

Please tell the family I am well and have prospered in Colorado as timber and land broker. The railroad and mining contracts have proven profitable. I am now in a condition to give support for my nephews and nieces, should they ever need it, although I am sure you and Libbie have well seen to their needs. Please convey my love to them.

With brotherly respect and admiration,
Callum

He stared at the letter. Tears brimmed in his eyes as he whispered, "I believe I've lost him."

Libbie came up behind him and put her arms around his shoulders. "It says he can't stand in your presence, not that he can't stand you. Sounds to me like he's saying he's unworthy yet. Whatever he means, Hamish, there's no sense blaming yourself. He always was something of a little boy. He might feel that he's been *your* little boy, even though he's only two years younger. It seems he needs separation to become a man, and if we love him we must allow him that."

Cashdown nodded, wiped his eyes roughly with his cuffs, and walked silently out of the kitchen. For the first time since opening Steptoe Station, he didn't lead the evening's festivities. That night he took a lamp straight to his bedside and sat with the King James and Callum's letter on his lap. But he didn't read. Lost in thought, he smoked a pipe, rubbed his temples, massaged his feet, occasionally got up to feed the stove and return to the bedside. When Libbie joined him, long after midnight, he was still sitting on the bed, pondering.

"Why don't you turn in, Hamish?"

"I've been going over the history, mine and Cal's, much as I can remember, at least. God knows, I've tried to be good to him, tried to give him best advice. I always thought he needed his elder brother to give him direction, don't you know. He never resisted or objected, always seemed grateful. I gave him everything our father would have, had he lived long enough. I wonder if he's gone off in the head."

"It could help you, Hamish, if you removed your thoughts from yourself and instead looked into Callum's heart, not just defend yourself. Give him time and distance, as he's asking. Give him credit for knowing what he's about and estimating the chore he's undertaken."

Cashdown changed into his nightshirt and got under the covers. But he remained awake for another hour before turning down the lamp. In the morning he was up before anybody else, seeing to the barn chores and the animals. When he came in for breakfast, he said to Libbie, "You are an angel and a sibyl, m'love. You're absolutely spot-on, and I'll just trust Cal to come to his senses in his own time." Libbie raised an eyebrow at him and said nothing.

Later that morning Cashdown said he was riding to Colfax to have lunch with Sam McCroskey and OP. Libbie said she would go with him.

"Why'd you need to travel to town?" he asked.

"I'm going to talk with Orestes about the suffrage bill. And I want to visit with Lucinda. Get out the gig, and we'll go together."

He hunched his shoulders and did as she said. The drive to town was uplifting, despite the brisk wind and the threat of snow rising on the southwest horizon. They drove the little cart almost directly into the late winter sun. Creases of dark soil appeared like ripples on snowfields across the loess hills, and the air was moist and smelled of the coming spring. Early blackbirds chirred on open ponds, and wedges of Canada geese rustled overhead.

In Colfax, Cashdown went to meet Sam and OP at the hotel.

Libbie walked up the hill to the Banks's cottage.

"It's about time for the new legislature to start work, isn't it?" Libbie sat erect on the parlor divan. Opposite her Orestes stretched out his long legs as he sprawled in an oversized horsehide armchair. Lucinda brought in tea and sandwiches.

Orestes grinned broadly. "Chester Warner has been seated, the House is in order, and the first order of business, I'm told, is our suffrage bill."

"Oh, wouldn't that be a miracle. How's chances for passage?"

"My intuition says it'll go through this time, and, at long last, women will have the vote in '84."

"Is there anything else we should do here?"

"Naught but pray the court isn't offended."

Lucinda was skeptical. "If it passes, and we women vote in the next elections, there are two ways, as I see it, that men in power will be offended. It will open the door for everyone to vote, Chinese and natives included. And it will properly threaten the liquor game."

Orestes pursed his lips. "I suspect the latter." He turned to Libbie to explain. "When I arrived in Olympia I was immediately offered a stake in the skimming arrangement. All indirectly stated, naturally, like an invitation to join an ancient cabal. I soon learned that half my fellow legislators and most office appointees were in on the scheme, and it was a very profitable brotherhood. That's why suffrage has been so difficult. My refusal was one of the causes of my being named a dissenter."

"Couldn't you run again—you'd be sure to get elected—so you could clean up that wickedness?" Libbie looked pleadingly at him.

"It's a fight I choose not to undertake, Libbie. It's pervasive; the setup includes the courts, all the way to the top. Let a lifetime politician well schooled in prosecuting corruption do the work. I have other schooling in mind."

Libbie looked quizzically at him and then at Lucinda.

"I'm thinking of becoming a teacher," he said.

Lucinda feigned a frown. "Now Libbie has the burden of keeping a secret. Shame on you, Orestes!" She went on, nonetheless. "He has received an offer of a professorship at the college in Walla Walla come next year. Dr. Anderson is leaving the University of Seattle, now that Whitman College has been granted its four-year curriculum, and he's going to become president of Whitman, and he wants Orestes to teach the law and politics."

"Oh, my heavens! You're not going away again, are you?"

"No, no. I can make weekly trips back and forth by rail, once the trains start coming to Colfax. I'd have to change twice, but we will find it to be tolerable. I want to teach, and if I have time enough, I might also keep my law practice here."

"When will you know for sure?"

"We know, but the contracts aren't finished yet."

"You can't expect me to keep it from Hamish. But he well knows how to keep a friendly secret."

Meanwhile, at the hotel dining room, Cashdown had joined OP and Sam at a corner table where Lycurgus had already seated himself. There were hearty handshakes all around.

"I was joyous to hear you were coming back to town, Sam," Cashdown said. "It's been months since we've seen your happy face and heard news of your family and the goings-on in Farmington."

"Always a pleasure to be with old friends. The family and I have no complaints or calamities. And Farmington's growing fast, maybe too fast. I now have over forty children at the school." He turned to Overman. "OP, the bank there is stretched to its limits. Have you given any thought to expanding up our way?"

"I have my hands full by adding Waitsburg and Dayton. I should say, have my hands tied. If I added another branch, we'd be required to join a central bank consortium, probably Boston or New York." He paused, eyebrows raised. "Troubles at your bank?"

Sam looked around the room and leaned toward the others. "Someone's been trying to buy the Farmington National, but we can't find out the particulars behind the offers. We know thieves are buying up little banks just to hide their money, so we can't afford to lose our local control, because all the crop lending comes from us."

OP confirmed the threat as a real and legitimate concern for the citizens of Farmington. He mused that arrangements probably could be made to share some underwriting and possibly provide help with credit lines as a limited partner. He would send Liam to Farmington for some consultations.

"That would be helpful. You might tell Liam to say I mentioned the town's growing population as a reason for his trip." Then, brightening: "Well, I didn't come to Colfax looking for help for the bank. I mainly wanted to see my good friends and do a little school business."

Cashdown stroked his beard and said, "Always savor a bit of gossip, Sam. So, what's that school business you're up to today?"

"I hope it's out by now, but, anyway, Ursula Hartjes will soon be assistant to the territorial superintendent. She'll oversee all the teacher standards and district accreditations. So, she's moving on to Walla Walla. We're going to start discussions on the future of the Colfax Academy."

Lycurgus cleared his throat. "I've been sitting on the story, at Ursula's request. More like her commandment. But now it seems that the story's out in the open. She and Mrs. Wheeler and the child will move to Walla Walla come June, and we're going to need a new headmaster or mistress. Any chance you'd be considering a return? It'd be hand-in-glove."

"No, no. I'm happy in Farmington and have lots yet to do there. We expect the railroad will come in by '85 at the latest, and it'll bring more growth and more prosperity. The way things outside the Palouse country are now, we feel very lucky. Besides, nobody's offered me the job here."

"Give us time, Sam, give us a little time," Cashdown said, flashing his sly grin around the table. "We only heard about it just now."

Within a week Lycurgus convinced Ursula Hartjes to allow news of her forthcoming move and new job to appear in the *Gazette*. Pinky complained to Cashdown. "What will I do now? Lettice is number two at Ponderosa House, knows everything, works like crazy! Now she goes off to Miss Hartjes, and I have no number three to make two! What can I do now?"

Cashdown had driven his farm wagon to Colfax for spring supplies. As was his habit, he'd stopped for a refreshment at the Ponderosa dining room. "Aye, Pinky, that's always the problem, isn't it, getting the right help for business. But you've got the Northrup chap, young Silas. He's smart and hard working, yeh?"

"Knows kitchen and dining room okay, very good, runs things fine, good to workers. But he is still young, knows nothing about business."

"Must be at least twenty now, not much younger than my twins. Any chance you could teach him the business?"

"Too busy. I want to change dining room, make it all restaurant, much bigger, fancy, top Chinese food, good American food. No time to train Silas in business!"

"If *I* didn't have enough time, I'd get *him* to turn the dining room into a posh eatery. Bet he could do that, maybe with a little help."

Pinky's eyes shifted side to side, and Cashdown knew she

took to the idea.

On the drive home, Libbie told Cashdown about Orestes becoming a teacher at Whitman College. She swore him to secrecy.

"How wonderfully things change here, and keep changing," he said. "Pinky's expanding at the hotel, adding a fancy restaurant, and I think that Northrup boy is going to be her majordomo. OP will be sending our Liam up to Farmington to sort out the bank there, help them stay independent. The twins have eyes on another section near Colton, and they're doing swell. Liam's married to a fine woman. Couldn't be happier Cushing's me in-law brother. Jack is learning the printing trade. Just think, Libbie, soon and at last, there will be another generation coming on. It's all a lovely turn of the wheel, ain't it?"

"Maybe this is a good time to tell you, Hamish, speaking of the turning wheel. That Northrup boy, Silas, wishes to call on Charlie. She's receptive, and he asks your permission."

Cashdown thought for a moment. "He's a good young man, though his family cast him out. Seems to have strong character, despite our first encounter. Good worker, Pinky says. But Charlotte's still a child. I don't know."

"Charlotte is eighteen, Hamish. Remember, I was married and already had Liam by that age."

"Where'd they meet, Charlie and Silas?"

"Church. He finished school over in Idaho."

After another pause, he said, "Why don't we have him out to dinner after church? He's to ask me himself."

Silas did ask, and Cashdown said he'd be pleased. A few weeks passed before it could be arranged, but one Sunday in late March Silas rode out to Steptoe Station on his young appaloosa. Charlie wore her commencement dress, originally Holly's commencement dress, and for modesty a lace shawl. Holly and Laura worked on Charlie's unruly red hair for an hour before consigning the curls to bows. Willie and Jack were warned to avoid teasing and sarcasm. Libbie said any pranks or off-color comments would be cause for their father to get involved.

Silas carried with him more than just good intentions to court a pretty girl. He had a message from Orestes and Lycurgus for Charlie's parents.

Cashdown greeted Silas at the front door, shook his hand vigorously, and welcomed him into the house. Although Silas had visited Steptoe Station with Pinky over the past year, Cashdown insisted on giving him a tour of the inn and its outbuildings. When they were back in the house and seated at the dining table, and after Charlotte and Silas had said their awkward hellos with the Musgrave family smilingly gathered around them, Cashdown asked Silas what he knew of Pinky's restaurant plans.

"Well, sir, she says I'm to dream up the highest-class place between Chicago and Astoria. And together we're going to assemble a right proper kitchen for both the American food and the Chinese. She's sending me to Walla Walla to gain an observation of what they have there."

"Can you cook Chinese?" Holly asked.

"Pinky said she knows a first-rate Chinese man who will render us assistance, and I can do the American, and we can oversee the kitchen together until I learn all about the Chinese cooking."

"And you'd be running the restaurant, then?" Cashdown asked.

"I hope to do so, sir. Oh, and I have news from Mr. Ames and Mr. Banks. They wanted me to inform you they received a telegram yesterday from Olympia. It said the bill on suffrage was signed into law, and as of yesterday women have the vote in Washington Territory."

"Oh! Oh, thank God in heaven!" cried Libbie.

"Splendid news! You are the blessed spawn of Mercury, me

lad," said Cashdown. "Bring that ale here. Let's all have a toast to the wisdom and long labors of our women and to all who have just made our politics fairer!"

They drank a toast and then another, and they enjoyed an exultant meal. They chatted about the coming crop season and predicted changes in Colfax and joked about prospects for Charlotte and Silas; they laughed at Willie's teasing and Jack's sarcastic remarks, and Libbie took no notice, for she was distracted and overjoyed by the news Silas had brought.

Chapter 21

The chartreuse haze of green-up blanketed muddy hills once again, the high creeks and rivers receded into their channels, boggy roads began to dry, and flocks of spring birds returned to their nesting sites. Silas came courting Charlie again and again, and sometimes he was welcomed to stay on for the late festivities. He invited her to socials in Colfax and the Fourth of July fair. By the end of the growing season, they were engaged to be married.

Liam, who had married Tessie McBride and was nearing thirty, immediately gave his approval to the marriage. When he appeared at Steptoe Station one sultry Friday afternoon in August, his parents thought it was a surprise social visit to congratulate Charlie. But as he rushed in the front door he was scowling.

"What's the trouble, lad?" Cashdown said.

"It's a damnable calamity, Pa. There was a robbery, and Mr. Powell was shot."

He described the event to his family. A man in a black duster and a bandanna over his face forced his way into the bank at closing time the previous day. He threatened all the employees with a revolver, locked the door, and after emptying the cash drawers ordered Liam to open the safe. Before Liam could comply, there was a scuffle outside, as Sheriff Carscallen pounced on the robber's lookout. In the confusion, one of the tellers tried to make an escape, and the robber turned and fired his revolver in her direction. OP leaped to shield the teller, and a second shot hit him beneath his left shoulder.

"They took him to Doctor Totter's office," Liam concluded, "but he was hit sure and bleeding fair bad. Doc doesn't know if he's going to make it."

"Ah, tragic. What a misfortune," said Cashdown. "What about the rest?"

"Our teller, Sarah, the one who ran, was unhurt. Just scared. Melissa, the other, fainted or pretended to faint, and she was unharmed, too. Arvind and Billy jailed the man they caught outside, but the robber made it out the back, and now there's a posse after him. Didn't take much, just a few small bills I put in the bag from the cashbox."

"Are you all right, Liam?" Libbie asked.

"I'm fine, Ma. Ashamed, that's all. And mad. But I fear for Mr. Powell's life."

"Such a calamity," Cashdown said. "If there were a God in heaven it wouldn't have happened. And thank our lucky stars you weren't hurt. But when a man has something of great value, Liam, he's vulnerable to terrible dangers. Ah, what a time we live in, boy, desperadoes with revolvers hanging off their belts still roving through towns, robbing banks and shooting each other in saloons if they disagree about who gets the next dance. A civilized place would see to it all guns are kept out of town or under lock and key and released only in case of insurrection. But even Orestes didn't see fit to go so far."

"Pa, I see yours hanging right there by the front door. You take it with you when you go to town, don't you?"

"Only because of the savage time we live in. Damn the war anyhow. If it wasn't for all the guns left over, people would have to settle things by reason and the King's English."

"People will always fight, Pa. There'll always be something they value greatly that someone else has control over, and they'll always be willing to risk greatly to get it, as you just said. If they can't get it by a revolver, it'll be by a knife, a club, fists. Any weapon."

"You're right, Liam, but the gun encourages the fight and lowers the odds, so to speak. Otherwise, things being closer to even, civility is encouraged. We're beasts, for certain, but we aren't without our calculating wits. The evener things are, the less mayhem we'll have."

"Well, Pa, carrying a revolver wouldn't have helped us yesterday, and now we must pray for Mr. Powell's life to be restored."

Liam apologized to Charlotte for his intrusion and congratulated her on her engagement. He assured her Silas was a properly ambitious young man with a growing reputation in Colfax. She said she'd been confident of that, as all of Papa's friends had investigated his character and reported favorably to her. Liam stayed for supper and rode back to Colfax under the first of two harvest moons that year.

When Liam arrived at home, Tessie told him to hurry to Doctor Totter's surgery. They were looking for him.

"He didn't make it," the elderly physician said. Clarence Totter had been looking for a successor ever since suffering a stroke a year earlier, leaving him with a crabwise gait and a right hand that dangled like a dead pheasant. "I couldn't bring him through," he said apologetically.

Liam placed his hand on Doctor Totter's shoulder. "It's a sorrowful loss. Has anyone told the family?"

"I sent the wife, and she's still there."

"I'd better go over," Liam said.

At OP's home above Main Street on the south hill, Liam and Mrs. Totter tried to comfort Florence Powell. In the hushed, dimly lit parlor, he offered to shutter the bank for a period of mourning, but the widow insisted that OP would have wished it to stay open, in service to the people and communities he had loved and supported. She asked if he would bring James and Jenny Perkins to visit, as soon as it would be convenient for them; he promised he would see them before returning home. As he and Mrs. Totter readied to leave, Florence asked him if Orestes might read OP's will and other personal papers—she was sure they were in order, but there was much she didn't understand because it was in legal language, and a lot of it was about the banking business. Probate would have to be started, notices needed to be published in the newspaper, bank regulators had to be told, once succession was arranged. She ticked off a list of tasks as if she had long been expecting this tragedy and had rehearsed the aftermath many times. Liam later said he could not decide if she was showing strength of character and a brave acceptance of events or was avoiding her grief by closeting a sense of loss to be opened later and mourned in private.

OP's bank branches in Colfax and Waitsburg and Dayton kept their normal hours, and over the next two weeks many people came to offer their condolences. Orestes examined OP's papers and sent a note to Liam, asking him to meet to discuss what should be done. When Liam arrived at the cozy law office above the newspaper, Orestes was standing at the window overlooking the bustling Main Street. He crouched as he gazed out in both directions.

"Strange how business goes on almost without regard to a great loss. Goes on and on, and with each loss something beneath notice is changed forever, the world is just a bit different but looks much the same." He turned toward Liam. "Liam Musgrave, you have been designated. It's your turn to take the reins and maybe to change the world just a bit, maybe as Overman Powell would've done. Or maybe in some ways he wouldn't have predicted. But you've been named."

"How's that? Named for what, Orestes?"

"Both the will and OP's plan for succession at his financial institutions authorize you as the next president and chairman of the bank. Two caveats were set: the stipulations are that, first, you voluntarily accept the mantle, and, second, you maintain in perpetuity the statements of purpose and guiding principles of the business. He had seen to the support of his family from his personal holdings, so the bank has no other fiduciary responsibility or recompense owing to them. Nonetheless, an offer of some limited shares might be considerate, in view of Florence's steadying influence on the bank since their marriage."

"Well, that's a mixed blessing, isn't it? I don't know what to say, Orestes."

"Give it your thought, Liam. As to the first caveat, remember to consider your own safety and your family's needs. As to the second, remember to think about how it both constrains you and facilitates your possible future as a banker. Let me know in due course. I'd like to complete both the personal and business probate within the month, if that's possible for you."

Liam told the news to his father over lunch at the Ponderosa Hotel. Cashdown said he was pleased and proud to learn that OP had such high regard for his son. He told Liam to take firm charge of running the bank and its two southerly branches.

"Think of the possibilities, boy," he said. "When the railroad comes in—and that'll be soon, for certain—this town and the prairie will truly thrive, newcomers will be pouring in, new houses and businesses to be constructed, new farms started, and all will need financing. You've got to grab the brass ring when it comes around, or you might never get another chance. There will be competitors."

Liam said that's what Tessie had urged, too, but he wanted to consider any other alternatives before deciding, not particularly alternatives for his future but for the best interests of the bank and the customers. There was the proviso about purposes and principles, and they placed the communities' welfare first, he said. It was a poor time to be a banker in the West, and he didn't want to preside over the bank's demise. By the following day he had decided, and a week after their first meeting, he and Orestes gathered with the directors for the installation of the bank's new chairman and head of all operations.

Cashdown planned an event at Steptoe Station to honor OP's life and commemorate his death, and to celebrate Liam's rapid ascent to the bank presidency. Before invitations could be sent out, however, a second unexpected event of the season intervened.

Returning on Peppermint from his orchard one afternoon, Cashdown noticed something odd at the barns. As he neared the high gate, he could see a brownish-grey plume of cloud roiling and rising above the back barn, where a new neighbor named Ridley, also a livestock breeder, had stored his fresh hay. Cashdown had offered a vacant bay for temporary storage, until the farmer could finish building a proper hay barn. Cashdown had always insisted that smoke and barn should never be seen together, and now he knew something was terribly wrong.

He dismounted and ran to open the big sliding doors. When he grabbed the iron handles, his leather riding gloves hissed and began to smoke. He ran to the house, a hundred yards north, waving his scorched hands and shouting, "Fire! Fire!"

Libbie, four of the hired staff, and five of the children rushed out to meet him, and they dashed to grab pails at the garden shed. Ferdy manned the pump; the rest formed a bucket line to the back barn. Filling and hauling as fast as they could, they swung water down the line to Cashdown, who threw it on the flames now flaring around and below the big doors. The noise from the fire inside rose from a crackling buzz to a thunderous rumble. Within minutes it became a deafening roar. More flames pushed through the doors and the tops of the sidewalls, and soon the roof caught fire. The ground under his feet started to smolder. Cashdown desperately hurled water upward but couldn't get it high enough to meet the growing sheet of fire. His hands burned inside his gloves, and his beard and hat brim were singed.

With a great creak and groan, the east wall tilted and collapsed outward, narrowly missing Cashdown as he leaped out of the way. The flaming roof and rafters collapsed into the bay. He stood facing a massive inferno, the interior of the back barn and on into the main barn now an impenetrable curtain of fire. The sound was furious, a monstrous beast bellowing as it devoured the massive structure and all its contents: carts, wagons, and carriages; harvest machines, grains, straw, hay and silage; tack, tools, and nearly a decade of accumulated supplies for the inn, farm, and orchards.

The fire raged on for hours until nothing was left but a charred hill of smoky, sparking wreckage glowing in the dusk. Blackened shards like shattered bones—posts, beams, rafters, and sills—angled out of the heap of flickering ashes. A black mound of burnt hay filled the chasm. Cashdown stood and watched the destruction for another hour. As he walked around the darkening perimeter, inspecting and poking with a rake into the still smoldering remains, he muttered to himself: "So this is how it's going to be. This is to be me fate, nothing but a stinking heap of ruined dreams. What a folly."

He stood aside and watched long into the evening before returning to the house.

"It's just good luck that the wind was light and came in from the north," Libbie said with a sad look. She turned a weak smile to him.

"Good luck would've been not to have a goddamned fire in the first place," Cashdown grumbled.

"What happened?" she said.

"Ridley's hay. Should've known and not let him store it. He cut too soon. I told him so. But I don't want to be un-neighborly, do I. Ah well, I told him I'd take no liability, and he said of course not. But the rest is my doing. Can't ask him for the barns and all our gear and grains."

"We'll rebuild, won't we, Hamish?"

He stood by the stove, rubbing a salve of yarrow and tallow into his burned hands, and looked up pleadingly at her. "What am I doing wrong, Lib? Why does something like this happen? Why did OP have to get killed? Why doesn't me own closest brother want me now?"

"It's that wheel turning, Hamish. We can't control everything, and there's much we can't predict. You had no part in OP's passing. In time Cal will come around. The wheel will turn again and move everything forward."

"It's been turning in the wrong direction lately, Lib."

"It can't be all happy news forever. It's the way of Nature. Everything has a beginning, and everything has an ending, every creature and every plant and tree, every year. Just like in the Bible. Even the mountains, they say, rise and fall away. Life is just that way, good news and bad news."

"Makes no sense to me. Especially when an ending's untimely. Sure and everything has a natural lifespan, and when it ends properly you're not surprised or angry. Saddened, maybe, but not cheated. Why should we need bad news at all?"

"We wouldn't be human without it, and we'd have no need for courage and no use for hope."

"Hope! Hope is for people who doubt their own power to make things happen." Cashdown went on rubbing salve into his hands and said no more. Libbie would later tell Liam his pa had been imagining the new construction and the way he'd tell the story of the fire so that his reputation and Mr. Ridley's dignity might be preserved.

The barns were rebuilt before the first snowfall in November, thanks to help from the twins and dozens of friends and neighbors. Mr. Ridley and his sons left off work on their own hay barn to help Cashdown. Every chance he had, Cashdown spoke of the need for fire brigades around Whitman County's outlying settlements. He argued before the county commissioners that a levy was needed to fund them. When his barns were finished, he restocked them from auctions on failing Palouse farms, of which there were many that year. The harvest had been a disappointment, enough to bankrupt some growers.

The trains nonetheless began arriving at Colfax on December first. A festive celebration greeted the inaugural passengers, all civic and railroad bigwigs, from Wallula and points south and west. The huge, glistening black engine was draped with red, white, and blue bunting across the cab and cowcatcher, and flags flew from windows of the two shiny coaches. Bands played, local leaders gave speeches, and Lycurgus and his photographer were busy creating their history of the great moment. Expectation of prosperity and expansion surged across the Palouse region.

The stagecoaches continued to stop at Steptoe Station through the mild winter, and the inn and mercantile did a brisk business. Cashdown happily held court whenever guests were lodging. He played his hornpipe or fiddle, kept a stream of ale and cider flowing, served oysters at midnight, and told stories about building freestone walls and wells in the old country, until he tired out the last lodger. When no stagecoaches came, he would grow gloomy in the quiet evenings and turn in early. The Northern Pacific's arrival at Colfax nonetheless cheered him, and he planned for future additions at the inn, possibly making it into a way-station hotel, against the time the track would be laid past his main gate.

CHAPTER 22

The runoff came early and gradually. By Saint Patrick's Day the Palouse River was flowing ice free within its banks, tricolored and yellow-headed blackbirds were chirring on pond reeds, and crimson buds of bearberry colonies were poking through receding snowfields.

The Friday following Colfax's Saint Patrick celebrations, the twenty-first of March, the *Gazette* published a feature story about Orestes. The headline said *Former Sheriff, Congressman Returns to School.* The article described how Representative Orestes Alton Banks "has swapped the legislative chamber for a classroom and his badge for a stick of chalk" and would travel each week to Walla Walla to pursue his new calling as college professor of history, politics, and the law. The newspaper assured readers they could continue to rely on the hometown hero for wisdom, influence in Olympia, and strong leadership in Whitman County: "Mr. Banks will remain among his fellow denizens of Colfax as a model of civic dedication, moral respectability, and honorable manhood for all to emulate," it concluded.

Lycurgus could hear the familiar, uneven thump of the lawyer's boots descending the stairs. "You let the nag out of the barn early, amigo," Orestes boomed as he stooped through the doorway.

"News is news, and rumors were starting to fly around. I thought it was high time to correct the record."

"I see. You do have a way of protecting the community from

its own excesses, Lycurgus."

"Just doing my journalistic duty," he said.

"I've heard intimations recently about your journalistic vocation," Orestes said. "Maybe you'll correct the record on the increasingly widespread canard that you're headed to Spokane."

"Can we hold that nag in the barn for a short while yet? Nothing's finalized."

Orestes smiled and turned to leave. "Sure thing, amigo."

Before Cashdown and his neighbors had finished their spring planting, Orestes started his twice weekly commute by rail to Walla Walla. New Whitman Seminary president Alexander Anderson needed his help to restructure the college. Together, he'd told Orestes, they would turn it into the premier institution for educating the finest students of the Northwest territories. But he would need Orestes full time.

Often at breakfast that spring Cashdown would tell Libbie of his dream the previous night about the trains. Always they would come chuffing up the track to Steptoe Station, all steam and smoke and shiny brass trimming. Hordes of gaily dressed passengers would debark at the inn and cheerfully pour into the great room for festivities. He said it gave him a happy feeling to awake and reflect on the dream. As soon as he had time, he vowed, he would see where the road gang was and figure out when he would need to start expanding Steptoe Station.

With the onset of the hot, dry season, Cashdown rode out in search of progress on the new rail line. At thirty-three years, Peppermint was no longer fit for long rides on the rough plain, so Cashdown took Buster, a young quarter horse gelding who would benefit from the work and added training. He rode west all morning looking for a work crew. He asked for information from the two groups he met on the way—drivers of a supply wagon headed to Rosalia and, an hour later, Mr. Ridley and his sons, who again were planting late. None of them had seen or heard about railroad men at work on the Palouse prairie. The eldest Ridley boy said he thought the rail line might not come through this year. Someone said it might be delayed because of squabbles over the right-of-way. Cashdown thanked them and rode on.

He looped south around Endicott, reasoning that progress might have been slower than he'd expected so the crews would still be coming up from the Colfax line. But crossing west to east just half a dozen miles above Colfax he encountered no signs of railroad activity. He saw immense vistas of bright-green bunchgrass edged by dark ponderosa stands and copses of poplars and cottonwoods in ravines; he saw lakes of blue camas flowers and higher up on hillsides the last of the buttery balsamroot blossoms, all vibrating on the breezes; he saw basalt outcroppings like iron ships' prows cutting through the mint-green sea of new wheat. But he saw no wagons and cranes, no roadbed being laid, no ties being cut or milled or set.

Still, it was a pleasant ride, and Cashdown relaxed in the saddle. From time to time he would pause for lessons to improve Buster's trail manners or smooth his gaits and to give the colt a rest. He would be seventy on his next birthday, and lately he'd begun to detect reminders that his years of easily traveling all day on horseback eventually would come to an end. Thus, he took special pleasure in the rhythm of his rangy gelding's stride and the sweet air they breathed and the sounds and landscape as they traveled, and he found the rest stops refreshing.

He paused for his lunch by a creek near Pullman. He was aware that the new Columbia and Palouse Railroad Company was building a line from Colfax to Pullman, which would be extended to Moscow, across the Idaho border. But that was to the southeast, and he was looking for a line north and east of Colfax, as Cleary and Anders had promised. After eating and refilling his canteen, he and Buster turned north toward Palouse City.

He was a few miles outside Palouse City when he topped a bald rise and spotted four men working near a buckboard and team in the broad plain ahead. They were doing something with sticks and flags and worked a small telescope on a tripod. One held a tall, paint-striped rod. Cashdown rode up and said good-day. The man steadying the rod tipped his hat and asked if they could help him.

"Looking for the railroad crew," Cashdown said.

"Found us," the man said with a gap-toothed grin. He spat tobacco juice beyond his boots.

"Looks like you're surveying something."

"Yup."

"Something for the NP?"

"Sort of."

"What might that be?"

"Marking up the road to Farmington. Long way to go," he added with a head shake.

"Aren't you supposed to be over near to Steptoe?"

"Nope. Palouse City to Farmington. All we've been told." He spat again. "For the C and PR."

Cashdown thanked the man and rode back to Steptoe Station.

His mood had changed from happy anticipation to angry disappointment, and the longer he thought about it, the more he imagined getting his hands around Anders's bony neck. Libbie cautioned him to first get the story directly from the agents, "before you go flying off the handle. And don't do anything rash," she added.

He fumed through supper and was only mildly distracted by the stagecoach guests who lodged at Steptoe Station that night. The usual revelry took place, but Cashdown seemed partly absent: he watched the dancers from his big chair by the wood stove, and there was no grand speech at oyster serving time and no late storytelling over cognac or port. An hour after midnight he was sitting up in bed, still mulling what the surveyor had told him.

The following day he rode Peppermint to Colfax. He told Libbie it would be good for his mule if he gave her moderate exercise from time to time. She replied that it would do him some good to take Peppermint, they were such old friends. "Not that Buster or any of the other horses is undeserving," she added, "but you always seem happiest when you've been off adventuring on that mule."

He was eager to get to town so he could summon Anders and Cleary. But he rode at a gentle pace and tried to calm himself by watching the distant klatches of pregnant does and the smaller animals he spotted along the trail—crouching rabbits and skittering pods of quail and tableaux of stalking coyotes. At Colfax he asked to speak with the NP agents. The clerk said they were "in conference" and wouldn't be available until late in the day. Cashdown told him he would wait. He doffed his stovepipe hat, took out a bit of lunch, and sat on a bench near the door.

Two hours later Cliven Cleary came out of the NP office on his way to the toilet. Cashdown stepped in his path and pressed his fingers into Cleary's chest. "I want to talk with you and Mr. Anders."

"A minute, just a minute," Cleary said and hurried toward the privies. Anders peeked out the door, and Cashdown spun around and marched into his office.

"Aha, Mr. Musgrave. How . . . how nice to see you again," Anders uttered.

"I doubt it. Yesterday I came across your surveying crew, over near Palouse City. They tell me there's no plan for a line out to

Steptoe. I'm here to learn what you have to say about that."

Anders tugged on his waistcoat and smiled. "Actually, Mr. Musgrave, we have nothing to say about that." His eyelids began to flutter. "It's all out of our hands. We have no connection to the rest of the Whitman County lines, existing or a-building."

"There's a line going up to Palouse City and on to Farmington. They're surveying it right now. I talked to them."

Anders lifted his chin, exaggerating the prominence of his Adam's apple. "Mr. Musgrave, those aren't our people. It's all being done by the Columbia and Palouse Railroad Company. We sold out to them. You'll have to speak to the C and PR agent, I'm afraid."

"Did you sell them your expansion plans?"

"They appear to be planning their own routes. For their own reasons."

Cliven Cleary was now hovering outside the door, listening to the discussion. Cashdown shouted, "Come in here, Mr. Cleary. You passed out assurances, too."

Cleary edged into the office and moved behind Anders's desk.

"Now, where can I find these Columbia and Palouse people? And give me a name," Cashdown demanded.

The two agents glanced at each other. Anders shrugged and said, "Ask for Twombly. Upstairs at the depot. There's an office. The plaque says 'Administration.' "

"Cashdown!" he heard when he crossed Main Street on his way to the train depot. James Perkins was grinning broadly as he jogged to catch up with him. "I have wonderful news. We're going to have a telephone in Colfax!" James had been elected to his second term as mayor, and he was promoting every new device and service he could acquire as modern advances for the town and county.

"A telephone, James? And what'll we do with it, now?"

"We can talk to somebody who's in Walla Walla, or even as far away as Olympia. We won't have to wait for the post. And we can talk and hear, not just write like with the telegraph, but talking, asking questions, explaining things. It's like magic."

"I s'pose." They were strolling arm in arm on the board sidewalk. "What would we talk about?"

"Business, all kinds. Sheriff might find it handy. It could help to run the government. We could even get news quicker. Anything we'd put in letters. There's always plenty to talk about. But it's the wave of the future, and I'll be damned if Colfax will be left behind."

"Aye, that's splendid, James. Now I have some talking to do with an agent at the depot. Seems the new line might not be going past Steptoe after all, but over to Pullman and up to Farmington. I've got to sort it out."

"Take it slow, my friend. I doubt anything's settled just yet." He slapped Cashdown on the shoulder and headed off to his office.

At the depot, Cashdown looked for a door marked "Administration." All the doors above the waiting and ticketing salon were unmarked but one. The plaque said "Private." He knocked loudly, and a man's high, creaky voice shouted, "Enter!" Cashdown let himself into a shambles, more storeroom than office. From behind a wall of boxes and file cabinets, stacks of chairs, desks laid on top of desks, and piles of scrolled maps, the scratchy voice said, "Yes?"

"Looking for a Mr. Twombly."

"Tromberly, Charles Tromberly, that's right. I am he, at your service." A tiny man with an enormous head came out from behind the piles of furniture and papers. He scrabbled forward on stunted, bowed legs, and though not fat, his body looked compressed in all directions. His torso was the same elliptical shape as his head. He offered up his hand, the incongruously thick, symmetrical mitt of a strong workingman.

"How d'you do?" he chirped.

Cashdown shook hands. "I'm Hamish Musgrave, and I own the Steptoe Station Inn, up by St. John."

"Yes, Mr. Musgrave?" Tromberly's voice was pinched and metallic, a laughing-gas sound.

"Over the past two years I've been given assurances by Mr. Cleary and Mr. Anders of the Northern Pacific that once rail service reached Colfax, a new line would go northward to Cheney or Spokane Falls."

"Yes, Mr. Musgrave?"

"Well, the new line was to include a stop near Steptoe Station."

"I see."

"And now I'm told it's your outfit that has the franchise on the Palouse Prairie. I'm told there's no plan for a line to Steptoe. And the other day I came across your surveyors laying out a line over to Pullman and up to Farmington."

"Yes, Mr. Musgrave?"

"Is all this true? And is there any plan for a line to my inn?"

"Yes, Mr. Musgrave."

"There is?"

"Oh. Yes and no. Yes, it's all true. Colfax one day will be connected to Cheney. And Spokane. No, no plan yet for a westerly line near St. John and Steptoe."

"Sure and why not? Great profits await you in my area. Not just passenger revenues, which will be abundant, but from our farm products and cattle and wheat production."

"Yes, Mr. Musgrave. But they've decided against it for now."

"What advantage does it give you to build to the east? You'd lose money."

"Oh, Palouse City has the brickworks, Mr. Musgrave, and they're floating logs down the river, you know. They also have cattle and cash crops and wheat, Mr. Musgrave. And abundant passengers."

"Who do I have to talk with? Who is making the decisions on routes?"

"You can write, Mr. Musgrave, to our owner, Oregon Railway and Navigation. But I shan't be encouraging."

The railway man watched impassively as Cashdown pulled on his stovepipe hat and abruptly left. Charles Tromberly waggled his massive head and went back to his desk behind the wall of debris.

"The line's not coming this way, Lib. Was given the double-shuffle from Cleary and Anders, and a dwarfish gent who speaks for the new railroad outfit says it's not in their plans."

Libbie was almost ready to serve dinner. "Calm down and sit, Hamish, and tell me what you're talking about."

He described his day in Colfax and concluded by saying that he might indeed write to the company president. "Couldn't hurt, could it?"

But first he talked with Orestes, and he learned the implied promises the Northern Pacific agents had made with him in conversations weren't legally binding on them, nor was the letter he had received. Subsequently, the rights-of-way had been sold to Oregon Railway and Navigation, which leased the territory to the Columbia and Palouse Railroad Company. Cashdown could not compel anybody, Orestes said, to construct a rail line anywhere. Cashdown appeared stunned, and Orestes apologized for delivering his opinion so abruptly.

"Nae, but I had to hear it from somebody who knows what they're talking about and who I can trust to be square with me. I'm obliged."

"No charge, amigo. Just remain mindful and happy that you can welcome your stage passengers for some time to come. So long as there's no direct rail service to Spokane or Cheney, they'll keep running the coaches, and you'll continue to realize the revenue and hold your shindigs, both of which seem to make you happy."

Cashdown nodded and pondered a few seconds. "You know, Orestes, I wanted to expand and grow me inn to be a real hotel with a grand ballroom and lounge. And expand the orchards to sell fruit across the territory, far as the coast maybe. That alone would require rail shipping. Cushing wants to sell his orchards and return to Almota, and I was thinking on buying him out. And there's more land available soon around the butte. I've already made Dolphus Sain an offer. What am I going to do?"

Orestes's face softened, and he smiled. "You'll find a way, amigo. You always do."

"Fancy a glass of port at the hotel?"

They stopped by Lycurgus's office on their way out. He eagerly agreed to go with them for a drink. As soon as their port was served at the round table in the rear of the dining room, James came in and joined them. The four drew straws for the privilege to invite Pinky to sit with them. As usual, she had been keeping watch from the balcony, where she sat at her business desk, an ornate basswood monstrosity she had imported from San Francisco. Her Ithaca coach gun stood in the umbrella stand next to her chair. It had become a ritual of courtesy to ask her to join the group of old friends. Besides, she had access to fresh rumors from outside the Palouse prairie, and she always had useful and entertaining things to say. James drew the short straw.

"My best gentlemen friends look so happy and strong like young boys," she said. "No headaches, Cashdown? You don't need treatments for a long time, so that's good, huh? But you don't look so happy like the rest of my boys. What kind of problems you got, Cashdown?"

"He just received some disappointing news from the railroad people," Orestes said. "We're cheering him up."

" 'Tis true," Cashdown said. "They're not going to build out past Steptoe Station. Leastwise not now."

"Oh, too bad. But travelers tell me new Columbia and Spokane Railroad Company will make a line coming down, Cheney to Colfax, maybe Spokane Falls to Colfax, not soon but could be after some years. Maybe then they come to Steptoe, huh? They goddamn better build it!"

"You tell them to do it, Pinky; they'll listen to you," James said. "We could well use a second line through Colfax, and then Cashdown could have his hotel, too."

Pinky grinned, eyed Lycurgus, and said, "Can I tell it?"

Lycurgus raised his eyebrows and shrugged in resignation.

"Stagecoach to Spokane Falls too hard, too goddamned slow. We need trains so we keep seeing old friends."

The rest of the group looked quizzically at her.

"Someone is going soon to Spokane Falls, and then, by Jesus, Colfax needs a new newspaper!"

All eyes turned to Lycurgus. "Well, half a dream come true," he said with an apologetic shrug. "Sorry, friends, but I just found out they want me, and we signed the contracts today, the city and county and my new employer."

"What new employer?" James exclaimed. "We need you and the *Gazette* here. What would we do without you?"

"You'd have to recruit a publisher, same way Spokane Falls did when their paper went on the rocks. But I've already put out the word, and I assure you, James, there is no end of interested editors and publishers who think Colfax is a promising place to start."

"So, what's the plan, Gus, and if we can't keep you here, how can we help?" Cashdown asked.

"Town fathers in Spokane Falls wanted a newspaper,

Republican-oriented they said, to provide truthful and objective news. All they have now is that redemption weekly. They're funding the *Sentinel* until it's profitable, and we're supposed to start publishing a daily, with guaranteed readership, by the nineteenth of next month. I've already ordered a press from Chicago, but it's behind schedule arriving. This one will go north, too."

"Aye, good for you. I know you've long wanted a daily in a bigger town. But what about all the friends you have here, we original seekers after the grail—what are we to do without your level head and the news you bring us? Aye, and what would we do without your wit and bloviating instruction?"

"The other half of my lifelong dream remains in Colfax. I shall continue to cultivate you ruffians, to bloviate and educate all my spirited companions, right here as often as I can muster the travel. As Pinky said, the train will be a boon, for all of us and in many ways. When we're connected to Spokane I'll be here opinionating again amongst you, more often than you'll wish."

"And when will this happen?"

"Two weeks, even if the press won't come in on time. Your Jack can secure the *Gazette* till a new publisher's found. I'll pay him well. I meant to tell you after the municipal contracts up there were done."

Cashdown turned to Orestes. "Seems all's changing, and too fast for me. That'll be about the time you're off to the Whitman school, yeh?"

"I should be there now, but I told President Anderson I would require some time to set my practice in order. You, my friends, need not worry for my abandonment, either. I'll be here constant enough to compensate for Editor Ames's temporary absence. I promise to continue exhausting you with my sermonizing and my occasional bloviating, with the enthusiasm but perhaps not the eloquence he has."

"Nae," Cashdown countered, "we'll grant you haranguing and all, but you're the least likely to be delivering any sermons."

Chapter 23

The dry season was coming on, and summer labors lay just ahead: the last of the fence mending, then planting in the gardens and wheat fields, a few weeks later the first cutting of hay, and felling and splitting wood for next winter. Calves and foals needed to be separated with their mothers, last year's colts would be gelded, tack and rolling stock wanted repairs. But Cashdown's head ached, and right now he needed a treatment.

The new Ponderosa Territorial Dining Hall was nearly completed. Pinky had bought the failed haberdashery next door, knocked out walls, and joined it to the hotel, thereby nearly doubling the size of the hotel restaurant and kitchen. Oak paneling was being installed, as well as a new bar-back with tall, beveled mirrors enclosed by mahogany columns carved in Chinese and Greek motifs. The bar dominated the wall below Pinky's balcony perch. She watched Cashdown admiring the details of the woodwork and came down to greet him.

"Kitchen still open, Cashdown. Silas in charge now. What will you like?"

"Ah, Pinky, I'm in need of the pins again. The headaches are tormenting me," he said with a grimace.

"Cheese?"

"Nae. I've been good. But the pain's back."

"How long?"

"Weeks. And I've much work to do. Can we sort it?"

"Come follow me." She led him to a quiet room at the back

of the hotel that served as her clinic. "Okay. Take clothes off and lie down belly up." She hummed softly as she administered the treatment, occasionally encouraging Cashdown to be calm and think soothing thoughts. After a while she finished his front side and told him to turn over. The same gentle humming continued, and soon he nodded off.

He awoke as Pinky finished removing the needles. "Take towel off your bum, get dressed now. I come back soon." She returned as he was buttoning his waistcoat. "You worry too goddamned much, Cashdown. Need to be more calmer, then you have smaller wrinkles, no headaches, okay?"

"The head feels better already. But the wrinkles won't be going away, and now I'm getting wrinkles atop me wrinkles. I'm getting old, Pinky. Everything sags just a bit more every week, it seems; everything gravitates to me feet."

"Buddha says everything that rises will fall again. He says when you okay with that, then you got no worries and last longer. Confucius says when he got to seventy he just follows his heart. Very good plan."

"Ah well, Pinky, I'm not the Buddha nor Confucius. Libbie is more like you and the Buddha, says everything changes like a wheel rolling forever. I'm just a romantic fool who can't stop wishing for the wheel to roll and then hating it when it happens."

"Yeah, change. Okay, everything is change. But still best if you follow your heart. We all are like fools sometimes, but we just try to help change a little."

"If only this heart were as pure as yours, dear friend." He put his dollar down on the table, and Pinky reluctantly accepted it. She held his arm as she walked him out the front door of the hotel.

After a few days the headaches were gone, and Cashdown resumed his work with vigor. When stagecoach guests lodged at

Steptoe Inn, he attentively entertained and played the jolly host for them. But he continued to reflect on what Pinky had said. Riding out to his orchards by the peak and gazing at the rolling hills and wildlife and flowers, he said aloud to Peppermint, "Everything will end, old girl. All that has a beginning has an ending, and that includes those syringas and larks and even the creek. Even those mountains, as Libbie said." He paused. "Even you and me."

The day arrived when Peppermint shied away from the halter, and Cashdown knew she no longer could work. Her topline drooped like a slack rein, and her hindquarters were dished. Her once thick, muscular neck had turned stringy and gaunt, and her coat had gone dull. He said, "You should be able to follow your heart, old girl. I'd bet it says now's the time to rest and enjoy what's left of your life."

She followed him to the paddock kept for sick or declining livestock. There was a deep shelter and a long, level turnout with views to the east toward Idaho's mountains, and to the southeast, where Steptoe Butte dominated the horizon like an extinct volcano. He brought in a lame, aged ram for company. He told her now she could look out forever at her favorite place, as if he knew she was as whelmed with love for the peak as he was, though last year he began dismounting before leading her to the top to gaze together across the Palouse prairie.

Now, every day after feeding he would pause and talk to her, even during harvest season, and sometimes he groomed her and rubbed her legs. She seemed to enjoy the attention, nickered in anticipation, but as autumn came on her eyes grew dull and unfocused. Cashdown knew her suffering had begun.

"I think old Peppy isn't going to make it through winter," he told Libbie. "The hard choice awaits me again, and I'm not sure I can do it."

"It's the kindest thing you can do for her, Hamish."

It took him a few days to screw up the courage to go through with it. At dawn one frosty morning in late October, he took down his Spencer repeater and trudged out to Peppermint's shed. He put a lead rope and halter on her and led her out of the paddock, past the main gate, across the road, and over the western hills far beyond view of the house. They walked for an hour, past the hay fields, through fence gates, along the rim of the breaks above the creek and into a swale near the edge of the Musgrave property. He talked to her as they walked, quietly reminiscing about the adventures they'd had together since she was a foal—the lessons he'd taught her as she was growing up in Wisconsin, their long trek out to the Willamette, the migration north to the Palouse, their hunting trips across the territory and over into Idaho country, the roundups of livestock and of Odis Bragg and his gang. He talked to her again about the joys they'd had on countless rides out to the orchards at Steptoe Butte, and she nickered as if in agreement as they walked along.

At a leafy rise in the swale, he ground tied her and walked away. She stood still and looked afar. Two hundred yards off, he lay prone on tufts of bunchgrass and duff, swung his Spencer around, and aimed at the tall mule's shoulder just below the withers. He was a master sharpshooter, but it was not in his heart to aim for a head shot. He squeezed the trigger, and the .56-caliber slug instantaneously struck its target. She did not slowly crumple or roll; she flew off her feet sideways, as if blown over by an explosion.

Cashdown knew she was dead, but he went to check anyway. She looked monstrous, lying on her side with her legs out straight, her ribcage a grey mountain of bone and flesh. There was a gaping hole, and a spreading pool of dark blood oozed from beneath her. He removed the halter and lead rope.

"I'm not a praying man," he murmured. "But I sure wish to

high heaven you could've lived forever. Farewell, old girl." Tearfully, he began the slow walk back to Steptoe Station.

Libbie tried to comfort him by insisting he'd saved the mule from needless misery. He'd given her a good life; he'd made a brave choice on her behalf, she said. But for a time he was inconsolable. He went silently about his chores to prepare for the coming winter, grimly hosted overnight guests, and joylessly drank his ale each night. He avoided Steptoe Butte and the orchards, until one day two weeks later Cushing McBride arrived with a contract to sell his part of them.

"Cushing. How grand to see ya. You know I lost me mule, Peppy?"

"I heard. That's hard, always is. I'm sorry for you. And that's the sorrow of loving our creatures. Just nothing we can do about that."

"I'll get over it," Cashdown said. "Just need to sort out the feelings."

"Here's the papers for the orchards." Cushing looked neither happy nor sad about the transaction. "Shall we sign our names?"

"Aye, we should do that. It's a fair price you've asked, and I'll be sorry not to have your company out there. But I wonder how it's necessary. Are your finances in good fettle?"

"I have obligations to the Nez Perces, you know, duties that're better served if I'm back on the river. But some of the settlers have taken to chasing away the Snake Indians, including our Paluses. I mean to help turn the tide back so the homesteaded bands can grow their fruits like before. Besides, it's a long way up to the butte for me. And you and I, we're not as easy in the saddle as we once were. But, my finances? We're okay. Your Liam has been keeping me solvent through the ups and downs."

"I heard about the evictions, and I admire your reasons. But Liam tells me we're about to be granddads again. Five months. I trust Tessie's well?"

"Says she's just fine. She told me last Sunday they might shortly be going up to Oakesdale, and she'll be in the care of old Doc Kenoyer."

"Oh? I hadn't been told. Going for a short spell, or . . . ?"

"Unclear, Cashdown, but it doesn't sound so. I get the idea they've offered him the bank. You should maybe ask Liam."

They laid out the contracts on the kitchen table, went over the details, and signed their names.

"I'll have Liam transfer the funds," Cashdown said. "And I'll ask him about this Oakesdale business. In the meantime, Cushing, any time you wish to come out and lend a hand at the butte, just for old times' sake, feel free."

"Whyn't we go take a look now?"

They rode out to the orchards, for a final inventory they said, but they passed most of the time pointing out what they loved about the butte and the landscapes and reminiscing about their years of raising fruit trees together. It was late in the day, and the sky began to darken as dusk and a line of storm clouds came in. They were about to collect their horses and return to Steptoe Station when they saw four riders slowly approaching from the peak's northwest flank. As the riders came nearer, Cashdown could see they were Paluses. Soon he recognized the man in the lead as Tomeo. The Indians rode directly to Cushing and Cashdown, halted, and remained mounted, staring stoically down. Their winter gear was tattered, buffalo greatcoats worn at the cuffs and torn at the elbows, their fringed trousers scraped thin and faded. Their dignity remained, but they looked much poorer than before.

"Ah, Tomeo. It's been a long time," Cashdown said. "I'd thought you were off to Yakima or Colville." He offered up his hand in greeting.

"Never, Mr. Cashdown. No reservation can be home for my family." They shook hands.

"What brings you men out here?"

Tomeo responded slowly and deliberately. "You said the railroads would not come for a long time, many years. Now a train goes from Wallula to the whites' town at Kulispel Lake. The railroad took more of our land, took more of the Kulispel tribal land. We wanted a homestead, but they took our land and said they had it first. In Colfax they say you want trains to come to your station."

In the silent tension that followed, Tomeo continued to stare down emotionlessly at the orchardists. A cold wind picked up from the southeast. After gathering his thoughts, Cashdown replied, "It's not right, Tomeo, for the railroad to take your land. I am sorry, but I have no control over them or over the United States government. You will remember we also talked about how everything changes, and sometimes all we can do is find a way to gain from it, because it will happen anyway. We make firewood from the old tree that falls in the wind. That's why I asked for a line out to my inn. It would not cross your land, and it would bring people for my inn when the stagecoaches end. But there is no line from Colfax to Spokane, and now that won't happen, and I'm out of luck."

Tomeo scanned the horizons, returned his stoical gaze to Cashdown, and said, "They have taken our little children. For the white schools and religion. Soon, if we can't homestead, we will disappear."

"You can claim a homestead under the Act, you know," Cushing interjected.

"We have heard about Major MacMurray and Mr. Hunter. But they have not come to help us."

Cashdown chewed his lip. He said, "Maybe we can help bring them to you. We will try."

"Thank you, Mr. Cashdown. That's good."

"Where are you living now?"

"With my family. Back at *Tahklite,* your Rock Lake. But life is no longer good there. Whites have driven away the deer and elk and smaller animals. They plow over the *quamash* and grasses. We have little to eat. We must homestead and become farmers or disappear."

Cashdown and Cushing assured Tomeo they would try to contact George Hunter, a prominent civilian agent and staunch advocate of tribal rights who helped many Indian families to establish homesteads. The four riders turned their horses and headed slowly into the gathering storm.

Cushing lodged at the inn because of the weather, and the two men talked late into the night about how to help Tomeo's clan at Rock Lake.

A few days later Cashdown told Libbie he needed to ride to Colfax again. "Whatever for?" she said. "The weather's turning foul, Hamish, and we still have work to do here. You just want to sit with your friends."

"I need to see Liam. About Tessie and the money to pay Cushing. I want to see if the rumor about them going up to Oakesdale has merit and why they haven't told us, if it is true. But I want to help Tomeo. Again, maybe Orestes can help, and I need to see him before he leaves for the school."

"I will worry myself sick until you're safely back here in this kitchen," she said.

"Go easy on yourself, Elizabeth. Your fretting always is twice what it need be."

But when Cashdown arrived in Colfax, he learned Orestes had already left on the train for Walla Walla. He met at the bank with Liam, who confirmed he and Tessie were moving to Oakesdale.

"I learned about it from your father-in-law . . . would've preferred to hear it first from you, Liam," Cashdown chided.

"Tessie told her dad, and I swore him to secrecy until I've sorted out my successor here. Florence no longer wants to be part of the bank, and I've made an offer to another person, a fine man who can be taught what's needed quickly. Pa, I'm still waiting to settle that part. I'm sorry you were left out."

"Never mind, son. It's understandable. Lately I seem to be fated for omission."

"As you and Ma have often told us, it's never all bad news and never all good news. You've had a string of setbacks lately, Pa, but much continues to be promising at Steptoe Station. You should head back soon, though. There's a blow coming in."

"I have to find how to reach Orestes first. Then home."

At the *Gazette* office Lycurgus said he thought Orestes already was in Walla Walla. Cashdown went in search of James Perkins and found him in front of the town hall. He told James he was frantic to reach Orestes so they might help Tomeo and his people avoid famine or worse. James pondered as they went inside.

"Have you ever spoken on the telephone, Cashdown?" James asked.

"Never even seen one."

"Come to my office, and I'll speak on it for you."

James led Cashdown to a rectangular oak box attached to a matching oak plate that was mounted to the office wall. The wood was stained amber and polished to a high sheen. Protruding from the top of the device was a stubby brass tube capped by a white porcelain funnel shaped like a horn bell. Above it was a brass bell housing. Thick fabric tubes hung from each side, and at the end of each tube a brass fitting held a black funnel, shaped the same but smaller than the white one on top. Beneath the box was a brass keyboard with two rows of white buttons, each button marked with a number from zero to nine. Cashdown approached the machine as if it had descended from heaven. "I'm speechless," he said.

"I would expect that," James quipped. "Most people are, first time they see one."

James cranked a magneto beneath the telephone, tapped the zero key six times, and sat down to wait. Shortly a scratchy voice could be heard emanating from the cloth tubes. James put the black funnel to his ear and spoke in a loud, slow voice into the white microphone.

"This is James Perkins, Mayor of Colfax. I have a citizen who must contact Professor Orestes Banks of the Whitman College president's office. Can you help?"

After a few moments the scratchy voice answered: "Stand by for one half hour. I will bring him to talk with you."

"Thank you," James shouted into the funnel.

When they spoke, Cashdown told Orestes about Tomeo's people and his promise to help bring George Hunter to their aid. Orestes said General Wright had become his friend, and he would ask him to direct Hunter to go to Rock Lake or to contact Cashdown at home. They promised to have dinner together when Orestes next had an opportunity.

"Are you done?" James asked.

"I think so. We stopped talking. Can't tell how you'd know you're done on this thing."

"I was told you just say 'Goodbye,' as if you were taking your leave."

"But I'm right here, and I might not be going anywhere. Mighty peculiar."

On his way to the town stable Cashdown saw that the sky had darkened ominously down to the western horizon, and flakes of snow like shredded batting had begun to drift in on a rising wind.

Chapter 24

He knew he should have taken Liam's advice to wait out the weather. He hadn't worn storm gear to town and was too busy thinking of his troubles to watch the sky for signs. Now he was halfway home on Buster, and both horse and rider already were layered in thick, wet snow that turned them to ghosts. After a while the temperature dropped suddenly, and a dense fog descended. They proceeded north, and the snowfall began to turn dry and hard, and the wind rose to a howl. The storm soon became a blizzard, piling up and swirling into high drifts.

When he failed to find Clear Creek, Cashdown realized he and Buster had lost the trail. It was growing dark, he couldn't see much farther ahead than Buster's ears, and the chill was penetrating his duster and slouch hat.

They dropped into a draw and came to a stand of firs and cedars. He dismounted, pulled out his wire saw from the saddlebag, and began cutting cedar branches. From blowdown sticks he built a tepee frame in an open area. He scraped snow away with his boots, threw some rocks into the center, and with osier shoots lashed the cedar branches up the framework like overlapping fans, leaving a gap at the top. He removed Buster's saddle and placed it inside the makeshift tepee, freeing the horse to paw snow for grasses under the close trees. With dry leaves he started a twig fire inside his shelter.

The blizzard keened in the tall firs and cedars, and snow piled up even in the ravine. Complete darkness shrouded the region. The little brush hut was soon transformed from a green tepee to a white mound, insulated as an igloo. Cashdown went out to scavenge for fuel and quickly ducked back into his shelter. He dried his coat, hat, and gloves, ate a bit of salmon jerky, and dozed.

At the inn, Libbie grew anxious as soon as the snow started falling. There were no guests that night, so she was left alone with the three youngest children and three hired hands. As darkness and the rising wind and mounting snowfall enwrapped the station, she began to wring her hands and move aimlessly about the kitchen, sitting and getting up to go to the windows, sitting and rising to go look again.

"No need to worry about Pa. He knows how to get on; he always has," Frances said cheerfully.

"I s'pose you're right. But he's not as spry as he used to be. Not that he's old, not too old, but still I worry."

"That's not ordinary worry, Ma. You're holding it in."

"What are you talking about, Mindy?"

"You look beside yourself, like when we left for the fort because of the Indians."

"Hmm. Well. Frances, you finish cleaning up. Mindy, you mind the fires for a while, but don't stay up too late. I'm going to bed."

"It's not even nine o'clock," Frances objected.

"Well, I'm going up to bed."

But she didn't get into bed that night. She sat by the bedroom stove and listened to the wind howling and imagined the blowing, drifting snow. She wondered where her husband could be, and she kept thinking about all the tragic events that seemed to befall her year after year. Little Henry, the Indians, pestilence, these terrible winter storms. She nodded off from time to time, but she was so frantic with worry that she couldn't truly sleep. The night dragged on, paced by gusts of wind rumbling around the eaves and chimneys like a massive machine.

Her neck hurt when dawn came, and she realized she must have fallen asleep after the last time she stoked the stove. The storm appeared to have passed, and ripples in the grey morning sky showed promise of clearing later in the day. She went downstairs, made a fire in the kitchen, and began to watch for Cashdown.

At his makeshift shelter, Cashdown kicked out the cedar boughs over the entrance, and snow cascaded down. Once outside, he brushed the snow off one side of the tepee and tipped the structure over. The wailing of the storm had vanished, and now there was a stunning silence. He called Buster to him, saddled up, and rode to the crest of the surrounding hills. Immediately he recognized where he was and what mistake he'd made in the storm. He was too far west and needed to head northeast, almost directly toward Steptoe Butte. The peak, rising under the milky sky like a tower of sugar against the greyer backdrop of Idaho's mountains, would be easy to follow in the morning's clear, frosty air.

It was a slow journey home. The snow had drifted in places too deep for Buster to pass, and they had to detour many times. When finally they arrived at Steptoe Station, he found Libbie in the barn, saddling Ginger and two other horses for a search party.

"Where're you off to, Lib?" he said.

"Oh, Hamish! Thank God you're home. We were going out to find you." She began to shake, both from joyous relief and from her rising anger.

"Nae, no need of that. I'm fine as the day. Hope something's warm on the stove." He began to remove the saddle and tack from Buster.

"Damn you, Hamish!" Libbie yelled, and she ran to the house, leaving Cashdown standing amid four nervous beasts.

He half smiled and returned to storing gear and turning out the agitated horses.

The winter was harsh that year, with frequent storms and long stretches of subfreezing cold through December and January. There had been the usual midwinter thaw and then two weeks of below zero temperatures, leaving the landscape hard and icy. More snowstorms came through, and the spring thaw brought flooding across the territory. Some of Cashdown's livestock did not make it through the worst cold and snow. The ice had damaged many of his fruit trees, and the stagecoaches were often delayed at Colfax or Cheney by weather.

It was an isolated season for Cashdown, and when no stage guests arrived, he grew restless for social contact. Some rare days when he became acutely lonely for his friends, he would ride to Colfax for lunch. He responded to Libbie's chiding by saying he had business in town, checking on the railroad developments and his funds, or lining up supplies for summer, or seeing to the search for a new newspaper editor. But it seemed Orestes was always in Walla Walla, and James had little time for leisurely midday meals. Liam had persuaded James to take over the bank, after Florence Powell declined the offer of Liam's tutelage and his other choice had failed to impress. Pinky was not at her usual surveillance spot on the hotel balcony, as she frequently was away on shopping trips for the hotel and restaurant, which were perpetually being redecorated. Lycurgus was so occupied with the inauguration of his daily newspaper in Spokane Falls that he had not once returned to Colfax.

Cashdown settled for lunches with Silas Northrup, who would wear his toque and apron into the dining room to join him, or with big Felix Warren, who had sold his Concord and jerker stagecoaches and now was thinking of going into politics.

Both Silas and Felix paid close attention to local rumors, and Cashdown found he could keep himself up to date despite his friends' absences. When he arrived home in the evenings, he proudly reported to Libbie what he had learned, as if he were an espionage agent.

A week after Christmas: "They tell me the suffrage law was upheld, Lib. Supreme Court in Olympia heard the case and said it's lawful and in accord with the Territorial Constitution." Libbie, as he expected, was delighted with the news.

Late January: "Felix says James is maturing fast as a bank president. Everyone's pleased with him. He's all too busy, though, running both the bank and the town. Felix also said the rail line's already down past Rosalia, regular service there from Spokane Falls and Cheney. Silas tells me they've got a roller-skating rink at Cheney now. Very popular with the young ones."

Libbie smiled and said, "That's nice."

Early March: "Big Felix is moving on to Lewiston. Says Idaho is friendlier to a Democrat like him, and he's already taken his herds from Alpowa up the river. I'll miss his company. But not his politics." Libbie told him she thought Felix was more restless than even he was. Cashdown also reported that he heard Lettice Wheeler had parted ways with Ursula Hartjes and was returning from Walla Walla to live in Colfax. Libbie just raised her eyebrows.

Old Doc Kenoyer was at the bedside when Tessie gave birth to Cashdown and Libbie's second grandchild, a girl Tessie and Liam named Miranda, after her sweet-natured aunt. Doc blessed the infant with a prayer, prescribed a week of bed rest for the mother, and drove his trap back to his farm. A letter from Liam said the grandparents would be welcome to come up to Oakesdale at their soonest convenience, and Cashdown excitedly declared he was ready to leave immediately. Libbie suggested that they first ready the inn and farm for their absence, which might last several days. The twins said they could ride over once or twice to assist Willie and the hired hands as they started the spring chores; Charlie said she could supervise the inn for the weekend, if Frances would promise to help. "There are fewer stages coming by," she observed, "so there might not be much work anyway."

Cushing and Vonda McBride had arrived at Oakesdale just before Cashdown and Libbie. Liam and Tessie's home was a tall Victorian, with a curved turret, triangular dormers on all four sides, and a wide wraparound porch. Set high on a west hill, it overlooked Main Street and a grid of residential plats. The young settlement was already a prosperous commercial center served by a new rail line and surrounded by well-tended farms.

"The town just officially adopted Oakesdale as its name," Liam explained. "After Thomas Oakes, you know, from the Northern Pacific."

"Oh, of course," Cashdown muttered, "the railroads."

"Your place has come up real fast," Cushing said.

"Aye, lots of frame buildings," Cashdown said, brightening. "Quick to erect and less costly than masonry. But you could've found somebody better to name the town for."

"Maybe so, Pa. But frame buildings, they're vulnerable. And cold in the winter," Liam said. "That's why we're rebuilding the bank in brick."

"Wouldn't you men like to visit with our new grandchild?" Vonda interrupted. Libbie nodded in stern agreement, and they trooped upstairs to the big bedroom to pay compliments to Tessie and coo over baby Miranda. Mother and infant appeared healthy and flourishing, and so the grandparents set plans to leave after the weekend.

Monday morning following breakfast, Cashdown and Liam went out on the porch to smoke cigars and talk. Below them

Oakesdale spread out like a bracelet of shiny charms, as the early sun glinted off dewy roofs and tin signs. Crocuses and snowdrops covered the yard, and the songs of early spring birds rode the light breezes.

Cashdown gazed around the property and over the town with an appraiser's eye. "You seem well fixed here, Liam," he said.

"It's a fine opportunity, Pa, and it looks like the future will be strong for us and for the bank and town. We're building a new school this year, bringing in well-trained teachers. It'll be a good one. We're thinking to raise our family here, stay on in this house."

"It's a grand house, Liam. You've done well, and Tessie surely is wonderful. I only hope you aren't forgetting your family, our family. We haven't seen much of you in recent years."

"I think every day of you and Ma and my brothers and sisters. But I'll bet you don't see so much of the twins or Ferdie and Willie anymore, either. Charlie and Silas are living in Colfax now, and Jack's so busy at the paper we hardly see him. They have their work to do and their lives to claim, just as I've done. Mindy's the only one left at home."

"Ah, Mindy. We're trying to find a way to get her to the academy, her schooling's been so irregular. Your ma's taught her just about all she knows, and Mindy—she's like a sop—wants to go on learning. But she can't board because of the chores required in the dormitory."

"Let me know if we can help, Pa. She might live with us, and she could go to school here."

"Thanks, Son. We'll sort it out in time, I suppose."

Cashdown and Libbie were searching for answers when a card arrived in the post from Colfax Academy, inviting parents of past and present students to attend a welcoming reception for Mrs. Lettice Wheeler, recently vice-superintendent for public instruction standards of Washington Territory. Mrs. Wheeler, it said, would join the academy's instructional faculty as head of pedagogy and curricula, beginning September 1885.

"Perhaps we ought to go," Libbie said.

Always eager to socialize with townsfolk, Cashdown enthusiastically agreed. They would take Mindy with them. There was a reception line in that stretched from the granite threshold steps of the academy's main building all the way to the rear of the great hall. As they neared the honoree at the head of the line, they saw Angela next to Lettice, smiling and chatting graciously with people receiving them into Colfax again. When Angela spotted Mindy, she whispered something to her mother and slipped away to join the Musgraves.

"It's nice to see you again, Mr. and Mrs. Musgrave." She turned and took Mindy's hand. "I'm happy you came, too, Mindy. Do you remember me? We met at your house a couple of times."

Mindy smiled. "You look wonderfully grown up, Angela!"

Libbie and Cashdown said hello to Angela, and the two girls huddled aside to exchange gossip. When the line moved forward, the parents, too, renewed their acquaintance, promising to meet later in the day for a more personal visit.

After the academy's official speeches were over and after much parading around the small campus, Lettice met Libbie and Cashdown at the Ponderosa Hotel for tea. The two teenaged girls sat together at a separate table. Silas personally took the orders.

"Thank you for traveling in for this event," Lettice said. "I'm so pleased to have a second chance to make my home here among friends."

"It's a comfort," Libbie said, "to see you again and hear about all the inspiring things you've done in the past few years. You must've learned so much!"

"I assure you," she said with a little laugh, "I've had a complete education about education. And about politicians and people with more self-interest than I could show."

"That part of coming back, the politics?" Cashdown asked. Libbie frowned at him.

"I felt it was time for a change, for personal reasons. And the politics—I'm not very good at that. Ursula had long wanted more from me than I could provide, more commitment than I wanted to make. Angela was eager to return to Colfax, and I wanted her to grow up here, and all I could think of was the academy. So here we are."

"Aye, it's a grand place to raise a child and a right welcoming town for everybody."

Lettice apologized for the day's commotion and her delay.

"A bit of hubbub's invigorating. It's like a special holiday," Cashdown said.

"I'm frankly surprised, stunned by it all. I thought they'd just quietly sneak us in during the dark of night."

"Now why should they do that!" he said. "You've done so well, lived so honorably since leaving here, we're all filled with admiration and happiness for you and Angela." Libbie nodded her agreement and eyed caution to her husband.

"Yes, my second arrival here is different. Angela's a young woman now. And Mindy is remembered as her favorite friend. She was so sweet toward her when we went to gatherings at Steptoe Station. I wonder if we couldn't arrange for them to get together more often now?"

Libbie and Cashdown exchanged glances. Then Libbie said, "That would be wonderful for Mindy. It would relieve her from the constant company of only her sisters and brothers, and I know she looks up to Angela. She would talk about her for days after your visits. Yes, let's do that. I wonder, have you found a place to live?"

"Maybe. Pinky told us about a cottage on the south hill, and we looked it over and loved it. I've offered to buy it, and James Perkins said I should be approved for the loan."

Libbie congratulated her, and they discussed the logistics of moving in and home decorating. Cashdown offered to give Lettice some furniture she would need for a second bedroom. For an hour they chatted like old friends about local news and family events, the recent successes of the suffrage movement in Olympia, and departures of friends and acquaintances. As they left, Libbie and Cashdown grinned at each other. They said they would visit again after Lettice and Angela were settled in. And, they said, they would surely bring Mindy.

As soon as they entered the front door, Frances told them Mr. Hunter had called while they were in Colfax. "He said he'd be back tomorrow. He needs to talk to Pa," she said.

Cashdown lingered around the farm all the next day, waiting for George Hunter to show up. Late in the afternoon, as the warm breeze calmed and squadrons of ladybugs began drifting toward aspen groves by the road, he spotted a rider heading in from the west hay fields. When the horse and rider neared, Cashdown recognized the man. He wore a swallowtail coat and high-crowned Stetson, both dusty from long hours on the trail, and he was unmistakable in thick eyeglasses and muttonchops.

"Ah, George. Welcome. My hand will see to your ride."

"Good afternoon, Mr. Musgrave," Hunter said formally. He was a bony man with a beaked nose. When he removed his hat, his greying hair stood upright, stiff as a wire brush.

"My apologies for missing your call yesterday. We had business in Colfax."

"I availed myself of the extra time to pay a visit to Husishusis Moxmox. He was at his cousin Piyuwaitin's home, over near Little Falls. He travels around, but most of his tribal kin remain on their holdings."

"Come in, George, and have a refreshment while we talk," Cashdown said.

When they were settled with whiskeys in the great room, Cashdown asked, "What have you heard about Tomeo and his family?"

"Alas, I am afraid you will not find it good news. By all appearances, they seem to have scattered like chaff on the wind. I endeavored to offer cordialities at every site on the Snake and Palouse Rivers, within and up all the drainages where Palus members have settled. There they well informed me that no sign of Tomeo's people has been detected in a year. Most tell me that what was left of his family, the stragglers they knew of, were removed to Colville or west to Yakima. They were starving to death, it was reported, and some others have gone into seclusion. Nobody knows about Tomeo."

"What's your guess about his fate, George?"

"It would be the Devil's own mischief to say. Tomeo was a traditional Palus man and one of Kamiaken's favored sons, and he was excessively burdened with pride. I am informed it nearly killed him to learn about the desecration of their grave. Surely you recall that?"

"Aye, indeed. It was a cruel insult, done in the name of science. Like the rest of science, ethnology ain't sentimental."

"I have heard, and I credit the reports as valid, that Tomeo grieved forever afterward. I shouldn't be surprised if his body right now is floating down the Columbia towards the open sea and into the arms of the Almighty."

"You think he's gone."

George Hunter nodded. "It would be his way. But, whatever the case, he's just disappeared, and I am regretful that I could not be of greater assistance to them and you."

Cashdown and Libbie invited him to stay for the night, but Hunter said he had promised his family he would return straightaway, and he had to get to Colfax to take the early train out toward the coast. They saw him to the gate and watched for a long time as his tall, erect figure rode toward the horizon and disappeared into the gathering darkness.

Trains now were running in multiple directions from Colfax: southwest to Wallula, with stops at Hooper, Winona, and Connell; and east to Pullman, where lines went southeast to Moscow in Idaho Territory, and north to Cheney with stops at towns along the way. It was becoming possible to ride by train to any destination in the Pacific Northwest. George Hunter would arrive home within a day.

CHAPTER 25

Over the next year, stagecoach arrivals became increasingly rare at Steptoe Station. Cashdown attended to his farm, livestock, and orchard work as always. He occasionally went to Colfax to visit Pinky and Silas at the hotel and to see Mindy, who was lodging with Lettice and Angela. He and Libbie would sometimes travel to Oakesdale for an overnight stay with Liam, Tessie, and their children. The twins and their new families—and the rest of the Musgrave children, now all adults—gathered at the inn for Christmas and for the occasional wedding reception. But Cashdown was forced by circumstances to be more solitary, and he sometimes seemed gloomier. The thought that sustained him was his confidence that there could yet be a spur from the new C&PC rail line being laid from Cheney directly south to Colfax. He and two of his neighboring farmers had written to the company's executives, as Charles Tromberly had suggested, arguing their case for a link from St. John out to Steptoe Station. The reply was cordial and gave assurances that petitions such as theirs "would receive first priority in considerations about connecting facilities."

In the spring of 1886 the stagecoaches stopped coming altogether.

In the mail bag arriving on the next-to-last coach was a letter from Willamette. Aunt Adelia's news dismayed Cashdown and Libbie. She said Uncle William had been taken ill and was now housebound. Their sons had returned to the farm, built two new houses on the property, and were trying to make a go of things. But it was evident that they were not prospering. Cashdown commented to Libbie, "I wish they'd come up here soon after we did. Life would've been better for them."

Adelia also wrote that Callum had returned to Oregon:

> He arrived at the station, in mid-January, after a hard travel, and he had changed so greatly, I scarcely recognized him, but he is fit, and flush, and I think he is going to stay around awhile, although he reveals nothing of his plans. He kindly offered to help the boys, with the farm work and such, and he asks after you, and your family, and is especially keen to know all the details about Miranda. I guess you had told him long ago about little Henry. Cal is even quieter than I remembered him, and seems pensive, much of the time, but cheerful. That is all I can tell about him now.

Cashdown asked Libbie to read the part about Cal again. She handed the letter to him. He studied it, stroking his beard and muttering quietly. "I wonder if she's telling everything she knows," he said.

"We can't control that, Hamish."

A few days later he told her he was thinking of going down to Willamette to see his brother. Libbie suggested that he first write to Cal through Adelia and William. "Give him some notice," she said, which he did. His letter was a veiled plea for reconciliation. He wrote,

> Adelia tells us you might stay there at Willamette for a while, and I thought it might be swell if we came down for a visit. We could ride the trains from Colfax all the way to

Portland. And it would be grand to see you again. I shall send a postal card when we have settled on the time.

He mailed the letter the following week when he traveled to Colfax to rendezvous with Orestes and Lycurgus for lunch. It was a rare event when all three could meet and enjoy exchanging news and gossip as they once did. On a whim, Cashdown stopped at the bank to say hello to James, and to his delight James was eager to join the group at the hotel. There were hugs and back slaps all around as the four greeted one another.

"How grand we could be here today, everyone," Cashdown said.

"Luckily for me," Orestes said, "I could come home early this week. It's recess at Whitman. And we have the rare privilege of seeing the esteemed Editor Ames once again."

"Things are now running smoothly at the *Sentinel,* thanks to my assiduous attentions and my heretofore undiscovered talent for putting matters in order," Lycurgus said with a smug grin. When the denials, contradictions, insults, and laughter died down, he added more evenly, "We're soon to be the *Spokane Sentinel-Review.* Taking over the *Falls Review* and making two editions. But what's the latest on the Colfax paper now? I've been so busy, I haven't paid enough attention."

James replied with a sigh. "Not flourishing under our present editor, Mr. Clayborne G. Pettijohn. And he refuses to let go the reins to Cashdown's Jack."

"Why don't you just kick him out?"

Orestes answered, "Can't do that. We already excommunicated one editor, and two in succession would set a poor precedent for future searches. In truth, we can't because he has the money—his group owns the enterprise outright."

"Can you buy him out?"

"I gave him a ripe offer," Cashdown said, "and he considered it, then told me his backers wouldn't go for it. Not nearly ripe enough. I can't afford more, and I don't think the town can pay his price."

James agreed. "We tried to get him interested in taking over the old paper in Lewiston, but he wasn't interested enough to talk with them, and they soured on him when they did their diligence and read some of his editions."

Orestes pursed his lips and frowned in thought. "I have been wondering if it would be possible to launch a competitor to Mr. Pettijohn's enterprise. Colfax and this end of Whitman County are now populous enough to support two newspapers, and if Lewiston and Moscow can do it successfully, why can't we?"

"There'd be a paper war, and however it turned out we wouldn't be the same afterward," James said. "But I'd bet there's room for a morning paper."

Lycurgus said morning editions were catching on in the newspaper business. "And I would gladly release the rights to the *Guardian* name, if that would help. And maybe Jack could help run it."

They ordered lunch, congratulated themselves for creating a new project, and began laying plans for recruiting a publisher. Lycurgus volunteered to organize the effort and canvass colleagues among his newspaper friends. Pinky's aerie was dark, her surveillance chair vacant, and the shotgun missing. When Silas took their lunch orders, he told the group she was out back, inspecting a delivery of artwork and leaded glass screens from San Francisco. Just as he finished excusing her, she raced into the dining room, shouting "All my favorite gentlemen, all together again. My lucky, lucky day!" She rushed to the table and hugged each of the friends, holding her coach gun out with one hand like a torch.

"Pinky! Happy to see you again," Lycurgus said. "But could you break that weapon before it goes off?"

She laughed and called a waiter to take her shotgun up to her desk. She pulled up a chair and joined the group at lunch. "Somebody's birthday?" she asked.

"Just a bunch of old friends with nothing to do on a late winter Friday," Orestes said. "How's your business?"

"I got too goddamned much business, need to find more workers, more good workers. Too many bums—no-good drifters want jobs but don't want to work. I need to talk to part-time mayor, ask him to get me some good workers. Hey, James, how about that?"

"You've already taken away all my authority, Pinky. I should be going to you for help."

"What's this?" Cashdown said. "Pinky's running the town now?"

James looked around and said, "A bit of unpublished information—if I may, Pinky?—and solely for old friends. Pinky's now a director of the bank and a major shareholder. She's helping us with business accounts and investments."

"Yah, and James takes all my money, too, hah-hah!"

Cashdown ordered sherry for everyone, and they toasted to Pinky's expanding influence in Colfax. Over lunch the talk turned to the growing presence of the railroads across the Palouse prairie. James said that the direct line from Cheney was supposed to reach Colfax by next spring, making it the second route to connect with the north of Washington and Idaho. "They expect to build down to St. John by fall."

"Keeping me eye on their progress," Cashdown said. "The plan for expanding our inn at Steptoe, you know, depends on a link to that line."

"Watch 'em closely, Cashdown," James advised. "That bunch are very tight fisted and short sighted. They're building south only because one of the partners farms wheat near St. John and around Colton—thousands of acres. They'll have a coaling station and grain elevator stop near Colton. We were just lucky they saw a gain in coming through Colfax."

After lunch, Cashdown told Orestes what George Hunter had learned about the Paluses and Tomeo's family.

"It's tragic," Orestes said, "and I doubt anything can be done to reverse it."

"Aye. But what happens now to their traditional lands? Whites continue to flow into the Palouse Prairie, and it looks ripe for the picking."

"Whatever shows up on the plats for homesteading is fair game, amigo."

Before they departed, Orestes told Cashdown to let Libbie know that the long knives in Olympia had taken the suffrage law to court. "It's almost certain to end in the Supreme Court later this year," he said.

"You don't sound sanguine over it."

"Not very much, though I'm trying to influence my contacts in the judiciary and legislature. We'll just have to wait and see," he said.

Amid handshakes, backslaps, and promises to gather again in a few months, the five friends went their separate ways. Cashdown walked up to the academy to see if he might say hello to Mindy, but she was away with Angela and some other friends on a half holiday. A light rain began to fall. Disconsolate, he slowly saddled Buster for the three-hour ride back to Steptoe Station.

For the next few weeks, he was buoyed by the lunch gathering in Colfax, the good news for Pinky, the plan to establish a competing newspaper, and the prospect of acquiring all of Steptoe Butte, now that the Paluses had no claim on it. He checked at the land office later in the spring and found that the sections map showed it as already partially his; the remainder was owned by the government's reserve trust held for Indians. It was available for sale, but not at homesteading cost. Cashdown bought it anyway, convincing Libbie that he had money-making ideas for developing it as a tourist lookout site.

He was uneasy, however, as he watched the C&PR line being built to the west. Once or twice a week he would ride out at dawn to observe the crews' progress. As the summer went on it became apparent that they had already passed locations Cashdown deemed to be good places for a spur toward Steptoe Station. By the end of harvest season he saw that wheat from the fields around St. John was being shipped north on the new rail line. Construction further southward would commence with the spring thaw of 1887.

Cashdown sent letters to the officers of the Columbia & Palouse Railroad. He wanted to know if there were plans for a spur to Steptoe Station. Perhaps they were going to add it after the line reached Colfax and extended down to Colton and Uniontown. Or maybe, he reasoned, they would choose a more southerly route below St. John. His letters went unanswered.

On one of his trips to Oakesdale, he pressed Liam to call the railroad on the bank's telephone and secure an appointment to talk with the president. The president, however, was unavailable. "I talked with the vice president, who's also chief planner. Better steady yourself, Pa. He told me there will be no branch lines from the Colfax direct route. I tried to get their reasoning, but he just said it would not profit them enough. I'm sorry, Pa."

Cashdown was stunned by the report. "What can I do?" he moaned. "The inn will fail, and our livestock and grains delivery will be later to market than farmers on the line, so in time the farm will fail, too. It's the bloody ruination of my lifetime's work!"

"You could haul your produce and sale livestock east to Palouse City and ship it from there. You might even consider starting up an inn or hotel there, or in Pullman."

"The profits'd be too small if I had to haul everything over there meself. And they already have too bloody many hotels over there!" he snapped.

Liam handed him a whiskey and suggested they should have a "family powwow" after they all thought it over for a few weeks. Cashdown calmed down and apologized for his ingratitude. He thanked Liam for his effort and good intentions.

His ride home was guided by Steptoe Butte, its summit looming over Palouse prairie hilltops and dominating the horizon like a lighthouse. Cashdown muttered his thoughts aloud, as he reviewed everything that made him feel isolated. Buster plodded along, his ears cocked back in attention to the complaints.

Over the winter months Cashdown fell into a deepening depression. Libbie tried to cheer him up, promising a big celebration at Christmas, but he remained gloomy and ruminated on his foreclosed future. After the holidays, when there was a break in the weather, Liam gathered most of the family at Steptoe Station to discuss the future of the farm and inn. For the previous week, however, Libbie had commented to Cashdown about his change of mood. He seemed to be happier, almost back to his old chipper self, she said. He would just smile and say, "I'm thinking about happier things now." At night he sat up late by the stove in their bedroom, writing and drawing in a notebook.

It wasn't long before the clan gathered for a Sunday dinner and their deliberations. Cashdown agreed to it, saying he thought it would please the children.

Liam opened the discussion after the meal, while everyone was still seated with port. "Pa seems to think the failure of the railroad to make a line out this way is the end of our farm and inn. I told him we might be able to come up with a way to help, maybe give him and Ma some new ideas for keeping the place going."

"Maybe we could just stick with raising livestock and forget the crop farming," Elbourne said. "Tray and I made a good profit last year from our beef cattle."

Trayton nodded in agreement. "We d-d-drove our herd to Colfax and p-pah-put 'em on the t-train there."

"If you take out the hilly acreage we have in wheat and turn it over to grazing range, I'll bet you'd double the profit on those fields," was Ferdie's contribution. Ferdie had a talent for calculations and his father's instinct for profits. "You could lease some, too."

Charlie and Silas had come out from Colfax with Jack to join in the discussion. "The inn could be converted to a full restaurant," Silas said, "with a bar and bandstand, and maybe, aside from raising livestock, it could stay open for weekend shindigs, higher quality than just a roadhouse or cantina. I could help you with that."

"People travel some distance for entertainments nowadays," added Frances, with a smile and little head nods of encouragement.

Libbie sat with her arms folded across her breasts, listening. As their children talked, she gazed at Cashdown. He beamed distractedly, as if lost in thought. "Well, Pa, what do you think?" she said.

Cashdown looked around the table at his family and stood up to speak.

"I'm tired of raising livestock, I regret to say. We work like steam pumps all year to birth them, feed them, fix them when they take ill, and fatten them for market. Some years we get a good enough profit, but many years we have such winterkill that we lose money. And it's heartbreaking to see the poor beasts frozen in the snow or rotting in the mud in spring. And I've long been unhappy with our horse breeding. Good Jesus, the natives do a better job of it, while we baptize the best ones, bring 'em into our home, and keep 'em like cousins till they pass on. The profit is small, and I have felt like we're selling our children each time we put the horses and mules on the market. Besides, I'm tired of the labors of ranching. I'm coming seventy this year . . ."

"Seventy-three," corrected Libbie.

"I'm getting old and creaky, and you don't want me to get cranky to boot."

Derisive groans issued around the table.

"Anyway, I've decided we won't be expanding or even continuing to farm and raise livestock as we've been doing these many years. It's served us well enough, but the comforts and financial good fortune we enjoy are not owing in the main to our husbandry and produce. Nae, it's due to thrift, wise investments, and your enterprise." He gestured grandly around the table, like a maestro at the end of a symphony. "And the future isn't in family farming enterprise anymore, what with the railroads and industry and all." Another dramatic pause, and the family waited expectantly.

Mindy broke the silence. "What about Silas's idea for a roadhouse restaurant, Pa?"

"I've been thinking on that for over a year, Mindy. I reckoned that without the regular stagecoach visitations, and with so much growth in places like Colfax and Palouse City and Farmington, why, we'd have a devilish hard time attracting merrymakers. There are too many new choices right where the people live for anybody to come all the way out here. So, I thinks to meself, if attracting people to our establishment is the obstacle, and we want to enlarge the offering we've been making at Steptoe Station Inn, we'll need something truly special." He paused again and looked around the table at his family. A wily grin overtook his face.

"I'm going to build us a hotel on top of Steptoe Butte!"

★ ★ ★ ★ ★

Part Three

★ ★ ★ ★ ★

No house should ever be on a hill or on anything.
It should be of the hill. Belonging to it.

—Frank Lloyd Wright

CHAPTER 26

"That's a crazy idea, even for you! No, no, no. We're not going to start that again."

"Start what, Lib? I've thought long about this, and I know we can make it work. We need to do something grand, something new, out of the ordinary."

The rest of the family sat in stunned silence. Cashdown flashed a manic smile. He sat down and clasped his hands behind his head.

"You sit there with your self-satisfaction, Hamish, but it's all just a vanity. Will you *never* stop building castles in the air!"

Charlie leaned over and placed a consoling hand on her mother's wrist. "Pa," she said, "the top of the butte is just too remote. And it's steeper than a gable roof. There's no road. And if there was one, it'd be so steep nobody could get up it in a carriage. So how would you build a hotel up there?"

Before Cashdown could reply, Ferdie said, "And there's no water up there. You know how much water we use here, Pa, and this is a small inn. Hard to say how much water you'd need for running a hotel up on that peak. Considering you could build one. You'd have to do something with the sewage, too, the night soil. You can't put a lagoon up there."

Elbourne chimed in: "And where would the paying customers come from, anyway? The coaches are gone. The railroad's not coming out here. So, what would draw people up some scabby rock three hours away from the city?"

Cashdown's smug expression had faded. He looked around at his family with disappointment and disbelief on his face.

Liam took the floor. "Let's give Pa the chance to explain what his thinking on this is. Let's not all strike the idea off before we know what it really is."

Eyes went downcast, feet shuffled under the big table, lips tightened. Cashdown rose from his chair once again.

"Thank you, Son. Now as to the clientele. I agree there must be an attraction to lure people away from the towns and cities hereabouts. There are hotels and flophouses aplenty on the Palouse. But few—with the noteworthy exceptions of Pinky's Ponderosa Hotel, and the Willows in Palouse City, maybe that new place over in Pullman—few have any elegance to speak of. Elegance, I'm aware, isn't enough on its own; success needs something more. Some offer location, like being close to the trains depot or in the center of a town. Steptoe Butte offers something no guesthouse, inn, hotel, or dormitory anywhere in all of Whitman County, possibly anywhere in all of Washington Territory, can boast of."

A dramatic pause. "Vistas. Yes, vistas. I have spent many a magical hour atop the butte, and whenever I gaze across this land all the way south to Oregon and west to the Cascades and east to the high ridges of Idaho, I feel like I'm witness to the greatest works of Providence and the most dignified labors of the yeoman. The patchwork quilt of farmers' fields is a grand work of art. It's a sacred place and an inspirational viewing site, good for the soul. No wonder our native brethren made it a holy mountain and the young braves made their spirit hunts there."

A clamor of objections and questions took over, until Liam raised his hand, and all quieted to hear what the eldest son would say. "We've been up there many times before, and we know how glorious the view is from atop the butte. And I think the idea of capitalizing on the spiritual power of the site has merit. But I can't help wondering, Pa, what would keep people from just hiking up the mountain to have a picnic and enjoy the view? And why haven't they already done it? Hoteling's a business, Pa, and I've never heard of a lodging that attracts paying customers by offering a view out the window that they could have by some other, cheaper means. What would be different about your hotel idea?"

Cashdown grinned in triumph. His hushed answer was almost a whisper. "A telescope."

"Telescope?"

"Aye. Think of this: with a magnifying instrument of considerable power, a person can see vast distances and the finest details, way beyond what any mortal can see without the instrument. He suddenly becomes more powerful himself. He becomes like an eagle; he feels like a god. I warrant that's a seduction and an addiction, more so than a firearm. People will come out because of their curiosity, and they'll return because of their euphoria. I'll have a belvedere atop the hotel and an observatory, where people can gaze full circle, all four directions, to the farthest horizons. I've me eye on an instrument already."

"What about the water?" Elbourne said.

"In the good months, use catch basins for rainwater and runoff. If we must, we'll haul it. We'd augment the catch basins by hauling from cisterns below. Mules, mash vats, good springs on the water wagon—we could haul it. And we'll haul the night soil down to pits below, away from the creek. A few good privies above and thunder mugs in rooms should be sufficient. We'll first off build a sturdy road, on the east and south faces, because it's a tad less vertical there, and we'll level off the top and finish it with stone. We'll make a plinth of it for the hotel, with room for wagons to stop and people to gather. The stables'll be down below. We'll decorate with the grandest woodwork and furnishings, bring it all in from the old country. I'll sort out the details, I know all the suppliers south of London. Oh, it will be splendid to behold, our palace atop the sacred mountain."

He looked so fervent and merry as he described his plan that tears came to Libbie's eyes. But she said nothing. She rose and began clearing the table. The other women did the same. Cashdown watched them and again turned forlorn.

"It would be grand to have your agreement," he said to their backs, "but that's not necessary. I'll go ahead anyway." He poured himself another glass of port.

"We want to join in your plan, Pa. But there remain some obstacles that becloud the vision of it succeeding," Liam said.

"Nothing that can't be overcome, m' boy."

"It sounds highly laborious and costly. Have you thought of the initial investment required? You'll have to hire a large crew and their equipment. Outfitting with finery shipped from Europe will come dear. Materials will have to be hauled from Palouse City and moved up to the summit. And there will be licensing and publicity costs, and expenses for new domestics. Conditions across America are making it so that none of us, none of the banks, can make loans for beginning enterprises anymore."

"I've me own nest egg that's been a-building all these years. I've been frugal enough, and now it's time to use our little cashbox to invest in the future. All our futures."

"These are not favorable economic times for risky investments, Pa. I know from my bank's experience of late. Yes, you have cash aplenty. But you'll pour all of it into such a scheme." The other men—Elbourne, Trayton, Ferdie, Jack, and Silas—nodded and listened attentively.

"James Perkins assures me that our funds are sound and plentiful. That will be sufficient." Cashdown got up from the table, fetched a cigar, and went outside, signaling that he'd made his case. His sons and Silas conferred for a few minutes before Liam went out to join his father on the porch.

"If you're decided to chase this pipe dream, Pa, we won't try to thwart you or abandon you. We will work with you and do what we can to make it good."

Cashdown had been studying the fence line across the access road with narrowed eyes. He turned to Liam and said, "Thank you, Son. I'll welcome your support."

As soon as the spring thaw subsided and the ground firmed up, lines of freight wagons began rumbling up the narrow road between Palouse City and Steptoe Butte. At first they hauled excavating machinery—scrapers, parts for a steam-powered dirt dredge, heavy plows—and began pulverizing rock. Later would come loads of huge posts and beams of milled fir and cedar, fasteners, sacks of mortar and plaster, bricks, finished windows and doors, and all the other materials for constructing a hotel.

Cashdown designed a snaking road to ascend the southwest grade of the citadel. He built switchbacks every few hundred feet and braced the outward edges with dry-stacked boulders. For powering the road machinery, he corralled twenty of his horses and mules near his orchards and taught and supervised the hired men, nearly two dozen idled miners and drifters, to drive the scrapers and plows. They first built stables for the animals. For over a month the crew gouged soil and rock for the switchbacks, scraped roadbed, plowed away debris, and laid down gravel by shovels and wheelbarrows. They installed run-off pipes under the gravel, groomed the road surface, and pounded it firm with iron tampers shaped like platters. Cashdown directed his men to level the top of the peak, over 1,700 feet above the surrounding Palouse plain. They hauled the dredge up and excavated tons of rock, then used scrapers and teams to make the half-acre site smooth and level enough to build the hotel.

Work on the road and building site went on through April and May. More men were hired and instructed in the finer points of drystone masonry. They built the foundation for the hotel and laid the stone apron for visiting wagons and teams to deliver guests. On rainy days the project proved itself capable of shedding and collecting water; the roadway held, and framing went on unabated. But the spring and summer of 1888 turned dryer than normal, and the favorable weather encouraged Cashdown to set July Fourth as the time for the grand opening of his hotel. In the rush, more idled miners and teamsters were hired. Most had carpentry skills, and all were grateful for the work.

Many of the men found it difficult to keep up with Cashdown's manic pace. He slept little, ate ravenously, and worked from first light at four thirty a.m. until ten p.m., when the last glow faded in the western sky and stars twinkled on like gemstones. He produced detailed drawings of the hotel and oversaw every facet of its construction. His agent in London sent half a shipload of estate furnishings—upholstered oak chairs with intricately carved arms; tall sideboards in walnut and beechwood; sumptuous divans and antique side tables and bookcases; mahogany wall panels and matching interior doors—everything hauled by freight wagon from the Colfax depot. He supervised the smallest details of their transportation and placement in the new hotel.

Three times he rode to Farmington to badger Sam McCroskey about a telescope; from the Alvan Clark Company of Massachusetts they ordered a brass refractor of six inches aperture, a treasure of an instrument that weighed more than its owner. Cashdown designed a pedestal, and he and Sam installed a German equatorial mount that doubled the weight of the telescope. The installation was on a raised platform within the observatory on top of the hotel, gained by a narrow stairway from the second-story balcony. Massive joists and beams supported it, to assure stability and to minimize vibrations. The observatory was glassed in against the weather but permitted views in all horizontal directions. He called it the Panorama Room. Believing his guests would not have competence for celestial observing, Cashdown made no provision for turning it toward the sky. He was astounded when he first viewed his domain through the gleaming new refractor.

"Good God a'mighty! I can read the sign on the granary doors in Wallula! I can see buildings in Pendleton!" he exclaimed to Sam. Swinging the instrument to the west, he said, "Mount Tacoma in all its glory. Bet I could pick out a goat up there. It's a miracle."

The week leading up to July Fourth was a blur of activity. Cashdown had choreographed the grand opening and booked both the Wheatland Whirlwinds Frontier Band and the Northwest Pipers for the event. He invited a group of politicians from surrounding towns, Whitman County, and the territorial legislature. Journalists were assigned by their editors to attend. Fireworks were ordered from Walla Walla, and the twins learned how to set them in place and ignite them. The last details of the construction were being completed late in the afternoon of Tuesday, July third. Doorknobs were installed, exterior trim painted, the cobbled stonework washed, and the last of the debris removed to a burn pit below.

Libbie came up with the galley staff from Steptoe Inn to inaugurate the new kitchen. Earlier in the day she and Cashdown had hung a sign on the old entrance gate. They had debated the exact wording and settled on *CLOSED FOR BUSINESS. CONTINUE AHEAD FOR HOTEL STEPTOE.*

"Shouldn't we paint an arrow or something to show the direction?" she asked.

Cashdown added a fist with the index finger pointing like a revolver down the access road. When they had suspended the sign above the driveway, he stood back and gazed around at the inn and barns and livestock pens.

"It's been a good life here, Lib, a good place to live. But, as you say, everything changes, and I'm ready to take up life anew on the butte. Today I feel like a young adventurer again." A satisfied smile spread across his face.

"You're not going to *live* up there, are you?"

"Of course we'll live at the hotel. Why would we stay here, when we've just brought up all our fondest luxuries? It's not only for visitors, you know. Besides, we'll be there every day from dawn to dusk anyway. No sense traveling back and forth."

"Oh, Hamish," she said and turned away, shaking her head.

There was no time for rehearsals. Jitneys, charabancs, surries, and traps began arriving by midmorning of Independence Day. Some guests came on horseback, and the Orrin Ewing family walked the six miles from their farm. Spooked by the steepness and elevation of the escarpment, more than one team balked at the third or fourth switchback and had to be calmed and led up by stable boys on foot. Soon teams and carriages going up encountered empties on their way down to the stables. Cashdown had calculated just enough space at turnouts for negotiating passage.

By noon the musicians had mounted a stage erected before the hotel's front doors. Red, white, and blue bunting decorated the stage and was draped along the packed roof walk above the second story. The bunting fluttered in the light breezes. A noisy crowd had gathered on the cobblestone parking apron, and Cashdown made ready to welcome all the visitors. Dressed in his shiny swallow-tailed suit and brushed stovepipe hat, he stood in front of the band and signaled the pipers to play. They wheezed and whined and shrieked out the first two bars of

"Always Believe." The crowd turned silent and pivoted attention to the stage.

"Friends, neighbors, distinguished honorees, members of the press, you bless us with your presence for the grand opening of our Hotel Steptoe. You see before you a splendid example of what the pioneering spirit and much honest work and hard-won experience can bring to the Northwest. It is unique in all the region, both in the elegance of its refined décor and in its unmatched location. Some would say it's audacious, being perched atop a remote mountain as it is, and maybe an affront to good sense. But I invite you to look to the horizons and behold the wider splendors of your own work—your cultivated fields and orderly settlements and prosperous towns growing up like eager saplings—and gaze upon the wonders of Nature rolling before you to the vast mountains afar. No lodging or gathering place on earth has finer vistas, and our aim is to guarantee that no lodging has more graceful service or more enjoyable festivities on offer. Welcome to Hotel Steptoe. There will be food and drink inside, and music for dancing upstairs in the ballroom; please join those folks on the top balcony, and shortly I will begin conducting tours of the interior and our special feature, the Panorama Room observatory."

He jumped off the stage, and a group of journalists from all the region's papers gathered around him to ask for details of the construction and the establishment's distinctive offerings. He happily regaled them with information and then led them to join a larger group for the first tour of the hotel. The band began to play, even as carriages continued to arrive and disgorge more visitors. The kitchen staff set out hors d'oeuvres and desserts and beverages on long rows of tables in the main dining room. There were fried oysters, pâtés, and slices of roasts and hams; sautéed mushrooms and glazed pigeons; nuts, cheeses, and fruits; baskets of breads and biscuits; platters of vinegar tarts and fruit pies; flasks of wine and jugs of apple cider, strawberry water, and lemonade. Tall copper and enameled tea samovars were placed strategically around the room.

People lined up on the gallery over the main ballroom to await their turn to ascend the stairs to the Panorama Room. From below, excited chatter, *ooh*s and *aah*s, and whistles could be heard as viewers looked through the telescope. After the tours and after the food and drink had been consumed, the band set up in the ballroom and began to play. Dancing took over the afternoon, and the festivities went on until nearly sunset, when carriages began arriving to fetch merrymakers for the ride home. The tables in the dining room were separated, and a late dinner was served for people staying overnight. Before the meal, Cashdown led guests outside to watch the fireworks set off by the twins. The lodgers were reluctant to turn in after eating; some stayed up to enjoy more of Cashdown's best port and conversation, some returned to the observatory to watch the western horizon against the fading afterglow, and others strolled slowly around the hotel's apron and talked softly into the night.

Long after midnight, Libbie and Cashdown sat side by side on the bed in nightclothes. They were in their private quarters next to the hotel kitchen.

"I must say, Hamish, they came out in numbers. And everyone seemed to have a good time."

"Aye, 'twas a right fine start, wasn't it?"

Libbie cast a probing glance toward Cashdown. "It would be a pretty ride back to Steptoe Station tonight, wouldn't it?"

"Indeed. They lingered outside and admired the nightfall." He looked around the room, as if planning where to place his treasures.

"That would be a pleasure, wouldn't it? After a long day's work here, to just turn it over to the night clerk and have a nice, slow drive home each night." Libbie continued to keep surveillance on Cashdown's expression.

He turned toward her, his face puckering. "Wouldn't be such a nice drive home in the deep of winter, I warrant."

"Oh, in the worst of weather there's always this room. Or we could winter at the inn."

"Libbie, darlin', I'm not going back and forth each day. I'm not going to be living at the station. I've sold the herds and have no reason to be there. The work's here, and I'm living here. To the end of me days." His voice and expression were calm but firm.

"Yes, I suppose you will," she said quietly, as she got under the covers.

Chapter 27

They later broached with friends the matter of what was to become of Steptoe Station. James Perkins advised them to sell it. Orestes and Sam thought they might find somebody who would want to lease the mercantile as a concession—after all, they reasoned, Cashdown might one day find living on the mountain too demanding and wish to come down to someplace more convenient. Lettice Wheeler told Libbie it was sad that the inn was unused and wondered if any of the Musgrave children could take it over. Nothing further was done about it, and the inn and farm were shuttered for the crops season and winter.

After the following year's July Fourth celebrations, Cashdown and Libbie talked with the twins and Ferdie, Willie, and Jack. They were willing to take the land, but none of the boys—now all in their twenties and well established in their own farms and businesses—wanted the house or the store and inn. "S-se-sell them and those f-five acres. Or m-move back into the house and l-l-lease out the rest," said Trayton. The others agreed.

Cashdown took no action that year either, saying only that he would reconsider it later. The winter of 1889 to 1890 was the snowiest in a decade. For two months no guests came to Hotel Steptoe, and there were stretches of weeks when the snowbound staff could not haul water up the mountain or waste barrels down. The firewood supply dwindled, and food stocks ran short. By day, Cashdown, Libbie, and their three workers huddled near the massive stove in the kitchen, reading, knitting, polishing utensils, anything to fill the time. They concocted meals from flour and snowmelt and whatever was left in the pantry. Cashdown went out hunting for any edible game, but he could not get far into the snowdrifts, and there were no large mammals on the mountain. He would settle for rabbits or small birds. They kept one stove going at night, and all slept in the same room. Chamber pots were emptied into overflowing barrels, only to freeze instantly. Nobody bathed.

When at last the spring runoff began, Libbie told Cashdown she wanted to go to Oakesdale to see her granddaughter. There had been no Christmas gathering that year, and she was, she said, "tired of talking to the same people, day after day for weeks on end."

"Soon as I get the washouts repaired, we'll go," he replied.

When the road was restored, they drove the surrey to Liam and Tessie's house, stopping sometimes so one could hand-lead the team while the other pushed the wagon through a muddy breach in the road. Arriving at Oakesdale, they needed to clean and dry their soiled outer clothing and boots. Tessie brought Miranda downstairs and joined the others by the fireside, where they talked happily about the baby's robust health and daily adventures. Cashdown and Liam discussed the hardships of the winter the Palouse prairie had just endured, the coming elections, the consequences of Washington gaining statehood; they speculated about the year's crop harvests and the possibilities for an economic upswing.

"With the rail line in, I might try again getting a spur out our way," Cashdown said.

"What would be in it for them, Pa?"

"We've a successful business, Liam, become a destination for adventurous spirits."

"Don't be surprised if they decline, Pa. The few passengers

your business might gain them in summer can't compare to their earnings from freight. They haul a lot of milled wood and grains now."

"At least I could get them to make a stop somewhere over near Elberton. Drop off and pick up for Pullman. Or Colfax and Spokane."

"You could give it a try. What's your thought on the coach inn now, Pa?"

"Well, I'm wondering would you want it for a retail business, the merc?"

"I have plenty to do here. No thank you."

"You could hire the labor, even someone to oversee the business."

"No time for that, Pa. The rest of us aren't interested, either. You could do the same. Maybe you should just sell it, if you're not going to live there."

"Maybe we shall, Son."

The trip home the following day was pleasantly dry and warm. The horses were so perky, Cashdown had to restrain them from trotting. Libbie was quieter than usual, and for a long time she nibbled her lower lip in thought. Cashdown commented on how different the landscape they were passing through looked when viewed from the hotel observatory.

Libbie placed her hand on his thigh. "Hamish, I'm going back to the house. I'm not going to live at the hotel, and I want you to live at the house with me."

"Ah, Lib, you don't want to do that. Stay with me on the peak."

"No, Hamish, you stay with me at home, our home, in the house we built."

"But there's no business there anymore, and I'm done with farming and raising livestock. We've much to do up on the butte every day. Why go back and forth, wasting our time? Why not keep a constant eye on our biggest investment?"

"Investment? You've spent our very last penny on that hotel. We have nothing if it doesn't pan out, nothing but our land and coach inn. Sell everything but the house, Hamish, but I'm not going to live on top of that mountain and get marooned every winter. And you shouldn't, either."

"Give me one good reason, aside from your unfathomable dislike for Steptoe Butte, why I should move back to the house."

"I want you at my side."

"You have that at the hotel."

"You're too old to live up there."

"What do you mean, too old?"

"The house is well fixed for hard winters. Plenty of game there and water and tools and provisions. We've good privies nearby and a year's supply of wood. We know how to live at home. For heaven's sake, we almost perished up there in January."

He looked askance at her. "Too old?"

"If things had got much worse, Hamish, I know you, you'd've tried to go off farther, hunting for food and firewood. You're coming seventy-six this year, my dear. Some one day soon you will have to admit that you can't do what you used to do. God knows I can't. But you'll kill yourself trying to make it right."

"If that's true, then how can we expect to operate the hotel?"

"Hire a man to run it for us. Shutter it in winter, if we must. If we sold out everything but the house, we could afford to do that."

"I'm no capitalist tycoon, and I have no intention of letting someone else run me business and take away the fun. And I'm not running back and forth from the inn to the hotel every day."

"So we live apart?" she said.

"If that's what will suit you, then we live apart," he said. And he let the team have their heads and trotted them the rest of the way to the butte.

That night Libbie said she was going down at dawn to open the house and make it ready for her return to living there. The twins came out from their farms for a couple of days to help her set up housekeeping. She had a team of horses and a mule, a cow, and some hens. They put by a supply of wood, hay, and feed. They restocked the cold hole, inspected flues and chimneys, and repaired corral fences.

Mindy finished school at the academy that June, and she returned to live with her mother. Lettice and Angela said they would visit as often as they could, but the girls grieved to be parted. Holly began coming out some weekends, and, whenever she did, she took her mother to church in Thornton on Sunday. Libbie looked forward to those times. She put in a good garden the first summer. The mail came through sporadically, delivered by Josiah Brickell on his gelding once or twice a week, but she often would be alone at home with her small menagerie.

Cashdown busied himself with repairs and upgrades to the hotel and grounds. He added a wide covered porch that wrapped around three sides of the building. It gave partial shade during the hot, cloudless summer months, provided a lounging veranda for guests, and would shield the lower sides of the hotel from snow come November. He went down to work his orchards each day after briefing the staff and Libbie, if she was there, on the day's agenda. Below, he also expanded the corrals and sheds, and redesigned and rebuilt the water wagon. As always, he cared lovingly for his horses, mules, tack, and wagons. He met hay and feed dealers, who filled the storage sheds, and he ordered supplies from Colfax or Farmington. He gave up pursuing the railroad.

At night he would greet each guest in the dining room and

invite them to join him after dinner in the ballroom upstairs. There they could dance and enjoy the beverages on offer, and later a midnight lunch, no extra charge. If the Wheatland Whirlwinds came out for the night's festivities, he would add his pipe or fiddle. If not, he would tirelessly play solo for the dancers. He was last to leave the ballroom, and he would make his final inspection rounds of the hotel before turning in.

As summer went on, Cashdown was so burdened by labors at the hotel he rarely went to Colfax. Sam McCroskey came down from Farmington in July, shortly after the second anniversary of the hotel's opening. He said he wanted to see how the telescope was faring, to make sure it did not need recollimation or a new eyepiece. He silently appraised the site and operation as he wandered around. Cashdown was delighted with Sam's visit. He posted a hastily-penned sign, Closed for Private Showing, on the Panorama Room access door, and they passed an hour alone, talking and peering through the telescope.

"Looks like your enterprise continues to do well." Sam measured his words.

"Aye, the house is full more nights than not."

"Must keep you busy."

"I'm sorry I haven't been up to see you, Sam. Haven't even had time to get into Colfax much and haven't seen the boys in months. But you have to serve the crowds, y'know."

"I had no expectation. You have your hands full."

" 'Tis true."

"They say there's always a high time in the after-hours. Still serving up oysters?"

"Oysters, aye. Everyone loves a good oyster stew at midnight. Or fried."

Sam refrained from saying what he had also heard around Whitman County: some gossips had started calling the hotel derisive names. They said that it had cost him everything, his savings and herds and lands, and now it appeared to be threatening his long marriage.

"Well, we keep talking it up in Farmington and Belmont. Nobody comes through that doesn't hear about Hotel Steptoe."

When Sam left, Cashdown stood at the edge of the stone yard, hands in his pockets and shoulders slumped in fatigue. He watched the horseback rider diminish into the gathering dusk below.

Chapter 28

Pinky came out at the end of the summer. It was the slow season at the Ponderosa and the last weekend of the high season at Hotel Steptoe. She had not been to the butte since the grand opening. She pulled a package out of her trap before the stable man took her team below.

"Pinky, how grand of you to come!" Cashdown rushed off the porch to greet her.

"I drive out because you never come to Colfax, so I'm thinking, he must have troubles, or he is busy making a fortune at his hotel. Maybe making a fortune gives you some troubles, too, ha-hah."

"My fate is to be just one step ahead of trouble and two steps behind me fortune. But come in and have lunch with me."

Over omelets and beans they chatted about business and Silas's growing reputation as a restaurateur and how the railroads were changing things.

"I told you long time ago, Cashdown, everything is change. Sometimes changing too fast, and we rush too much to keep up."

"Aye, seems like I've been rushing too much this summer. It's easy to make mistakes then."

"Some people say Hotel Steptoe has new name. Cashdown's Folly I heard. That's good, not mistake, huh? I like it having your name. But I don't know so much about folly."

"You don't know what it means?"

"Maybe it means something funny?"

"A folly's a kind of stage show, like a silly entertainment."

"Hmm, silly. But not something bad, huh?"

"Well, folly *can* be bad, it can mean something like a foolish mistake. But they don't mean that. I've heard it before. They're probably just hankering or envious about our music and dancing upstairs. But business is good, and I'm making money. Not a fortune, but it's paying."

"Oh, okay, that's good," Pinky said. "Me, too. I bought my husband."

"You did what? Who?"

"Most Chinese men buy wifes to get married, even here. I got plenty of money now, so I thought, by Jesus Christ, why not buy Wang-an? He is a good man, strong, works hard, always clean, quiet. I need husband so other men leave me alone; he needs wife so he's not alone. He's getting old. So, we decide . . . decided getting married is good idea."

"Wonderful indeed! When did this happen?"

"July. We had some problems before wedding. Goddamned county judge says, 'You can't marry. Man has no papers, woman, too, and she has bad past.' " Pinky imitated a man's gruff, low voice. "So, James and Orestes just help us go to the state court and get permissions. Two weeks go by, and county judge decide it's okay, we can get married. Hah! Orestes sure can tell them something, by Jesus."

"I shall get you a wedding gift. We must have a celebration. We'll close the hotel for a day and invite everyone out for the party."

"Oh no, no thank-you. We keep it quiet. Lots of people thinking we are some Chinese gang, just control all Colfax business. Making too much noise is not good for our hotel and laundry. We need to stay sneaky, ha-hah!"

She handed the package to Cashdown.

"What's this?"

"Got it in San Francisco last time. Good luck Chinese silk."

"It's beautiful." He looked puzzled but said nothing further.

"Maybe you can give it to Libbie. She can make nice dresses with it, very pretty."

Cashdown's eyebrows pinched. "For Libbie?"

"They say she lives at Steptoe Station Inn, but you live here. I say that's goddamned crazy."

"Ah, that's it. Thank you, Pinky. This silk material will be sure to please Libbie. But she is happier at the house, and I need to be here at the hotel, just like you at your Ponderosa Hotel—you live there and always keep watch on everything, don't you?"

"Okay, I understand. Not my business anyway. I just want happiness for you. Being sad is no good for your headaches."

"Thank you, Pinky, but it's all fine. Now back to my son-in-law. Does he well have the kitchen under control?"

They chatted over lunch and spent an hour at the telescope before Pinky left for Colfax.

When Libbie came up to Hotel Steptoe the following Monday morning, she brought a letter for Cashdown.

"From Callum, looks like," she said.

"Ah, about time."

"Did you write to him recently?"

"I was waiting for him to extend a hand," he said sheepishly. Cashdown hastily opened the envelope and saw there were three photographs with Cal's letter. He recognized the images, though he hadn't seen them in twenty years.

My dear Brother, the letter began.

All is well, here on the Willamette. Our Nephews and I have sorted Adelia's farm, and have it productive once again. She is well and happy. I have a small holding, above the river, to grow hay and market crops. It does well, but I'm thinking of going up to British Columbia, one time soon, and expand my businesses. If I do such, I shall come see you, on my way.

I enclose three photographs Adelia wished you to have, as they are of your Liam and the Twins. You might remember the time, shortly after we arrived in Oregon, and we all sat for pictures. William kept these, which perhaps you thought were lost, and Adelia wished you to have them after he passed.

It would please me to no end, if you were to write back, and tell me of your news. I well miss all the Family there, and much enjoy knowing what each is doing now. Please give my fondest greetings to Libbie, Mindy, and all the other Children, and to our various Friends, on the Palouse. Remember your faithful Brother,

Callum

"Well now, isn't that a right big surprise. Remember these pictures, Lib? Cal was right, I'd thought they were lost." He handed the photographs to her. The images of their three eldest sons as children, each seated next to a cardboard fern, were fading like sun-bleached newsprint.

"What a lovely gift," she said. "Shall I keep them at the house? They will preserve better in the album."

"I suppose," he replied. He took her hand and gazed beseechingly at her. "We could bring the album here, along with your things, and we could enjoy living together again." His voice was trembling.

"It's too hard on me, Hamish. I am truly sorry, believe me. But I won't be moving up here."

"You never approved of the hotel, did you, Lib?"

"That's beside the point. It's me. I don't sleep well here. It frightens me, this peak. And I have no peace through all the good months, and the winters are impossible. You need to reconsider and move back to the house." She said this last with such conviction that Cashdown averted his gaze and just shook his head.

"So, there it stays," he said.

That night, sitting on his great Black Forest chair, he composed a reply to Callum.

Dear Brother Cal, it was splendid to receive your letter. Thank you, and Adelia, for the photographs of the boys. Libbie has placed them in our album. I am made happy to learn you've been farming and helping Adelia get on her feet. Also that all of you are well. It would be a godsend for you to come up here, I haven't seen you in so long that I fear you would not recognize your old brother. My beard is long and white as linen now, and my skin is saggy and crinkled. But despite my aging body and my aches and stiffyness, I am well and full of gunpowder for each day to begin.

Cal, you should consider the opportunities here on the Palouse Prairie. It's a glorious country, fruitful and populated by good people in fine towns, and now we have the railroads crisscrossing the land to serve our shipping needs and for convenience of passengers. You could expand your businesses here. If you have such an inclination, I would make available to you our Steptoe Station inn and mercantile and the house very favourably priced. I find it hard to imagine a more suitable arrangement for us in our old age than for you to be living and farming right nearby. Nothing would give Libbie and your nieces and nephews more happiness, either. Give it some thought, will you?

Love, from your Faithful Brother, Hamish

He took his letter with him for posting the next time he rode to Colfax. As it was Friday, Orestes was at home from the college for a few days. They met for lunch at the Ponderosa Hotel, and Pinky came down from her balcony lookout to join them.

"How's business these days, Pinky?" Cashdown rose from his chair to greet her. Orestes stood at attention, as if royalty had entered the room.

"Oh, two of my favorite gentlemen return, both with best manners! Business picking up, better than last year. People come to your hotel yet?" The three friends moved their chairs close together as they sat down. Pinky and Orestes ordinarily spoke in commanding voices, Pinky's piercing as a rookery, Orestes's like the low notes of a church organ. But they knew Cashdown was losing his hearing, and they didn't want to disturb other patrons with shouted conversation.

"Some. They're just starting to come out. Not as many as this time last year, but we serve different kinds of travelers, don't we, you and I."

"In your kind of hospitality business, it undoubtedly takes as much patience and persistence as routine hard labor," Orestes said.

"Aye, as Pinky will attest, it's a hard business. But so far, so good."

"So far, so good," repeated Pinky. "But Hotel Steptoe needs new publicity."

"What's wrong with our publicity?"

"People say, start saying, Hotel Steptoe having some ghosts. Some say Indian boys."

"Nae, never heard such." He turned a questioning face to Orestes, eyebrows raised.

Orestes shifted in his chair. "I've heard stories of that sort, and a few other rumors derived from superstitions."

"Other rumors?"

"I overheard some visitors say they saw little fires flaring up on the slopes of the butte at night. It was here, in Silas's dining room, and a group of elderly ladies were right over there talking about their outings to Steptoe. They gossiped with outspoken delight and bewilderment, and, I admit, I listened. One said she heard the cries of wild animals in the darkness, and they speculated whether it might be wolves or some other creatures. Another said she heard chanting and drums, as if from a great distance."

"Someone's trying to damage me business."

"So far it appears to be innocent. These things always happen, Cashdown, when something new appears. They imagine more threat than what's plain and obvious. Recall what it was like when the electric telephone arrived. Work of the devil, attracts lightning, they said. But what I heard wasn't quite plain and obvious. Those fine ladies never said they'd stayed at Hotel Steptoe. They might've been on a tenting trip at the butte before you bought it. They might've heard those stories from somebody else. They might have been entertaining one another. The problem for your enterprise is that you don't know where they got those stories, and you don't know how many people they've told them to."

Pinky followed with interest. "People say, many years ago said, my Ponderosa Hotel was filled by ghosts, dead men buried under basement, so at night ghosts walk through my hotel to find murderer. I say horseshit, but it doesn't stop. They still say we have ghost of dead man under my hotel. But business is better and better, so don't worry, Cashdown, just do good publicity."

He did worry about the rumors, enough to tell Libbie about them a few days later and ask her if she thought some publicity to counter them would help. "Maybe something in the *Gazette,* or a handbill to circulate around the towns?"

"You might be giving the rumors a cloak, dear. We don't know their extent, and publicity about ghosts and howling animals might plant seeds in people's minds."

"I suppose," he said. But he continued to be uneasy about what people in Colfax had been saying, and he began eavesdropping on his guests' breakfast conversations.

His preoccupation with the rumors was interrupted when another letter from Callum arrived. For over a year Josiah Brickell had refused to bring mail to the hotel, dropping it off instead at a box by the stable below. Cashdown wanted the mail handed over personally from postal carrier to him, no unreliable stable hand involved, so he offered Josiah a lure. He was invited to stay for a free lunch, complete with a glass of Lewiston's fine red wine. For Josiah, the lunch and wine quickly became the central purpose of his ride out to the hotel. As he was leaving one June afternoon, he stepped off the porch, thanked Cashdown over his shoulder, and headed for his gelding.

"You did bring mail, didn't you?"

"Oh, must be getting forgetful!" He fetched a bundle of envelopes from his saddlebag and handed them over. Cashdown waved goodbye absently, as he riffled through the mail and pulled out the envelope from Oregon. He sat on the edge of the porch and eagerly opened Cal's letter. It was brief.

> My dear Brother Hamish, Yours received and much appreciated. I am still thinking of exploring British Columbia. I well know the Attractions of your Palouse Prairie. You make a generous offer, as you have done, many times before, but like before, I fear it would not work out well, for me. I hope you have success in selling your Place. Perhaps I shall see you and the Family, if I come through, on my way North. Your Hmbl & Obd't Brother, Cal.

Cashdown slapped the letter on his thigh. "Now ain't that a rude kettle of fish!" he said to the cloudless sky.

Chapter 29

The summer of 1891 was not profitable for Hotel Steptoe. The number of people arriving for overnight stays dwindled, possibly because the long depression dragged on, as deflation and unsettled currency policies had reached Whitman County. It might have been because the Palouse prairie towns where rail lines converged were growing into cities with diversions of their own. Cashdown at first blamed the weather, which had been unusually dry and hot from May through autumn. Creeks dried up, wells went down, and some crops failed for want of moisture. Wildfires were larger and longer lasting than usual, so the scenery was shrouded in smoke. He also wondered secretly if he had already exhausted the potential clientele for his hotel. When he went to Colfax to consult with Pinky, she said her business was about the same as always during the summer months.

"But not so many Colfax people stay now," she said. Her lodgers were mostly travelers, she pointed out, and more people were coming through on the trains as Pullman and Palouse City expanded like mushroom beds. The military college in Pullman had welcomed its first class; and the new state-funded Agricultural College and School of Science was approved, prompting speculative development near the proposed site. In Palouse City the timber harvests from Idaho's mountains were processed at a new mill, and the brickworks had expanded to keep up with increased building demands.

"I've been wondering if the wellspring of me guests hasn't dried up," Cashdown confessed. "What's changed around the Palouse, Pinky? Hope it's not our reputation." He looked uncharacteristically doubtful.

"You have reputation like gold; everybody loves Cashdown, no problem. Maybe electric keeps people home now, some people got real good lights, stay home, play cards, read books, do *nuganug.*" She flashed her impish smile. "Maybe more places like Reaney Hall getting so goddamned popular, I don't know."

"How's that?"

"In Pullman? Upstairs of Reaney's Pullman is some kind of opera house. People love it, by Jesus—now everybody goes to opera houses for entertainments."

"Ah, I heard about it. Even Orestes and Lucie have been over there for the opera. I hope the attraction doesn't spread."

"Yeah, well, got a goddamned big opera house in Walla Walla; people say soon opera houses open in Oakesdale and Rosalia. Maybe you need better events at Hotel Steptoe, maybe something different from operas."

"I'd bet you're right. I'll give that a good think."

Late in the season Lycurgus stopped at Hotel Steptoe on his way to Lewiston for the annual gathering of newspaper publishers. He hadn't seen Cashdown for nearly two years.

Lycurgus quipped, "As the Moscow Swedes say, 'You don't know what will happen before evening.' "

"Aye, regrets for aging so, and I'm still trying to figure out what's already happened," Cashdown retorted. "I'm trying to revive me hotel business. It's been slow this year, Gus, and it's unclear why."

They talked over dinner about the devastated markets and Washington's economy. Lycurgus said his views were distorted by the rapid successes of Spokane and his newspaper. “It’s booming up there, Cashdown. People flowing in, new businesses popping up. We’ve even started a city transportation line by rail, and we’ve put in better street lighting than San Francisco has. The population has more than doubled just in my six years there. Since the fire, we’ve built a magnificent downtown, Cutter designs up and down the center of the city. Granite and brick and ironwork structures, all of it. You should come up and see it. And stay with us.”

“Soon as I restore health to this business. Pinky thinks I need a new attraction, something besides just hoteling. So, I’ve started publicity for the ballroom as a place for weddings and club gatherings, political gatherings, too, if they’re of the right sort.”

“Any luck?”

“We’ve had some interest, seen some improvement. Getting it sorted.”

The events did help balance accounts for the year. For a time, Hotel Steptoe became known among Colfax and Palouse City couples as a choice venue for wedding receptions. It always was a grand, festive time, people said. The annual meeting of the Washington Daughters of the American Revolution convened as guests for two days in September, and before the first snow fell Hotel Steptoe was host to a group of retired army officers who had served at Fort Benton and Fort Walla Walla. But after the cold weather set in and the snow piled up on Steptoe, all arrivals ceased. Libbie stopped coming to the hotel each day. She began to pay a visit once or twice a week, and occasionally Cashdown would ride to the house for a meal, and to have Libbie update the hotel’s accounts, if the trail was passable. She was alone at the station now, as Mindy had returned to Colfax to live with Lettice and Angela. Libbie could not deny her that happiness.

In November Cashdown staged a party at the house to celebrate Libbie's seventy-fourth birthday. Pinky, Lettice, Angela, Mindy, and the Perkinses rode up together from Colfax, followed by Silas and Charlie. The twins and their families came in from west of St. John just as Liam, Tessie, and Miranda arrived from the north. It was a noisy affair, and for a few hours all seemed almost as it had been half a decade earlier. Cashdown presented Libbie with a new mangle, claiming it was superior to anything at Hotel Steptoe. Pinky said it was newer than what Wang-an had at his laundry. The children gave their mother seed packets and new planting tools for her gardens. She shyly thanked everyone for coming to honor her, but her smile was subdued, and she was quiet and downcast much of the time.

Alone together after the farewells had been said and the last visitor rode out the main gate, Cashdown and Libbie talked affectionately of the children and grandchildren, argued politely about keeping or selling the property, and struggled to boost each other's flagging spirits. Nothing was resolved, and Cashdown headed back to the hotel in a dark sleet, hunched in the saddle like an injured man.

The winter passed much as the previous one: wave after wave of storms from the west, repeated campaigns to bring up water and dispose of sewage, dwindling firewood and food stores, and too much idle time for Cashdown and the three workers he retained through the gloomy season. He divulged to his cook and his stable hand that he missed Libbie's company; and, whenever the weather permitted, he went down to check on her at the house. Each time he did, he stayed until after supper and tried to convince her to join him at the hotel. But she was adamant, repeating her argument that she was no longer fit for the rigors of winter at the mountain top. It was not that she did not want to be at his side, she would say, but she could not do as he wished. He continued to say he was needed at the hotel, to safeguard their investment and supervise the workers.

For only the second time since their beginning in Wisconsin, there was no family Christmas celebration that year. All roads were impassable for the holidays. Cashdown was temporarily marooned at the hotel by a heavy snowfall, as was Libbie at the house. The twins snowshoed the dozen miles from Trayton's farm to see their mother through the worst of it.

But the spring thaw came early, blackbirds and migrating ducks arrived in late February, and green-up started before the equinox. Cashdown was busy repairing the winter damage and laying plans for new publicity and improvements at the hotel, when Josiah Brickell came up for lunch and carried with him a letter from Callum. It was even shorter than the last one.

> My Dear Brother, I have decided to come North. I shall leave our Kinfolk, here at the Willamette, after Easter, April 2nd. I should arrive at your Cottonwood Creek location abt. two weeks following. I am looking ahead, with joy in my Heart, to seeing the Family again. Perhaps we can talk then.
>
> Your Brother & Hmbl Svt, Cal

Cashdown flapped the letter on his thigh. Josiah was discoursing over his sandwiches and wine about the challenges of rural mail delivery, but Cashdown was lost in thought. Later, he rode down to the house to show the letter to Libbie.

"Says here he's returning to us. What a godsend, Lib!"

"Don't get your hopes too high. Remember, earlier he said

he was off to British Columbia. He might just be passing through."

"But it's clear as the day. 'I have decided to come North.' And there's no mention of further north, nothing of British Columbia."

"We'll just have to wait and see, won't we." Libbie turned and gazed out the front window to the main gate.

"Just in case he *will* be remaining here with us, maybe we could offer him the house and inn again. We'll give him a thief's price. Though I'd bet he can well afford any."

"And where does that place me?"

"He could help you here. You'd become a lodger of a sort. We could put that into the bargain for him."

"Oh, Hamish. I'm too tired to fret over this now," she said, twisting her wedding band.

Cashdown got the news out to Liam and Tessie, Elbourne, Trayton, Charlie and Holly. Charley sent notes to Ferdie, Laura, and Willie, who told Jack and Frances. Mindy learned of Uncle Cal's coming when Holly drove her out to the house Easter Sunday. Cashdown attended church at St. John with Libbie, Holly, and Mindy—it was the first time he had been to services since they settled on the Palouse prairie. On the way, they talked about the expected visit.

"Pa," Mindy asked, "when do you think Uncle Cal will arrive?"

"I'm expecting middle of April, likely the sixteenth or seventeenth, just as he said. He's always been very punctual." Cashdown held the reins loosely. He had dressed in his best suit and stovepipe hat. Robes covered laps against mud splatters.

Holly said, "Shouldn't we have a gathering? Maybe we could bring everybody up to the hotel for a day." She sat next to her father on the surrey front seat.

"Aye, I've been thinking so. We could have the pipers out;

he'd like that. But I want him to lodge at the house. We've much to talk about."

Holly poked her father on the shoulder. "What could two brothers have to talk about? It's only twenty years you've been apart." The three women laughed, but Cashdown looked over at Holly disdainfully.

"We've written letters, we have. We've kept up. Cal just needed to be away a good long while. Sort things out, you know."

"Holly was joking, Hamish," Libbie counseled. "But it's a big change for him to write us about his visit. We should just be thankful."

Cashdown thought a moment before replying. "I warrant the best thing to do is treat him as always, part of the family. Ease him right in, as if he's only been down to Walla Walla to buy seed."

"We shall see," Libbie said.

"I'll pray on it, when we're in chapel."

Notice went out to the Musgrave clan to be ready for Uncle Cal's arrival around April 16. The hotel staff started spring cleaning early, and Cashdown spruced up the reception area and porch, clearing away the residue of winter and laying a new rug in the hall. The pipers reserved the seventeenth for a celebration at Hotel Steptoe.

But Callum was no longer as predictable as he once was thought to be. On the sunny afternoon of Tuesday, April 12, 1892, he rode through the inn's entry gate on a tall sorrel gelding. On his head was a chocolate bowler, and he wore a three-piece striped brown suit under his duster. He dismounted and strode up to the front door of the house. Libbie was alone.

Chapter 30

"Oh, my God! Callum! What a surprise. We weren't expecting you for another three or four days." She was wiping her hands on her apron. "Come in, come in."

Cal took off his derby as he entered the front room. "Hello, Libbie," he said. His smile was easy and confident.

"Well. So. Here you are." Libbie fidgeted and offered her hand. Cal took it, then cautiously pulled her toward him and briefly hugged her. He released her and looked around the room.

"Yes, at last. Nice place here. Things sure have changed in my absence."

"It's been a long time, Cal. Sure, this place has changed, is changing, everything's growing, towns and railroads and lots of new people coming in, in spite of the Depression. Why, we've all the modern conveniences here, you know, even streetlamps in Colfax, and telephones and electric in the houses. Some of the better houses, not here yet, but soon it's going to come out this way. And of course all the children are grown now. Liam's the president of the bank in Oakesdale—did you know that? Married the McBride girl, Tessie, and they have a family started, little William and our granddaughter named Miranda. And the twins have a big farm over near Endicott. Elbourne is married, and I'm sure Tray will be soon, too. Hamish probably already told you all that. The girls are all doing fine, Holly and Laura, and, oh here I am nattering on so. I'm sorry. I just didn't expect to see you this soon."

"It's all right, Libbie. I want to hear all about the children, especially about Mindy."

"Wouldn't you like to freshen up? I'll fix us some coffee and cake. Do you have effects?"

"Just my saddlebags. I shipped all the house goods and personal things ahead. I'm earlier than I'd said because I took the train. Found out I could put the horse on it, too. We didn't leave Oregon till day before yesterday. Yes, I'd like to wash, if I may, and a coffee would suit me just fine. Hamish around?"

"He's up at the hotel, but I expect him any minute now. He comes down Tuesdays so I can do the bookkeeping on the weekend receipts. He'll be so surprised." She showed Cal the way to the washroom and went to prepare coffee.

As she was putting the pot on the stove, Cashdown came in the front door. "Lib, has your mail come yet? Josiah didn't come up for lunch."

She called from the kitchen. "No mail yet. Callum just arrived. He's washing."

"So that's who's riding that fine beast outside." He entered the kitchen and shouted for Cal. "Where's me little brother?!"

Cal came out, straightening his waistcoat and tugging at his sleeves. He extended his hand to Cashdown.

"Hello, Hamish," he said evenly. The serene, self-assured smile animated his face.

"Ah, Callum, ye took us by surprise! How splendid." Cashdown looked up at his brother and gave him a hug and backslap. "You've filled out a bit, eh?"

"Adelia has fed me well, yes. We're both a bit filled out, Hamish, you and I. Happens over time, if we're lucky enough."

"Aye, not just gained an extra pound or two, but look at us, we've both gained snow on top, too, and crinkly all over. And I, for one, am shorter. Ah, here's coffee. Oh, and cakes, too. Thanks, Lib."

They sat at the kitchen table and talked about Adelia's farm and her children and the saga of adjusting after William's death. Libbie and Cashdown told Cal about each of their children and grandchildren. Josiah Brickell came by with the mail, and Cashdown took the packet for the hotel. As the sun neared the western horizon, Cashdown was still holding forth about all the developments that had happened since Callum left the Palouse.

"Ah, there's so much to tell you, Cal. About my old friends from Colfax and around, and the orchards, and the fate of the Paluses. I wish to hear all about your adventures, too. We'll make time to talk it out shortly."

"I should be getting supper on," Libbie interrupted.

"They're waiting for me at the hotel," Cashdown said. "Dinner's already in the ovens, and there'll be plenty for us. Why not come up for the night? We have only three rooms booked." He looked pleadingly from Libbie to Callum.

"That will be fine," Libbie replied.

"I would greatly like to see your hotel," Callum said.

Cashdown prattled all the way to Steptoe Butte. As they reached the top in waning light, Callum looked around at the darkening quilt of farms and bare rolling hills and strips of forest below. The mosaic seemed to extend to infinity, as night and lowland mist set in, blurring the horizons.

"Surely do have a view from up here," he said.

"Aye, that's why I chose the site. And the peak has a sacred history. It's always attracted people by its wonders. Reverent people, ambitious and visionary people."

Libbie muttered, "Indians. And you."

Callum turned a questioning look to her.

"That's all that used this peak before us. The natives," she said. "They sent their boys up here in some Indian ritual to turn them into men. The boys were supposed to have visions. But ambitious? Hah."

Cashdown appeared to be not listening. He already had dismounted and was headed for the hotel entrance.

Over dinner that night, Callum related details of the years they had been apart. He began by asking their forgiveness for his abrupt disappearance. "My anguish," he said, "was made unbearable, especially as I learned of Henry's death. But by then I'd drifted away from the Willamette as if in a dream and was in Colorado under the influence of two grifters who had lured me into some crimes. Eventually I was detained and served my time in a Durango jail."

He didn't say what caused his arrest, but he was deeply embarrassed about it. He was troubled by many things, he said, and he spoke of them to a Jesuit missionary, who asked him to help in his ministry to an Indian tribe south of Durango. There he met a shaman, and that encounter changed his life.

"Inside and out, top to bottom, changed everything," he went on. "That holy man helped me learn how to see into myself and understand why I had been so broken as a person. He led me in his rituals, and those rituals revealed the truth of our place in the firmament. The Great Spirit, I learned in the visions, is in everything and connects us to each other like rain to wheat to the soil below. We all are the Great Spirit equally. And we all are our own selves, different from one another. We have a first duty, I learned, to live out our own lives to the fullest. Now I understand myself, and I can understand the sanctity of this mountain."

Cashdown had been silently listening. He wiped his beard with his napkin and stared at his brother with a look of fearful disbelief, as if he'd come across a threatening new species in the forest. He paused before responding.

"It's a comfort, Cal, to learn what's happened to you over the absence. But meantime we've built up our holdings, twelve hundred acres now, put in all the orchards you saw around the butte, moved most of the livestock over to Elbourne's and Tray's farms or sold 'em off, and built this hotel. It takes all our time, entertaining guests and overseeing the staff and repairs and whatnot. The farmland's for sale. Lib still runs the house below. Has her team and a few hens and a cow to care for, and she does the receipts for me, sometimes helps out here. So, we both are strapped for time. Neither of us is getting any younger, either. You, you look young and fit, if I do say so, much fitter and straighter than I am. I'd wager you could settle in right comfortably and be a grand success."

"Sounds like you're a salesman trying to close a deal of some sort, Hamish," Callum said.

"We've been thinking maybe you'd like to take over the house and merc and the whole farm. I might even throw in the orchards. It's a fine house, and the mercantile will do a bang-up business for outfitting, soon as the rail line comes out this way. I've been agitating for years with the railroad people to bring it in, and they've been very promising. We could offer you a wondrous low price, so long as you'd keep it hushed." He grinned expectantly.

Callum stared attentively as Cashdown spoke. The serene smile returned and softened his face. "That sounds very generous of you, Hamish. I shall give it careful consideration."

" 'Course, Libbie would still reside at the house. You might take her as a special boarding tenant. She's a splendid cook, you know."

Callum sat a moment in inner deliberation, his eyes wandering above their heads. He appeared to be asking himself questions. Cashdown poured more wine.

"I see," Callum finally replied. "That's quite unexpected. I'll think on it for a bit."

Nothing more was said for the next few days about Cashdown's offer. Word went out to round up the family for the reunion. In the meantime, the brothers toured the orchards, rode their horses to every corner of the farm, and inspected the old inn, the house, and the outbuildings. Cashdown described the virtues of every aspect of the property, pointing out how profitable the farm and inn were and suggesting ways they could be restored and improved. Callum listened and nodded, sometimes uttering a compliment on the sturdiness of a shed's construction or the wise placement of a fence line or fine condition of the mercantile store. But neither spoke of Cashdown's offer.

It was a festive reunion when the family gathered at Hotel Steptoe on the fifteenth. Cashdown invited paying guests to join them in the ballroom, but they politely declined and returned to their rooms or wandered around the peak. Callum had brought small gifts for each of his nieces and nephews: wafers of Colorado gold, "to start your fortunes," he joked. They in turn gave him mementos of the intervening years: photographs of weddings and graduations and awards won at fairs, handcrafted bits of tack, and, from Mindy, two small drawings of their first Palouse farm under construction. One showed Uncle William's carriage in the background.

They partitioned off half the dining room and enjoyed an afternoon-long feast. Everyone told tales about their relatives and competed for the loudest jeers. Cashdown concluded with his story of Great-uncle Ricketts.

"Built up a fantastic circus show, Uncle Ricketts did—lions and tigers, kangaroos, and most especially his grand stallions. They were trick horses, sixteen hands and more, and he could turn cartwheels on top of them at a full canter. It was the first horse circus in the world. He traveled all over Scotland with his show, don't you know, even down to London and the South. Then he aimed for America. Came over to Philadelphia, and his horse circus was an instant smash, every performance sold out, and every newspaper wrote about him. People had never seen a leap like his. They'd string a line four meters off the ring floor, and he'd ride his stallion at a wild gallop right for it, and he'd be standing on the withers and leap over the line in a tumbersault and land on his feet, still at a full gallop, and the people would cheer madly. So, on he went to other cities, opened a second circus in Baltimore and made a fortune. But then, in the blink of an eye, both his shows burned down flat in the same month. No one knows why. Ruined him financially, so he headed back for England. On the way, his bark got caught in a bad storm. The ship was dismasted, and it rolled. They found the hull but never recovered old Uncle Ricketts."

"Now we know why Pa loves to entertain so much," Ferdie said.

Liam added, "We've heard that many times, Pa, but before it was only three meters high he'd jump, and he rode a mare!"

When the hooting and clapping died down, Cashdown suggested a little musical entertainment. They trooped upstairs to the ballroom, and he handed a concertina to Callum, took up his fiddle, and they began to play the old songs. The rest listened and clapped for a while and then began dancing. The wine and cider flowed, the dances were rollicking, and the brothers grinned to each other as they made the festive music together. The celebration went on until the children and their families prepared to leave for home. Callum stood on the porch and, murmuring, "Farewell, darling," he hugged each niece and nephew and kissed each baby.

The next morning, when Cashdown came down to the kitchen, Callum already was seated at the table. He had eaten breakfast and was packing fruits into his saddlebags.

"Going off for a ride?" Cashdown asked.

"Time for me to get moving north, Hamish. I'll be late if I don't start now."

"Late for what? What about our offer?"

"I've considered your kind offer, thinking I might perhaps change intentions. But I have decided it would not be right for me to remain here, don't you know. I prize your willingness to have me back, but I'm headed north, above the border."

"Not right? Why not, man? It's a fine opportunity, and all your kin are here."

"There are fine opportunities across this continent. I learned while I was away that I can be my own man, and now I must continue to be my own man. Now, Hamish, I know *how* to be my own man. You've always known how, always had ideas, and you've always been in the lead. And I was at your side, as your aide de camp. In everything. You've been a protector and champion for me, but you wrapped me in a comforter that became a cloak over my life. If your cinch was slack, I tightened it. If you offered a lure, I took it. I was pleased to please you and be your inferior because I had no other life; I was both derivative and grateful. I've needed to get out from under the blanket of your force and your ideas and protectiveness, dear Brother, into the sunshine of my own life, to recover my soul. I've since made that choice."

"And what will I tell the family? What about Libbie?"

"Tell them the truth. And I wouldn't think it's a wise idea for me to take Libbie as a boarding lodger in her own house. There are many reasons why that would be unfair. You'll find help for her, if she needs it."

"Well, that Indian surely gave you a new voice. Never heard you speak so. But I wish you would reconsider and stay. Why go today?"

"I am taking the train at Spokane and directing shipment of my belongings for the change to another line. I meet up with friends there, and we'll travel to the Okanagan to claim our new properties. You are welcome to come up for a visit, once I'm settled there. I'll notify you by post."

They silently walked down to the stables, where Callum tacked his horse and made ready to leave. "Give loving farewell for me to Libbie, won't you?"

Cashdown was stunned. His cheeks were red with anger, his eyes cinched with remorse. It was as if he had lost his brother, not to death but to something more insidious and equally final. He nodded, embraced Callum, and turned away. As he trudged up the steep road, he heard Callum ride off in the bright April morning. All the way up Steptoe Butte, Cashdown watched the diminishing figure of the man and horse rising over hills, vanishing in ravines, and rising into view again, until it disappeared. He decided against trying to follow him through the telescope.

Chapter 31

The creeks receded into their courses, farmers began planting the new crop, camas flowers came into full bloom, and Cashdown made the hotel ready for the summer season. June, he thought, would be a banner month, what with all the weddings coming up.

But he would be disappointed. Few wedding parties asked for bookings, and the only club gathering at the hotel that summer was Lycurgus's newspaper editors and publishers, who stayed overnight on their way to their annual meetings in Lewiston and Colfax. He told Lycurgus all was fine, bookings would pick up when the dry heat of high summer subsided.

"Me brother Cal came through in April," he said, "for a reunion. He is now constructing a grand estate in the Okanagan, starting life anew after making his fortune in Colorado."

Lycurgus said, "You're a restless clan, you Musgraves. You're not going off to join him, are you?"

"Nae, nae, Libbie wouldn't hear of it. Besides, there's the bairns, the grandkiddies."

"It must've been a joy to see Callum once again. It's been a long time."

" 'Tis true, Gus, I've missed him greatly, and it was a grand visit."

"He didn't want to settle hereabouts?"

"I offered him the house and inn, and the mercantile, all at a thief's price, what's left of the acreage, too. He turned it aside, didn't want to have Libbie as his housekeeper. Maybe he thought he'd have to take care of her someday . . . who knows?"

"Did he say why he declined the offer?"

"He's changed, grown up you might say, during his absence. Has his own ideas now."

Lycurgus looked skeptical. "You'll miss him again, won't you?"

"Hard to say. I'm relieved he's gone, because he needs to please himself. If he'd stayed here, taken up me offer, it'd be awkward. Alone in the house much of the time"—he shook his head—"just wouldn't be right."

It just wouldn't be right: he would mutter that judgment to himself again and again.

The heat of July and August gave way to a dry autumn. The ninebark turned early to bronze and amber, and the wheat stubble became a golden fur on the fields. Evenings brought a welcome chill, wedges of geese barked overhead on their way south to the river valleys, and ground fog often hovered far below the peak in the mornings. Still the bookings did not come, and Cashdown fretted constantly to learn why Hotel Steptoe was being shunned. He puttered in his orchards, groomed and worked the horses at the stables, and spent hours at the telescope identifying and recording regional points of interest. He visited Libbie at the house. Whenever any of the children came up to see him, he would confide somberly that Libbie was losing her vigor. "She's showing lassitude," he'd say. The children vowed to go see their mother more often thereafter, and he was comforted.

Cashdown thus was caught off guard by the news Josiah Brickell carried one mid-October noon. The sky was threatening a cold rain, possibly snow—the temperature hovered a bit above freezing—and the wind was gusting from the west. Josiah rode up the butte as if being chased by brigands. When they reached the top, his little gelding was lathered and wheezing like a bellows. He jumped off, tossed the reins to the stable hand, and ran into the hotel, all the while calling out for Cashdown.

"Josiah. You're in a mighty rush for lunch today. But I'm glad you came, even late!"

Josiah was panting as he grabbed Cashdown by the shoulders. "Cashdown, sit over here." He gestured to Cashdown's throne. With an unsure grin, the old man sat.

"There's been a tragedy, Cashdown, a calamity," Josiah said.

"What's happened, man? Whose calamity?"

"At the house. Libbie didn't come out to fetch as usual. I banged on the door and peeked in. Couldn't see nobody, so I fixed to just leave the mail on the kitchen table, as I done before. Nobody was around. On my way out, I caught sight of something stirring down near the barn, just by the big door. Looked like some cloth flapping in the breeze." Josiah started to blubber. "Libbie's housedress. She looks to have passed out right there going into the barn—must've been fetching something. But she was gone, Cashdown, not passed out but passed away. She was gone. I'm just awful sorry."

Cashdown stared incredulously at Josiah. He shook his head vigorously. "Nae, nae, you have it wrong. Probably she's just fainted from exhaustion. She always overworks herself. You just leave her there, lying at the barn door? Good God, man. I'd better go see to her."

"I checked real good, Cashdown. There's no breathing. Her eyes were just starey. I thought you should be the one to move her. I'll go with you."

Cashdown shook his head again. "C'mon, then."

It had begun to spit snow when they dismounted at the inn and ran to the barn. Libbie lay crumpled over one arm, a leg turned askew, her mouth and eyes agape. Cashdown knelt by her inert body, felt her neck and wrist for a pulse, placed his cheek next to her open mouth, and then drew her eyelids closed. He stayed kneeling over her for a few moments and then rose, looking mournfully at Josiah. He began to weave, as if the ground were moving, and he was trying to keep his balance. He grabbed the barn wall and steadied himself as he stared out the doorway, across the entry gate, over the western fields, and away to the far horizon.

Josiah put his arm around Cashdown's shoulders. "Let's go on up to the house. Figure out what to do," he said.

Libbie was buried at a glen east of the access road above the inn. It was the spot she and Cashdown had spoken about over the years as a good place for a family cemetery. The children had suggested putting her next to Henry's gravesite, but Cashdown said nobody had been to that place in many years, and, anyway, it now belonged to another family. There was a funeral, and in addition to the Musgraves, dozens of people from Colfax and nearby towns and farms attended. Some congregants from the St. John church, most of the neighboring farm families, and a small group of suffragist friends came to pay their respects. Lycurgus and Genevieve came down from Spokane by train and horseback, and Cushing and Belle drove their gig up from the Snake. Pinky, Lettice and Angela, Orestes and Lucinda, and James and Jenny joined them. Dr. Kenoyer officiated.

When the coffin was lowered into the grave, Cashdown tossed in a handful of gravel, turned his back on the gathered mourners, and walked down the road to the house. Later, Holly and Charlie set out food and drinks and rounded up the people for a remembrance of their mother's life. People told amusing anecdotes about her, laughed a bit too loudly, and praised her kindnesses and diligence. Cashdown sat silently by the stove.

Liam and the twins drew up chairs next to their father and chatted quietly with him.

"It's a terrible loss, Pa. But she must have suffered dearly in recent months without telling anybody. That'd be like her. So her passing must've been like a release from pain, don't you think?"

"Perhaps so, Liam, perhaps so. I hadn't seen." His voice was hopelessly weary.

Orestes joined Cashdown and his sons. He placed a hassock in front of Cashdown's seat and squatted down on it facing Cashdown. He placed his hand on the old man's knee and squeezed for emphasis as he spoke.

"Such is the inevitable turn of the wheel, my dear friend. My heart aches, but I can scarcely guess how much more does yours. You have many friends and admirers, Cashdown. I am chief among them, and you must remain mindful that all of us stand by to help and guide you in the days and months ahead of us. I wish I knew what to do now to give you comfort."

Cashdown struggled to organize and understand what he'd just heard, as Orestes continued to gaze at him. Tears came into his eyes, brimmed, and ran down his cheeks into his beard. When he finally replied, his voice was a barely audible croak. "Orestes, what in goddamned hell am I going to do?"

"Go on and go on, amigo. What else is there? Just remember her and go on. That's our duty and our blessing."

"What would *you* do?"

"We are two differently feathered birds, Cashdown. My example might be useless to you. But me? If I were in your circumstance, I would sit with my grief for a while and then sell out, everything—the farm and orchards, the inn and mercantile, the hotel, most especially the hotel—and I would fly away. Maybe move to Colfax, where friends are at hand and something's on, day and night. I might travel a bit, too, take the trains to San Francisco or out to Chicago maybe. You, my friend, must reckon with your need for company and dancing and music. Pinky's looking for an entertainments director. You could preach to people, teach people, lead people. You might even think about politics. But it's too soon to decide."

"Why especially sell the hotel?" He appeared to perk up, and he wiped his eyes.

"The rail line isn't coming out to Steptoe; you now know that. And soon your paying guests will come to nothing. It's about to be bypassed by new changes in the towns and cities. I'd sell out before its value is entirely gone."

"Changes. Oh, aye." He paused a beat. "But why? Why must there always be changes?"

"People are fonder of convenience than toil, and away from home they're generally fonder of innovation than repetition and routine. You get fewer and fewer returning clients because it's toilsome to reach Hotel Steptoe, and once they've seen the innovation of peering through your spyglass, they're off searching for some new diversion. All the towns hereabouts, up and down the states and territories, now have dancehalls and operas and offer convenient entertainments, sometimes next door to a good hotel, or even part of it. It's the railroads, Cashdown. They've brought changes that are reweaving the fabric of life in towns."

Cashdown thanked Orestes, patted his hand, and said, "I'll try to get it sorted."

They stood and embraced awkwardly, before Orestes joined the crowd and prepared to leave for home. Cashdown turned a sad face to his sons and trudged off to his and Libbie's bedroom. Before he left, Orestes pulled Liam aside and said, "I think your father will be just fine. He won't forget this loss, but he's already thinking about his future."

Sam McCroskey was in Olympia to testify about education

when Libbie's funeral was held. He came down from Farmington two weeks afterward to deliver his condolences.

"Our hearts are broken over the loss of Elizabeth. And for you, Cashdown. It must be too awful to bear just now," he said.

"Thank you. 'Tis heartbreaking indeed," Cashdown replied, his voice beginning to quiver, "and made all the more so because it was sudden, such a surprise. I never expected . . ."

"How can I help?"

"Just being here is fine enough, Sam. You've always been a balm, no matter the situation. Just being here. That's what me brother Callum should've known. I wrote him right after she passed and haven't heard a word. And, of course, if he'd taken up our offer, he would've been here, and none of this would've happened."

"It's not like you to resent and blame, Cashdown. We have to make amends or be consumed by bitterness."

"I've never dwelt on the past for long, but, for the first time ever, I have no plan for me future, and it sets a person adrift."

They were at the Hotel Steptoe, and Cashdown was pouring tea as they smoked cigars. Sam said, "You're still strong and ambitious. You'll surely have many years to devote to new enterprises. You're a fine orchardist. Why not expand the fruit production? You could create new varieties and find new markets. Rail lines are going everywhere now, so you could ship fresh. You could hire young men to do the hard labor, and you'd have time to enjoy your reading and go on visits to your grandkids."

"Rail lines, aye. I warrant they've been me bane. I'd sooner travel by mule or afoot than get near a railroad train again. No, this peak is home and destiny. I just don't know what to do to keep it going at a profit. And the old eyes are too weak to do much reading."

"It may all be too soon to think about. Take your time,

because it takes time to regain your feet. If you have faith in nothing else, have faith in yourself. And be patient."

Sam promised to return whenever he could get away from Farmington. Now that he was principal of the school, it could not be as often as he would like. Cashdown rode with Sam as far as the orchards, where they said their farewells. Afterward, he walked through the apple and pear trees and reflected on Sam's admonishment to be patient. He scrutinized the last blowdown fruit he found under the trees, pocketing some that looked still edible. Despite Sam's advice, Cashdown knew it was not his nature to be patient, and he already was plotting schemes to revitalize his hotel.

By the time he returned to his horse, he had considered several possibilities and rejected half of them. He could convert the ballroom to a roller-drome, but that would require shoring up and refinishing the floor and buying skate-boots. The roller-drome in Cheney already had failed. He thought of bringing in traveling theatrical and vaudeville shows; but he realized he knew nothing about booking and marketing entertainments of that sort, and they always stopped first in the towns. He might buy a fleet of bicycles and offer guests cycling tours around the Palouse prairie, perhaps guided by the children of local farmers. The success of that idea would be limited by weather, of course, and it would necessarily be seasonal. Besides, many of the guests he had had in the past could not ride a bicycle. He also thought of creating an art gallery, or a museum of oddities and antiquities, or a gambling casino. The latter three remained on his mind as he returned to the hotel. Over the next week, from his morning tea until his last dram of whiskey before bed, he sketched and scribbled and figured in his notebook, intensely testing ideas.

Late in November the last guests of the year arrived, half a dozen missionaries from Vancouver on a tour, they said, of the diocese and hinterlands. They booked five days and well enjoyed the hotel's hospitality, happily staying up each night with Cashdown over port and cigars. They traded stories, and when they learned of the hotel's need for a new attraction, they conferred and suggested he might instead turn it over to the church to be used as a convent. He could profit by such a move. Cashdown told them he "would give it a think."

After the missionaries departed, he began to ruminate about what he saw as Cal's willful avoidance. He kept asking why, why would he not come to her funeral? And, behind that, why did he refuse the generous offer of the inn and the rest? Could it have been an aggressive shunning? He recalled something Orestes told him many years ago: "You can't guess what's in a person's mind or heart. The best you can do is ask them. It's easier to discern the truth from what they tell you than without it. That's why we bring witnesses into courtrooms."

He decided to write to Callum.

My Dear Brother Callum,

It now has been near to two months since my darling Libbie's passing. It remains hard to accept, but I am sustained by work at the Hotel and the ministrations of the children and friends. We hosted a group of missionaries from around the Western Region, looking for opportunities in the growing areas for their superiors. The Palouse, it seems, attracts all sorts.

I wish it had been sufficient to attract you and hold you here with your family. I wish you would tell me what convinces you it is right and proper to refuse the offer from your brother that is nearly a gift of property. I wish you would also say why you still haven't seen fit to come pay your respects to your deceased sister-in-law but remain aloof somewhere in the North.

I recognise my impatience with you, and for that I apologise, as it is not my purpose to chagrin you. But you said you are now your own man. A grown man knows and performs his duties, a grown man renders comfort as his family needs, a grown man honourably does what is difficult and does not take the easy way. Perhaps you believe your absence in some way achieves all this. I do not, and I wish you would tell me why, so that I might reconsider.

We both are old men now, Cal, and thus in a time of life when we should be sharing the company of one another. Far as I know, we are both without a helpmate now, but each could be a solace and anodyne in our coming age of decline. Please give it some thought, and please write back soon.

Your loving Brother,
Hamish

It would be a long time before he received any response from Callum. Through the silence of the long winter, Cashdown devoted his idle time to making detailed plans for remodeling the ballroom. There was much work to finish before he could open his gambling casino in the spring.

CHAPTER 32

As the weak sun dropped over the hills west of Colfax and temperatures dipped below freezing, Cashdown walked to the town stables, groomed and fed Buster, and ambled idly up and down Main Street by the rising river. Before he returned to the Ponderosa Hotel, he saw Lettice Wheeler approaching. She was on her way home from the academy—now reconstituted as the Colfax Preparatory College—burdened with an armload of portfolios and ledgers and smiling absently.

"Ahoy, Lettice. Grand to see you," he hailed her.

Her smile broadened, and she looked him up and down appraisingly. "Well, Cashdown, you seem downright jaunty, especially after such a hard winter. How are you?"

"Getting along fine, thank you. Help with those files?"

"Oh, no, thank you. I'm used to it, my homework. What brings you to Colfax tonight?"

"Ah, I came to see Orestes, to set up me new business. But he's at Walla Walla, so I'm here till tomorrow. Pinky's out of town as well. Perhaps you'd care to join me at dinner?"

"Third choice? I'd have to think that over carefully." Her expression turned coy.

"Didn't know you'd be about. It's mandatory, don't you know, to ask Pinky, when she's here. What say?"

"In that case, it would be my pleasure. Mind if the girls come, too?"

"All the better, that."

Lettice, Cashdown, and the two young women sat stiffly at a round table in the Ponderosa dining room. Mindy was twenty-four, Angela a year older and now engaged to be married. Cashdown could have been taken for the grandfather of the reverent family, with his long, white beard and wispy hair, his creaky voice, and his black stovepipe hat under his chair. Lettice wore her church-going crinolette dress, and her grey-streaked auburn hair was swirled around her head like a loose scarf. Mindy and Angela smiled and listened, as if obeying prior injunctions, hands folded demurely in their laps: daughter and granddaughters, eavesdroppers might think.

Cashdown asked about progress at the college and the competition from new campuses in Pullman. Lettice assured him all was well, and there were plans to start a course in stenographic writing soon. They talked about changes in the morning newspaper's editorial slant and the chances that the rhododendron would become the state flower.

As their meals arrived, Lettice turned serious. "Cashdown," she asked, "how are you getting along at the Hotel Steptoe these days? Business okay?"

"Slow now, but the season's not yet started. I've a plan to boost interest."

"Your new business? And you have a plan—a secret plan, or can you tell?"

"Nah, 's not secret, and I should get to advertising it. I'm going to open a gaming room, turn part of the dancehall into a casino," he said proudly.

Lettice looked aside in thought. With a bright smile, she turned back to him and said, "You still have the spyglass, don't you?"

"Aye, me telescope. That continues. People marvel over the views and still come out to look through it."

"Maybe we could arrange day trips for students at the college to come use your telescope. We couldn't stay overnight, of course, but it would be something the new science school in Pullman can't offer. And we could pay a fee."

Cashdown said that would be splendid, a jolly time. But Lettice's face betrayed a suspicion that problems lay ahead for his new attraction.

Orestes confirmed her suspicion. He returned from his teaching post the following morning and met Cashdown in his office above the *Gazette.* "Let me get a clear understanding of what, in particular, you intend to offer, Cashdown. You say 'casino,' but I need to know what activities would be on hand."

"Oh, you know, games of chance, cards, maybe Chinese games like the spreading-out one that Pinky talks about. Like that, maybe more, depending."

"And the payouts, how would that be set up?"

"Oh, a little fee to play, they'd throw into the pot. Fee would go to the house. No big bills, no skimming for the hotel."

"I must tell you, my friend, even that is not possible. Not legally."

"They're doing it down in Walla Walla, raking in a fortune."

"I wish I could lie to you and make you happy. But the truth is they'll soon be shut down, and you can't do it."

Cashdown stared at Orestes as if he were facing the Jabberwock. "But I need it; the hotel can't go on without it. It's no good just to have rooms and a telescope anymore. People aren't coming. I'm losing money, more each season."

"I dislike intensely having to bear disappointing news, Cashdown. But all forms of gambling are outlawed by the Washington Constitution. And now there are laws on the books that lay out the penalties. They're not lenient in the least."

"Well, what in the bloody universe am I supposed to do now?"

"I'm sorry, amigo. Your alternatives are to find another attraction or live with your losses. Or undertake something entirely different."

Cashdown thanked Orestes for his legal briefing and paid him before leaving. They went for a drink at the Ponderosa and talked of other things.

Back on Steptoe Butte, he burned all his sketches and business plans for the casino. He brooded and mulled and sullenly went about his daily chores and rounds at the hotel. His staff avoided him whenever possible. When he was in a pouting silence, he was like a thunderhead on the horizon. After two months with no guest arrivals, the head housekeeper left. The spring rains ended, and the long dry season began, and still no overnight guests came. Cashdown told the rest of the staff—the day clerk, the stable hand, the cooks and maids—they could leave, too. The widow Mrs. Hanrahan, one of the cooks, said if he would continue to pay her she might stay on through summer's end. The others solemnly packed up their belongings and quietly departed. All except Jasper Philpott, the stable hand.

A party of twelve came to Hotel Steptoe to celebrate the Fourth of July. It was a day outing for the two families, and, even though they wouldn't be staying the night, Cashdown was overjoyed to welcome them. He gave them a guided tour of the observatory, took them through each room of the hotel while relating the history of the antique furniture and rugs, and walked them down to the orchards to show his apples and plums and pears already ripening. Before they departed, Mrs. Hanrahan prepared and served a four-course meal. Cashdown saw them off from the porch, tearfully waving goodbye until the last of the group disappeared below.

After classes at the preparatory college started up in September, Lettice and one of the teachers brought a group of schoolkids for a day of scrambling around Steptoe Butte and gazing through the telescope. They asked Cashdown to lecture about the geographic points of interest and the history of settlements that could be spied from the Panorama Room. He happily complied. He entertained the children by playing his hornpipe and telling stories. He had tea with Lettice and the teacher while the students were on a treasure hunt around the peak, looking for bits of gold or silver; they would find only veined basalt and mica flakes.

Lettice was saying, "The rumor in town is that business is poor everywhere. I hear you've let your workers go, it's so bad."

"Aye, 'tis bad," Cashdown replied. "It's the economy being run into the ground by the nobles of industry back East. Depression, they're calling it now. Lots of banks going under. Affects every honest farmer and western business."

"I'm sorry your new plan didn't bear fruit. Will you be okay?"

"Oh, aye. Got me savings in gold; never owed anything. Converted it and withdrew everything in May. Son Liam's holding it. You?"

"We'll make do. As long as Colfax College is open, I can work. If it closes, I'll find something else. We have many friends in town now."

"It's the same for me," the teacher said.

Cashdown's sourness expanded. "We need to get rid of the fools in Washington, in the government. And get rid of the bloody big capitalists, excuse me. Bankers and railroad barons and such. They don't care a button for the working person, not the politicians nor the money men. And we should replace the lot of 'em with strong, hardworking, sensible farmers and laborers. And teachers, aye. Get away from the gold business, too. Cleveland knew better."

"But you're a capitalist, Cashdown. And you've kept your

savings in gold."

"No choice. I've had to, what little I've got."

The financial panic would deepen and soon would be labeled the Great Depression of 1893. It would spread to countries across Europe and South America, where its germination and roots lay deep in Argentina's economic and banking soil. The Hotel Steptoe would see no more guests that year, and Mrs. Hanrahan would leave in October to work at a rooming house in Pullman.

Only Jasper the stable hand remained over the winter. He had his choice of rooms, and he would keep Cashdown company through the long stretches of snowstorms and isolation. Jasper had limitations as a companion. He was illiterate and dull witted, knew no more of the wider world than hay farming and tending to horses, and was interested mainly in whittling animals with his pocketknife. Though middle-aged, he had always been a loner and had few social graces. Nonetheless, they prepared meals and ate together, swapped chores to avoid boredom, and often worked together at the stables and orchards whenever the weather permitted. Jasper listened patiently to Cashdown's stories and complaints, no matter how repetitive or lengthy. It was a dreary winter, amid months of freezing temperatures, modest snowfall, and a late runoff.

Spring finally came again, and soon the sides of Steptoe Butte were splotched with buttery clusters of arrowleaf balsamroot. The seasonal birds returned with their cheering calls, and Cashdown watched the green-up on the region's farms through his telescope. To Jasper, the old man seemed neither happy nor unhappy to greet the new season. He understood Cashdown's carping talk and disappointed mien as merely bad temperament. By the end of March, he too was prepared to leave the hotel.

"Mr. Musgrave," he said, "I figure I can get steady work in Palouse City. At the flouring mill. They still pay real good, last I hear. 'Course, that was fall. So, may I leave?"

"Good Christ, man, you're not in prison. Yes, of course. I'll pay your wages and give you a favorable letter, too. Say farewell afore you're off."

Perhaps Jasper merely forgot to say goodbye, but he silently vanished like a Palus ghost. Cashdown was alone on the mountain, and the high season was about to begin.

The crowds never came. The guest registers for April and May were blank. The Catholics came again for a brief tour in late June, just for the day. This time they brought the bishop, who was still searching for a site, they said, to establish a convent and rest home for aged nuns. The bishop's secretary suggested to him, just within Cashdown's hearing, that the hotel might also be useful as a retreat site, which might help defray costs of maintaining and provisioning the convent. The bishop, whose cassock and cape were spotless and smoothly pressed, appeared intrigued by the idea. He whispered something about the impressive furnishings. As he moved about, he clasped his soft, chubby hands before him, as if in prayerful humility.

Cashdown escorted the entourage on a tour of the hotel and the outbuildings and orchards below. The hotel's small farm and stable had chickens, pigs, goats, and a cow, and a shed large enough for a dozen horses. A vegetable garden was flourishing just above the orchards. The bishop saw that a convent and retreat center could be supplied from sources immediately at hand.

Before they left, the bishop and his group asked Cashdown to sit with them for a sherry. Cashdown poured while they chatted among themselves. When he was settled in his Black Forest chair, the missionaries went right to the point.

"We would like to make you an offer, Mr. Musgrave," the secretary said, glancing toward the bishop.

"Offers are what makes the world go 'round, Father," Cashdown replied. He grinned broadly. "I'm all ears."

"We observe that your hotel is not serving you well as a business enterprise, but it might serve adequately for our purposes," the secretary said. Again he averted his eyes, as if he were speaking to the bishop instead of to Cashdown.

"You want the hotel, Father. And how do you propose to achieve that?"

The bishop interceded. "We would make you whole. We've heard of your reputation, and, credit being such a devilish burden now, the diocese would cover your original investment entirely in cash. Gold, if that were necessary."

Cashdown flashed his eyebrows, stroked his beard, and looked around the table. He sipped a bit of his sherry. He tapped the tabletop with his fingertips. " 'Course, I'd need the furnishings and me telescope and such. When were you thinking of consummating this offer, Your Holiness?"

"We could prepare a formal offer within weeks. We must first obtain concurrence of my superiors, but they strongly favor development of eastern Washington. If we were to reach agreement, I'm confident that we can sign the papers before we're too far into autumn."

"And what, Your Eminence, were you thinking would be a fair price? How would you value me years of investment? There was great cost in labor for many dozens of men, all the materials and provisions, just building the structure and roads."

"I'm not the Pope, Mr. Musgrave. The valuation would come first, and we could determine a price together. By reasoned discussion. But you will make a profit."

"Suppose I give it a good think and send you a decision by

post—a counteroffer, so to speak?"

A smile flickered across the bishop's face. "Say within two weeks?"

"Aye, that would be about right."

They rose, and the troupe immediately left for Colfax and Pinky's hotel, where they would stay on their way south to the Snake.

The only other guests at Hotel Steptoe that summer were a few day visitors who came out to satisfy curiosity. They had heard stories about a strange hotel atop the most prominent peak on the Palouse Prairie. Some people said the place was haunted, others that it was sacred and had rejuvenating powers. Josiah Brickell still came up with mail from time to time.

Cashdown consulted Liam about the bishop's offer. Liam said the bank was fighting for its existence, and the bishop was right about credit. He advised his father to take the offer and move to Oakesdale. Cashdown replied that most of his children lived nearer to Colfax, but he would continue to see Liam and Tessie and the grandchildren anyway. He committed to nothing and said he'd talk it over with his old friends before deciding. Liam later told Tessie he was surprised by how aged his father looked, at seventy-nine, and how oddly unsure of himself he'd become. She reminded him that Libbie was gone, and everything in his world was now changed. "Besides," she said, "he's adored that mountain and the amusements and all the people ever since the beginning."

Liam replied, "I got the idea Uncle Callum didn't take to the mountain. Or maybe it was the hotel he was puzzling over. Probably wouldn't have done what Pa did. But he should sell it."

A week passed, and Cashdown went to Colfax to seek the counsel of his friends. Luckily, they all were in town, and he invited them to lunch at the Ponderosa. Pinky asked Silas to have the kitchen prepare something special and join them. She sat with James, Orestes, Silas, and Cashdown. Sam McCroskey was back to help Lettice revise Colfax College's curriculum, and shortly he arrived at the table. The server brought out a sparkling wine and some steamed Chinese appetizers. The friends talked of the devastated economy, businesses going bankrupt, and the lack of investment money for Colfax's expansion. Cashdown interrupted the gloomy discussion.

"I've some news of interest to tell, interesting for me, anyway."

"We could all use a measure of good news," Sam said.

"Not sure if it's good, but the bishop from Fort Vancouver came by a week ago, with his priests, same as were out last year. They're thinking of buying the Hotel Steptoe, he says."

"What would they do with it? The bishop doesn't run boardinghouses," James said.

"Or observatories," Sam added.

Orestes asked, "Do you think they're serious?"

"Nunnery of some sort," Cashdown said. "Place to stable the elderly sisters. They've brought in a lot of those girls, and one day they'll be too old to work. I think they mean it."

"Lucky people all someday get too old for working, even you, Cashdown," Pinky said.

"Aye, but that day's not here yet. They've offered me a cash deal, a profit guaranteed, fair price to be set together later. But I don't know about it. I'm not sure if I should sell."

Sam said, "What's making you hesitate? You think they'll try to devalue the hotel?"

"I'm not clear on what's making me unsure, Sam, but it seems a strange future for me mountain."

"Once you sell out, sadly enough, it's theirs to do what they want. What do you mean, strange?"

"Oh, maybe those sisters might be better served by living

nearer to the city."

"Sam's right, legally," Orestes said. "Choose your buyer wisely, the saying goes. But I suspect there's something about abandoning the place that troubles you. You'd miss being up there and having people come up to stay with you, I'll wager."

"Can't imagine what else I'd do, where I'd go. I do miss the people, but they're not coming anymore anyway. Aye, that's been a bother. I'm up and down and up, you know that."

"Your answer's there," Orestes said.

Cashdown paused a long while before replying. "Well, I confess, whenever I see m'self at a new place, I picture a view, always a certain view. On the near horizon there's the peak. Wherever I go, I must be able to see Steptoe Butte, even if there's church people aswarm on it."

While they were eating, the friends decided the solution would be for Cashdown to sell Hotel Steptoe and what was left of the farm and inn and relocate somewhere nearer Colfax. Then he could farm again and become master of festivities at the Ponderosa Hotel. Of course, any place he chose to buy would have to include a clear view of his beloved pinnacle.

Cashdown admitted it sounded appealing. " 'Course, I'd have to take the instrument and the rest of me treasures."

A few days after the lunch, Lycurgus came to Hotel Steptoe on his way to meet his publishers' group in Moscow. Cashdown told him about their friends' ideas for his future, and Lycurgus added his approval.

"That's a fine way to resolve your predicament. I'll be grateful if you'd let me help. Just ask. You going to do it?"

In response, Cashdown grinned broadly, handed him two letters, and asked him to post the letters in Moscow. One was addressed to the Nesqually Diocese in Vancouver; the other was to *Mr. Callum Musgrave, In Care Of General Delivery, Penticton, Brit-*

ish Columbia, Canada.

To the bishop he had written:

My advisors have concurred it would be agreeable to receive your offer to purchase Hotel Steptoe. We must make a sale contingent upon my retaining ownership of the optical instrument from the observatory and contingent as well upon my retaining ownership of the orchard plots surrounding the east and south faces of Steptoe Butte. All furnishings, animals, and related equipment also shall be removed, at time of sale. This, as previously discussed and agreed upon.

If these contingencies are acceptable to the Diocese, I shall be pleased to meet with you or your representatives at the soonest date to settle on an agreeable price.

Thank you.

He labored long in composing the letter to Callum. His dejection over the hotel had subsided, now that a new horizon was opening for him. He still rankled at the distance his brother was keeping between them, but he didn't want to alienate him further—with each passing year he wished more ardently for Callum's company. He also wanted Callum to be aware of the potential resolution to his business problems, which he believed had been brought on by the railroads and the national depression. He began cautiously.

Dear Brother Cal,

You perhaps have wondered how we've fared through the many months since Libbie's passing. It has been difficult for me to learn how to get along without her, but I have been blessed with the succor of the children and grandchildren. Also, many friends have been at my side.

I've continued to operate the Hotel at Steptoe Butte, but this year has been the worst for business since we came up here from Oregon. If things go on this way for long, I shall be saddled with an entirely useless hotel and a failed business.

Luckily, I've received an offer for purchase of the business, lock, stock, & barrel. By the time you read this, Hotel Steptoe could be officially owned by the Diocese of Nesqually, and I shall be living at a new location. The farm is up for sale, as well, and we've some interest in it already. I've an eye for a bust farm on a slope just south of St. John, half closer to Colfax, some eighty acres and an established orchard and good well and outbuildings. From there, with the Clark telescope, I can keep watch over the goings-on at Steptoe. I can ride to town in half the time as now, a favourable aspect.

It will be grand, Cal, and the only improvement I could wish for is your presence and company. I haven't heard word from you since well before my last. Please write and tell me when you can come down, even just for a brief stay. Also, tell me if you'd want me to hold off sale of the farm, just in case you might consider having it yourself. I would rather it go to you than to anybody else. Write me at General Delivery Colfax.

Your loving Brother,
Hamish

The bishop's secretary replied immediately. The diocese would send a delegation, including the bishop, to Colfax to discuss the price and, if agreement was reached, to sign the necessary documents. The letter asked that Mr. Musgrave designate his legal representative and banker and suggest a place for meeting. Cashdown quickly replied, naming Orestes as his attorney and Liam as his banker.

A second letter from the diocese arrived a week later. The secretary wrote that the bishop would like to have all the furniture, rugs, and tapestries, as well as the vases, urns, sterling serving sets and utensils, samovars, paintings, and the telescope—for the pleasure and support of the sisters, should they one day be settled at Steptoe Butte. They might wish to create a museum of sorts, he wrote, as an attraction to their religious retreat. A most favorable offer, full credit for the accoutrements, and eternal gratitude of the diocese would be forthcoming.

Cashdown immediately wrote back with his refusal. The bishop, he said, had agreed in principle to his original offer of just the hotel, stables, and garden areas. He would welcome a delegation only under those conditions.

A week passed, then another, and no word came from the diocese. Nights were growing colder, and, when Cashdown carried out the slops in the grey dawn, ice topped the waste barrel, a skim at first and then a thick lid that invited blows from an axe handle. As the first pellets of snow arrived with the final cold rain of the season, a brougham bearing the bishop and his secretary arrived at Hotel Steptoe.

"Have you rethought the offer, gentlemen?" Cashdown ushered the priests into the ballroom. They sat by the massive, nickeled stove, and Cashdown served tea.

"We could discuss the property, Mr. Musgrave, but in fact we were just passing on our way to Colton to confer with Father Frei, and we thought to pay a social visit. Are you still thinking of selling?"

"We're always interested in beneficial transactions, Father, anything that well benefits both sides of a sale and purchase."

The bishop blew silently on his tea and sipped pensively. "It's most peaceful here, very quiet. No guests just now, Mr. Musgrave?" he said.

"The season ended not long ago, Your Grace."

"Hmm," murmured the bishop. He searched around the ballroom, as if he were taking mental measurements. "And how do you use all this space between the seasons? Must require some considerable labor to keep it warm." He returned his attention to his tea.

"Close it off." Cashdown clenched his jaw and frowned.

The bishop shifted in his chair and smirked. "Our superiors were not terribly enthusiastic about the conditions you placed on the sale of the hotel, Mr. Musgrave. I was pleased that they approved—reluctantly though it was at first—ah, consented to our original thought of purchasing it for the sisters' residence and retreat. They were most insistent, I'm afraid, that the appointments be included in any such arrangement. To be frank, the cost of purchase and transporting all the furnishings and accoutrements required would be too burdensome, and I could not persuade them otherwise. So, there you have it."

"Aye, 'tis a sorrow, the cost of things these days." He paused and appeared to be pondering the burden the diocese would bear. The bishop sipped his tea and kept his eyes on Cashdown.

Cashdown continued pensively. "I suppose a person could live without some of the large fittings and decorations, maybe without the kitchen tools, those big sofas and chests. Maybe some of the carpets and such. But a person couldn't part with other things. Surely not the bar and long table, and the owner's suite entirely."

The secretary said, "The telescope?"

"Nae, never the telescope."

"Hmm," said the bishop. A long silence ensued, and Cashdown poured more tea. They sipped in silence for a time.

The bishop rose and turned toward the door. Over his shoulder he said, "Thank you for your hospitality, Mr. Musgrave. Pleasant to see you once more. If ever you change your position on sale of the hotel, please do write to us again. Good day."

The secretary followed him out, and they paused and looked back for just a moment before continuing to their brougham. The coach headed down the grade, and Cashdown was left alone, sitting by the great stove and listening to the rising storm.

Chapter 33

"The fathers wanted everything I own here," Cashdown said to Liam. "If they can't afford to replace a few furnishings, they surely can't afford the price to make me sell all I own."

Liam had stopped at Hotel Steptoe on his way back to Oakesdale from a bankers' meeting in Walla Walla. He and the rest of his brothers and sisters had begun checking on Cashdown from time to time, now that he was living alone on Steptoe Butte. Liam and Tessie had invited him up for Thanksgiving, and he had stayed for three days. But, otherwise, he was alone at the top of the butte. When days were dark with storms and he could not work outdoors, he would build a fire in the kitchen stove and a second in the great room and pace from one to the other, talking to himself. He would name the furnishings and paintings and tapestries he might sacrifice, against the time the diocese showed renewed interest in buying, each morning adjusting the list of sacrificed possessions until he was sure of his final position. He would caution himself about making too generous a counteroffer, and he rehearsed negotiations he would have with the bishop. He would pass hours in this reverie, until more wood had to be brought in, or it was time to feed the stock, or he became too hungry to further delay the next meal. But he was constantly alone now, with only his dogs to talk with, and no sign of the bishop's renewed interest in the hotel came. He began to grow used to his solitude and the silence from the diocese, and it led him to feel increasingly hopeless.

He made a capricious entertainment director at the Ponderosa Hotel, sometimes not appearing for weeks at a time. Despite his isolation at Steptoe Butte, he rarely undertook the ride to Colfax. Pinky never complained, and she told Silas she considered it a good sign that Cashdown showed up erratically with the band. "He must be happy now," she'd say. But Cashdown's ardor for parties and gaiety had cooled along with his expectations of a new offer from the bishop. It was a duty to go to Colfax for an evening's entertainment, and he never stayed overnight, preferring to ride nearly three hours in the dark to be home on the butte.

Rarely in his entire life had he been sick, but deep in December's long freeze he caught a cold. Sneezes and a cough turned into heavy congestion and a fiery throat. He took to his bed and got up only to ladle out more soup or make himself a tea and whiskey. He had dried balsamroot and willow bark on hand and added them to his teas for relief. But his illness persisted, and he grew weaker. When the twins came by just before Christmas, they found him incapable of rising from his bed.

Trayton rode to Colfax to fetch help at the Charity of Providence hospital. He returned seven hours later with Sister Margaret Joseph, a nurse whose Ursuline order had recently arrived on the Palouse prairie. Her medical skills and saintly compassion already were gaining her an admiring reputation. She examined Cashdown and immediately pronounced pneumonia. She used a tiny spoon for scooping powders from several vials she carried in her satchel. She mixed the powders in folded strips of newsprint, two dozen carefully measured out, and folded over the tops to seal the packets.

"Dose him one of these powders mixed with good water, just water, morning and evening, till they're gone. They'll help him feel more comfortable, and he'll breathe better." The twins paid close attention to her stern instructions. "Every hour or two, thump him on the chest four or five times, stout blows but not to break his sternum. Turn him over and do the same to his back, right about here." She pointed to the area on Cashdown's torso between his shoulder blades. "Keep doing that until I come out again. We don't want to take a pus bath."

Elbourne and Trayton looked at each other in bewilderment. Elbourne said, "So we must stay with him at all times?"

"I will remain here until day after tomorrow. After that he will need someone at his bedside, possibly for two or three weeks. Come for me if he makes a sudden improvement—that could well be a danger signal—and certainly when he seems to be healed."

The twins paid Sister Margaret Joseph and thanked her, went home, and arranged to return in relays. They cared for their father for the following two weeks, administering the powders and thumping his lungs as instructed. Gradually the sputum began to clear, his croupy cough subsided, and his oscillating fever steadied at normal. Trayton brought the nurse out again. After examining him thoroughly, she declared Cashdown quite recovered. She cautioned him against hard labor for the rest of the winter and showed the twins how to help keep his lungs clear by suspending him head down on a steep slant board a few minutes each day.

Before she left for Colfax, Sister Margaret Joseph lectured him like a schoolmarm. "You are well known hereabouts, Mr. Musgrave, and I hear testimonials from countless people who admire and have gratitude and affection for you, despite your irreverence. Don't disappoint them by allowing a recurrence of your illness."

Later, Cashdown told the twins, "Sounds disrespectful, but it was just her way of saying take care of m'self."

★ ★ ★ ★ ★

But it happened again the next winter, and the twins had the Ursuline nurse out again. They added Silas to their rotation of caretakers for a month. Cashdown recovered, but it was obvious that he was weakened.

Still no clients came to the hotel. During the dark months there was little work to do at the mountaintop but maintenance chores. Cashdown spent long hours at the telescope, gazing across the Palouse prairie, spotting game, and watching events at farms and ranches around the region. When the cellar was low, he would go hunting on the lower slopes and return exhausted but satisfied, with quails and rabbits in his game bag. Between storms he would care for the livestock in the pens and sheds by his orchards below. But he was alone, day and night, week after week, the solitude broken only by one of the children making a house call or a mail delivery by Josiah Brickell. He would be overcome by joy when someone arrived, and tears would fill his eyes as he watched a visitor go back down the mountain.

Working by himself around Steptoe Butte became risky, too, because for the first time in his life he suffered accidents. Early the following summer, he was knocked unconscious by his mule. Daydreaming while shoeing, he dropped his pull-off, which struck the balance hock and startled the animal. He told nobody about the injury, but it was days before he felt normal again, and he had lost several hours of memory.

The incident moved him to dig a hole. He chose a spot just west of the hotel, on the downward slope, where a few feet of topsoil had escaped the ancient scouring. He worked slowly, as he had lost much of his strength and endurance, and there was rock to break through. He had lost none of his persistence, though, and a week later he had a hole three feet wide by six feet long and five feet deep.

"What in the world are you doing, Pa?" Liam had stopped on his way to a bankers' meeting in Lewiston and found his father standing in the hole.

"Liam. Hello. Just made me grave."

"You wouldn't want to be buried here, Pa, would you?"

"Why not? It's convenient, no trouble to anybody. Just drop me in, Son. I've already started on a casket, down in the tack shed."

"Pa, you should be buried, when the time comes, next to Ma over at Cottonwood Creek, in our cemetery. We should all be buried together; we're a family."

"Aye, Son. We're a family. But who knows where you'll be when your time comes? And what about the others? Nothing's to say they won't migrate again. I've spawn all over the place anyway—the infant back in Wisconsin, little Henry out near St. John. They're family, too."

"They didn't have any choices, Pa. You don't have to choose here."

"Well, I choose this place. I came here sure it'd be a final resting place. I'm satisfied with that."

Liam shook his head and escorted his father back to the hotel for lunch.

On a frosty morning that autumn, Cashdown slipped while fencing at an icy creek by the orchard and fell into the water, hitting his head. He awoke after some seconds—or perhaps many minutes—had passed, when his horse nuzzled him. It took him nearly half an hour to return to the hotel, and he was wet and shivering cold. The pneumonia returned.

Some days later, before any of the family came by to visit, Josiah Brickell arrived with the week's mail. He wore a long storm coat and slouch hat against the intermittent snow squalls. His knock at the front door of the hotel got no response, so he walked around and peered in windows. Inside, it was silent and unlighted. A skim of snow was beginning to cover the rough boards set over Cashdown's grave.

Josiah let himself into the hotel and found it stone cold, no fire in the great-room stove, none in the kitchen. He hurried to Cashdown's bedroom. The old man lay in a rumple of bedding. Thick, yellowish phlegm crusted his beard, and his eyes stared balefully at the ceiling.

"Oh, good Lord Jesus," Josiah groaned. "Not again."

For years afterward, Josiah would sadly tell anyone who listened that he was the one who found both Cashdown and Libbie Musgrave upon their deaths. He attended Cashdown's funeral, along with nearly two hundred other mourners. It was held during a rare warm spell early in December. The cortege of wagons stretched back half a mile as they bore the casket from Steptoe Butte to the Cottonwood Creek cemetery. His boys, in a somber ceremony, had filled in the hole on the mountain's shoulder. They buried him next to Libbie near Cottonwood Creek and marked his grave with a tall granite obelisk.

Chapter 34

Liam wrote to Uncle Callum, describing the death and funeral and asking him to come for a visit. When spring finally arrived, Callum wrote back, promising he would. He arrived at Oakesdale a month after posting his letter. Liam and Tessie welcomed him, offered their hospitality, and prepared a room. He thanked them and said he would ride out to Hotel Steptoe the next morning. He apologized for responding so late and remaining so briefly: he had been establishing new business ties and had been away for some months.

"I wish to see how Hamish lived at the end," Callum said. He looked fit and energetic despite his age. "And I wish to have one more tour around the Palouse terrain before I head back. I'll stay over in St. John. Can't tarry, though, as I've urgent business in Vancouver."

"Vancouver? We thought you homesteaded near Penticton."

"My business now is in the city. And across the ocean. I'll see m'self out in the morning. Perhaps I'll stop in on my return, if I can reserve the right trains. The next time I come to the Palouse, perhaps we'll have a family gathering."

Liam turned serious, possibly fearing this might be his only chance to speak with his uncle of difficult and important matters. He asked Callum to sit in the parlor with him for a while and poured two brandies.

"I've wondered for long and must ask, why didn't you write to us after Ma passed?"

"Ah, yes. It's difficult to explain, Liam, but I shall try. I couldn't. I remained too confused about responsibilities, about mine and theirs. I came to see my absence was a loss to you and the rest of the children. When we were young—your father and mother and I, back in Ohio—well we, both of us, sort of took a shine to her. For a time, we quarreled over the other's attentions and resented our competition for her affection. Your father, I'm sure you know, is . . . was . . . a lively sort, even domineering, you might say. And he knew what he was about. I was quite the opposite. And, besides, I was in fact uncertain about how I felt. I then suspected I was just, well, peculiar. Much of this I cannot explain, but the awareness awakened somehow, beginning when I found I must rely solely upon myself in confronting men who had me in their clutches. There was nobody to come aid me, because I couldn't speak of it, and I had only myself to blame. I did it, and it was a freedom, and that awareness was followed by a decade of wandering and exploring, much of it with the wise man I told you about. He taught me that love is more than a flash in the heart. It is a recognition of your true need and a decision, and then a true commitment to that decision. And true commitment is possible only if you care enough for yourself to be respectful. It blossoms only through a long time of consistent acts, so I knew then what I would do. Men who held me before no longer would cause me fear and disgust. I would find love and commitment my own way." He paused a moment. "Don't know what else to say."

"I believe I understand, Uncle Cal," Liam replied.

"There's something else, might seem a little thing." He sat on the divan opposite Liam's chair, leaning forward with his hands on his knees. "The peak that seduced your dear father, and his hotel business—it was how we saw the world differently."

"The butte?"

"The butte, aye. Before, when I was receiving his letters about his desire for the mountain and then his orchards and the plan for his hotel, I thought it was all wrong. He wished to own it. But it wasn't his to own. I've thought long about this and believe now that your father could appreciate only its beauty and power and was incapable—he who I always believed was capable of anything, just like our father before him—he could not recognize the hypocrisy. It continues to remind me of the hypocrisy, that hotel. I wished not to confront that difference, and I could no longer do his bidding or place myself in a condition to have to refuse it."

"I understand, Uncle Callum." Liam patted him lightly on the arm.

"But I loved my brother dearly, Liam," he said, rising from the divan, "for all our lives. I'm just grieved that he dared to put his hotel on top of that peak. It should never have been."

Callum departed the next morning. He spent two nights at an isolated roadhouse near St. John; by day he rode out to the abandoned Hotel Steptoe. There he inventoried what was left of the furnishings and trim. There wasn't much. Elbourne had removed the Clark telescope the day following the funeral, and the rest of the fine imports had been taken by the family. The remaining furniture and décor—even much of the woodwork—had been scavenged by vandals. Callum also noted the scant items of worth remaining at the stables below. He walked the acreage and inspected the condition of the trees and fences. He would later send his lists to Liam.

The second night, alone at the roadhouse but for a hired houseboy, he drifted in and out of sleep and rose an hour before midnight. He was restless and paced around the dark rooms for a few minutes. He lit a lamp and went out to his horse at the stable. After quickly saddling up, he rode off in the dark. An hour later he was back in the roadhouse kitchen, where he made a fire in the stove to heat water. He stood in semidarkness at the frosty parlor window while drinking his tea and pondered an orange flare growing on the northeast horizon. It appeared like a pulsing eidolon, and he smiled with satisfaction.

In Oakesdale Liam was up late, assessing bank fees and auditing balance sheets, his family asleep upstairs. A throng of noisy people with torches passed before the house, and he rose from his desk to see what the stir was about. The crowd was moving up the hill from the center of town, talking excitedly and gesturing toward a pulsing red cloud to the south. Liam dressed and joined the last of the hikers. When he arrived at the crest, he found the gathering hushed, all faces turned to the coral dome on the southern horizon.

Clusters of people climbed above the rimrock on Colfax's north side to follow the glow. Some thought it was an aurora, some shouted encouragement to move higher and see more. At the top their awestruck gazes turned silently northward across the rolling prairie.

At about the same hour, three night-stalkers with their dogs had finished hunting on Moscow Mountain and were trudging back to their wagon in the dark. They joked about their coming penalties for arriving home in Farmington much later than usual. As they topped the last western hump of the range, they stopped short. The dogs whimpered and gathered at the hunters' feet. In stunned silence the men stared at the incandescent western sky.

On a hilltop above Alkali Flat a lone Palus elder paused one last time on his journey from the Colville reservation. He turned his horse toward the luminescence in the northern sky that had followed him for over an hour. He well knew its source, and he again recalled how Mr. Cashdown promised him fine fruits forever at Eeyomoshtosh and how he said he would honor and revere it forever.

Earlier that night, three young brothers from Thornton had been larking through the shadowy town, tipping outhouses at random. A merchant closing late at the settlement's verge fired his shotgun in their direction as they escaped, carrying a jug of whiskey and a packet of cigarettes stolen from his store. The boys scurried off to a friend's farm, where they sat in the barn to regain their breath and sample the whiskey. The jug went around twice before the oldest boy suggested they borrow some horses—it wouldn't be stealing, he said, if it's from friends and they return them shortly—and ride out to the derelict hotel on Steptoe Butte. Nobody would pursue them there, and by dawn they would be back in their beds at home, like all good boys. Besides, the shell of a hotel had become a place for young people to court in privacy, or do just what these boys were thinking, to enjoy a brief party.

They raced bareback across the rolling hills. It was a clear night with a waning quarter moon about to set, and they knew the way. One of the boys stopped along the trail and foraged some tree bark, twigs, and a long hank of dried grass. They dismounted at the summit and entered the cavernous structure, most of its contents and much of the woodwork—the moldings and chair rails and wainscoting—now missing. Even some windows and doors were gone. It resembled a dry, empty skull with bits of debris clinging inside.

It was dark as a mine in the dining room. The eldest brother said, "We need a torch." The youngest boy wrapped the bark and twigs inside a frayed handkerchief found on the floor and tied them to a stick. He lit the fistful of grass with a match and held it to the cloth until it caught fire. He stomped the still-glowing grass on the two large slabs of granite that once served as a stove hearth. The twigs and bark began to smolder and then fluttered into a cluster of little flames.

With the torch, the boys could examine the vast room they

were in. Names, initials, drawings, and cautions were scrawled or carved on the walls: "CB/AR," "Willie Love Sal April 22," "Beware Of Ghost." Strips of wallpaper had been torn off, and the stairs had gaps where treads were missing. The balcony above was collapsing; one section had been pushed out and hung like a broken pendulum over the dance floor. They looked out the windowless holes in the walls and saw that the moon had set, the sky now a river of starlight. It was a cold, perfectly clear night, and they felt the gathering chill. They collected bits of wood downstairs, and their torch became a small campfire on the hearth. They sat on broken cabinets torn from the kitchen walls, used previously as seats by other visitors, and passed around the whiskey bottle. They smoked cigarettes.

After an hour of tipsy storytelling, joking, and singing, one of the boys said, "Getting late. We better be moving on home." They rose as one and pissed together on the granite hearth. The campfire hissed and went out.

The three brothers would return the depleted horses to their friend's farm and make it home undetected. They later would be called to task by the shopkeeper in Thornton for the theft, and their father would whip them for the offense. History would blame them for what happened on the peak later that night.

At the summit, a breeze came up around midnight. It arrived from the west in gentle puffs at first, then rose over time to a strong blow. The gusts ruffled shreds of wallpaper in the dry building, circled around the dining room like impatient ghosts, dispersed bits of litter, and came upon the germ of a fire. They stirred the tiny pile of embers, urged it to renewed life, and scattered the red nuggets and pink-edged ashes across the seasoned floorboards. They fanned the flecks of glowing debris into bright flames that ignited the skittering litter. Spawning flares quickly bit into the well-oiled floorboards and burst into a bonfire, and the fire grew and flew apart and raced on the wind down the length of the building and up the north and east walls, consuming ragged draperies, dry lath, and beaded ceiling boards as it spread.

It began eating into the sturdy bones of the structure. Half an hour later the entire hotel was ablaze in a colossal stack of colors—white and orange, pink and coral—shooting hundreds of feet above the summit. The plume detonated like a bomb when the ballroom floor collapsed into the dining room below and again when the walls caved in, bringing down the deck and observatory with them. The conflagration consumed the massive sills and joists that held the hotel fast to the ground. The mountain top heated like a furnace, and rabbits, foxes, and coyotes fled from the butte; voles and snakes retreated deeper underground and were roasted in their burrows. The peak cracked and hissed as if all memory of visions by countless boys over thousands of years was being released and vaporized in the inferno.

The fire could be seen from every peak around the compass, as far away as the Blue Mountains in Oregon and Ryegrass Summit halfway across Washington and Idaho's Latour Peak to the east. As dawn began to light the eastern sky, the magnificent blaze at Steptoe Butte had settled to a crimson dome, and a tower of smoke ascended a thousand feet and slid off eastward. By full daylight only the waste remained, a massive heap of crisp, ashy rubble, still smoldering and glowing.

Snowstorms would come through and cover the ruins. Afterward would follow spring rains and then the dry winds of summer and autumn. Many seasons would come and go. With the passage of enough years and endless cycles of Eeyomoshtosh expanding and contracting in frosts and thaws, the scattered shards of crockery and metal and chips of charcoal would be absorbed into the thin soil or blown across the vast loess hills below. In time, only a few cracked foundation stones would remain as traces of Hotel Steptoe.

ABOUT THE AUTHOR

Stephen Preston Banks is the author or editor of five previous books. His novel *Kokio* is based on the life of early twentieth-century travel writer and espionage agent Neill James. He has taught at the University of Idaho, Arizona State University, the University of the Basque Country, and the University of Southern California. He currently is at work on a novel inspired by African-American pioneer George Washington Bush, one of the earliest and most influential settlers north of the Columbia River and sometimes called the other George W. Bush.

Banks lives on an island off the coast of Washington State, with his wife and their two dogs and two cats. When not busy with writing projects, he devotes his time and energy to gardening, volunteer work for environmental organizations, and hiking in the Pacific Northwest.

The employees of Five Star Publishing hope you have enjoyed this book.

Our Five Star novels explore little-known chapters from America's history, stories told from unique perspectives that will entertain a broad range of readers.

Other Five Star books are available at your local library, bookstore, all major book distributors, and directly from Five Star/Gale.

Connect with Five Star Publishing

Website:
gale.com/five-star

Facebook:
facebook.com/FiveStarCengage

Twitter:
twitter.com/FiveStarCengage

Email:
FiveStar@cengage.com

For information about titles and placing orders:
(800) 223-1244
gale.orders@cengage.com

To share your comments, write to us:
Five Star Publishing
Attn: Publisher
10 Water St., Suite 310
Waterville, ME 04901